# MIRAMONT'S GHOST

# MIRAMONT'S GHOST

## ELIZABETH HALL

LAKE UNION
PUBLISHING

Published by Lake Union Publishing, Seattle

www.apub.com

Amazon, the Amazon logo, and Lake Union Publishing are trademarks of Amazon.com, Inc., or its affiliates.

ISBN-13: 9781477820469
ISBN-10: 1477820469

Cover design by Cyanotype Book Architects

Library of Congress Control Number: 2014946050

Printed in the United States of America

*For June*

# PROLOGUE

*Manitou Springs, Colorado*

She sat at the piano, fingers still poised over the now-silent keys. The notes of the night serenade dissipated in the cool air, ghosts of sound, lingering in the periphery of light and shadow. The sun had set. Shadows crept across the room. But Adrienne stared straight ahead, lost in a trance of remembering. The music had carried her away, to another time and another place, when she was young and in love and the future still sparkled with possibility.

Somewhere on the hillside a dog barked and jolted her from her reverie. Adrienne turned her head toward the window, filled now with the blue dark of evening. She stood and moved to the glass and stared out into the dusk.

Color faded from the sky. Stars winked in the canyons. Lights in the houses on the hillside flickered to life, bathing the windows with gold and spilling out into the streets. She could hear them—families gathering for dinner, plates clattering on the table. She could smell what they ate—garlic and tomato in the house below her, chicken with rosemary at the house across the street.

The little girl who lived in the blue house on the corner rode up and dropped her bike on the sidewalk. She turned and looked up at the castle, and for a moment, their eyes locked on one another. The girl stared for an instant longer, and then ran up the steps and in the front door of her house. Adrienne heard the screen door slam, watched as the girl raced into the amber light of the living room.

It had been many years since anyone had actually *seen* her, actually looked at her. Those eyes, locking on her own, sent a jolt like a bolt of lightning into the core of her being. Connection, however small, was something she hadn't experienced in far too long.

But as soon as the little girl turned away, as soon as that connection was broken, Adrienne was flooded once more with the weight of her isolation. She thought she had managed to put all that away from her; she thought she had become adept at living with seclusion and silence. Now the force of her solitude threatened to knock her to her knees. She ached with longing—a longing she had not felt for many, many years.

The pine trees were completely black now, only silhouettes against the almost-black sky. Shades of gray filled the streets, as if all of life's color had drained away with the setting sun. Adrienne wrapped her arms around her chest and stared at the falling darkness. Outside the window, crickets chirped. Wind rattled the leaves in the cottonwood tree. They click-click-clicked as they hit against each other. An owl hooted, his voice low and sad.

Memories of her dream came back, enveloping her like the gray of a rainy day. She was in the confessional, in a church she could neither see nor remember. The space was close and small. She watched the light, dim and dappled by the confessional screen, as it fell across her skirt and the hands resting in her lap. She could smell the onions that the priest had had for lunch. He was the priest from her childhood, Père Henri. As a child, the smell had always made her draw back and wrinkle her nose, but she remembered his voice as being deep and kind. He always listened quietly to those oh-so-innocent sins of her youth. She had pulled her sister's hair. She had made a face at her aunt Marie. She had raised her voice to her mother. She remembered how hot and red she had become when she confessed that she had told her sister to "go to hell." He never laughed, never minimized her sins or blew them out of proportion. He seemed to know instinctively that Adrienne was one of a handful of souls who took everything to heart. If she mentioned something, then it was because it weighed heavily on her mind.

How was it, then, that as she got older and her sins became greater, she had ceased confessing? She could not recall the last time she had stepped inside the confessional, could not recall the last time she had unburdened her heart. But waking from the dream last night, and now, as she stood at the window staring out into the dusk, she remembered how she always left that small, dark space feeling lighter. She could smile and laugh, and know as soon as she had said her five Hail Marys that all was well, that she was free to start fresh, to begin again, unshackled by guilt or shame.

And oh, how she would love to start fresh, to unburden herself of all that had happened. Because no matter how she had tried over these many years to justify her behavior, no matter how she tried to blame the situation and the circumstances that had led her to that point, the truth was that she had committed the worst of all possible sins. She had taken a life—and in fact, more than one.

She had thought, at the time, that it would end her torment, would allow her escape. But that was not the case. If anything, she was more trapped, more isolated, more haunted than before. And just a few moments ago, when she looked into the eyes of that young girl in the blue house, she felt once more the heavy burden of guilt and shame that she carried.

Adrienne looked back at the blue house. The family was sitting around the dinner table, lit up like a Norman Rockwell painting. They were laughing and talking and enjoying their evening dinner—a perfectly normal family and a perfectly normal evening. Normal. Adrienne sighed, and laid her forehead against the glass.

# CHAPTER ONE

*Beaulieu, France—1884*

Four-year-old Adrienne leaned out her window into the warm May morning. She smiled and closed her eyes, giddy with the perfumes of spring. She smelled the lilacs, the chestnut trees, Grand-père's tulips and roses in the garden below. She turned her head, toward the Pyrenees Mountains to her left, and sniffed again. She could smell the mountains, the scent of pine trees wafting on the air, and a faint whiff of spice that could only be from Spain.

She opened her eyes and drank in the sights of the little village of Beaulieu in the valley below her. Whitewashed walls, red tile roofs, birch trees and chestnuts and pines. The steeple of the church rose above it all, a finger reaching into the sapphire sky. Smoke curled from the chimney at the *boulangerie*; three boys ran down the road toward the river, their arms and legs jerking about like puppets on strings. The river separated the château grounds from the village like a shiny gray ribbon. She loved how small the village looked from her window on the hill, as if it were a collection of toy dollhouses built just for her. Standing in this window, surveying the kingdom, she felt like a fairy princess, straight out of one of Grand-père's storybooks.

The white curtains billowed inward, and Adrienne's eyes locked on a sharp stab of light, the sun reflecting on a window in town. For a moment, she couldn't breathe. She stared at that bright flickering gold spot, and her mind drifted. A story opened up before her. Adrienne could see Madame Clemenceau, standing before the mirror in her bedroom. She was admiring herself in her new hat, turning her head this way and that, inspecting the peacock feathers and the blue-black velvet, and the pleasing way it set off her eyes in the glass. Adrienne watched as madame's eyes grew large and her features froze with fear. The woman moved quickly, snatching the hat from her head and stuffing it in the hatbox. She dropped the box to the floor, and shoved it with her foot so that her skirts covered it. Adrienne watched as the woman's husband entered the room, his face puffy and red. He looked like one of the seven dwarfs, and Adrienne covered her mouth with her hand and giggled.

Another reflection caught her eye, and once again, Adrienne saw things that were not actually visible from her window in the château on the hill. Monsieur LaMott had his arms around Madame Binoche, kissing her in a way that made Adrienne blush. The woman's robe could not conceal her breasts, and he bent and kissed each of them. Then he opened the door of her kitchen and left, blowing her a kiss, and whistling as he walked down the back street to his own home, two blocks away. Adrienne watched as he composed his face into something serious and walked in the back door of the patisserie, where he lived with his wife. Madame LaMott was stirring a pot of cereal on the stove, but when she heard him, she turned, her face contorted with rage. Adrienne could see her, yelling, trying to hit him with the spoon. Monsieur put his arms up to protect himself from her assault. Adrienne winced, as if she herself had been struck.

"Adrienne? Adrienne?"

Adrienne heard the voice of her governess as if from a great distance. She turned her head toward the sound, but it was as if she was at the end of a long tunnel. It took a moment or two before she recognized Lucie's face, before she remembered her surroundings.

"Adrienne?"

Lucie let out a long sigh. "Your grand-père is waiting." She held Adrienne's sweater in her hands.

Adrienne slipped her arms into the sweater and ran through the room and down the hallway.

The Comte de Challembelles waited at the bottom of the wide staircase. His own blue eyes sparkled, a mirror of Adrienne's, as he watched his little granddaughter hurrying down to meet him. He was smitten with the child, as she was with him. The comte was now in his eighties, easier with this granddaughter than he had ever been with his own children. His hair was a soft, milky white, his eyes cobalt, his jawline still strong. The traces of the lieutenant colonel who had served under Napoleon still rested in the proud lift of his chin, the strength and dignity of his shoulders and stance.

"I'm ready, Grand-père!" Adrienne hopped from one foot to the other, trying to be patient as he reached for his hat.

He took her hand, and they strolled out the front of the castle and down the hill to the village. The sun was warm, the air thick with the aromas of spring. Birds sang, a chorus of tiny bells and flutes in the trees.

Adrienne dropped his hand to run after a butterfly. She stopped and sniffed the bluebells at the side of the road. The comte smiled. Her joy at the sights and sounds of the spring morning was contagious. There was nothing like this grandchild, giddy with the wonders of spring, to make him forget the ache in his knees. It was so different than what he had had with his own daughters. When they were young, he had been much more concerned with the issues of discipline, with instilling good behavior and creating proper French ladies. He had often been called away from home, burdened with the duties of a comte. Now he had time to enjoy the intricacies of little-girlhood. He had the resources to spoil her, and damn the consequences. Truth be told, neither of his girls had ever displayed the joy in life that Adrienne seemed to possess. She savored everything, from snowflakes to dragonflies, and in her eyes, he saw the world anew. He, too, could see the wonders in a pink tulip; he smelled afresh the heavy scent of the pines.

They wandered down the dirt road that connected the château to the village, walking past vineyards and farm fields, over the creek that separated the village from the estate grounds. When they reached the village, the comte stopped and looked down. "Would you like a pastry, my sweet? We won't tell your mother," he whispered with a wink.

Adrienne's smile faded. She turned her gaze to the window of the patisserie. "Not this morning, Grand-père, thank you. Madame LaMott is in a sour mood."

The comte's eyebrows went up. "Oh?"

Adrienne stared into the window and sighed. "She and Monsieur LaMott are fighting." Adrienne leaned forward and lowered her voice to a whisper. "He was kissing Madame Binoche." Adrienne raised her hand to stifle a giggle. "And she did not have all of her clothes on." She raised her eyebrows, as if she actually understood all that her words implied.

The comte stared at the window of the patisserie, as if he could see into the lives of the LaMott couple. He turned to face the little girl. "Adrienne . . . what makes you think this?"

"I saw it. When I stood in my window this morning."

The comte looked back up the hill toward the castle. Though less than a mile away, the distance was too great; trees obscured the view. "How could you see it?" He leaned down on one knee, and put his hands on Adrienne's waist.

Adrienne sighed. "Sometimes . . . when I look at something shiny . . . I see this little picture. Here." She touched her fingers to the middle of her forehead. "I can see what people do. I can hear what they say."

She leaned close to him, lowered her chin, and looked up at him through thick eyelashes. "I heard what Madame LaMott said when monsieur came home this morning," she whispered. "It was not very nice, Grand-père."

The comte swallowed. The icy finger of the past brushed against his neck, making his hair stand on end. He stood, wrapped Adrienne's hand inside his, and they wandered down the street. "What else have you seen?"

Adrienne turned her head and stared at the milliner's shop, hats perched on display like peacocks, strutting for the customers.

"I saw Madame Clemenceau in her bedroom. She was standing in front of the mirror, looking at the hat she bought yesterday." Adrienne scrunched her nose. "It looks like a dead bird."

The comte smiled at her expression.

"But then she yanked it off her head and put it in the box, and hid it. Her husband was coming," Adrienne explained. "He doesn't like for her to spend so much money."

The comte pressed his lips together, and turned his head toward the village chapel, attempting to hide his amusement. Monsieur Clemenceau was often heard complaining about how much his wife spent on "fripperies."

Adrienne stared at a little gray bird, splashing in a puddle at the side of the lane. "And Maman's new baby? The one in her tummy? It's a girl," she said with a frown. "I know she wants a boy . . . She talks about it all the time." Adrienne shrugged her shoulders and heaved a deep sigh. "But . . . this baby is a girl. She has yellow hair. Like Maman."

The comte looked down at the reddish-brown curls, catching the sunlight like jewels. So similar to his late wife, this little girl, with her auburn hair and blue eyes. The comte stopped in the lane, his brow tense as the memories flooded over him. Marguerite, too, had been able to see. She, too, had known things that she should not have known. She knew that their daughter, Genevieve, Adrienne's mother, would have yellow hair. But there was no joy, no anticipation, in that knowledge. She saw the blond hair of that baby, but she also saw her own body, lifeless and still. She knew, almost from the time she became pregnant, that this yellow-haired daughter would cost her her life. The comte had tried to reassure her, tried to tell her she was only nervous, that it was just the normal jitters and fears of carrying a baby. But her knowledge hung heavy on them both. She'd wake up at night, bathed in a cold sweat, her hands on the child growing inside her. He would pull her close and wrap her in his arms, but she could not be consoled. She knew what she knew, and there was no way to pretend otherwise.

Adrienne stopped walking, and turned back to him. She stood still in the middle of the lane. The comte stared straight ahead, lost in memory.

"Grand-père? What was my grand-mère like?"

The comte turned back to his granddaughter, and exhaled slowly. "Hmmm? She was much like you, Adrienne. Her eyes, her hair."

"Did she see pictures? Like I do?"

The comte looked down at the girl. His throat burned. He nodded. "Yes. Yes, she did." His Adam's apple bobbed above his collar. "She knew that your maman would have yellow hair. Even before she was born."

Adrienne smiled.

The comte looked toward the river on their left. He remembered other visions, other things she had known. Like the way she knew that their son, their only son, would not live to his first birthday. He remembered the times she had cursed her gift. She had hated seeing the pain that awaited them both—hated that she could do nothing to change things. The visions had torn at her, leaving her exhausted and often lost in her own melancholy.

The comte put his hand on top of Adrienne's head. She was rapturous with the joy of spring at the moment, completely innocent. She had no idea that the pictures she saw were anything more than fairy stories, like the ones in her books. They were entertaining, nothing more. He stared at her, his eyes filled with sadness. He would not have wished this gift on his worst enemy.

Adrienne gave his wrinkled hand a squeeze.

The comte sighed, and glanced up the hill. "We should be getting back now. Your aunt Marie should be here soon."

"Yes, I know." Adrienne frowned. She dragged her foot back and forth through the dirt. "She isn't very nice, is she, Grand-père?"

The comte stared at his granddaughter. She could not possibly remember Marie; she had been only a few months old the last time Marie had been home. But she was right. Marie was not very nice, though he would never say so out loud about his own child. Though petite, only five feet tall and ninety pounds, she was quite a forceful woman. More than one man had been cut by her sharp words, her icy glare, the force of her iron will.

Guilt washed over him once again. He had neglected Marie after the death of her mother; he knew that. Marie was thirteen at the time, and the loss had hit her hard. She had become sullen and angry. But the comte had been lost in his own pain, his own guilt. He went to Paris as often as he could, trying to evade the memories that hung in the air of the castle. And that meant leaving baby Genevieve with her nurse, Marie with her governess. They had all suffered, but privately, in their own separate worlds, unable to connect to one another.

He'd come home from Paris to find that Marie had taken over the role of lady of the house. Even at the age of thirteen, she had mastered the art of managing the servants. But her bossiness and manipulation did not stop with the servants. She was equally harsh and demanding with her baby sister, and with anyone from the village who happened to cross her path. He had hated returning to Beaulieu back then, hated the way she reigned over the castle like a queen.

The comte exhaled, trying to rid himself of the darkness that remembering that time always brought. It wasn't until the birth of Adrienne, this granddaughter who stood beside him now, that he had finally been able to make amends for his neglect. To Adrienne, he gave all the attention and love and concern that he was unable to bring to his own daughters in those dark days.

Adrienne looked up at him. "She brings you a present, Grand-père," she confided. "It is a . . . ray . . . re-tab-lo. A little wooden saint. The Indians in New Mexico make them."

The comte tipped his head and nodded. "Ahhh."

"Grand-père . . ." Adrienne tipped her head to one side. "What are Indians?"

The comte studied Adrienne's face. She was such an intriguing mixture of knowledge and innocence. So like his late wife. He felt very old, suddenly. As if he had aged a decade since they left for their walk.

# CHAPTER TWO

The air in the castle sparked with electrical energy, like the air before a thunderstorm. The hair on the back of Adrienne's neck stood on end. Butlers and maids flew around the rooms, their faces creased with tension. The whole estate was in the last stages of being polished and groomed, as if they were expecting visiting royalty.

Things were no better when Adrienne went down to dinner. The maid seemed to be all jitters and nerves, and she splashed a drop of water on the white linen tablecloth as she moved to fill their glasses. Adrienne watched as her hands began to shake. Her eyes jumped. The pitcher nearly slipped from her grasp.

"What's wrong with you?" Marie snapped, her lips and brow and forehead creased with irritation. "Can you not pour water?"

*"Désolé, madame."* The maid's face fell.

"Maman?" Adrienne leaned forward, staring across the table at her mother. "Why are you sitting there?" As long as Adrienne could remember, her grand-père had sat at one end of the long table, and her mother at the other.

Genevieve did not answer. Her eyes fluttered nervously to her older sister, and back to some invisible spot on the tablecloth. "I . . ."

Marie held her spoon perfectly still, arrested in its strategic assault on the soup. "There are rules, Adrienne. When your grand-mère was alive, this was her seat. Since she is no longer with us, and I am the oldest daughter, I am now the head of the household."

Grand-père cleared his throat at the other end of the table.

Marie glanced at him. "The female head of the household, that is. When I'm not here, your mother is allowed to take my place."

Genevieve lowered her head, and slumped in her seat as if she had been beaten with a club.

Adrienne bent her head and sipped from her soup, thinking how different the two sisters were. Through her eyelashes, she watched her mother, sitting with her head bowed, directly across the table. Genevieve looked like a jewel, the candlelight sparkling in her golden hair and blue eyes. She seemed the perfect match for the sapphire necklace around her throat. Her dress was a lustrous blue silk. The mound of her tummy under the silk only added to her glow. Everything about Genevieve glittered.

Marie, on the other hand, looked more like a piece of coal. She was petite, with a head of dark curls, gray sprouting at the temples. Her eyes were the color of steel and had the same hard, unyielding quality. Despite the fact that her husband had been dead for over a decade, she continued to wear the dreary black, unadorned crepe of mourning. Everything about her was dull and hard.

"Are you accustomed to staring at your elders, Adrienne?" Marie reproached the child.

"No, madame." Adrienne dropped her eyes to her soup bowl. Her ravishing hunger of an hour before was disappearing quickly in the tense atmosphere.

Both of the comte's daughters had been raised with wealth and power, but Marie wore it differently. On Genevieve, it looked like a decoration, a tiara that made her even more becoming. On Marie, it was more like a weapon, an axe she wielded to get exactly what she wanted. Those privileges had filled the shell of her being and flowed into every part of her. The way she tilted her head slightly when Grand-père spoke, the way her fingers held her wineglass, the way her shoulders were thrown back, all spoke of a woman who was accustomed to having her way, and entitled to whatever she wanted. She made certain that everyone knew of her position, whether as the daughter of the comte, the wife of a French diplomat, or now as the mother of the chancellor to the archbishop in the largest diocese in the New World.

Marie sipped her soup. "Don't you think she's rather young to be allowed at the dinner table, Genevieve?"

Genevieve's eyes flitted about like butterflies, darting first to Marie, then to Adrienne, then landing, once again, on the middle of the table. "Well, I . . ." she stammered, unable to finish her thought.

"She is, for the time being at least, an only child," Grand-père said. "I see nothing wrong with her joining us."

"Julien was an only child," Marie responded. "We never allowed him to join us at table at such a young age."

No one responded. The family kept their heads down, focused on their food. The only sounds were the spoons tinkling against the soup bowls, the swallows and slurps of eating.

"I cannot imagine how we would have managed, had his father allowed him at table. Diplomacy is an art; it requires finesse. Children must be old enough to understand the subtleties." She stared at Adrienne, as if it were quite obvious that Adrienne would never grasp subtleties.

"Fortunately, Marie, none of us is in the diplomatic corps," Grand-père said. "No kings and queens at this dinner table." His eyes crinkled at the corners, and Adrienne sent him a shy smile.

Marie ignored the comment. "Of course, once Julien reached the proper age—I believe he was around ten or so—his father allowed him to join us. Gave him exactly the training and experience and background he would need to be a renowned diplomat himself." Marie tipped her head to one side, took a bite of her roll. She looked down her nose at Adrienne, and Adrienne turned her face back to her own meal.

"Yes. After all that training, how unfortunate that he chose the priesthood instead." The comte and Marie stared at one another, as if he had just fired the first shot in the next round of battle between them. The subject of her son and his work was a sore spot with Marie.

Marie bristled. His comment took her back to so much that she would rather forget. Her marriage to Jacques Morier had been arranged by the families, and had been, at least to the outside world, very successful. She was only eighteen at the time and was overjoyed at the prospect of leaving her father and Genevieve behind. Jacques worked in the diplomatic corps of the French government. They traveled extensively, dined with nobility, stayed at all the finest places in Europe. Marie reveled in the life of diplomacy. It served her love of power and prestige and control.

Privately, though, the marriage did not live up to its promise. After their important guests had left for the evening, the air between the two of them was icy and quiet. Jacques escaped into the arms of his many mistresses as often as he could.

Marie tolerated his philandering. He was discreet; she was a good Catholic. Divorce was unthinkable. She had exactly what she wanted. She relished the influence and status that being the wife of a diplomat afforded her. That was much more valuable to her than the relationship itself.

But he abandoned her completely when he died of a heart attack at the age of thirty-seven. She missed their travels, the dinners hosting heads of state. She missed the control she had once wielded in European political circles. She missed the importance of his position, and the way that importance transferred to her. But she did not miss him.

And for the second time in her life, death had left her deserted by someone she had relied on. Jacques's death brought back all the instability and fear she had felt at the death of her mother and the neglect of her grieving father. Once again, she was forced to make her own way in the world, to figure things out without anyone to help her. It solidified her belief that the only person she could rely on was herself, that it was only through absolute control that she would survive. She was compelled to return to her childhood home at Beaulieu, to live with her sister, Genevieve, that golden-haired beauty who had captured all the attention and all the sympathy after the death of their mother. It grated on Marie, this fall from power, this loss of prestige. She was determined that it would never happen again, no matter what that might take.

She turned all her skills, all her power, manipulation, and control, to their only son, Julien. He was thirteen when his father died, devastated by the loss. Marie was determined that he, too, would become a diplomat, and return her to her rightful place at the tables of European power. Julien did as he was told. He studied in Paris, did well in school. And just as he neared the fulfillment of her dream, Julien, too, suddenly rebelled.

On his own, he would never have gone against his mother's wishes, never have had the courage to mutiny. But just before he was scheduled to finish his diplomatic studies at university, Julien announced that he was entering the priesthood. He said it was God who called him. Marie could not argue with God; he was the one being outside her sphere of influence. The young man insisted that God called him to give up his diplomatic studies and attend seminary at Clermont.

When Archbishop Lamy, himself a graduate of Clermont, recruited Julien for the archdiocese in Santa Fe, New Mexico, Julien jumped at the opportunity. It was half a world away from Marie. But his escape was short-lived. She had joined him in Santa Fe less than a year after he left France.

The comte rested his fork on his plate and watched as his eldest daughter fought to control her emotions. He could not remember a time when they had been only father and daughter. He and Marie were like opponents in a game of chess, each searching for the other's weakness, ready to use it to advantage should the need arise.

Marie's gaze locked on his for a moment. She dropped her eyes to her plate, and raised them again. The glare was gone; her training had returned. "He could not have chosen more wisely, as it turns out. I know Archbishop Lamy is very grateful to have someone of Julien's high caliber to help him. The place is so desperately in need." Marie's perfectly composed features bent slightly to take in a bite of the veal.

The comte fought off a flicker of a smile. This reminded him of the battlefield when he was a young man, or a serious game of poker, predicated on the ability to make your opponent believe something that may or may not be true. The comte took a deep breath. He knew well all the subtleties of the game. "And how do you like the West? Is it true, everything we've heard? Indians on the rampage and all of that?"

"It is still very rough, that's true, but it has improved a great deal since the archbishop first went there. Most of the Indian tribes are confined now—on reservations. Of course, there are still Indian attacks, but not nearly as often as ten years ago. And the journey across the continent is much easier now as well. They just finished building the railroad into Santa Fe. Before that, everything had to travel by wagon." Marie took a bite and chewed thoughtfully. "The archbishop told us all kinds of stories about the trips he made, by wagon train, across the prairie, through Indian territories. I cannot even imagine how difficult *that* must have been. I found the trip quite arduous even on the train, and of course, I never had to face those ghastly Indian horrors.

"But the archbishop did it several times. On one of his trips, he had a wagonload of items for the church in Santa Fe—things that had been donated by all his supporters here in France. They crossed a river, swollen with spring runoff, and the wagon was swept away. He lost almost everything. It is amazing that he survived. Even so, he has been able, over the years, to bring so many fine things back with him. Books. Proper dishes. Silver and crystal for the church altar. He even managed to haul in plants for his garden. You should see what he has done with the church gardens! I guess it does give one hope that the place can ultimately be civilized." Marie took a sip of her wine, and swooped the wineglass out in front of her with a flourish. It was evident that she loved being the center of attention, being the one who had all the interesting stories.

Genevieve sat silently, her eyes traveling back and forth between her father and her older sister. She did not attempt to speak; she broached no questions about the New World.

"God knows they need every bit of culture and refinement that he can manage. But the archbishop is getting older . . . I'm afraid he's not as strong as he needs to be for such work. It's a good thing he has Julien there to help him now."

Marie tipped her head to one side, and cut another bite of her veal.

"What is Santa Fe like? Is it much like here?" The comte was fascinated with all subjects related to Julien's station in the New World, from the flora and fauna in the mountains of New Mexico Territory to the history of the tribes that lived along the Rio Grande.

"I felt dirty the whole time I was there," Marie said. "Dirt streets. Dirt floors. Houses made of mud bricks. Everything is always coated in dust, except for those rare occasions when it rains. Then everything is coated in mud. I never thought I could be so grateful for a rough plank floor." Marie raised her wineglass once again, her eyes sparkling.

Adrienne had lost track of the conversation; she was no longer paying attention to the people at the table. She studied the water goblet in front of her plate. Light rays from the candles hit the crystal and bounced in different directions. She stared at the amber light, pulled into the strange new world that opened before her. She lost track of where she was; she could no longer hear Marie's words. Rays of sunlight poured through a bank of gray clouds and onto the dirt streets of Santa Fe. Adrienne could see the snowcapped mountains behind the town; she could smell the faint whiff of piñon and sage and juniper, even though she would not have been able to name what they were.

Her vision showed her the little mud houses, some of them surrounded by fences made of thin branches, standing upright. She heard the creak of wagon wheels, the clop of horses' hooves. She watched the dark-haired women, wrapped in woolen shawls, as they moved along the streets.

The street curved to the right, and Adrienne's eyes grew huge. She smiled at the scene that unfolded before her. "Is that where the little church is? The one with the round staircase and the big colored-glass window?"

Marie stopped, her fork poised in midair. "You mean the Chapel of Loretto?"

Marie cut another bite of her veal, not waiting for an answer. "It's not far from the cathedral the archbishop is building. He's had a struggle, poor man, finding enough money to keep going. The sisters, though—they were able to get their little chapel built fairly quickly." Marie seemed lost in her own story. She did not notice Adrienne.

"Too quickly, I'm afraid," Marie continued. "They forgot to put in the staircase. And then when they realized their mistake, there wasn't enough room for a proper staircase." Marie looked up at her audience.

"Yes. That's the one!" Adrienne said. She turned to her aunt, her own spell broken, but the story fresh and exciting in her consciousness. "And they prayed to God for help. And then one day, this man rode up on his mule. He is old, like Grand-père. And he built the staircase. He made it round. And then he rode away, before they could pay him. So now they call it the Miracle Staircase." Adrienne beamed, enthralled by the scene that had just played out before her eyes.

Marie's gaze narrowed. "Just how do you know so much about the staircase, Adrienne?"

Adrienne almost glowed with the fairy tale story she had just witnessed. She bounced in her chair with excitement. "I saw it! Just now. It is so beautiful. The colors in the window. The round staircase with the dark wood. And that old man was so nice. He had white hair . . . like Grand-père." Her gaze shifted to her favorite man, sitting at the other end of the table.

The room grew very quiet; even the servants stopped moving. Everyone stared at Adrienne. Genevieve's eyes grew large. She swallowed without chewing her food. Lucie's mouth hung slightly open, breathless.

The comte could feel it in the air, as if the ghost of the comtesse had just flown in through an open window. He was flooded with memories of those months right after they married, and he brought her here to live with him. It had started slowly, just a feeling he had, like a finger running down his spine. Unlike many other men of his class, he had learned to pay attention to those feelings. They had served him well during his years in the army, making him hyper-vigilant of his surroundings, of the threats that he could neither see nor hear. As a young lieutenant, he had learned very quickly that the soldiers who survived were the ones who followed their own visceral sense of the situation.

At first, he thought that what he noticed might be jealousy. Marguerite possessed the kind of beauty that made everyone uncomfortable: women were envious; men were dumbstruck. She had a natural reticence in company. Her reserve had sometimes made her seem distant and haughty.

Gradually, though, he began to notice a pattern. He would enter rooms to find servants staring, struggling to avert their eyes from the face of the comtesse. Sometimes he would walk into a shop in town, and everyone would stop talking. It was disconcerting, this feeling that they were being watched, that their lives were subject to such scrutiny.

They tried so hard to keep her visions a secret, to make sure that no one found out. It was impossible. Stories leaked out, just a trickle at first: servants in the next room who might have overheard; people in the village who had reasons for latching on to any bit of gossip that made its way from the château. The talk had never completely disappeared. Even now, thirty years after her death, he knew that the stories were still alive, still brought out and shared, like a family keepsake. He could still feel it, now and then, walking into a shop in town, and sensing the hush that fell over the room.

Grand-père glanced at Adrienne; he assessed the faces of everyone around the table.

He could tell by looking that Lucie already knew the secret of Adrienne's visions. Genevieve seemed completely surprised by Adrienne's story. He had no idea if she knew about her own mother; it was not a subject that he had ever felt the need to discuss with her. Marie's eyes met his across the length of the table. She knew about the comtesse, but he could not be certain just how much she remembered about those visions.

Adrienne continued. "I could see the town . . . the streets . . . the 'dobe houses . . ." Her voice dropped off, as if she were no longer sitting at a table in France, but had been magically transported to the scene of her story.

The comte held his breath. Marie had not used the word "adobe." She'd called them mud houses. He was amazed that Adrienne had come up with the word.

"And then I saw the little chapel." Adrienne's voice was a soft whisper, and everyone strained forward to hear her. "I saw the man ride up on his mule. I could see him build the staircase."

Marie's voice turned to ice. "Perhaps your mother told you about this. I distinctly remember writing to her about the chapel. Perhaps she read the letter to you." Marie's features were completely devoid of emotion, her body stiff.

Adrienne's eyes went back to this stranger at the dinner table. "No. I saw it . . . just now." Adrienne sat back in her chair, her blue eyes defiant.

Genevieve was immobile. The servants, though appearing to stare straight ahead, intent on their work, were hanging on every word.

"Well, that's quite an imagination, Adrienne," Marie hissed.

"It's not 'magination," Adrienne declared. "I saw it. Just now. When I looked at my glass." She crossed her arms in front of her.

At the other end of the table, the comte felt Marie's gaze. Their eyes met in a tightrope of tension.

He cleared his throat and pushed his chair back. It scraped along the marble floor. "Adrienne, it's getting late. Perhaps we should skip prayers this evening and get to bed." He walked to Adrienne's chair and stood, holding his hand out to her. She looked up at him, her adoration suddenly eclipsing everything else.

She climbed down off her chair and took his hand, a child once again. Lucie stood and laid her napkin on the table.

The comte tipped his head to Marie and then to Genevieve. "*Bonne nuit*, ladies."

Adrienne slipped from the comte's grasp and ran around to her mother. She stood on tiptoe to kiss her mother's cheek. *"Bonne nuit*, Maman," she whispered. She turned slowly and looked at her aunt Marie once more. Marie did not return her gaze. *"Bonne nuit*, Tante Marie."

# CHAPTER THREE

In the cool light of morning, the dining room had lost all of its charm. Gone were the dancing flames of candlelight, the shadows that softened the corners of the room, the warmth of dinner. Despite the bright sunlight streaming through the terrace doors, the room was harsh, hard, and glaring. The marble of the floor reflected blinding rays of sunlight. The chairs were lined up around the table, stiff and formal like soldiers at attention. The ceiling soaked up every attempt at conversation, the feeble words disappearing in the height of the room.

Marie presided over the breakfast table like a general, perfectly at ease in the strict formality. The comte was not at his seat.

Adrienne slipped into her chair, her soft *"Bonjour"* barely audible in the cool air.

Silverware clinked against the china plates. The clock ticked. China coffee cups hit their saucers with a ringing sound. Adrienne swallowed one bite of scrambled egg. She laid her fork down.

"Maman?" Her voice came out rough and coarse. Adrienne stared at her mother across the table. "May I be excused?"

Genevieve's eyes left her plate, flitted over to her daughter's face. She was lost in her own thoughts, and had not noticed her daughter. Nothing seemed to register, in her eyes or her voice. "Hmmm?"

"Adrienne, you've barely touched your breakfast," Marie observed.

"I'm not very hungry this morning," Adrienne whispered. "Maman? May I go?"

Genevieve's eyes were back on her plate again. "Yes. Fine. You're excused."

Adrienne slipped off her chair, and she and Lucie went outside for a stroll in the morning sunshine.

Marie cleared her throat. She held her coffee cup before her, both hands wrapped around it, and gazed at the door to the terrace. Adrienne and her governess were walking in the distance. "Genevieve, I'm not sure you understand the severity of this situation," she began.

Genevieve sighed, wishing she could escape from her sister. "What do you mean?"

Marie took her time answering. "It's obvious that Adrienne has a very active imagination. But the way you and Papa coddle her, she has begun to think her imagination is real." Marie raised her delicate china cup and sipped from her coffee, her gray eyes locked on her sister. "You must not encourage such behavior—all these stories and fantasies and imaginings."

Genevieve's hands rested in her lap; her fingers toyed with her linen napkin. Coffee and juice sat before her, untouched. "But Marie, the story she told was true."

"Of course it is." Marie sipped from her coffee cup, her elbows resting on the table. "I wrote to you about the chapel. I distinctly remember that. You and Papa may have discussed it. Perhaps you even read the letter out loud."

Genevieve searched her memory. She did have a vague recollection of such a letter. She never cared much for what Marie had to say, and would often let letters from her sister sit for days without opening them. It seemed that her sister had two main themes in any of her communications. They always centered on the perfection of her son, or on what Genevieve was doing wrong. Genevieve had long ago grown weary of both topics. But the comte was fascinated with the New World. He read everything Marie sent. He purchased every publication he could find about Indians, or the Wild West, or life on the American frontier. He probably *had* read the letter out loud.

"She's young; she's sensitive to everything she hears. She seems bright enough. Perhaps she has heard the whole story, from that letter I sent, and remembers much more than most children her age." The prim set of Marie's lips left no room for argument.

"Perhaps," Genevieve conceded. She looked at the terrace doors, at the bright sunlight washing over the flowers outside, and felt relief at such a simple solution. Genevieve did not have the energy to figure out what was going on with her daughter; and Marie's idea made so much more sense than the idea that Adrienne might actually have *seen* the events she described.

But there was another part of Genevieve that did not want to agree with her older sister. She did not want Marie to be right; she did not want Marie to have all the answers. She could well remember all the years of Marie telling her what to do, what to think, how to behave. She remembered coming downstairs, at the age of fifteen, in a silk dress the color of spring leaves. Genevieve loved the color; she felt so grown-up and beautiful that evening. She had walked into the parlor, and Marie had turned from her place by the fire, her face contorted in an expression of horror.

"Genevieve, darling, hasn't anyone ever told you that blondes should not wear green? You look as if you might be ill." Genevieve's pleasure crashed to the floor and shattered like glass. She suddenly felt ugly and stupid and completely inept. She fought hard to keep herself from crying, and for the rest of the evening she barely spoke, never raised her eyes from her plate.

In the years that Marie had been home, living here at the château, Genevieve had never been strong enough to disagree with her. Any time she had come remotely close to rebellion, Marie would make a veiled comment about their mother, and Genevieve would be plunged back into a sea of guilt. She was the one, after all, who had taken their mother's life, and it seemed to her that Marie would never forgive her for that negligence.

"I'd be very careful how you respond to these stories of hers," Marie continued. She laid her napkin next to her plate and pushed her chair back. "She mustn't be encouraged to think that she actually *sees* these things. We cannot allow the servants—" At that Marie glanced up at the maid who was removing dishes from the sideboard. She lowered her voice to a whisper. "We cannot allow *anyone* to talk about her. We don't want these fantasies of hers to . . ." Marie stared out into the sunlight. Her eyes flicked back to Genevieve.

"You may not remember this, Genevieve, but Papa and I have seen some major upheavals in France in the past thirty years. Something like this . . . if it got out . . . I hate to even think how people might respond. You must be very strict with her on this. I know you don't want the family to be the subject of idle gossip." Marie's eyes narrowed. She stood and pushed in her chair, the legs scraping with a screech. "We both know how devastating gossip can be."

Genevieve looked up at her sister, searching her face for information, for evidence of some knowledge that Marie had and Genevieve did not. Their eyes locked. The corners of Marie's mouth lifted slightly, and she turned and strode from the room, her heels clicking on the marble floor.

Genevieve watched her leave. Her stomach did a flip, as it often did these days when the subject of gossip was raised. She felt sick. She put one hand on the mound of the baby she carried, and stroked it absently. Gossip had followed her for as long as she could remember, and lately she had to wonder if the talk was about Pierre.

Why was it that he found so many excuses to stay in Paris? He rarely came home anymore. Adrienne was growing up without a father; Genevieve was left alone far too often. She wanted to live in Paris with him. She wanted all that the city had to offer. But somehow, the time was never right. Pierre always seemed to have some reason why moving his family couldn't possibly work *right now.*

She raised her eyes to find the sunlight and flowers of the terrace once again. Adrienne walked in the grass, her governess close behind her. She carried her doll and began running and laughing in the bright sun. She seemed so much happier, so much more at ease with her governess. Genevieve frowned, her brow knotted with the weight of Marie's warning.

# CHAPTER FOUR

onjour, madame," the woman at the patisserie greeted Genevieve. Madame LaMott radiated cordiality; it glowed in her cheeks and sparkled in her brown eyes. Her graying curls burst from the bun at the nape of her neck. That sunny disposition had proven very useful, drawing the gossip of the little village to her like a magnet. She and monsieur had been operating the patisserie for as long as Genevieve could remember, and madame had her nose in all the secrets of the village.

"*Bonjour*, Madame LaMott," Genevieve answered. Lucie and Adrienne followed her through the carved wooden door.

The patisserie was located in the lower portions of the LaMotts' home, and a brick fireplace dominated one wall. Warmth glowed in the soft amber walls, and wafted through the air on the smells of fresh pastry. Wooden tables were scattered around the room, chairs perched in total disarray, as if they'd had a wild night of drinking. Light from the huge window shimmered in the lace curtains and spread soft, undulating patterns across the brick floor. A glass case of pastries stood near the back of the room, and Adrienne dropped Lucie's hand and ran to examine the contents, her eyes wide with the wonders of the cakes and napoleons and tiny fruit tarts.

Genevieve and Lucie sank into chairs at a table by the window, and Genevieve began pulling off her gray kid gloves, one finger at a time. Madame LaMott brought a small pot of tea and china cups to their table, and began pouring.

"Maman, may I have a strawberry tart?" Adrienne ran to her mother, glowing with excitement.

"Of course, my sweet." Genevieve pulled out a chair for Adrienne and held her arm as she climbed up. Genevieve's eyes burned with fatigue; her shoulders slumped with weariness.

Lucie leaned over to Adrienne and began unbuttoning her little sweater.

"I'll have a piece of that chocolate cake," Genevieve murmured.

"And you, mademoiselle?" Madame LaMott turned to Lucie.

"A strawberry tart also, madame."

Genevieve dropped a lump of sugar in her tea and fell back in her chair. She stared out the big picture window, studying the street. A few women were out shopping. Several children ran past, chasing each other and laughing.

Madame LaMott returned, bearing a tray with their pastries. Adrienne's eyes lit up as her tart was placed in front of her. She stared at the ruby color of the strawberries, ran her finger around the tiny pink flowers on the edge of the plate.

"And how is monsieur?" Madame LaMott asked in a friendly tone.

Genevieve looked up at her. "He's been working very hard, as usual."

"Yes, I'm sure the consul keeps him busy. It must be difficult to have him so far away." Madame LaMott placed forks and napkins on the table beside the pastries. "Will he be home soon?"

"We expect him this weekend, actually." Genevieve smiled.

Adrienne looked up at her mother, but she sat perfectly still. "Not this weekend, Maman," she stated with certainty.

The air grew heavy with the sudden silence.

Madame LaMott placed the now-empty tray at her side and looked down at the little girl with the auburn curls.

The eyes of the three waiting women locked on Adrienne. There were certain times, and this was one of them, when Genevieve could see traces of her handsome husband in Adrienne's face. The girl had certainly inherited the best traits of both sides of the family.

"He can't come home this weekend. He is staying with his other family," Adrienne said firmly. "The little boy is sick."

Genevieve felt her face flush, embarrassment flooding every pore of her being. It didn't take a genius to see the way Madame LaMott blushed, to notice the way Lucie was suddenly absorbed with her plate. The suspicion had been gnawing at Genevieve for some time now. Pierre Beauvier was an incredibly handsome man. Though he had hurried home from his work in Paris when he and Genevieve were first married, his visits had become much less frequent in the past year. Genevieve suspected there was more to the story than the demands of his job, and she felt confirmation of her fears in the faces of the two women. She looked at Madame LaMott, wondering just how much the woman might know. The feeling tore at Genevieve—the idea that everyone knew more about her husband's behavior than she did, including her four-year-old daughter. She forced herself to swallow the lump in her throat.

The feeling was one she'd known her whole life, even before Pierre. For as long as Genevieve could remember, she had been the object of too many staring eyes, had walked into too many rooms to find conversation completely stopped and all eyes on her. It was as if the whole village, and all the servants at the castle, knew things that she did not. She had asked her father about it once, when she was seven or eight, and she remembered clearly the way he had replied. "They are only jealous of your beauty, darling. Do not let it trouble you." Even then, though, the words had rung false. It felt as if everyone in her life had conspired to keep her in the dark, to keep her from having to face the truth.

Genevieve's eyes flashed, a dart of anger shooting at Adrienne. Tension filled the room, and Adrienne sat back in her chair. She blinked rapidly, fighting tears.

Genevieve crossed her arms over her body, rubbing them as if she were cold, as if she were trying to protect herself from the sting of the words. She had known that something was amiss, had felt it deep in the pit of her stomach. She had fought her growing suspicions as his excuses for staying in Paris became more frequent. But she couldn't allow herself to think about it. *Of course he's busy*, she told herself again and again. Her hand went unconsciously to the baby she now carried. *Perhaps, if I give him a son . . .* she thought, not for the first time. Genevieve rested her hand on the mound of the baby she carried. She looked up to see Adrienne staring at her.

Adrienne twisted in her seat and turned toward Madame LaMott. "Did you know I'm going to have a baby sister? She has yellow hair, like Maman's." Adrienne took a huge bite of her tart, struggling to capture the whole strawberry at one time.

Genevieve's jaw clenched. She wanted to reach out and slap Adrienne, to tell her to keep her thoughts to herself. Instead, Genevieve forced herself to breathe, turned a watered-down smile toward Madame LaMott. "Adrienne has quite an imagination, as you can see."

"But, Maman, I saw her," Adrienne insisted. "The baby is a girl."

"Finish your tart, Adrienne." Genevieve's words were clipped and short, forced through clenched teeth.

Adrienne stared at her, but said nothing else.

Madame LaMott stood silently for a moment. "Well, I'm sure it will be a beautiful baby," she said in a too-loud voice. "Boy or girl." She turned and headed to the back room.

Adrienne took up her fork once more, and started playing with her tart.

"Aren't you going to eat your cake, Maman?" Adrienne asked after several silent moments.

For a moment, Genevieve forgot her daughter; her mind was focused on Pierre. Adrienne's question brought her back. Genevieve swallowed hard and murmured, "No. I guess I'm not feeling well. Perhaps we should go home now."

"Of course, madame." Lucie began helping Adrienne with her sweater. They stood and Genevieve reached to put coins on the table, not wanting to face Madame LaMott again.

Madame LaMott emerged from the kitchen just as the three made their way to the door. "Good day to you, madame," she called. "Good day, Adrienne, mademoiselle."

Adrienne turned and waved her hand gaily. "*Au revoir*, Madame LaMott. My tart was delicious!" she added with childish exuberance. Lucie took Adrienne's small hand and followed Genevieve out. No one spoke on the walk home. Genevieve climbed the hill to the château in silence, slightly behind the others, as if trying to distance herself from the cause of her unease. Adrienne ran and skipped on the road, bending down to examine a beetle, picking up a rock with flecks of shiny mica in it.

When they reached the front hall, the maid rushed to take Genevieve's wrap. Genevieve turned and her eyes brushed lightly over her daughter's face. "Lucie, please take Adrienne for her nap." She turned on her heel without waiting for a response.

"But Maman. I'm not tired," Adrienne insisted to her mother's back. "I'm too *big* for a nap."

Genevieve stopped, but she did not turn. "You need a nap, Adrienne." Her words cut through the air, sharp with impatience. Genevieve strode quickly away from them, through the parlor and into the morning room. She sat down at her desk, leaned on her elbows, and rested her head between her hands. She rubbed her temples, listening to Adrienne's chatter as she and Lucie climbed the stairs.

Genevieve sighed. Fatigue filled every fiber of her being: the strain of carrying this baby, of dealing with Marie being home, full of judgment and criticism. Her uneasy feeling about Pierre had been gnawing at her for months. She was agitated enough without Adrienne's embarrassing behavior and distressing stories. Where did the girl come up with these ideas?

She opened her tired eyes to find the envelope staring up at her—delivered while she was out. Her own name blazed at her, written in his dark, slanted hand, and she felt bile rise in her throat.

Her hands shook as she picked up the thick, creamy paper, and slit the top. She pulled the note from inside, and opened the single fold.

"My dearest Genevieve." His handwriting was so bold, so sure and certain, like the man himself.

*I'm sorry, dear, but I find that business is too pressing for me to take the time to come home this weekend. We are meeting with the consul from Guatemala, and I will be unable to leave. Give my little darling a kiss, and pat the baby for me. I'll be home as soon as things slow down a bit.*

*All my love, Pierre*

Genevieve's eyes burned. She swallowed, trying to fight back her anger. Bitterness flooded her bloodstream—waves of anger at Pierre, at her situation, at Marie. But just as troubling was this bizarre behavior that Adrienne had been demonstrating lately. How did Adrienne know? And why couldn't she just keep the information to herself?

# CHAPTER FIVE

Adrienne and Lucie sat at the desk by the window. Books towered around them—floor-to-ceiling shelves, gleaming dark wood that held the collections the family had amassed over many years. Grand-père sat in his favorite chair, on one side of the marble fireplace. He held the newspaper from Paris in front of his face. Smoke curled up from the edges of the paper, and the sweet chocolate scent of his tobacco permeated the air, weaving soft gray figures into the sunlight.

Genevieve sat in the chair opposite him, her knitting needles clicking. Gray circles ringed her eyes. Small baby booties formed in her lap, the blue yarn jumping and spinning as she pulled.

Adrienne eyed the blue yarn and sighed. Then she turned her head back to the primer in front of her on the desk. She sat on her knees, leaning far over the book, elbows locked on each side of it, her face in her hands, as she turned her head back and forth. "Sssss," she said, in response to Lucie's finger on the page. "Sssss," Adrienne continued, looking up at Lucie and wrinkling her nose. "Like ssssun . . . and ssssnake."

Lucie beamed. "*Très bien*, Adrienne. And this one?"

Adrienne turned her head back and forth between her palms, studying the squiggles on the page. "Mmmm." She drew the sound out with a flourish. "Mmmm . . . like Maman. Mmmm." She let her eyes travel around the room, searching for another *M* word. Her gaze drifted from her grand-père, to his newspaper, to the blue booties in Genevieve's lap. She searched the library shelves, the rose-patterned carpet. "Mmmm . . . like . . ."

From the hallway, they could hear Marie, charging down the stairway, cracking out orders to the servants around her. Her voice snapped like a whip. Adrienne looked in that direction. Her smile melted away like candle wax.

Grand-père lowered his paper, his pipe still clenched between his teeth. Genevieve's knitting needles stopped clicking, now still and silent in her lap. Everyone had tensed at the sound of Marie's approach.

Marie swept into the room. "Stefan, pack the entire collection of the lives of the saints." Her arm swept out toward one shelf of the collection.

"*Oui, madame.*" Stefan bowed just slightly, and began removing books from the shelf.

Marie turned slowly, her eyes sweeping over the contents of the room, oblivious to the people watching her. "Oh . . . and those silver candlesticks will be perfect. He can use those on the altar." She reached for one of a matched pair, and held it in her fist, her eyes appraising its value.

Grand-père took his pipe from between his teeth. "Are we vacating the premises, Marie?"

"Hmmm?" She turned to him, her brows pulling together, as if she'd just noticed there was anyone else in the room. "No. No, but I am."

"Oh?"

Marie beamed as she pulled a letter from the pocket of her black dress. "Yes. I've just had a letter from Julien. He's been promoted." Pride radiated from every pore of her being.

"That's wonderful." The comte locked his blue eyes on his oldest daughter.

"Archbishop Lamy has given him his own parish. Can you believe it? And he's only twenty-six! I knew the archbishop would recognize Julien's worth. It was only a matter of time." She flipped the letter open with one hand, the candlestick still poised in the other. "Let's see—it is a little place called . . . Santa Cruz de la Cañada." Her eyes found her father again, after brushing over Genevieve's blank look. "Julien says it's north of Santa Fe about twenty-five miles."

"Well, this is wonderful news." The comte smiled and lowered the paper to his lap. "I'm happy for Julien." He took another puff from his pipe. "You'll be joining him, then?"

Marie replaced the letter in the pocket of her skirt. "Just as soon as I can book passage." She placed the candlestick on the table, and picked up a heavy volume of poetry. "I can imagine it will be very difficult for him, alone in the wilderness like that. That parish is over seventy square miles," she added. "That's a lot to take care of. I'm certain I can be of help in running his home."

Adrienne looked at Lucie, her eyes widening, then back at Marie. She continued to sit on her knees, leaning on the desk.

Marie pointed toward a crystal vase on one of the tables. "That vase, too, Stefan. Only pack it carefully. That's leaded crystal from the queen of Spain."

Stefan stepped down off a stool and turned toward Marie. *"Oui, madame."*

The comte frowned. The paper crackled underneath his hands. "Are you taking the entire contents of the château with you, Marie?"

Marie turned to him. "Oh, Father. There is so much here, you can hardly miss these few things. But this place—this Santa

Cruz—is very poor. I believe the parishioners are mostly Mexicans and Indians." Marie's nose turned up slightly, and there was no mistaking the disdain in her voice. "Julien says the church has dirt floors. He says the entire area is poor and backward. At least in Santa Fe, the archbishop tried to provide us with some of the comforts of civilization. Now it looks like that will be up to me."

She turned and swept a lace doily off a table and held it out to Stefan. "Imagine the possibilities. Julien can bring so much to those poor people. We'll bring the beauty and comforts of civilization, an appreciation for music and art . . ." Marie stopped for a moment. "Just like when my late husband and I traveled in Europe. Julien will be able to bring a little bit of France into the remotest corners of the New World." She smiled.

"Hmmm," the comte murmured. "I would think that a priest's main function is to bring the word of God, to administer the sacraments." He sat up a little straighter.

Marie's lips settled into a thin, grim line. "That goes without saying. But Julien is not an average priest. A man of his learning, his background, his ability, can bring so much more. A sense of refinement . . . a sense of . . . progress. Culture at its finest."

She turned her head toward the window, and a smile crept back into the lines of her mouth. "I knew it was just a matter of time. Julien's gifts are too great not to be noticed."

Genevieve swallowed, and her eyes dropped to her knitting. She exhaled sharply, and clicked her needles together, her knuckles white with tension.

Adrienne's eyes locked on the window in front of the desk. Sunlight poured through the glass. Golden beams shot from the panes. Adrienne stared, her eyes wide and dark. She relaxed into the vision that pulled at her.

Suddenly, Adrienne gasped, her mouth dropping open in a soft O. She climbed down from her chair and ran to her grand-père, scampering up into his lap despite the presence of the newspaper and the pipe.

The comte held his arms out and dropped the newspaper to the floor. "What's this? Finished with lessons for the day, Adrienne?"

She shook her head and pressed her face against his jacket.

The comte placed his pipe on the table beside him and lifted her chin with his finger. "What's wrong, my sweet?"

Adrienne swallowed and looked first at Marie, and then up at her grand-père. "I don't like that church. The one with the dirt floors. It feels bad. Like something bad is going to happen."

The noises of packing and moving died away, as if all the air had gone out of the room. Genevieve looked up, as did Marie. Stefan stopped moving, his arms full of books, his eyes discreetly lowered, but his body obviously straining toward Adrienne's words. The servants had been talking. Everyone who worked in the household had started paying closer attention to the little girl and her stories. Word of Adrienne's outburst at the patisserie had swept like fire through the village, and the servants had learned of it before the day was done. Everyone was talking about the little girl, and those who were old enough to remember were also talking about the girl's grandmother.

Marie turned slowly, her black skirts swishing.

"Someone wants to hurt Julien," Adrienne whispered.

Grand-père cleared his throat, and wrapped his arms around her. "Don't worry, sweetheart. Julien is a smart man. He can take care of himself." He pulled back a little and looked his granddaughter in the eye. "And your aunt Marie will be there to help him. She would never let anything bad happen to him."

They both turned their gaze toward Marie. She was frozen in the midst of what she had been doing when Adrienne's words leaked out into the room. She held a crystal candlestick in one hand, her eyes locked on her niece. Slowly she raised her eyes to her father, and a look passed between them, heavy with memory.

Marie's brow pinched with fear, but in less than a moment it was swept away, replaced by perfect calm.

Marie cleared her throat. "There is nothing to be afraid of, Adrienne. New Mexico might be poor and the buildings might be mud brick, but it is not one of your fairy tale stories." Marie rolled her eyes dramatically. "Honestly, Adrienne, your imagination is running away with you."

Marie turned to face Lucie, still seated at the table in the corner of the room. "Perhaps it would be best if you don't allow her any more of the Brothers Grimm. Those Germans—always planting the seeds of fear, with their wicked stepmothers and deep dark forests. It is obviously too much for the girl."

The release of tension was almost audible. Stefan returned to packing. Lucie let out a sigh. Genevieve watched for another moment, and took up her knitting needles once again. The comte picked up his pipe, and Adrienne could feel his chest relax.

Adrienne watched them all. Why did they keep glancing at her? What had she done that was causing everyone to act so strangely? She felt their eyes on her, and she scrunched down in the seat, trying to hide her face in her grandfather's jacket.

# CHAPTER SIX

The bells of the village church chimed in the air. Renault, the comte's driver, pulled the carriage beside the curving stone path that led to the church doors, open now to absorb the parishioners and the warmth of the spring morning. People milled about, hats bobbing in the sunshine like jewel-toned tropical birds. Lilacs framed the whitewashed building, and their perfume made everyone tipsy with spring.

Grand-père stepped down from the carriage and reached to help Genevieve. She was back to her old slender self and wearing a stunning periwinkle silk gown, a knitted shawl wrapped about her shoulders. Lucie stepped down next, holding baby Emelie, the child's golden hair catching the sun. Grand-père offered his hand to Adrienne. Age was slowing him. His straight shoulders had rounded. His hands shook, just a little, and she held on to him, even after she was down on the ground. His hand seemed thinner, almost as if the fingers she clasped were made of fine bone china. She looked up at him and smiled.

"*Bonjour*, Comte." Two older widows stood outside the church doors, still wearing black, despite the brilliant spring sunshine, despite the fact that their widowhood had spanned several decades.

"Ladies." The comte tipped his hat, still holding the hand of his little granddaughter.

"Have you heard from Marie? How is she faring in that wild New Mexico Territory?" The two women seemed anxious to hold on to the comte, as if they could pin him down with their questions, and Adrienne squeezed his hand possessively.

"She is well. Julien is very busy, I believe. It is very isolated there; we don't get as many letters as we used to."

"I imagine they both have much to do, what with running a church and a school and trying to learn the language." Madame Silva smiled and her gloved hands fluttered like jittery birds.

"Yes, I imagine so." The comte removed his hat and flashed the two ladies his most dazzling smile. "If you will excuse me." He tipped his head to them, and followed his family into the church.

Genevieve led them up the wide aisle, and entered the second pew from the front, on the left side. It was the same spot the Challembelles family had been sitting in for generations. She knelt for a moment, made the sign of the cross, and then settled back into the hard wooden pew. Lucie sat beside her, arranging Emelie's blanket. Adrienne sat down next, and copied Lucie's movements exactly, arranging the small blanket that covered her own little doll. Her father had brought her the doll from Paris, a gift when Emelie was born, and Adrienne had taken to motherhood with gusto. Grand-père smiled at the top of her head, and settled himself into the pew, his arm stretching out behind her.

Lucie sighed, followed just seconds later by a heavy sigh from Adrienne. The music began, the altar boys and priest trailed slowly up the center aisle, but Adrienne, like Lucie, stayed seated. Care of young babies excused them from the normal ups and downs and kneeling of the rest of the congregation.

Adrienne stared at the sunlight, streaming through the clerestory windows in the nave of the church. Dust filled the amber light, and Adrienne wondered where each little particle landed. She followed the beams of light, the dancing dust, down to the altar at the front of the church. Père Henri was swinging the censer back and forth, incense weaving and winding its way into the dust motes.

Adrienne examined the play of light at the front of the church. She looked at Jesus, hanging on the cross, his blood brilliant red in the stained-glass window behind the priest. She watched the way the sunlight played over the whitewashed walls, the way it disappeared in the vaulted ceilings that had always made her feel small, much too little for God to notice. She watched the dust motes as they landed on the priest's bald head, the way they scattered when he waved his arms during the homily.

The priest stepped behind the altar, and began the words of the communion. The table was covered with white satin cloth, trimmed in gold. Silver dishes held the bread and the wine. Père Henri raised the silver chalice to the heavens. Light beams shot out like stars.

Adrienne watched as the room became very dark. The windows disappeared; no sunlight streamed onto the altar. The floor turned to dirt, the walls to brown; the wood pillars lost their sheen and became rough and crude. And the priest, raising the chalice in his hands, was suddenly much younger. This man was slender and small, with a dark beard and mustache, both neatly trimmed. There was no stained glass behind him, only the dark brown wall, and a rough wooden painting of the Virgin Mother. The altar had turned to dark wood, legs swirling upward in a carved pattern, but the wood was jagged and rough.

Adrienne viewed it all as if from a distance, as if she were sitting in a darkened theater, watching the scene play out below her. She could see the bowed heads of the parishioners, all of them with dark, blue-black hair. There were no fine dresses, no sparkling silks in that crowd. Many of the ladies wore striped woven shawls over their shoulders, in shades of gray and brown and beige.

The younger, smaller, darker priest began the words of the consecration. He offered the bread, the body of Christ, and held it high in the air. He raised the silver chalice, the one piece of wealth, the one piece that sparkled, in that poor brown building. Adrienne recognized that chalice. Marie had packed it last year, when she was preparing to join Julien in America. Adrienne glanced at the priest in her vision again, and knew suddenly that this was her cousin, the one she had never met. Julien, Marie's son.

He lifted the chalice in both hands, raised it in the air, and repeated in a solemn voice, *"Hic est enim calix sanguinis mei, novi et . . ."* The words of the Latin rang in the air.

He brought the chalice to his lips, drank a slow swig of the wine. His hands lowered the cup, revealing his face. The face transformed before her eyes, changing from the calm and peaceful look of a priest communing with God into a grotesque monster. His eyes bulged. His skin turned clammy and gray. He looked as if he had seen the Angel of Death standing right in front of him. The chalice dropped to the floor with a thud, and Julien clutched his throat. His eyes rolled back in his head, and he crumpled to the ground. Marie, sitting in the first pew, rushed to his side. Several of the men who helped with the service followed her, and knelt beside the stricken priest. His mouth bubbled with blue-white foam.

Marie's eyes, round with fear, rose to the man across from her. She shouted, in French, "Milk! Bring milk!" The man stared at her, uncomprehending. *"Leche!"* she shouted.

One man ran from the building. Marie loosened Julien's collar, and reached for the chalice, on its side a few feet away. She picked it up. The wine had spilled into the dirt, leaving a trail of wet spots on the dirt floor where it had fallen. She brought the chalice to her nose and sniffed, then placed it beside her as Julien continued to retch and gag. The chalice tipped over, and rolled a few feet, forgotten in the heat of the moment.

45

The young man who had run out returned, holding a battered tin cup in his two hands, milk sloshing over the top as he handed it to Marie. Marie held Julien's head. Another man held his shoulders. She pushed the rim of the cup between his lips, already slightly blue in color. His eyes were dilated, huge, unfocused. "Julien, drink. You must drink this," she said. She managed to get a few sips of the milk into his open lips, and watched as he swallowed. She poured in more. Time seemed to stand still, the men around him watching, waiting. Their eyes were dark and unreadable, their faces set like stone. Marie forced more milk into his mouth.

His lips lost some of the bluish color, but his face looked bleached and pale. A sheen of sweat could be seen on his forehead. "Help me," she whispered to the men around her. They understood. One man lifted the priest in his arms, and carried him down the aisle and out the doors of the church to the rectory next door. The parishioners stood and watched. Most of the faces were unmoved, unemotional, stoic, as if the entire congregation were chess pieces carved of marble.

Adrienne blinked, brought back to the bright light streaming in the windows of the church in Beaulieu. Père Henri, sunlight bouncing off his bald head, was replacing the chalice on the altar.

Adrienne leaned forward slightly, turned toward her mother. "Maman," she said, her voice echoing off the walls and ceiling of the church.

"Shhh," Genevieve whispered.

"But Maman." Adrienne's knowledge was too much for her to contain. She reached around Lucie to pull at the sleeve of her mother's dress.

Genevieve glared her. "Shhh," she commanded, her eyes and voice pushing Adrienne back into her seat.

Adrienne turned her eyes to the front of the church once again. She watched, her body refusing to sit still, as the priest raised his arms, and led the congregation in a final song. Everyone but

Adrienne and Lucie stood. Adrienne watched as he made the sign of the cross, and uttered the words of the blessing.

"The Lord bless you and keep you. The Lord make his face shine upon you. The Lord lift up your countenance, and grant you peace." Adrienne could barely contain herself, impatient to speak about what she had seen.

The priest started slowly down the aisle, followed by the altar boys. His robes swung leisurely from side to side. Adrienne stood, almost jumping up and down. In her excitement, she forgot her own baby, and let it hang from her side, dangling by one arm, brushing the floor.

"Maman," Adrienne spoke again as they stood and moved into the center aisle.

Genevieve pinched Adrienne's shoulder, shot her another glaring look, and Adrienne bit her tongue, wriggling with the excitement of what she had seen.

They moved slowly toward the doors at the back of the church. Grand-père and Genevieve greeted the people of the village, Grand-père shaking hands, Genevieve offering her slender, gloved hand to a few of the local women. They stopped at the door. The priest took Genevieve's hand in both of his, swallowing her hand in his rough red paws. "And how are you today, madame?" He smiled.

"*Je vais bien,* Père Henri, *merci.* Wonderful message today." She smiled.

Adrienne grew impatient. Her mother had not listened to the priest's homily; she never did. This news that Adrienne held inside her was too important to wait while Genevieve charmed the villagers like some exotic hothouse orchid.

Adrienne tugged at her mother's skirts. "Maman, we need to go. Julien and Aunt Marie are at the castle, waiting for us." The insistence of her voice drew the attention of several people who stood nearby.

Genevieve's smile dropped from her face, and she looked down at Adrienne, as did the priest and Grand-père.

"We must go, Maman! Someone tried to kill him. In church, during the mass." Adrienne was insistent. "He is sick, Maman. He almost died. With *poison*." Adrienne drew out the last word dramatically. "I knew there was something bad about that church."

By now the entire area had gone completely quiet, all voices stilled as they caught the words of the little girl.

Genevieve looked up at the priest. She tried to smile, but it slipped away, cracking like a china teacup dropped on a marble floor. All of the radiant beauty of a few moments before had evaporated.

The priest blinked. He looked at Genevieve, suddenly rendered speechless.

"Such an imagination," Genevieve exhaled, her voice ruffled with fear. "We are quite beside ourselves with her stories, sometimes. I don't know where she comes up with these things." Genevieve tried another feeble smile.

"I understand, madame. It is not unusual, at her age, to imagine things. Children can be so creative."

Genevieve sighed gratefully. Her face had turned green; she refused to meet the eyes of any of the people around her.

Grand-père did search their faces, looking for anyone who might remember his late wife and the stories that had somehow escaped about her. Most of the parishioners were watching Adrienne and Genevieve, not looking at him. But when he turned to make his way to the carriage, his eyes met those of Madame Ettienne. She was almost the same age as the comte, ancient compared to those around her. She did not nod, did not acknowledge their glance in any way, but the comte knew, as he reached to take Adrienne's hand, that at least one person in that congregation had remembered Marguerite, and made the connection. He wrapped his hand around that of his granddaughter, and with his other hand, took Genevieve's elbow, steering them both toward the carriage. Lucie followed, folding the blanket over Emelie's face. Grand-père opened the door of the carriage, helped all the ladies inside, and folded himself into the seat next to Adrienne.

They heard the crack of the whip, and the carriage jolted forward. The horses trotted off, their hooves clicking on the stone street. Renault turned the carriage toward the château. When they were safely away from the ears of the village, he leaned back slightly, his voice low. "Monsieur? There is . . . news. Madame Morier and Père Julien are at the castle. Père Julien is very sick, monsieur."

Genevieve's eyes met those of her father across the space between their seats. The comte swallowed, his Adam's apple moving up and down. He doubted that Genevieve knew anything about her own mother. He could not imagine that anyone from the village or any of the servants would have dared to speak to the daughter of the comte about such a distressing subject. Certainly he had never discussed it with her. He turned to look out the window, feeling the glaring inadequacies of his parenting. Should he have told her? Would it have made any difference?

Genevieve held her lace handkerchief, locked inside her gloved hand, in front of her mouth. Lucie sat in the corner of the carriage, jiggling the baby, who had begun to whimper. Lucie kept her eyes held discreetly on the child. Adrienne sat across from her, next to the comte, staring out the window, and jiggling her own baby doll.

"Shhh," she whispered to her doll. "We're almost home. Shhh."

# CHAPTER SEVEN

The carriage stopped in the circular drive in front of the castle, and Renault held the door and offered his hand to each of the women as they stepped down. The maid, Henriette, opened the door as the family trailed up the steps. She curtsied, and took Genevieve's wrap.

"We had arranged for luncheon on the terrace, monsieur, but it looks as if a storm is coming. We will move everything to the dining room. Whenever you're ready. And Madame Morier is waiting for you in the library." She curtsied again, and left the hallway.

The comte looked at the group in the hall. "Why don't you girls go change out of your Sunday clothes? We'll eat after I've had a chance to speak with Marie."

The women started up the steps. Genevieve and Lucie did their best not to stare, but both took advantage of the curving of the staircase to try to catch a glimpse of Marie, standing like a statue in her black crepe. She stood before the floor-to-ceiling window in the library, but her face was turned to the view outside. She was like a paper cutout, nothing but a dark silhouette with the light behind her.

The comte braced himself. At one time, he had loved a challenge, loved the adrenaline rush of dealing with difficult situations, and testing his own abilities. The coming encounter only sapped his already depleted strength. He felt every moment of his age, every ache in his body. He stepped into the library and closed the door behind him. "Marie," he said, turning toward his oldest daughter, "how good to see you. We weren't expecting you until August. Julien is with you?"

Marie turned toward him, her eyes nervous and tired, more fragile looking than he had ever seen her, and he found himself feeling relieved. Perhaps they would be able to avoid a battle. They kissed each other's cheeks, and her hands rested on his forearms for a moment. "Yes. He's upstairs resting. The trip was quite a strain on him. He's not been well."

The comte searched her face. She looked haggard; her skin was pale; dark shadows hung at her eyes. She seemed uncomfortable with his gaze, and turned back to the long windows, seeking the sun. She rubbed her arms as if she were cold.

The comte searched his jacket pocket for his pipe, and began to load and tamp it down. He kept his eyes on his work. "Julien is sick?" He kept his words as level as possible, and focused on lighting his pipe. He exhaled, and smoke curled up around him. He inhaled again and moved to the window beside her.

Marie turned and met his gaze. The blue of the walls cast a harsh shadow on her skin, making her look gray and sickly herself. "Yes." Her voice caught, and she swallowed hard. "His stomach. He's had a very rough time keeping anything down. I thought it would be best—that he would recover better if he were here."

She took a deep breath, and the comte noticed that her body almost shook with the effort of appearing calm. "Yes," Marie replied. "He's upstairs resting. Perhaps the waters of Vichy can work their magic on him."

"I'm surprised you dared to travel so far, if he's that ill." The comte took another long drag on his pipe. He stared out into the green lawn, the deeper green of the woods beyond. Servants were on the terrace, gathering up the plates and silverware, crystal and linen, from the outside table. Wind gusted, lifting the edges of the tablecloth as they worked.

Marie nodded, and turned toward him. Her eyes were brittle. "He can get better care here," she said. "Better doctors. And servants"—she raised her eyes to the floor above them—"to help."

"Have you any idea what might be wrong?" The comte inhaled, and blew smoke toward the window.

Marie seemed to be finding it difficult to get the words out. "We thought it might be the water. Conditions are so primitive there. Perhaps something has contaminated the well." Her words sounded rehearsed. Both the comte and his oldest daughter were well trained at maintaining composure, at framing information in the most beneficial way, but the air was thick with what was not being said.

The comte took another deep drag on his pipe, let the smoke out slowly. "I see."

Marie turned her head toward the window. She sat down on the arm edge of a chair, her body stiff and brittle, like a china doll perched on a shelf.

The comte stood beside her, but did not turn to look at her. "Marie, I have not survived eighty-five years of French politics because I'm a fool. One does not run halfway around the world, with a man who is deathly ill, because of bad water. You could have drawn water from a different source—drilled another well. You could have moved him to Santa Fe." Smoke curled around his head. He turned to Marie.

Marie met his eyes. They stared at one another. "Tell me the truth," he said.

She turned her gaze back to the baby green of spring outside the window, and let her breath out in a long, slow stream. She wrapped her arms around her chest. The comte could see that her eyes were full. "Julien almost died." She swallowed, and one tear dropped from her eye to the bodice of her dress. "He was poisoned. At the chalice—during mass." She braved one quick glance at her father's face. "It seems that someone wants him dead."

The comte exhaled slowly, and turned to look at the view again. Adrienne's words at the church hung in the air, specters of the story she had almost shouted as they stood in the doorway. He shuddered, and stared out at the horizon. Clouds were piling up over the mountains, heavy and gray with the promise of rain. When he spoke, he spoke to the glass. His voice was low. "Have you any idea who did this? Why?"

Marie sighed. She shook her head. "No."

"Has he done something, Marie? Something to anger one of his parishioners?" The comte turned toward his daughter. She glanced at him and then focused her eyes on the thunderstorm building in the distance.

"He's done something to anger almost every one of his parishioners, I imagine. There isn't a priest over there—not from France, anyway—that hasn't felt the anger, the resentment, of the people in New Mexico Territory."

The comte studied her face and raised his eyebrows.

She turned to him, and the anger in her eyes could burn holes in the carpet. "It's awful. I don't understand those people at all. They are completely locked into their own way of doing things. I've never met people so stubborn, so resistant to the ways of civilized society. And it's obvious to me that they don't understand Julien. He's only trying to help . . . trying to get a school going . . . trying to administer the sacraments. But they don't want his help. They don't want to better themselves or their children at all. I don't think they have any idea how hard Julien is working to improve things for them. They cling to their old ways, their old superstitions."

Her eyes went back to the window, and she stared at the approaching storm. Fingers of rain reached down and brushed the ground in the distance. The trees near the château began to sway in the wind. They could hear branches creaking in the chestnut tree just outside.

"It isn't just Julien, either. They resent everyone. They hated the Spanish—drove them out and kept them out for a hundred years after a very bloody revolt. Then they had to deal with the Mexican government. Now the Americans, and they *really* seem to hate them. They seem to dislike everyone outside of their own little group."

The comte exhaled slowly. "And the archbishop? Has he . . . ?"

"The archbishop has had all kinds of problems. He excommunicated two Mexican priests, just up the road from Julien. One of them had a wife and children, and yet he continued to perform baptisms and weddings—even after the archbishop ordered him to stop." Marie shook her head. "The people seem to have this idea that they can manage by themselves. That they don't need any of us. That the rules of the church don't apply to them.

"And this isn't the first time they've resorted to poison at the chalice, either. There was an incident in a parish in Albuquerque, just a few years back. Only that priest was not so lucky." There was a sharp intake of breath, as if the words she uttered had stabbed into her chest. Their eyes met, and the comte saw her fear, saw the brush with death that now permeated her being. She bit her lip and turned back to the window.

Marie ran her hands up and down her arms. The temperature was dropping. A gust of wind, thick with dust and the smell of moisture, rushed in an open window, and Marie closed it. "I really don't know how Julien can even consider going back. I don't believe those people are even remotely interested in salvation. They seem perfectly content to stay locked in their own little world, oblivious to the possibilities of something better."

Her eyes filled with tears. She was visibly struggling, trying to fight her emotions, trying to keep her fears from completely enveloping her. "I cannot imagine that the situation is going to get any better. But he insists . . . says they need him.

"Maybe they do need him, but they certainly don't want him. How is he ever going to make a difference? They agree to your face, nod their heads. But then they'll go off and do whatever they want anyway. They still practice their old ceremonies—but they do it in secret. And the very idea—" Her voice caught, and she swallowed. "The very idea that they would . . . that someone could do something like . . ."

Marie cleared her throat. The comte waited for her to continue, watching as she fought the fear that swirled like a whirlwind all around her. He could not remember more than one or two times in all of Marie's life when she had not maintained strict control of her emotions.

"There is another priest at Santa Cruz. It's a large parish—far too much for one man. Seventy square miles, and Julien has to make the rounds to all these small villages. Father Medina was appointed to help, but . . . I think he does more harm than good. He is one of them— his family is still part of the community. Trained at the seminary in Mexico, of all places. As if anyone could receive proper training in that godforsaken place." She looked up at her father, and back outside. "He and Julien have not gotten on so well. He is very sympathetic to the Indian people in Santa Cruz. Too much so, if you ask me. Sometimes it has hurt the authority of the church . . . Julien's authority."

The comte turned toward Marie. "Sounds like difficult circumstances for a young priest in his first parish."

Marie nodded. She turned to him. Her eyes were clear and hard. "I can't imagine anything *more* difficult. Understanding the Indian race is far more difficult than European politics, I'm certain. No wonder the Americans have a policy of putting them on reservations. But even so, they still persist in hanging on to their old ways. Perhaps the Americans were right to pursue a campaign of complete extermination."

The comte shuddered. He did not agree with her, but this hardly seemed the time to discuss such an issue.

Marie sighed heavily, and they both watched the storm as it broke against the castle, water pelting the window. Lightning flashed in the western sky; thunder hammered the air. The rain beat a heavy, pounding rhythm on the stones of the terrace outside.

"Father." Her voice was soft, almost drowned by the storm. "Let's keep this between ourselves, shall we? I cannot expect the rest of the family, or the villagers for that matter, to understand the intricacies of life in the New World." She turned to him, her eyes clear and hard. She was recovered, her stiff shell back in place, her shoulders and chin firm. "I cannot abide the thought of people talking . . ." She sniffed and took a deep breath. "When they have no way to understand."

Their eyes met, and the comte thought he could see a glimmer of what it had been like for the child Marie, the little girl whose mother had been the subject of so much talk. He swallowed a tight knot of pain. Despite how thorny Marie could be, despite her demanding, argumentative nature, he understood how difficult her life had been. She'd lost her mother; she'd lost her husband; and now she had almost lost her son.

He moved the pipe to his right hand, raised his left arm, and pulled her close. For one moment, she leaned into him. He could feel how frail she was underneath that tough exterior. She was too thin, her frame so slender and brittle that he feared crushing her.

After a moment, she drew back. She sniffled, and drew a handkerchief to her nose. She turned and left the room, careful not to meet his eyes after her moment of vulnerability. He heard the click of the door as she closed it behind her.

The comte blew out a puff of smoke. He turned back to the window and stared at the grounds of the castle through the veil of the storm—lands that had been in his family for generations.

Below the window, stretching away to the woods, were his vine-yards. Chestnuts and cedars surrounded the grounds of the castle, protecting it from the eyes of the villagers.

Despite all the unrest in France in the previous century, he had managed to retain his family's holdings. He was proud of that: so many other families in the nobility had lost everything, had been forced to flee France. But he had learned, partly from watching his own father, how to negotiate the minefields of political change. When the peasants and locals in the village of Beaulieu had fought against the high taxes imposed by the king, and the tithe imposed by the church, the comte had not remained rigid and unyielding, like so many of his acquaintance. During years of bad crops, he had excused part of their tax obligations to him and his family. He had allowed the villagers to hunt on his lands at certain times of the year, free of charge. He listened to their grievances against one another, or against the church, and helped to negotiate peaceful solutions. He helped to raise money for a school in the village. He never locked himself away—shut up in the riches of his own castle, waited on by servants—or turned a blind eye to the sufferings of the village. He made it a point to walk in at least a few times a week, to speak with those he passed on the street.

And now here he was, at eighty-five years of age, tired of the battle, exhausted by the endless rounds of power struggle and nego-tiation. The comte stared out the window as rain pelted against the glass. He could see his own reflection, faint though it was in the dim light. And now this. There was one pressing problem that he had not dealt with—one issue that could cost them all dearly.

There had clearly been talk about Adrienne and her stories all over the village for months now. This latest episode, with Adrienne's outburst at church this morning, and the arrival of Marie, sick son in tow, would only spark more gossip. He knew he should speak to the child, that he should do something to contain her, to teach her to speak only to a few trusted souls. There were only two trusted souls that he knew of, only two who would listen to the girl without judgment or recrimination. Lucie loved the girl; that was obvious. She didn't seem threatened or frightened by Adrienne's gift. But a governess was little more than a paid servant, and she had no power to either protect Adrienne from the wrath of others, or advise the girl on politically correct behavior. And he knew that Genevieve had neither the desire nor the skill to manage the situation.

He was the only one who could protect her, and he knew that he would not be around forever. He felt the ravages of his own mortality more every day. Every time he and Adrienne walked into Beaulieu, he was a little slower on the walk home. His breathing was not as deep, not as easy as it once was. He ached, and on days like today, when the air had become cold and damp, he felt his age in every joint of his body. If he really wanted to protect his grand-daughter, he needed to talk to her, to teach her, to somehow convince her that it was best to remain silent, to keep the stories she saw and heard to herself.

The comte stared out the window. Rain poured from the skies; thunder shook the glass; lightning flashed across the gray. The memory crashed into his consciousness, carried by that streak of lightning. He remembered the first time he had seen Marguerite. He was thirty-five years old, and he and his father were hunting with Seigneur Teyssier, on the Teyssier estate several miles down the road. A storm had come up, just like the one before him now, and each of the hunters had taken shelter wherever they could. The comte had found a rock overhang, along the side of the hill, and had stood underneath, watching as the water poured down around him.

Marguerite was with her governess. The two of them had been caught in the rainstorm, out riding horses, and had also taken shelter. As soon as the rain had started to let up, they had galloped past him. Both were sodden. But even soaking wet, even in that gray day, he had seen the reddish glints in her hair. She was wearing a cloak of cobalt blue, and the color had popped out against the gray of the day and the copper of her hair. She turned to look at him, as if she knew he would be standing there under the rock, sheltering from the rain. The look that passed between them went straight to his heart. It was as if she already knew him, had expected him to be waiting there.

He mentioned her to his father a few days later—the girl with the reddish hair. His father seemed unaware of the girl's existence, but as he thought back, he realized that there had been a young daughter mentioned years ago, at the Teyssier household. She had never been allowed out in public, had never even, as far as he knew, been allowed to sit at dinners held for guests at their estate. It was as if she had disappeared from consciousness within a few years of her birth.

Seigneur Teyssier had seemed stunned when Matthieu and his father approached him about a possible union. Matthieu never thought to question it, never thought to wonder why the girl had been hidden away for most of her life. He ignored the warnings from his own father, who insisted there must be something terribly wrong or they would not have kept the girl from society. He had begged his son to reconsider, but Matthieu had thrown caution to the winds. There was something about that young woman in the blue cloak, something about the way her eyes met his, something about that look of *knowing*, that had arrested Matthieu, had turned him into a captive even before they had actually met. When they met a few weeks later, at a dinner arranged by Matthieu's family, he was even more entranced. She was quiet, reticent to speak, especially in front of her family, but when she did, she displayed a keen intellect. Matthieu could see that nothing escaped her notice.

Later, when Matthieu and Marguerite had been married a few months, Matthieu had learned why she had been hidden away, why Seigneur Teyssier had done his best to keep her out of the public eye. Her visions, her stories, just like Adrienne's, had been cause for alarm, and her father had made sure that none of that talk would leak out to the surrounding countryside. As Marguerite learned to trust her husband, she began to talk about the things she saw. She told him that their first child would be a dark-haired daughter. She warned him to stay away from Paris one fall, and they learned weeks later that there had been a riot with several people killed. They agreed to keep her visions to themselves, and they had done their best to guard her secret.

For the most part, they succeeded. There were occasions, relatively few, when the comtesse would drift off, and come back with some startling new story that somehow managed to leak out. She told him about the family in Clermont who was forced to leave the country, forced to leave their possessions, because the father had argued with the village priest. She asked him to send their cook, Edith, home to Nice, knowing that the woman's mother was on her deathbed and would not live another month. There were times when servants overheard, even the rare occasion when a servant would come to her, asking for help. Edith was one of those. She had been dreaming about her mother, had come to Marguerite and asked if Marguerite could help—if there was anything that Edith should know.

It was when Marguerite became pregnant with Genevieve that the trickle of gossip turned into a raging torrent. The comte felt the wind rush out of him at the memory, and he dropped into the chair beside the window. Even now, over thirty years later, the memory had the power to knock him to his knees.

For months, she had begged him, trying to convince him that they should try again. She wanted so much to give him a son. He was reluctant: she wasn't strong to begin with, and the loss of their son a few years earlier, and two previous miscarriages, had sapped her of strength. What worried him most, though, was her state of mind.

When their boy died, at only ten months of age, she had grieved in a way that left him frightened, alarmed at what might become of her. They were both torn, but Marguerite had become sullen and quiet, sometimes completely unapproachable. There were days when she didn't bother to take care of herself—days when she sat in her chair by the window, staring out at the grounds of the estate. She would not dress; she would not allow the servants to do her hair; she would not eat. It had taken more than a year before she came back to herself.

When Marie had turned twelve, and was leaving for another term at the convent school, Marguerite started in on him with full force. Didn't he want a son, an heir, to pass the estate to? Marie was getting older; Marguerite was getting older; the time was *now*. She pleaded with him, almost desperate for another baby.

And it was true, the things she said. He very much wanted a son. He worried about what would happen to the Challembelles estate without a male heir. He often wondered if Marie could handle such a huge burden. So when Marguerite came to him one morning, and told him that she had had a dream that the baby was a boy, and all would be fine, he believed her. He wanted to believe her. He looked into her eyes, and saw the flame of her desire. He heard what he wanted to hear—that they would have a son. He believed her because he wanted to believe her.

She was only a few months into the pregnancy when he saw the change come over her. She refused to confide in him, refused to tell him that she had begun to have visions about the baby. He would find her sitting in some darkened corner, and when he asked her what was wrong, she would whisper that it was only the normal queasiness of early pregnancy.

She was halfway through her term before he learned the truth. December had fallen on the countryside with lead-gray skies and shrieking winds and bitter cold. Marie was home from school. She had asked to bring a friend with her for the holiday, and Madeline Fortier had joined them at the château. Her father was a duke in

Brioude; the families were slightly acquainted through the comte's work in Paris.

Matthieu had found Marguerite, sitting in a chair by the window in the greenhouse. Tears were streaming down her face; her shoulders shook. He knelt before her. "Marguerite, what is it? You have to tell me."

She pulled her hands away, and covered her face. She rocked back and forth in the chair. She shook her head. "No, Matthieu . . . I cannot."

His anger boiled at her refusal, and he raised his voice to her. He stood up. "Marguerite, this has been going on long enough. What is wrong? What are you keeping from me?"

Her shoulders stiffened, and she dropped her hands from her face. Tears had left trails across her cheeks; her eyes were those of a wounded child.

The comte regretted his harsh tone almost immediately.

"You want to know? You really want to know? So that you can be as miserable as I am?" Her eyes blazed with fire when she turned to look at him.

He felt as if the world had started spinning too quickly, as if he were about to fall. Suddenly he wasn't sure that he wanted to know. But watching her like this—more disheveled and emotional than he had seen her in years—could not be borne. He forced himself to take a deep breath. "Yes, Marguerite. I want to know."

She turned her face away from him. The low gray light turned her tears into luminous gray pearls, sliding down her cheeks. "The baby is a girl. A girl . . . with yellow hair."

He stood there, gazing at her, hit by a wave of shock that things could be so different from what he had believed for several months now. "But . . . I thought you said . . . I thought you had dreamt . . ." His mind clouded with questions.

She turned to him, suddenly calm. Her shoulders no longer shook, but the tears continued to glimmer on her cheeks. "I lied to you, Matthieu. I never had a dream about the baby. I never had a vision that it would be a boy. I lied to you."

He felt as if he had been kicked; his air escaped in one quick rush. "Marguerite, you know how dangerous this is . . . what the doctor said. How could you lead me to believe . . ." Anger made his voice sharper than he had intended.

"I wanted to try, one more time. I wanted to give you a son. I know how important it is to have a son to take over the estate. There was always the chance that the baby would be a boy, and I . . ." She stopped and exhaled. "I wanted another baby. I needed another baby, after . . ."

Matthieu raised his hand and rubbed it back and forth on his forehead. He was trying to absorb it all, but he had believed, absolutely believed, that they were going to have a son. He had taken her words about the dream at face value, having learned many years ago that her visions could be trusted. But now this—there had been no vision. His mind fought its way through this new information. She had lied to him, and the deception suddenly made him question everything he thought he had known about her. He stared at one corner of the room, not aware of what he was seeing. He raised his hands to his mouth and nose, breathed into them for a moment, trying to quiet his racing heart.

At last, he took a deep breath and turned to face her. "It doesn't matter, Marguerite. It doesn't matter. A baby girl is still a baby . . ." His voice broke off. His assurances sounded hollow and false, even as they left his mouth.

She looked at him, calmer now, as if telling him the truth had lifted some of the burden she had been carrying. "But it does, Matthieu. It does matter. I *lied* to you. I used my"—she paused, searching for the word—"my *vision* . . . to get what I wanted. Without thinking of what it might do to you . . . to Marie."

They stared at one another. Even then, even at that moment, Matthieu had known that things would never be the same for them, that a dark cloud had descended on their marriage and would never lift.

Marguerite turned her head, looking toward the room where Marie and her friend were engaged in a game of chess. "What kind of person am I? I have failed you both. As a wife, as a mother. As a person." She turned to look at him again. "My whole life . . . I've been . . . defective. My father hid me away. Made me stay in my rooms." He could see the depth of her despair.

"And now I am having visions about the baby. Matthieu . . . the baby will live. She will be fine and healthy." She stopped, watching as understanding dawned in his mind. "But I will not."

His breath caught; he shook his head. "No. No. This is not possible. What are you saying?"

She winced, both of them aware of the accusation in his voice. She turned to look out the window once more, avoiding the shock and fear in his eyes. "I can see it, Matthieu. My eyes are closed. I can see my body laid out: my skin very pale . . . almost gray. There is blood everywhere." She turned back to face him. "I will not live to help you raise this baby."

He stared at her, his mind fighting to push away every word, every image that she laid before him.

"I've ruined everything." Tears flowed down her cheeks. "It was bad enough, everything I've put you through, with the *real* visions. And now this. I lied to you. And nothing will ever be the same."

He had tried to swallow his own anger at what she had done, to go to her, to reassure her, but she had pushed him away, shaking her head, her face sloppy with tears. She turned and fled from the room.

The comte exhaled slowly, his eyes back on the storm outside the window. He could remember turning, the tension still thick in the air of the room, and seeing the dark eyes of Marie. She and her friend Madeline had been in the next room, playing chess, when they had heard the shouting, the beginnings of the disagreement. He remembered looking into the eyes of that other girl, the girl who would go back to her family and tell them about the crazy woman at the Château de Challembelles. He well remembered how the story had traveled the countryside, quickly coming back to the village of Beaulieu. And he remembered turning his gaze to Marie, shame and embarrassment written in every line of her features. In her eyes burned something even worse than shame and embarrassment, something that made him cringe even now, all these years later. Marie fairly vibrated with anger.

Adrienne looked so much like her grandmother. Not just in the coloring, the copper-colored hair and blue eyes, but in the way she walked, in the way she held her head slightly tipped, her chin pointing to the left, whenever a vision came to her. He felt a lump rising in his throat, and his eyes burned. He would do anything to protect this little girl, anything to keep her from the gossip and stares of the villagers.

But lock her away? Kill her spirit and force her to stay hidden and quiet? Like so many times over the past year, he pushed the thought away from him. Not now. Not today. He could not, would not, do anything just yet. He swore to himself that he would deal with this. Soon.

# CHAPTER EIGHT

Adrienne followed Lucie down the long hallway toward her bedroom. They passed a guest room on the right. The door was ajar, and Adrienne slowed, tipped her head slightly so that she could see inside the room. Julien lay in the middle of the bed, his face almost as pale as the white linen sheets surrounding him. His eyes were closed. He didn't appear to be breathing. Adrienne stopped for a moment in front of the door, staring at this cousin she had never met. He had the dark hair, the dark beard, she had seen in her visions. Julien began to cough, a horrid, crackling cough that wracked his entire body.

Lucie appeared in front of Adrienne and held out her hand. "Come, Adrienne. He needs to rest. You can meet him later." Her words were barely audible in the hushed atmosphere of illness.

They entered Adrienne's room down the hall, and Lucie began to unbutton the girl's church dress. "Adrienne, do you know who did this? Who poisoned Julien?"

Adrienne shook her head.

"How can you be certain he was poisoned?"

"I could see him—Julien. In the church. It is very dark there. No windows. The floors are dirt." Adrienne stood patiently while

Lucie slipped a day dress over her head. "Not that one, Lucie! Can't I wear the pink one, with the roses?"

Lucie stopped and smiled. "I suppose." She made another trip to the wardrobe.

"Tell me, Adrienne. What you saw."

"Well, he took the cup in his hands. The silver one that Marie took from the library, the last time she was home?"

Lucie nodded, and turned Adrienne slightly so she could tie the ribbon at the back of her dress.

"And then he raised it up, like this." Adrienne pretended to hold a cup in her hands, and raised it above her head. Her eyes lifted to the ceiling. "He said a bunch of words I couldn't understand . . . just like Père Henri says."

Lucie nodded.

"And then he took a sip, like this." Again Adrienne demonstrated. "And then his eyes got big, and he dropped the cup, and his hands came up to his throat." She acted out each sentence. "And his eyes rolled back in his head . . . and then . . ." Adrienne let her eyes roll back, and she dropped to the floor, like a rag doll.

"Hmmm," Lucie commented. Her lips were pressed together, as if trying to hide a smile.

A heavy silence filled the room. Adrienne opened her eyes. The roses on the rug were a deep crimson, shaded with cream and pink. And at the edge of one cabbage rose, two pointed black boots stood, black skirts swishing around them.

"That's very amusing, Adrienne." Marie's voice cracked in the air.

Lucie jumped. She had not seen Marie come in. Adrienne swallowed and sat up.

"I don't know where in the world you get these stories of yours." Marie stood at the edge of the rug, stiff and severe. A whiff of lavender escaped from her black skirts, and Adrienne coughed.

"But there is a great difference between imagination and the actual truth." Marie's eyes were narrow and hard.

Adrienne felt as if she'd been stung. "But I—"

"Enough!" Marie did not shout, but her words cut the air as if she had. "There is no way for you to know what happened on the other side of the world. And I will tolerate none of these stories. Is that clear?"

Adrienne swallowed. "Yes, madame." She met Marie's gaze.

Adrienne sat in the middle of the rug, where she had been demonstrating the story to Lucie just a few moments before. Her lower lip pushed out; her eyes burned with rage. But she did not cry.

# CHAPTER NINE

Père Henri stopped for a moment to catch his breath. He leaned against the trunk of a chestnut tree, and pulled a handkerchief from his pocket. Though it was only late May, the sun was hot on his bald head, and he mopped it down for the third time since starting his journey. It was a mile from the rectory to the gates of the Château de Challembelles, though it felt much longer, and it would never do for him to arrive looking nervous and sweat-drenched.

In truth, he was nervous and sweaty. It was not yet eleven, but the day was already unseasonably hot and humid. The incline on the road to the château was slight, but it was an incline, and for some reason it seemed much more difficult today than it had in the past. It was partially due to the effects of time: he was approaching sixty, and he was overfond of good food and fine wine and blessed with a housekeeper who kept him supplied with both.

But at least part of the difficulty lay in the visit itself. He'd been there many times, of course, as a guest of Genevieve and the comte. There'd been a dinner after baby Adrienne had been baptized, and another just a few months ago, when Pierre was home from Paris for the baptism of baby Emelie. He well remembered the marriage of Genevieve and Pierre Beauvier seven years ago. The whole affair had been quite lavishly done up, as he recalled, and the food had been excellent. He still remembered the crispy skin on the roasted duck, and the memory provoked an annoying growl from his stomach. Over the years that Père Henri had been the priest in Beaulieu, there had been several occasions to visit, but all of them had been through invitation. He could not recall another occasion when he had taken it upon himself to visit the château, uninvited and unannounced.

It wasn't that Père Henri was particularly interested in the gossip of the village. But whenever his housekeeper, Madame Cezanne, served him some delicious concoction from her overflowing kitchen, she usually spiced it with some tidbit or two that she had heard while at the market. Yesterday evening, she had served him a wonderful beef roast, slightly pink and swimming in juice, just the way he liked it, and roasted new potatoes, drenched in butter and flecked with chives from the garden. He had closed his eyes and inhaled the aromas, drinking them in, savoring the feast before he had tasted a bite. Indulging her penchant for sharing the latest gossip seemed a small price to pay for having such a wonderful cook in the house. But the news that she had served with last night's meal had been particularly interesting, since it tied directly to the outlandish story Adrienne had blurted out as the family left the church yesterday morning.

"Madame Morier is back from America," the woman said quietly, her eyes on the potatoes that she heaped on his plate. "The cook is all in a state—seems madame came back without any prior warning. Cook is positively mortified, since madame is very particular about how things are done when she is home."

Père Henri looked up at her, but she kept her eyes discreetly on the work of dishing up his plate. Her cheeks were red; her graying hair escaped in little vagabond curls from the bun at the nape of her neck. "And her son is with her. Cook was quite beside herself. Says she's going to have to make *two different* selections for each meal. Père Julien is sick, apparently, and having quite a time keeping anything down."

The story was particularly troubling, especially given Adrienne's outburst after the mass. Père Henri had assumed, at the time, that Adrienne was simply demonstrating her remarkable creative abilities. He liked the little girl. She was very beautiful, for one thing, quite like her late grandmother, according to his housekeeper. She was bright, precocious even. She showed an interest in everything. And since the addition of her governess just a few years ago, Adrienne had begun to demonstrate her creative abilities in several avenues. She had played a lovely little piece on the pianoforte for Emelie's baptism dinner. She had been most anxious to show the priest a little painting she had done of the lilacs in the back garden.

So when she'd shared that outlandish story as they left the church the day before, Père Henri had assumed that it was nothing more than her imagination, a little girl watching the priest as he performed the rites of the Eucharist, and expanding on that scene to create a story.

The father walked through the heavy iron gate that blocked the road to the Challembelles estate, and started down the lane toward the front entrance. Chestnut trees lined the path, and the temperature dropped a few degrees in their shade. His stomach danced with nervousness; his mind flittered from one prepared comment to another. He had told himself over and over again on the walk out here this morning that it was not simply curiosity that propelled him. If it were true that the younger priest had been poisoned at the chalice, then they might need him, Père Henri, to help them get through this difficult time with the ministrations and spiritual guidance that only an older priest could offer.

The maid announced him, and he was shown into the morning room, where Marie and Genevieve sat at their desks writing letters.

The comte sat in a chair by the fire, burning brightly despite the heat of the day outside, reading a newspaper.

The comte stood and offered his hand, and Père Henri noticed, not for the first time, that it shook slightly. "How good of you to visit, Père Henri. Please sit down. Would you like coffee?"

"That would be lovely, thank you." The priest shook the comte's hand, and turned to Marie. "Madame Morier! Such a long time has passed since I last saw you. It is so good to see you again."

"Likewise, Père Henri." Marie allowed her hand to be swallowed by his two enormous mitts.

"Madame Beauvier." Père Henri nodded to Genevieve.

"Please sit down." The comte took his pipe from his teeth, and indicated the sofa in front of the fireplace. Marie and Genevieve joined them, and Père Henri felt beads of sweat gathering on his forehead as he sat down across from the fire.

The maid returned with a tray and poured and served the coffee, beginning with their guest. He took the cup, stirred the sugar, and held his nose over the steaming brown liquid. He turned to Marie. "I understand Julien is with you."

"Yes, he is."

"I haven't seen him in . . . oh, years, I suppose. Not since he first left for America," Père Henri said. "He seemed so young, to be traveling halfway around the world." He took a sip of coffee, and placed it on the table in front of him.

"He is not so young, now, I'm afraid." Marie smiled. "Seems to be a common malady, this growing older."

"Yes, yes, quite so." The priest's eyes jumped from Marie's face to that of the comte, sitting across from him. He reached again for his coffee cup, unsure of how to proceed. He sipped again.

"I understand Julien is unwell."

"Yes, he is very ill, I'm afraid." Her eyes dropped to the floor.

Père Henri waited for her to continue.

Marie swallowed and placed her cup on the table. "Julien has been in South America these past two months."

The priest's eyebrows went up. "Oh?"

Both Genevieve and the comte raised their eyes to look at her.

"Yes." Marie met his gaze again, her eyes hard and flinty and totally unreadable. She folded her hands together in her lap. She leaned forward slightly. "I wouldn't want this to get out, Father, but . . ."

The priest leaned toward her, completely spellbound.

"Well, he's been on a mission for the French government. A secret mission." Marie let her eyes scan the room, as if checking to see that there were no ears to hear this. She leaned toward the priest again, her head lowered slightly. "A very delicate matter, I'm afraid."

The father leaned back and nodded. "I see."

Genevieve lowered her coffee cup and stared at her older sister.

Marie let out a long sigh. "They needed someone who understood diplomacy. You know that Julien trained in Paris?"

The priest nodded.

"And they needed someone who spoke Spanish. Someone who wouldn't call attention to himself. As an emissary of the church, Julien seemed to be the perfect choice. I'm sure you understand."

The priest nodded, his coffee momentarily forgotten. This situation was getting more interesting by the second.

"He did his best, I'm certain. But the conditions were . . . primitive, shall we say? Julien caught some kind of bug. He believes it was the water, but then . . . one can never be sure. It might have been something he ate." She met the priest's eyes again, reached for her cup, and wrapped both hands around it.

The priest fidgeted in his seat. "I had no idea he was . . ." His eyes jumped nervously from Marie's face to that of the comte, who held his gaze. He let his eyes flicker on Genevieve's face, but she kept her eyes down, staring into the coffee cup in her lap.

He turned back to Marie. "I had heard that he was sick, but I had no idea he had been in South America. I . . . ah . . ." He glanced nervously at Genevieve. "I had no idea."

He looked back at Marie again. "This is most dreadful! Will Julien be all right? Have you consulted a doctor?"

"We saw a doctor in Paris, on our way home. He seems to think Julien will recover—that it is just a matter of time. He prescribed rest . . . bland foods. Julien will be taking mineral waters."

"I've heard that the waters of Vichy can be very healing," the priest offered. He felt so much more comfortable now that he had the true story and it did not include attempted murder.

"Yes. Quite. I'm sure we will make use of them." Marie sat back and sipped from her cup.

Père Henri relaxed back into the cushions of the sofa, his shoulders loose, his face soft with relief. "When Julien is feeling better, I would love to visit. I've always wanted to hear everything I can about America. It sounds like quite a wild place, the West." He smiled broadly. "I would imagine South America is quite fascinating also . . ." His face changed when he noticed Marie's frown.

"Père Henri, this is . . . quite sensitive. The government insisted that this mission be kept . . . confidential. I'm afraid we are not at liberty to discuss it."

"Oh, yes. I'm sorry. I did not mean to pry."

They sat for another moment, silence stretching between them, like a cat awakening from its nap. A bird twittered outside the open windows. Père Henri could hear the snip-snip of the gardener's hedge trimmers as he worked near the terrace.

"Well, it has been such a pleasure to see you again, Madame Morier, but I must be going. Today is my day for visiting." The priest stood and placed his coffee cup on the table.

He bent and kissed Genevieve's hand, shook hands with the comte, now standing as well, and offered his hand to Marie.

"Give my best to Julien. I will look forward to hearing all about New Mexico Territory when he is recovered."

Marie stood and put her hand on the priest's forearm. "I'll see you to the door, Father."

They reached the main hall, and Père Henri leaned close to her, his hand covering her smaller one. He smiled awkwardly. "I will say a novena for Père Julien."

"Thank you, Father. That will be much appreciated." Marie looked back over her shoulder toward the morning room. Genevieve and the comte stood by the fireplace. Marie looked back at the priest, and leaned closer to him. Her voice dropped. "Father? Could you . . ." She swallowed, as if trying to swallow a bitter drink. "Would you mind . . ." Her eyes came up to his.

The priest tipped his head. "What is it, madame?"

Marie swallowed again. "Would you mind saying a novena for the girl? Adrienne?" She met the priest's eyes.

Père Henri was puzzled.

Marie glanced back at the morning room again. "I think there is something . . . not quite right about her." She let her eyes drop to the floor. When she looked up at him again, there were tears in her eyes. "She . . ." Marie bit her lower lip. "She tells these stories. Preposterous stories."

The priest swallowed. "Oh?"

Marie glanced back at the morning room again. "It seems to be getting more and more out of control." She sighed. "I'm afraid there is no one here who can handle the situation. Genevieve has other things on her mind, what with the new baby. And my father . . ." The sentence hung in the air between them. "You can see it, can't you? Age is taking its toll on him." Her eyes searched those of the priest again. "I don't think they see what is really going on here."

The priest stared at her.

"I'm afraid the girl may be"—she leaned in close to Père Henri, and her voice dropped to a whisper—"mentally unwell."

The priest drew back. For a moment, he was stunned. "I see."

"But, Father . . . please don't let this get out . . ." Marie glanced back toward her sister, once more. "It could be . . ."

The priest squeezed her hand. "I understand, madame. I will be happy to pray for the girl."

"Thank you, Father," she said, holding the front door open for him.

Père Henri started down the lane, stopping once to look back at the castle. Marie had already gone inside. He stared for another moment, then hurried his steps toward home. Madame Cezanne would be sure to find this latest news as fascinating as he himself did.

# CHAPTER TEN

Julien lay stretched out on a chaise on the terrace. The August sun was warm, even at ten in the morning, but given his emaciated, weak condition, it wasn't quite warm enough. He had a blanket over his legs, and still he had moments when he shivered uncontrollably. Not much different from Grand-père, Julien thought sadly. The old man was sitting in a chair nearby, wearing a sweater, despite the heat. He dozed, and his head was tipped forward, toward one shoulder. In the years that Julien had been abroad, the comte had aged considerably. Julien caught a glimpse of the comte's very slender wrist, poking out from the sleeve of his sweater, and shifted his gaze to his own bony knees, holding the blanket up like a tent. The two men looked like skeletons. It reminded Julien of the Dia de los Muertos, and the Mexican love of portraying skeletons in all types of clothing and scenery.

Grand-père's aging wasn't the only change since the last time Julien had been home to France. Genevieve had never truly seemed like "Aunt Genevieve" to Julien—they were much too close in age for that. There were, after all, thirteen full years between his mother and her younger sister, making Genevieve closer to Julien's contemporary than she had ever been with Marie. They'd never related like

contemporaries, though. Julien could well remember coming back
to the Château de Challembelles to live at age thirteen, just after
the death of his father. Genevieve was nineteen at the time, and
quite beautiful. He'd been stunned by her beauty, still an awkward
and slender preadolescent himself. He had been more than usually
shy in her presence. But it hadn't taken him long to see that she was
mostly illusion and very little substance. Genevieve's preoccupation
with appearance and beauty was just one of the reasons that Julien,
as he grew older, found himself increasingly annoyed with females.
Julien's father had been bright and funny and always curious about
the cultures that he lived in and the people that he worked with in
their diplomatic travels. He loved art and music and food and language, interests that Julien shared.

When all of that was ripped away by his father's sudden death,
and he and his mother had returned to her childhood home to live,
Julien had become bored very quickly with the narrow-mindedness of
the village of Beaulieu and its inhabitants. Genevieve, more concerned
with the cut of her latest gown or the way her earrings caught the
light, lost all her charms in just a short time, to his way of thinking.

Now, over ten years later, she seemed to be a faded rose, past
her prime though still relatively young. At nineteen, she had been
stunning, and her confidence in her beauty had only added to the
allure. All trace of that confidence had fled. Her failure to recapture
the attentions of her husband only added to the dullness in her eyes
and skin, the tentativeness of her smile. She was weak and passive
and it annoyed him.

Julien sighed and glanced toward his mother. Marie was walking the grounds with the gardener, no doubt pointing out all the
mistakes he'd made since the last time she was home. The man nodded and kept his head down as they ambled through the rose beds.
Julien looked away.

Where Genevieve was weak and passive, Marie was exactly the opposite. She had been orchestrating his own life for as long as he could remember. When he was a child, all she had to do was set her lips and shoot him one of her piercing glares, and he would freeze on the spot. He had escaped her clutches, briefly, when he first went to the New World, but by the time he was offered his own parish, just two years into his new life, she had made herself indispensable once again.

Julien felt a momentary twinge of guilt. She had saved his life a few weeks ago. He did not want to seem ungrateful. If she had not acted so quickly, he wouldn't be here now. But there were times when he deeply resented her control, times when he would give almost anything to escape from her prim mouth and perpetual correctness. Since their return to France, for instance, she had rarely left him in peace for longer than an hour or two, and then only when he was sleeping. Just this morning, when he had insisted on sitting outside for a while, she was adamant that he take an extra blanket and limit his exposure to the elements—correctly, as it turned out. He was suffering from occasional shivers, and was already beginning to feel tired. But he wasn't going to let her know that she was right. Julien intended to stay out here in the sun, feigning energy that he did not feel, rather than admit she was right, and be forced back indoors.

Grand-père shook himself awake, and squeezed Julien's shoulder as he rose and headed back inside. Julien spotted Adrienne and her governess coming across the grass from the meadow. Lucie carried a large bag containing their paints and easels, and Adrienne carried her painting in front of her, occasionally glancing at it as she skipped along the stone path. She stopped skipping, lowered her painting, and stared at Julien as she walked more sedately toward the terrace.

"Good morning, Adrienne." Julien smiled. "Have you been painting?"

She nodded, and glanced toward Marie, still walking with the gardener.

"Might I see it?"

Adrienne smiled slightly and rushed up to stand next to Julien's side. The painting was a small one, about eight inches square, and showed a view of the meadow and the vineyards beyond. Julien had often looked out at this same view in the years he spent at the château as a teenager.

"I wanted to paint Phillipe, working in the vineyard," Adrienne explained, pointing to a spot where the paint had been scraped. "But I have trouble with figures."

"Perhaps. But you do quite a nice job with scenery, Adrienne. How old are you?"

"Six and a half. Lucie is a good teacher. You should see her paintings. She can do figures. She can paint almost anything and it looks right." Lucie had joined them on the terrace, and stood a few feet away, waiting for Adrienne to finish her conversation.

Julien looked up at the governess, and let his eyes roam the length of her body. *Yes,* he thought, *she does figures quite nicely.* He pulled his eyes away and looked back at his young cousin.

"You like painting, then?" Julien continued.

Adrienne nodded. "And reading. And playing the pianoforte. And I'm learning a little Italian, too."

Julien's eyebrows went up. "How fortunate you are, to have a good teacher, and such broad interests."

Adrienne smiled.

Julien started to cough, and he turned away from her slightly. He covered his mouth; his legs jerked with the effort. Sweat broke out on his forehead and upper lip.

Marie rushed up and moved between Julien and the girl. "Adrienne, off with you. Can't you see he's too ill for your foolishness?" Marie scowled.

"But . . ." Adrienne stood staring. "But I want to hear about trains. And Indians. And ships on the ocean."

Marie knelt beside Julien, and offered a glass of water. She turned to Adrienne again. "Can't you see how sick he is? Leave us. Now."

Adrienne moved slowly in Lucie's direction, her painting now forgotten and hanging at her side. She stopped and glanced back at this man she barely knew.

Julien was exhausted from his coughing fit, but he could see that the girl wanted to talk to him. He turned his head toward Adrienne and gave her a weak smile.

Adrienne stared at Marie's back, hunched as she knelt over her son. Quickly, before anyone could catch her at it, she stuck out her tongue. Then she turned and fled into the house. Julien was the only one to see.

# CHAPTER ELEVEN

A current of tension ran through the estate, and it wasn't just the normal tension of Marie and her demands. This was subtle, more pervasive; it affected every moment of every day, for everyone who lived and worked at the château, regardless of where Marie might be or what she might be doing. This apprehension was all centered on the little girl and her visions.

The servants knew, and it had been whispered about endlessly, that Adrienne had predicted, almost a year ago, that someone would try to hurt Julien at his new church assignment. They knew what she had blurted out at church, even before the family was aware that Julien and Marie were back from America. They had all heard the story that Marie had told—the story about the secret mission for the French government that had taken Julien to South America. No one was quite sure what to believe.

While talk about the grandmother had lain dormant for many years, the rumors had begun to circulate once again, brought to the light of day by the girl's behavior. Everyone kept an eye on the little girl, watching her for any sign that she might say something about one of them. Everyone in that household had secrets, the normal secrets of humankind, but still, there were love affairs and shameful behaviors that none of the servants wanted to be made public. They had all begun to send sideways glances at the girl every time they passed her or were in the same room with her.

Not everyone resonated with this new vibration. Julien could think of nothing but his own health, the way his stomach revolted at almost anything he put in it, of his thin limbs and weak-kneed attempts at walking, of the unending necessity for rest. Getting better took every ounce of energy he possessed. Genevieve was lost in her own thoughts, and with the profound hope that the new baby she was carrying would finally give Pierre a son. Only on rare occasions did she give any thought to what might be wrong with her oldest daughter. It did not trouble her enough to take her away from her other concerns for longer than a few moments, at best. Not knowing what to do, not knowing what it was she was dealing with, she had a tendency to shove it aside, to ignore the tiny sparks of foreboding that would occasionally creep up her arms. It was easier to pretend that nothing was amiss, to smooth down the hairs that were standing on end, and pick up the latest fashion magazine from Paris, and dream of the day when her figure would be restored once again.

The comte knew, the way a former officer in the army would know, that people were talking. He knew he needed to do something to protect Adrienne from the deleterious effects her stories could produce. But like Genevieve, he shoved the idea aside, unable to summon the energy. He was tired, tired in a way that he had never been, and family and servants often found him asleep in a chair. He kept his eye on the girl, he kept his eye on Marie, but he did not deal with the situation the way he might once have done.

Most of the burden fell on Lucie. She was young, much too young to be put in this position, but she was the only one who had the quick-witted intelligence, the depth of curiosity, and the overarching concern for Adrienne, which kept her abreast of everything. She made it her business to keep a close eye on everyone in the château. She watched over Adrienne like a mother hen, and she also kept a sharp eye out for any predators. She watched Marie through lowered lashes. She listened to the conversations of the other servants whenever she had the opportunity. She was sure of only two things: the servants, and by extension the village of Beaulieu, were talking, and she was convinced, the more she watched Marie, that the woman had something she was trying to hide.

Adrienne had nothing new to offer in the circumstances. Lucie had pressed her, privately, to see if the girl had any idea who might have poisoned Julien, to see if there were any further visions to explain what had really happened to him. But Adrienne was not caught up in the intrigue. It was just a curious story she had seen, a little like one of her fairy tale books, and she was able to put the whole thing aside just as easily as she did Cinderella.

Lucie had begun keeping a journal. She waited until Adrienne was asleep, waited until all sounds in the household had ceased, and then she crept from her own bed, in the room adjoining Adrienne's, and sat at a desk in her nightgown and woolen shawl, scribbling away by candlelight. She kept the journal in her suitcase in her wardrobe, a suitcase her father had given her years ago, the only item she possessed that had a lock and key. She wrote down every vision that Adrienne had shared with her. She wrote down Marie's reactions. She wrote about her own fears, the suspicions that continued to feed on the stares and silences and whispers of those around her. The more she wrote, the more she observed, the more certain she became: someone in this household had something to hide. Sometimes she would lie awake, mulling over the day's events, telling herself to just let it go. But she could not. The compulsion to record what was happening would not let her sleep. She had to get up, had to scratch it all out on paper. Only then, after she had locked it away, and blown out her candle, could she return to bed and find slumber. As if, by the act of recording it all, she could somehow find the answers.

One afternoon, she and Adrienne walked out past the lake and up over a hill that looked down on the grounds of the estate. They brought their paints, and set up easels in the grass. The day was a glorious blue, that crystalline blue of September, when the air has just begun to cool down at night. The view before them was splendid: the château in the distance, the lake, the vineyards and farm fields that belonged to the comte, pressed all around by the deep green of the forest.

They sketched and painted, mostly in silence, and Lucie was absorbed in her own composition. She had left the cares and stress of the castle behind, and for the first time in several weeks, she relaxed. It wasn't until they were beginning to pack up their supplies that she looked at Adrienne's painting. Her calm evaporated.

Normally, the girl did her best to capture the beauty of the land around her, and she was becoming more and more proficient at following the lines of tree branches and leaves and the roll and sway of the ground in the near distance. This piece was very different and Lucie could not hide her shock at today's work.

Adrienne had painted the forest, not from the vantage that was before them now, the deep greens and browns and blacks in the distance, fringing the fields. This painting showed the trees and branches and heavy vegetation as if the viewer were in the midst of it, enveloped by the darkness and quiet. Tree branches were drawn like hands, their long fingers reaching out to grab the unwary traveler. The knots in the bark of the trunks stared out like eyes. The effect was startling, and left a dark, ominous taste in Lucie's mouth.

Lucie glanced at Adrienne, who stood staring into the forest in the distance. "This is very interesting, Adrienne," she murmured. "Quite different from the other things I've seen you paint."

Adrienne turned to Lucie, and there was something in her eyes, some mix of apprehension and knowledge, that Lucie had not witnessed in any of the girl's other visions. "They're watching me, Lucie."

Lucie felt the hair on her arms go up. "Who is watching you?"

Adrienne met the eyes of her governess, but she looked as if she was lost in another place entirely. "Everyone. Marie. The servants. The people in the village. I can feel their eyes on me when we go to church. I can feel their eyes in the castle, every time I go into a room. I can feel them right now, staring at me. Watching me."

Lucie glanced around uncomfortably. She could not see a soul, and they were a good mile away from the trees in that forest. The château was almost as far. The only movement in the pastoral scene was the trace of the breeze, bending the grasses, fluttering the leaves of the birch they'd been sitting beneath.

Lucie swallowed her own apprehension. "Your painting looks a little like the forest where Snow White lived. Perhaps there are some friendly dwarfs beyond these trees?" She pointed at the trees in Adrienne's painting.

Adrienne shrugged. She looked at her own painting. "It feels more like the wicked stepmother. Or a witch, like the one in 'Hänsel and Gretel.'"

Lucie exhaled slowly, forcing her fears down and her heart to slow. She reached for Adrienne's painting, and wrapped it in a cloth, putting it into the satchel along with the rest of the supplies. "There's no such thing as witches, Adrienne. They are only part of fairy stories. They're not real." She reached over and ran her hand down Adrienne's small back.

Adrienne looked at her, her blue eyes large and serious. "My grandmother was real."

A hush descended. All movement stopped; every leaf and blade of grass completely still, as arrested by Adrienne's words as Lucie was. "But your grandmother was not a witch."

Adrienne got very quiet. Her eyes moved to the château, the village of Beaulieu barely visible beyond it in the distance. "Some people say she was."

"Which people say that?"

"Madame LaMott. Her cousin. The housekeeper that takes care of Père Henri. A lot of people."

Lucie knelt down on the grass in front of the little girl. She put her hands on Adrienne's shoulders and turned her so that she faced Lucie directly. "Adrienne, your grandmother was not a witch. I don't care what anyone says. That is just people talking. Sometimes, when people are jealous of someone, or envious of what they have, they say mean things. Do you understand? You cannot listen to what people say." Even as the words left her mouth, Lucie thought of just how often lately she had been doing just that—listening for every veiled comment or conversation, searching for the knowledge that she lacked. She knew nothing about this grandmother, nothing other than the fact that she had died when Genevieve was born.

Adrienne stared at Lucie, but she said nothing. She shifted her gaze back to the village in the distance, to the steeple of the church rising into the clear blue sky. "I heard other things, too," Adrienne whispered. "At church a few days ago."

Lucie's breath caught.

"Remember when I ran into the churchyard? To get a flower for my mother?"

Lucie nodded. She always hated it when Adrienne took off like that, even though she was within sight. She remembered watching Adrienne as she looked through the mums, planted beneath a hedge of elderberry bushes.

"There were some girls behind the bushes. Noemie and Claire and someone I don't know. They were talking about my grandmother." Adrienne shuddered. "And then"—she paused, trying to get the words to come out—"Claire said I was just like her. She said I was . . . touched." Adrienne demonstrated by putting an index finger to her temple. "What does that mean? Touched?"

Lucie exhaled, wishing she could get her hands on Claire and those vicious little girls. "It means you are different from her. It means you can do something that she doesn't understand." Lucie stopped for a moment. "And Adrienne, those girls are much too young to know anything about your grandmother."

Adrienne was quiet for a moment. "They said my grandmother was a witch. That she had to be locked up. And that I needed to be locked up, too." Tears made a soft trail on Adrienne's cheeks, and Lucie knelt down next to her. "Lucie? I heard them say that Julien was not poisoned in church. That I was wrong. That I made it all up."

Lucie exhaled. "Adrienne, those girls don't know anything about what really happened to Julien. You need to forget what you heard—they don't know what they are talking about."

Adrienne's eyes wandered to the château in the distance. When she spoke, her words were low and quiet. "Do you think she will try to hurt me?"

"Who? That little girl? What could she possibly do—" Lucie began.

"Not her," Adrienne whispered, her eyes still locked on the château, as if she could see into the rooms. "Aunt Marie."

Lucie stopped breathing. That thought *had* crossed her mind. Her worries about Adrienne were many, but Marie had loomed over them all like a storm at sea. She forced herself to inhale. "Your grand-père would never let that happen," Lucie said. "And neither would I."

Adrienne turned and looked up at her governess. Lucie met those blue eyes, and for a moment, she could almost see the future. A thick sense of dread filled Lucie's bloodstream. She stood and stared into the distance.

# CHAPTER TWELVE

The great hall was lined with trunks and luggage, filled almost to overflowing with the things Marie and Julien were taking back to America with them. One carriage had already been packed, in preparation for their early-morning departure. Eight months had passed since they had returned to France. Julien was stronger, not nearly as pale. He was able to eat again, although in small quantities and mostly only very bland foods.

The family sat in the parlor. A fire blazed in the fireplace, straining to heat the tall room. The castle had been covered in snow for a fortnight, and the chill permeated every inch of the stone structure.

Grand-père was in his wing chair, smoking his pipe and holding Emelie, who snuggled in his lap, her head resting comfortably against his chest. Genevieve sat on the settee, her knitting draped over the mound of the new baby she carried. Marie occupied the wing chair opposite Grand-père, a white linen cloth in her lap, her needle poking in and out in a percussive rhythm. In the corner, slightly away from the family, Lucie knitted.

Julien sat at a chair by the window. "Game of chess, Adrienne? Might be our last chance for quite a while. I'm not sure when I'll be getting back to France again." He smiled at her. "You could be all grown up by then."

Adrienne smiled and joined him in the chair opposite the table. "Tell me again, Julien. I want to hear about the trip—the ship and the trains and the wagons."

The two kept their eyes on the chessboard. Adrienne made the first move.

"We'll take the carriage to Brive. Then the train to Clermont. Another train to Paris, and then the coast. From there, we take a steamship to New York."

At the mention of New York, Adrienne brightened. "Have you seen the Statue of Liberty?"

"Yes, we have. Several times, actually. They haven't yet held the formal dedication ceremony, but it has been up for a while." He moved his hand to the board.

"Then we take a train to St. Louis. That's about halfway across the continent . . . and then another train to Santa Fe. And then a buggy home to Santa Cruz." He smiled at Adrienne.

"I wish I could ride on a train."

"I imagine you will, someday. Perhaps you will come to America when you are older."

The comte gazed at the two of them, his grandchildren, so different, and so far apart in age. Julien would be leaving tomorrow, back to the New World, and it was highly unlikely that he would be back again any time soon. The comte knew that he would probably never see this grandson again, and somehow he sensed that Julien was feeling that same sense of finality. For this one evening, at least, the comte managed to shake off his fatigue. He wanted to enjoy every moment with Julien before he left.

"Your mother tells me that you have been doing some work with the railroads out there in the West." Grand-père removed his pipe and blew a stream of smoke into the air. "Something about the Chili Line, I believe?"

Julien looked up at him and smiled. "Yes, I have. It's a narrow-gauge train, smaller in size than a regular train. They are designed to handle the steep curves of mountainous areas, and they are constructing narrow-gauge lines in many of the places where gold or silver has been found. The Chili Line starts at a small town in Colorado and runs down next to the Rio Grande River. Even stops at Santa Cruz, where I live."

"Have you ridden on it?"

"Only part of the route. It's not completely finished yet. Maybe this summer they will have it completed. They want to take it all the way into Santa Fe." Julien's eyes dropped back to the board. "Money is always an issue, though. And land. The railroad has to buy up all the land before they can get started. And most of the landowners are Mexican or Indian. That's where I come in," Julien continued, his eyes on his next chess move. "I do the interpreting for the railroad when they are buying land."

The comte smiled. "So your training in diplomacy has come in handy, then?" He sensed Marie's back going stiff in the chair next to him.

Julien threw back his shoulders. "Many times, actually. I believe it has played an important role in my being able to move up so quickly in the church."

Adrienne looked up at her cousin. "How do they know where to put the tracks?"

"They send out surveyors. Men take instruments, and make measurements. How steep the slope is—how sharp the turns are. They look for places where they might have to go over lots of rocks, or over steep canyons, that kind of thing. The Chili Line has all of those—steep slopes, sharp curves. They've been working on a bridge over the Rio Grande Gorge. It should be quite a sight when it's finished."

"If I were a younger man, I would do my best to get over there and see it," the comte continued. For the past few years, he had been vicariously living out life in the Wild West through this grandson and his letters and stories. "Your mother tells me you have been working with some important people in the region. You know General Palmer?"

"General Palmer lives in Colorado. He fell in love with the West as soon as he first saw it. You would love it, too, Grand-père. The mountains and pine trees. General Palmer started the town of Colorado Springs. People are flocking to it—beautiful mountains, clean water, dry climate. They're calling it Little London." Julien glanced at his mother across the room. "I'd love to be transferred there, actually. It's a beautiful area.

"General Palmer is the one who started the Denver and Rio Grande Railroad—that's how he first saw southern Colorado and the New Mexico Territory. And that's the company that is putting in the Chili Line. And since I speak Spanish and French and English, even a few of the Indian dialects, they contacted me to help with the interpreting when they need to buy land from the Mexicans or the Indians."

"It's hard to imagine, Julien, you having direct contact with the Indian people. Living amongst them, working with them. I've been fascinated with those stories since I was a boy." The comte puffed his pipe.

Julien sighed heavily. He stared at the chessboard for a moment. "It is hard to imagine how different they really are. I guess when I first set out to join Archbishop Lamy in the New World, I was very naïve about it all.

"I thought they would be happy to have us . . . happy to have someone bring them the way to salvation." Julien looked up at the comte. "But that is not the case at all. They resent us—all of us, I think. Even the archbishop, and he has done nothing but good for them. They cling to their old ways, their old ceremonies. Their faces stay calm, they nod their heads at my suggestions, and then they go off and do what they want to do. As if nothing I say or do really matters to them.

"And those dark eyes . . . those dark faces . . ." Julien stopped for a moment, and his gaze seemed to drift into the distance. "It is so hard to know what they are thinking. All of their secrets are hidden behind the depth in their eyes, as if that darkness is a curtain that hides everything they feel." He brought his gaze back to the chessboard. "With Europeans, I feel like I can look in a man's eyes and get a good feeling for what kind of man I'm dealing with. But not there. I look in those dark eyes, and I cannot see anything."

"Perhaps it is just a matter of time. Maybe they will come to trust you after you have worked with them longer." Grand-père wanted to believe his own words, but even as they left his mouth, he doubted what he said.

Julien shook his head. "I thought so, too, at first. That we could find a way to connect. That when they saw the benefits of the school, of having their children educated, they would come around. But they don't trust anyone from outside. I have begun to doubt that we will ever make a difference in their lives."

Julien looked up at Grand-père. "They resent the Americans. I can understand that, at least partially. I mean, many of the people who live in New Mexico Territory have been in that area for generations. The Americans are newcomers, really. And some of them— the Americans, I mean—are quite uncivilized." Julien paused for a moment. "Certainly nothing like the French priests that the archbishop has brought in. And yet the people there treat us as if we are just as bad as the Americans, as if we had designs on their land."

Adrienne stared at her cousin. Her head tipped to one side. Her eyes were glazed, lost. "Julien? Do you . . . do you make money . . . when you help the railroad?"

Even with his frailty and age, the comte could feel the effect of those words on the rest of the room. The whole room had gone quiet; the comte noticed how Julien's back stiffened, how his brows knit together when he looked at the little girl.

"Of course, Adrienne. Very few people can interpret the languages. The railroad pays for that service. I never keep the money, though. I put it right back into the church coffers. For the school. Everything I do is working for their benefit. In the end, selling that land to the railroad helps every one of us."

The comte watched the two of them. He could see that Julien was defensive; it was written clearly in the set of his shoulders and the spark in his eyes. The comte sighed heavily. He'd spent too many years negotiating the minefields of tension between rich and poor. It made sense to him, suddenly, why Julien might have been poisoned. The comte let his gaze brush over the others in the room. Adrienne was looking at the chessboard. Julien was staring at the little girl.

Grand-père examined the two grandchildren for a moment longer. "As much as I hate for this fine evening to end, it's getting late, and you and Marie have a long day ahead of you tomorrow." He handed Emelie to her nurse and stood. "I think it's time for prayers. Julien, if you would . . ." Grand-père held his arm out.

The family shifted and moved, placed knitting and stitching into baskets, and knelt on the thick rug, scattered about close to where they had been sitting. Julien knelt, near the center of the room, and began the words of the rosary. His voice rose and fell, lilting, almost as if the rosary were a work of musical genius. His eyes were closed. He swayed back and forth with the rhythm of the words. All the tension of a few moments before seemed to have passed.

The comte gazed at Adrienne. Her eyes were open, her brow knit together like she was trying to make sense of something. She kept raising her head to look at Julien, kneeling on the carpet in front of her. Without moving his head, the comte let his attention shift to Marie. She, too, had her eyes open. She, too, was focused on Adrienne, and the anger that radiated from her posture and eyes was lethal. The comte shivered. *Oh, Marie,* he thought. *Let it go. Just let it go.*

Julien's voice led them. "Oh, my Jesus."

All their voices rose in the words of the prayer. "Forgive us our sins, save us from the fires of hell and lead all souls to heaven, especially those in most need of thy mercy. Amen."

# CHAPTER THIRTEEN

L ucie?" Adrienne's voice was faint, trembling.

Lucie sat at her desk, her journal open before her. A candle at the edge of the desk flickered golden shadows across the paper. Her journal had been growing thicker. She still recorded Adrienne's visions, but ever since the poisoning, she had begun to record her own observations about Marie and Julien, to give voice to her own uneasiness. She thought that perhaps by writing it all down, she might be able to find the thread that led to the truth.

Lucie had been waiting for hours for this moment, for this chance to write it all down before time had made it less acute. Just this morning, she had gone downstairs alone. She used the servants' steps, something she rarely did, since she almost always had one of the children with her. She hadn't been deliberately deceptive. But she moved quietly, and the two servants who were whispering together in the pantry were not aware that Lucie was standing steps away, just inside the doorway leading to those back steps. Lucie could see the two of them through the slim space between the door and the wall.

"She's just like her grand-mère, you know," Henriette whispered to the other girl. Henriette was nowhere near old enough to know anything about the comtesse, but she was an expert at picking up every tidbit of gossip. "They say it skips a generation."

"What does?" Noelle was the young girl who helped with the laundry.

"Clairvoyance. The sight," Henriette whispered, as if she had become an expert. "That's why Marie and Genevieve cannot see things."

Henriette glanced around nervously. "They locked her up, you know. The grandmother. The comtesse." She leaned in close as she shared this latest bit of information. "Kept her in her room. They didn't want everyone to talk about her."

Lucie had held her breath, and stood without moving. Every fiber of her being strained toward the whispers coming from the butler's pantry on the other side of the door.

Noelle whispered in confidence, "I heard she died in childbirth. With Genevieve."

Henriette looked over her shoulder, but seeing no one, she continued. "That's the story they told."

"Story? You mean it's not true?"

Henriette's voice was louder in her excitement. "All that blood, a week after the baby was born? Who ever heard of dying in childbirth a week later?"

Noelle was quiet for a minute. "I had a cousin who got some kind of infection when her baby was born. She died four days later. It's possible."

Henriette dropped her voice to a whisper. "Yes, it's possible. But doesn't it seem rather odd? Here they were, keeping her locked up, away from people, because of how embarrassing her stories could be."

"I don't understand."

"Maybe it just *looked* like she died in childbirth."

Lucie bit her fist to stifle any sounds from escaping her mouth.

"What are you saying? Do you think she was . . . *murdered*?" Noelle's whisper was so soft that Lucie found herself leaning forward, straining to hear every syllable.

"All I'm saying is, this family has secrets. And the comtesse knew them all. There had to be people who wanted to make sure she stayed quiet." Henriette drew her pause out dramatically. "Just like Adrienne. That little girl would be wise to keep her mouth closed."

⁓

Lucie sat at her desk, and turned to stare out the window on her left, her thoughts turbulent. Everyone knew Henriette loved to talk, that she loved gossip and stories, that she loved being the one with all the inside information. Lucie knew that the information she had overheard could not be trusted, but the story still left her with a shiver. And there were probably very few people alive who knew the truth. The comte, of course, and perhaps Marie. She was thirteen when her mother died. If there was anyone who knew the real story, it was probably she. Lucie was lost in the tangled web of her thoughts, and when she turned her head, Adrienne stood in the doorway between the two bedrooms.

"Lucie?" she whispered again.

"Adrienne? What's wrong?" Lucie laid her pen on the paper, and stood. Adrienne ran to her and threw her arms around Lucie's flannel-clad legs.

Lucie maneuvered them both into the rocking chair in front of the big window. She pulled Adrienne onto her lap. The moon was full. Moonlight bathed both girls, in their white nightgowns, turning them into luminous pearls.

Adrienne buried her head in Lucie's shoulder. "I h-h-had a bad . . . dream."

Lucie rubbed the girl's arms and hugged her closer. "There, there. It's only a dream."

The girl continued to shake, and Lucie pulled the shawl from her own shoulders and wrapped it around Adrienne.

"I was . . . I was in this little room. It was small and cold and dark. Very high up. I could look out this window, and see the ground a long, long way below." Adrienne kept her head against Lucie's chest. "The trees looked tiny from up there. I was cold." Adrienne shivered.

"And I walked over to the door. I tried to open it, but I couldn't. It was locked. I couldn't get out. It was so dark, and so cold. And I got scared. I started to call for someone to let me out. I banged on the door with my fists. I called for Grand-père. And Maman. And you, Lucie!" Adrienne sat up for a moment and looked into Lucie's dark eyes. Then she leaned back into Lucie's warmth again.

"But no one came. And after a while, I gave up. And I went and sat down on the bed. And while I was sitting there, the stones . . . the stones that were part of the wall? They started to bleed. There were little drops of blood, coming out of all of them. The blood was getting on my hands, and on my clothes, and on the bed where I was sitting. I screamed! And then I woke up."

Lucie continued to rock slowly back and forth. The chair creaked against the floor. Her slippers brushed against the wood. "It's only a dream, Adrienne. It's not real." Even as the words left her mouth, Lucie was struck by the similarity of Adrienne's dream to what she had overheard about the comtesse that very morning. Locked up in her room. Blood everywhere.

Lucie forced herself to swallow.

"You're right here with me, aren't you?" Adrienne nodded against Lucie's chest. "And we're not so high up. And the door is not locked. And the walls are not bleeding."

Lucie's slippers made a *sh-sh* sound on the floor. Adrienne relaxed into the sounds and her breath slowed.

"It was only a dream," Lucie whispered once again. She had to force herself to say it, had to convince herself it was true. "Only a dream."

They rocked in silence for a few moments. Adrienne raised her eyes, caught the flicker of the candlelight on Lucie's desk. "Lucie? Do you miss your daddy?"

Lucie's breath stopped. She nodded. "I miss him very much."

"How old were you when he died?" The two girls held tightly to one another.

"I was seventeen. That's when I came here. Not long after he died." Lucie put her chin on the top of Adrienne's head. She remembered that time, the months after her father had died. She was scared. Alone. Penniless. She was lucky to have found this position, luckier still that she had found Adrienne. Sometimes, like now, when Adrienne was curled against her and breathing softly, Lucie could almost pretend that Adrienne was her own daughter. It was certainly hard to believe that Genevieve would ever care as much about this little girl as Lucie did.

"He was coughing?"

"Yes, Adrienne. He was coughing. He was very sick, at the end."

"Why do I see so many yellow roses?"

Lucie smiled into the moonlight. "Hmmm. My maman loved yellow roses. She had all kinds of them in the garden. Yellow with orange on the edges. Yellow with pink in the middle. Yellow roses that climbed the porch. She loved yellow roses." Lucie's voice smiled with the memory. She could almost smell her mother, the rosewater she sprinkled on her wrists every morning. She could see her, moving about the kitchen, singing, her hands covered in flour as she kneaded bread.

"She died when I was seven." Lucie's voice lost its smile. "After she died, my father took care of those roses. Loved them as if . . . as if she were a part of them. As if my mother came back every spring in those roses."

Adrienne sat up and looked into Lucie's eyes. She laid one hand on Lucie's cheek. "Lucie?"

Lucie felt tears pooling in her eyes. She looked down at Adrienne. "Yes?"

"I wish you could be my mother." Adrienne leaned back into Lucie's arms again.

"So do I, Adrienne. So do I."

They rocked back and forth. Outside the window, an owl called out to them in a low, sad voice.

"Lucie?" Adrienne's voice was soft. "You won't let them lock me up, will you?"

# CHAPTER FOURTEEN

Winds rushed down from the mountains, filling the canyons, moaning, keening. They whipped the trees and whistled through the eaves. Icy pellets of snow smashed against the windows and the roof. Tree branches scraped against the windows, like fingernails, as if the trees were trying to claw their way inside.

Inside the castle, the silence was heavy. It weighed like stone on the shoulders of everyone there: servants, Lucie, Genevieve, Adrienne. Everyone moved about in hushed seriousness. The comte lay dying. What had started as a small sniffle had worked its way into his lungs. His fever soared. His cough was wrenching. His skin was pale and clammy.

The doctor, who had been to the château every day for a week now, straightened and stood. He took the stethoscope from his ears and turned to Genevieve, a few feet behind him in the dim light. He shook his head.

Genevieve clamped her knuckle between her teeth and fought back tears. The doctor laid his tools in his leather bag and touched the comte gently on his upper arm. The comte grimaced but did not open his eyes.

The doctor swallowed and let his hand rest on the comte's arm for a moment. Then he turned, took Genevieve's elbow, and guided her toward the door. "The fluid from the pneumonia is getting worse." His eyes traveled back to the comte, propped against several pillows. "I don't imagine it will be long now. You might want to send for the priest."

Genevieve swallowed. Her eyes filled; her face glistened in the pale gray light from the windows. She brushed at the moisture on her face, and nodded.

"I would stay, if I could," he whispered. "But Mademoiselle Fro—a young lady in the village is in labor, and I do not think she will have an easy time of it."

"Yes. Yes, I understand. *Merci, docteur.*"

"I am sorry, madame. He is a wonderful man, your father." He looked back at the frail old man on the bed. "It is hard to imagine Beaulieu without him in it." He touched Genevieve's shoulder and walked away. The door closed behind him with a soft click.

Genevieve stood, trying to breathe, watching her father as he lay there, his chest heaving with the effort of breathing. She turned and opened the door. Lucie and Adrienne sat on stiff chairs in the hallway, facing the doorway. Adrienne had situated her chair so that she might catch a glimpse of her grand-père whenever the door opened.

Genevieve glanced at her and then turned her eyes to Lucie. "Lucie, could you ask Renault to prepare to go to Nice? We will need to send a telegram to Marie and Julien." She stepped into the hallway, turning her shoulders to block Adrienne, and whispered to the governess, who was now standing. "And send someone else for the priest." Genevieve bit her lip and turned back to the sickroom.

*"Oui, madame."* Lucie curtsied, her eyes growing dark and clouded. "I'll be right back, Adrienne. I need to do a few things for your maman."

Genevieve closed the bedroom door behind her and went to her father's bedside. The day was so dark and gray; she had kept the bedside lamp burning long past the night. She dipped the wash-cloth into a pan of water on the table and brushed her father's brow and his cheeks with the cool cloth.

She sat down in the chair beside his bed and pulled her rosary from her skirt. "Hail Mary, full of grace. The Lord is with thee." She whispered the words, which threatened to choke her, to make her gag.

The light of the gas lamp flickered, casting amber spirits into the gray gloom. The comte began to cough, his whole body wrench-ing from the effort, jerking up from the pillows as he tried to expel the fluid in his lungs. Genevieve stood and held a cup beneath his mouth. He spat several times and leaned back.

His eyes were open. She looked into their blue depths, the same blue that shone in her own eyes, and in Adrienne's. She couldn't imagine a world without those twin lakes of wisdom and calm, watching over all of them.

"Adrienne . . ." he muttered. "Bring her to me."

Genevieve helped him lie back against the pillows and nod-ded. She opened the door and looked at her daughter, sitting stiff and fearful on the chair across the hall. Adrienne tipped her head, caught a glimpse of Grand-père on the bed behind Genevieve. Adrienne's eyes swept up to her mother's face.

"He wants to see you, Adrienne," Genevieve whispered. She was so exhausted she could barely stand.

Adrienne slid off the chair. She turned and placed her rosary on the cushion she'd just vacated. She pressed her lips together and tiptoed through the door to Grand-père's room.

"Not too close, dear." Genevieve's voice was soft. She laid a gen-tle hand on Adrienne's back as the girl crept forward.

Adrienne forgot to breathe. She inched forward, petrified at what she might find. She stopped near the foot of the bed. Her hands hung at her sides. She stared at her grand-père. His eyes were closed. He was thin, frail, delicate, and fragile like the finest bone china. She could almost see through his skin, to the bones underneath his face, the bones in his hand, resting lightly on the cover. He reminded her of a delicate white bird, like the dove she had found one morning, after a storm, its slender body broken and smashed against the ground. She shook her head, trying to rid it of the image.

The room was gray, filled with the dimness of the storm outside. The bedclothes looked gray and dingy in the dim light. Grand-père, too, was gray.

She shuffled another step forward, let her hand creep over the covers to find his own. She pressed it softly. The comte opened his eyes and let out a long sigh, as if the sight of her was a tonic, the one thing he'd been waiting for.

"Adrienne," he whispered, his voice hoarse. *"Ma cherie."* He began to cough, and pulled his hand away from hers to cover his mouth. It took several moments before he lay back against the pillows, and the coughing quieted. Genevieve stood at the opposite side of the bed, holding his shoulders as he spasmed.

He turned his eyes back to Adrienne, drew in a long, careful breath. "Be careful, my girl. Be careful what you say. Even when you know you are right . . . no matter what it may be . . . be careful." His hands lay on the cover. "There are some things better left unsaid. Your aunt Marie . . ."

Adrienne swallowed. Her throat burned, as if she had swallowed broken glass. She stood perfectly still.

He reached for her hand, and squeezed it gently. "Promise me? That you will keep what you see to yourself?"

Adrienne nodded. Her voice was soft. "I promise, Grand-père." Tears slid down her face. She did not want to cry in front of him. But she did not want to move her hand to brush away the moisture, to draw his attention to it. She stood still, her small hand inside his, and nodded again. She met his eyes through the curtain of her tears.

He smiled, and squeezed her hand once more. "That's my girl," he whispered.

His eyes closed and he began coughing again. He pulled his hand away, his body strained with the force of the cough. Genevieve held him, held the cup in front of his mouth as he spat and choked, the phlegm spotted with blood.

"You'd better go now, Adrienne." She motioned toward the door with her head.

Adrienne backed away, her tears warping everything she saw. She stopped at the foot of his bed. Waited. When his cough had subsided, and he lay back again, exhausted, she put her hands on the wooden foot rail at the end of his bed. "Grand-père," she whispered, leaning over the rail. "I love you."

He did not open his eyes.

"Adrienne, go. Please." Genevieve's voice was sharp.

The door to the bedroom opened, and Père Henri moved inside, Lucie right behind him. Adrienne stared as the priest lit a candle, took out his oil, and made the sign of the cross on the comte's forehead. The oil caught the light and made a shiny reflection on his skin.

"Through this holy anointing, may the Lord in his love and mercy help you, with the grace of the Holy Spirit." The words hung in the air, heavy and full. Genevieve stood to one side, her hand pressed to her mouth, her handkerchief wadded inside her palm.

"May all the saints and elect of God, who, on earth, suffered for the sake of Christ, intercede for him." Père Henri moved slowly around the bed. "So that, when freed from the prison of his body, he may be admitted into the kingdom of heaven."

Adrienne felt the pressure of Lucie's hand on her shoulder and looked up. Lucie guided the girl to the hallway.

The words of the priest could still be heard. "Through the merits of our Lord Jesus Christ, who lives and reigns with the Father and the Holy Spirit, world without end. Amen."

❦

Servants lined the hallway, up and down outside the comte's door. They were coming up the stairs, moving into the hall, quiet and somber. They knelt. They took out their beads. Mimi, the cook who had been with the comte for sixty years, knelt by a chair, her head down, her beads in hand. Her face was shining and wet in the gray light. "Pray for us sinners, now and at the hour of our death," she whispered.

All of the servants were dropping to their knees, whispering the words of the prayers they had been saying their entire lives. Many of them were crying.

Adrienne felt the sting of her own tears. "No," she cried, trying to see her way between all the kneeling bodies and feet. The words of their prayers pressed against her on all sides. "No!" she said louder. She held her hands to her ears. "No. Stop it!" She shook her head back and forth, pressed hard against her own ears, as if, by stopping their voices, she could make this whole ordeal end, make the comte be well again.

Lucie stopped and knelt in front of the little girl. "Adrienne . . ." Her own eyes filled. "You must . . ." She couldn't finish the sentence. She knelt in front of the little girl, her hands on each of the girl's arms. Her eyes sought Adrienne's, pleaded with her.

Adrienne threw her arms around Lucie's neck. Henriette, kneeling nearby, reached over and put her hand on the child's back. She rubbed small circles into Adrienne's dress.

Lucie pulled Adrienne back. She stood and led the girl down the hall to her own bedroom. Adrienne climbed onto her bed, on top of the covers, her face turned toward the gray window. Snow and sleet hit the glass and slid down, just like tears. As if the house itself were crying.

She would do as Grand-père had asked. No matter what she saw in her visions, no matter what voices she heard in her mind—she would never say another thing. She would bite her lip. She would refuse to listen to what the voices told her. She would erase the pictures. She would never again give voice to her knowledge.

She pressed her lips together, and a tear escaped from the corner of her eye and traveled a long, slow path to the pillow, forming a pool of darkness on the linen. "Oh, Grand-père," she whispered. "Don't leave me."

The storm wailed and thrashed against the walls of the castle. The wind sighed, picked up force again, keening and moaning as if it were the mother of a child, lost in the cold and darkness. As Adrienne lay weeping, the comte exhaled for the last time. Adrienne spoke only to his spirit.

# CHAPTER FIFTEEN

*Beaulieu, France—1896*

Autumn flamed on the hillsides. The chestnuts, beech, English ivy were all decked out in fiery jewels of carnelian, amber, coral, and amethyst. They decorated the hillsides, like ladies at a ball. The air was filled with their perfume, the sweet scent of decaying leaves. The yellow plums had dropped from the trees, and birds sang as they picked at the remains.

Sixteen-year-old Adrienne knelt at Grand-père's grave in the cemetery on the hill. Sunlight flickered through the leaves of the oak tree, casting lacy shadows on the graves of Grand-père, his wife, and their infant son. A breeze played with the curls at Adrienne's face and neck as she knelt to her work.

She had brought a trowel, and toiled at removing the grass that had grown up around his stone. She laid the trowel aside, brushed the hair from her face with the back of her hand, and swept the dried leaves away. She turned and reached for the bouquet she had brought him: crimson mums, yellow birch leaves, bright orange berries from the bittersweet vine. The best of autumn's color.

Adrienne slumped to one side, moving her knees out from under her. She loosened the tie of the brown velvet cloak around her neck. She stared at his stone. "She's coming back again, Grand-père," Adrienne whispered.

Marie had been back a few times in the years since the comte had passed. Julien had come only once. Each time, Adrienne felt her stomach clench and flip. Her throat tightened. Her head pounded. She forced herself to be vigilant, on guard, so wary of visions and voices that she could smell her own sweat.

"I've done it, Grand-père. Exactly what you asked. I've kept quiet." Adrienne let her head drop. She toyed with her skirt.

The silence had other consequences, and she herself did not understand the connection. But here she was, sixteen years old, and there were huge pieces of the past nine years that had disappeared from her consciousness completely. It was as if, in her effort to still the voices and visions that tried to come through, she had erased everything—even the memories of those events she had actually lived.

One day melted into the next, a somber pool of brown water. She rarely went anywhere, not even to the village. Her weekly trips to church were horrid, and she dreaded Sundays. She could almost hear the whispers of the townspeople, feel their eyes boring into the back of her head and neck. She couldn't meet their gazes. She kept her eyes down and her mouth closed. She rarely spoke. She often feigned illness just to avoid the whole ordeal.

Lucie spent most of her time with Emelie and Antoine, the son Genevieve had given birth to after the death of the comte. Adrienne was left to herself: to her books, her paints, her music. She took long walks on the hillside. The loneliness weighed heavily on her. It kept the corners of her mouth down, her gait measured and somber, as if she were an old woman, and not a girl of sixteen. She could not remember the little girl who had run and skipped down the hill with her grand-père, the girl who chased butterflies and dragonflies, and tried to imitate the wrens. This Adrienne did not run, did not skip. She rarely smiled. She rarely spoke.

Adrienne stood and dusted off her skirt. She gathered her tools into a basket and closed the wrought-iron gate behind her. It creaked, and she heard the click as the bolt slid into place. She turned and started back toward the castle. The whole countryside was bathed in gold. The dried yellow grasses were gilded with the softened light of shorter days. Leaves flickered like jewels, bright colors catching the sun. Adrienne topped a hill and started down the incline to the house.

Twelve-year-old Emelie ran through the tall meadow grass at the back of the castle, her hair flashing like metal in the sunlight. Antoine, now a boisterous nine, ran behind her, screaming and laughing as he waved a snake at his sister.

The scene brought back a snippet of memory, a picnic, one or two summers ago. Time seemed so hazy and nebulous to Adrienne. But she could remember sitting on a hillside, under the shade of a chestnut tree. She and Lucie were sitting on a blanket, the remains of their picnic lunch spread at their feet: grapes, apples, bread, a block of cheese. The picnic basket was open, cloth napkins tossed carelessly over the sides.

Antoine and Emelie were standing in the grass, just as they were now. In the memory, though, Antoine was smaller, no more than seven years old. He had found a frog, and he and Emelie were bent over it, studying the creature. Suddenly Emelie screamed, and Antoine started chasing her, frog held out in front of him. Every time Emelie stopped running for a moment, he raised the frog high in the air and made screeching noises.

Adrienne remembered how her spirits had lifted, watching the two of them. Antoine had been terrorizing his sister since the age of two. Most of the time, it was exasperating, but on this particular day Adrienne could tell from the way Emelie screamed and ran and laughed that she was enjoying this caper just as much as he was.

"I wish that could be you, Adrienne," Lucie had said, sitting quietly on the blanket beside her.

"The one with the frog, or the one being chased?" Adrienne asked.

Lucie smiled. "Laughing, having fun. I haven't seen you doing that since . . . since you were very young."

Adrienne's smile, her momentary joy at the two children playing, evaporated. She felt as if she'd been stabbed in the lung; for a moment, she lost the ability to breathe. She had a vague memory of running after a butterfly, in a field much like this one, Grand-père not far behind her.

Adrienne looked away, to the hills on her left.

"Do you still have them, Adrienne? The visions?" Lucie's voice was soft and low; she kept her eyes on the children in the grass.

In all the years since the comte had died, Adrienne had not spoken of any visions. Adrienne swallowed hard and picked at the fuzz on the blanket. It was a coarse gray wool; leaf shadows from the chestnut tree danced over its surface, over the skirts of the two females, legs stretched out in front of them.

Adrienne pulled her knees up to her chest and wrapped her arms around them. "Sometimes," she murmured.

Lucie sat up straight and turned to look at the girl, trying to read what might lie hidden in her silence. "I wondered if maybe they had stopped. You never talk about them anymore." Much of the tension that had vibrated through the air back then had disappeared. With Marie gone most of the time, and Adrienne no longer sharing startling stories, even the servants had relaxed. And truthfully, Lucie, too, was relieved that the stories had stopped. Since that moment, years ago, when she had overheard the servants talking about the death of the comtesse, Lucie had felt a thread of apprehension running through her. The thought of what might become of the little girl had always stayed in the back of her mind.

But she wasn't convinced that this silence was any better. She had watched Adrienne change before her eyes—from a little girl who was natural and light and full of joy to one who rarely smiled, never laughed, and seemed to hold herself rigid and straight and carefully in check at all times.

When she spoke, Adrienne looked away, as if she had caught a glimpse of Lucie's thoughts. "What is there to talk about? Visions are nothing but trouble. No one really wants to know."

"I do. I want to know what you see." Lucie meant what she said. She had always been fascinated by Adrienne's uncanny abilities. Yes, it was frightening sometimes, and yes, she worried about what would become of the girl. But it was intriguing to hear the things that she could see.

"Why? It only makes people angry. Or afraid. Or they think I'm some kind of—" Adrienne stopped, and drew in a sharp, quick breath. "Some kind of lunatic."

"Joan of Arc had visions. She became a heroine because of them."

Adrienne's eyes met Lucie's. "A *dead* heroine. Burned at the stake for all her trouble." Adrienne's words stabbed the air. "It's dangerous to be different. To know secrets."

Lucie sighed. "She saw things that were important. Things that helped her country. Not everyone can do it, Adrienne, and it seems to me that you might have visions for a reason. I guess I just wondered if you still had them, or if they had gone away."

Adrienne turned her head away. Yes, she still had visions. And she hated them. Hated them in a way that she could never explain. Just a few days before, she had been gazing out the window, staring out over the vineyards, and had spied Renault in the drive, returning from a trip to buy supplies in Lyons. Renault was the driver of the coach; he took care of the horses. His wife, Madeline, was an upstairs maid. They had married two years before, and she was about to give birth to their first child. Both of them had been glowing with anticipation and happiness.

Adrienne felt her shoulders and neck go stiff with the thought. Lucie and Madeline had become friends. Lucie was as excited about this child as the parents-to-be. She had seen Renault smiling as he worked in the stables, whistling as he went about his chores.

Adrienne turned and met Lucie's eyes. "Yes, I still have visions. But believe me, no one wants to know what I see. *You* do not want to know what I see. What good does it do to see the future if one can do nothing to change it?"

Lucie exhaled slowly. She shuddered.

"My visions have nothing to do with saving France," Adrienne said, turning her face away from her governess, away from the questions that filled the young woman's eyes. "My visions have nothing to do with saving anyone." Adrienne swallowed, the taste of her own knowledge bitter and sharp in her throat.

❦

Lucie stood on the terrace, picking up the books the younger children had been working on. She stopped and watched as Adrienne walked toward her. It was obvious from the basket of tools and Adrienne's somber expression that she had been up to the cemetery again. Lucie still missed the young Adrienne, the one who had smiled and laughed and skipped after butterflies and inhaled the nectar of the flowers. That younger version had been easy and light. She lit up the room when she entered.

Now, when Lucie looked into Adrienne's eyes, she saw only the melancholy notes of loneliness, the heavy oppression of silence. Lucie understood it now, the burden of Adrienne's ability to see the future. Since that day at their picnic over two years ago, since that day when her friend Madeline had bled to death in childbirth, Lucie had felt the misery of Adrienne's visions, of her differences, almost as much as the girl herself did. Adrienne had been almost as distraught at the death of the young maid as Lucie or Renault. She blamed herself; she confessed to Lucie what she had seen in her visions. Adrienne felt enormous guilt for not having spoken up. She could not stop wondering if perhaps she had spoken, if the doctor had been sent for sooner, Madeline might still be living.

Lucie sighed. "Nice walk, Adrienne?"

Adrienne nodded. Her cheeks flushed red; her hair strayed from its bun, from the exertion of her walk.

"Come. Let's work on the Schubert piece."

Adrienne slipped her cloak from her shoulders and dropped it on the divan. She and Lucie sat down at the pianoforte. Adrienne stretched her fingers, and they began to play. Adrienne's fingers were clumsy and lumbering, as if frozen. She hit two keys at once, unable to stay on the appropriate note.

Lucie, too, was making mistakes. Apprehension about Marie's visit sat on both of their shoulders like a dark cloud; it ran down their arms and into their fingers, forcing both women to stumble. Adrienne had not divulged any secrets at any of Marie's other visits. All the whispering and speculation that had followed the girl when she was younger had quieted. But they both sensed that all the gossip and conjecture about Adrienne and her sanity had only gone underground. With a little wind, it could easily flame into a full-scale fire once again.

Antoine plopped on the sofa and held his hands over his ears. "*Yecchhh!* It sounds like you're torturing the cat! Spare us, Adrienne! Spare us!"

Adrienne stopped playing and focused on her little brother. She stuck out her tongue. He grinned. Adrienne glared at him. Antoine pulled his mouth into a grimace, rolled his eyes back in his head. He pretended to fall over dead on the carpet.

The sounds of the horses' hooves clopping on the gravel and the wheels of the carriage in the drive made everyone in the room freeze for a moment. All eyes turned toward the front hall. Antoine got up off the floor and brushed at the dust on his pants.

Her voice reached them through the open door. "Be careful with those trunks, Renault. They've been in the family for years—I don't want them scratched."

Marie swept into the castle, and servants moved quickly to take her hat and cloak, to carry her bags.

Marie turned. "Stefan? Bring tea into the parlor. And light a fire. It's much too chilly in here."

Lucie met Adrienne's eyes. She watched as Adrienne tried to swallow, but her whole body had tensed with Marie's appearance. Lucie saw Adrienne's jaw tighten. She sensed the veil of silence that fell over Adrienne's features, as if she were deliberately numbing herself.

Marie entered the parlor like visiting royalty, and the children dipped their heads toward her. Even Antoine had grown quiet. She examined the boy. "Antoine, tuck in that shirt. You look like a street urchin." Marie moved toward the chair by the fire, pulling her gloves off, one finger at a time. The scent of lavender followed her like a shadow.

Antoine did as he was told. He moved more slowly than a few moments before, quiet and sedate now, and kept his eyes on the rug.

Genevieve trailed in a moment later. "Marie! How good it is to have you home again."

Adrienne rolled her eyes at the tone in her mother's voice.

"Are you home long?" Genevieve asked, slipping into the chair opposite Marie's. Everyone in the room held their breath, waiting to hear the words from Marie's mouth—like criminals, waiting to hear the sentence from the judge.

Marie smiled and held her hands toward the fire. "A few months, perhaps. Until Julien finishes building his castle in Manitou Springs. What with all the construction, it isn't a very restful place to be right now. But, oh! When it is finished." She sighed and smiled. "At last he is in a place that is much more fitting for who he is. A place where he is appreciated."

Marie continued, obviously lost in her story. "Manitou Springs is *so* beautiful—a lot like here, in fact. Mountains, pine trees, beautiful vistas. And the people." She moved her head from side to side. "Finally, he has been assigned to a place that is civilized. He is once again among Europeans, thank God. I thought we would never get away from all those wild heathens in New Mexico Territory."

~∽

Dinner dragged on and on, as if every moment were stretched into ten. Adrienne kept her eyes on her plate, watching the interactions between Marie and Genevieve from under her lashes. She studied her coq au vin, and did her best not to look directly at Marie. She pushed her food around the plate. From her sideways glances, she saw that Emelie did the same.

"You should see what Julien is building," Marie continued, and leaned back in her chair. She sipped from her wine, sparkling deep garnet in the candlelight. "The initial plan calls for forty-six rooms. And he's designed the whole thing himself, borrowing from all the different types of architecture that he saw in the cities where we lived before his father died. Everything glorious in European design will be incorporated into that home."

She leaned forward again and took a bite of chicken. "And all of it, nestled in the mountains, at the foot of Pikes Peak. Have you heard of Pikes Peak, Genevieve?"

Genevieve shook her head. Adrienne noticed that she, too, was not eating much.

"You, children? Have any of you heard of it?"

Emelie and Antoine shook their heads. Adrienne stayed still and kept her eyes on her plate.

"Hmmph!" Marie turned her chin up, slanted to the right. "Perhaps you need to expand their geography lessons, Lucie."

*"Oui, madame,"* Lucie mumbled.

"It is breathtaking," Marie continued, her eyes locked on some spot above their heads. "A beacon to travelers. Riding across the plains, in wagons or on the train, you can see that mountain for miles." Marie's shoulders rose, and she let out a long sigh. "Almost as beautiful as our own Puy-de-Dôme.

"Manitou Springs is a refreshing change. And Colorado Springs is just a few miles away. Filled with Europeans. They call it Little London." Marie beamed. It didn't matter if anyone responded. She had a captive audience, sitting at the head of the table, expounding on her worldliness. Now, in Colorado Springs and Manitou Springs, she could be among her own class, among people with whom she felt comfortable. Many of them spoke French, and she was relieved of the need to try to decipher the horrid squawks of the English language.

"Manitou is much smaller, of course, and is built in the foothills. The town boasts several mineral springs—just like Vichy. People travel from all over the world just to sample the dry, cool air and the healing waters."

Adrienne glanced up between her lashes. Marie held her wineglass between both hands. A smile played at the corners of her mouth.

"It is becoming a haven for tuberculosis patients. And you know Julien's great concern for the sick. He has a special understanding of illness, I think, especially after all he's been through himself." Marie's eyes shone. "He intends to give the Sisters of Mercy the home he's living in right now, just as soon as the castle is finished. To use as a sanatorium. The number of patients going to the area is growing faster than they can possibly accommodate in their current quarters."

"How generous of him," Genevieve muttered. She reached for her wine and held the glass before her.

The children did not speak. Marie's words were punctuated by the clink of silverware on the china, the occasional sip of water. Antoine burped, muttered, *"Pardonnez-moi."* He smiled triumphantly, as if he'd just managed a perfect score on his math, and then tried to hide it. Genevieve shot him a look.

Marie frowned at him, and Antoine dropped his smile to his lap. "This is just so much more to Julien's taste . . . so much more suited to his unique gifts," Marie continued. "The people are much more like us. It finally feels as if he has found his place in the world—his place in the work of the church."

She attacked the coq au vin with her knife and shook her head. "The people in Santa Cruz never understood Julien. Never appreciated him. But I feel certain that he will go far, now that he is in Colorado. Thank God the church finally recognized his worth. They were wasting his talents in New Mexico Territory."

Adrienne felt her jaw go tight. She reached for her wineglass, and suddenly she was in New Mexico Territory. She could see them, the people of Santa Cruz. Shuffling on the dirt roads, their eyes down whenever Julien was near. He wouldn't eat their food, refused it whenever he went to someone's home. It was the worst of insults, in those poor homes—to refuse the food they so generously offered. She watched as he refused a wooden carving of the Virgin, made by one of the village men, telling the man that his work was too "primitive" for Julien's taste. They hated him; they hated his arrogance; they hated his callous disregard for their own long traditions. She could feel their hatred thick like smoke in the clear blue air of her vision.

Adrienne stared at her wine goblet, her hand resting on its base, but did not lift the glass or take a drink. The vision swirled, like smoke, and changed. She could see the town of Manitou Springs, just as Marie described it. She could see the town clock on Manitou

Avenue; she could smell the pine trees. She could see Miramont Castle, being constructed before her eyes, hugging the hillside. She watched as builders set the heavy stones of the back of the castle right into the hill.

It hit her like a bolt of lightning, a charge of electricity that made the hair on her arms stand up. Something—or *someone*—was buried in that hillside. She didn't actually see a body, and Adrienne's mind raced to make sense of what she saw, what she felt. She couldn't say exactly what it was. But the stones of the castle were covering it up. Something that neither Julien nor Marie wanted anyone to know about. She came back to the present and found herself staring at her glass, her mouth half open in shock.

The room was completely silent; there were no sounds of forks or knives scraping against the plates, no sounds of eating and drinking and swallowing. Marie was staring. Antoine and Emelie were looking at her, and so was Genevieve. Adrienne looked back at them, covered her mouth, and pretended to cough. She lifted the wineglass to her lips and took two small swallows. She replaced her glass, picked up her knife, made an effort to eat dinner. The room slowly returned to normal. The children turned their attention back to their own plates.

Adrienne's mind raced. At certain intervals, she surreptitiously let her gaze wander to Marie's face. What was going on over there in Manitou Springs? And was the secret Julien's alone, or did it belong to Marie as well? It was as if her vision had been only a small burst of sight—only a fragment of the whole story. Before now, she had seen snippets of stories, little vignettes that were easy to interpret. Easy to understand. This was not the same.

Adrienne shivered, as if she'd been touched by a ghost.

# CHAPTER SIXTEEN

A drienne bolted upright in her bed, holding the covers up to her chest. She gasped. Moonlight spilled through the picture window to her right, bathing everything in a blue glow. She scanned the room. There was her wardrobe in the left corner. Directly across from the foot of the bed was the fireplace, cold and gray in the early hours. To her left was the dresser, the mirror reflecting the image of the door directly across the room. It was closed. The light caught a cut-glass perfume bottle, a tiny frosted dove, wings outspread, floating on the lid. Her father had given it to her last Christmas.

Her eyes moved to the picture window. The white curtains looked pale blue-gray in the moonlight, shimmering and dancing like spirits above the window seat.

Adrienne sighed and lay back against the pillows.

In the dream, the room was very small. There were no mahogany furnishings, their tops covered in creamy white marble. There was no wardrobe, no fireplace. In the dream, the room was cramped; it held only one narrow bed, one tiny table. A small window looked down to the street, far below. The moonlight caught the leaves of the tree, not tall enough to reach its arms as high as the small, dark room. In the dream, Adrienne had tried the door. She rattled it in the frame, but it wouldn't open.

She sat down on the bed. The room was cold. Dark. She heard the drip-drip-drip as tiny beads of moisture plopped on the floor. The smell was overpowering: a dense, metallic odor. She dipped the tips of her fingers in the pool at her feet. They came away dark, covered in something slick and thick, like oil. She brought her fingers to her nose and sniffed. The tangy smell of blood flooded her senses.

Adrienne's breath quickened; her heart began to race as the images of the dream came back to her. Fear tightened her throat. She sat up, threw the covers off, and stepped over to the window.

She'd had this dream before, long ago. She'd been very young. But she knew she had seen that little room before, had noticed the stones, the tiny drops of darkness that seeped, and grew bigger, and plopped to the floor. What wasn't clear was whether it was Adrienne herself in that room, or someone else. Some other woman that Adrienne sensed through the woman's own eyes, her own hands?

Adrienne shook off the images, and threw open the window. She leaned out into the cool fall air, forcing herself to take long, slow breaths. She closed her eyes and inhaled deeply, breathing in the night. It smelled of snow. She remembered standing in this very window as a young child, breathing in the scents of spring. She remembered a time when her visions made her smile, as if they were stories and secrets designed for her amusement, like fairy tales. Now they left her with questions, with a deep sense of something dark and foreboding. An owl hooted, somewhere in the trees to the left. In the village, she heard a dog bark. A street away, another dog added his voice to the chorus.

Adrienne leaned back into the window seat, resting her back against the sidewall. She pulled her knees up underneath her nightgown, wrapped her arms around her legs, and laid her head on her knee. She stared at the sky.

Everything had become so much more complicated. When she was little, the visions were clear and easy. She thought of the times that her visions had shown her the truth. She had known about Emelie and her yellow hair. She had seen the death of the maid, Madeline, in childbirth. But there was so much that she didn't know—and could never know for sure. She had seen Julien, poisoned at the chalice, but was that what had really happened? Or was it true, the story she'd heard, that he had been on a secret mission for the French government?

This was different. Not just what she had seen and felt at dinner a week ago, but this dream tonight. And she knew that she had dreamt the same thing years before. This required skills of interpretation that she did not have. Was it the past, or the future? Was it happening to her, or to someone else?

She stared out into the dark. She thought of the story in the Bible of Joseph being sold into Egypt and interpreting dreams for the pharaoh. Seven fat cows, seven skinny cows. How do you interpret things like that? How do you understand what it means for stones to bleed?

In the near distance, she could see the west wing of the château. Built of white limestone over three hundred years before, the château had been in her family for many generations. The moonlight turned the stones into a soft, glowing pink, and Adrienne stared, watching as the shadows of trees and leaves danced across the walls.

She sat up with a jolt, her back straight, her eyes fixed on the walls of the other wing of the castle. Maybe it wasn't a secret in Manitou Springs, in the new castle that Julien was building. Maybe the secret was here. Maybe her dreaming mind had jumbled it all up. Because just now, in the dim light of the moon, she could swear that it looked as if the stones were bleeding.

# CHAPTER SEVENTEEN

Stefan stepped into the morning room, his face almost hidden by the stack of boxes he held in his arms. He was followed by Renault and another servant, each of them bearing a similar burden. The boxes were wrapped in brown paper, tied together in bundles of three or four. They placed them on the rug since there was not enough table space to hold everything.

Adrienne and Emelie had been leaning together on the settee by the fire, examining a new piece of music. It fluttered to the floor in the excitement, and they both moved to examine the packages, looking for handwriting they recognized, a return address.

Genevieve looked up from her desk in the corner. "What's this?" Sunlight streamed across her desk. It highlighted the tiny lines around her eyes.

Stefan stepped forward and handed her a letter. He bowed and he and the other servants left the room.

Genevieve stared at the envelope. It was from Pierre, gilt flourishes framing the envelope. She opened it, her hands shaking, and let the envelope drop to her desk. Marie looked up from her own desk, in the opposite corner of the room.

The corners of Genevieve's mouth quivered as she read, as if she fought to keep her smile in check, as if she couldn't believe what she read.

"Your father . . ." she began, and had to stop. She scanned the letter again, making sure she had read it correctly. Her eyes flew up to meet those of her daughters. "Your father wants us to come to Paris." Her smile was firmly fixed now. "He wants to take us to the opera. He wants to take Antoine to the embassy." The note fluttered, like a nervous white bird, from the trembling of her hand. Her smile grew, radiated into her eyes, which had looked so tired and haggard just a few moments before. It lifted her shoulders, traveled down her arms and into her hands. "The boxes are things he picked out for us to wear. He says we may have to do a few alterations, but he hopes we will find them suitable for the opera."

Genevieve clutched the letter to her chest. She was suddenly luminous in the early-morning light.

Adrienne and Emelie turned toward one another, and Emelie grabbed Adrienne's hands. She began to skip in a circle, trying to get her serious older sister to dance with her around the room.

Antoine jumped up from his geography book. "Let me see that," he demanded, with ten-year-old manliness.

Genevieve pulled the letter away from his grasping fingers, and held it above her head. "No, you don't, young man. This is addressed to me." Genevieve's smile returned again. "Just be thankful for the invitation. Your father wants to introduce you to his work." She beamed. "As he should. That's what fathers do with their sons."

Antoine began a gangly and awkward dance around the big room. He took Emelie's hands, and the two of them reeled and spun. Antoine's streaky blond hair spilled across his forehead.

Adrienne stood in the center of the room, watching them. She turned to look at Lucie, sitting quietly at the corner table. Their eyes met and Lucie smiled.

"Well, let's look, shall we?" Genevieve moved to the boxes, her letter opener in hand, and began slitting the paper and handing out gifts. Emelie, Antoine, and Genevieve could not contain their joy. It bounced off the walls and windows and ceilings, threatening to break statuary.

Adrienne opened the box with her name on it, and her eyes flamed with color. Inside the layers of tissue paper was a pale teal-colored taffeta, spun here and there with copper threads. Tiny embroidered roses climbed the bodice. She gasped and held the dress to her chest. It was done in her favorite colors, like the ribbon she'd been admiring in the fabric shop just last week.

Emelie was dancing around the room, holding her sky-blue gown against her chest and singing, an awkward and ear-splitting version of an aria from *La Traviata*.

Marie watched them from behind her desk. Her lips were pinched, that same thin line of disapproval she always wore. The corners of her mouth went neither up nor down. They revealed nothing about how she felt. "So . . . when does this excursion take place?" she said.

Genevieve looked up from her own box of treasures. Happiness was etched in every line of her features; she smiled in a way that made her look years younger. "Two weeks from today." She clutched deep-green velvet to her chest. She looked at Marie. "Of course, we'd love for you to accompany us, Marie." Her voice did not quite match her words. "The embassy has a box at the opera house. I'm sure there will be more than enough room."

"I have missed the opera, since the death of my husband," Marie answered. "That would be lovely."

Lucie beamed as she hung Adrienne's new dress in the wardrobe. She put one hand on Adrienne's waist, grabbed her hand with the other, as if they were dancing partners. She spun her around the bedroom. "Oh, Adrienne! The opera! Isn't this wonderful?" Her skirts continued to spin, even after Adrienne broke away and collapsed in the chair by the bedroom fireplace.

Adrienne watched her governess, watched the joy that radiated from her hands and arms as Lucie pretended to dance with a partner, her skirts sashaying around the room.

"Lucie . . . did you do this?"

Lucie stopped swaying, stopped her humming. She moved to the package on the bed and folded the shawl, the opera gloves, the tiny beaded handbag that had all been part of Adrienne's box. She sat down on the edge of the bed.

Adrienne studied the dark eyes of the governess. "Did you write to my father?"

Lucie's gaze flickered to the window for a moment. "I had to, Adrienne." Their eyes met for an instant. "It breaks my heart, the way you live here. The way you've been so shut off from everything beautiful and wonderful in life. You are alone far too much. And lately, it seems as if you have been even more distant than usual. More lost in your own thoughts. So I wrote to him. I suggested, as the governess, that a trip to Paris could be highly educational for all the children. I told him that here you are, sixteen years of age, beautiful and intelligent, and that it is high time you were introduced to society." Lucie stopped for a moment. "Well . . . not in those words, exactly."

Adrienne stood and walked over to her governess. Adrienne was now a couple of inches taller than Lucie. She stood behind her, put her hands on Lucie's arms. She stared at the image of the two of them in the mirror.

"I had no idea how your father would respond," Lucie continued. She smiled into the mirror they faced across the room. "This is far more than I expected."

Adrienne rubbed her hands on Lucie's arms.

"Thank you," she whispered. She closed her eyes, her chin pressed into Lucie's shoulder. For one brief moment, she smiled.

# CHAPTER EIGHTEEN

The footman held Adrienne's gloved hand as she stepped from the landau. It was like stepping directly into a fairy tale, her slippers turned to glass. She scanned the scene before her. There had to be a handsome prince, an old green frog, a wicked stepmother, a pumpkin coach, and little mice footmen somewhere in this incredible scene.

The opera house blazed with golden light. The sky was a deep blue, a fine line of pale turquoise at the horizon. A few stars blazed in the deepening dusk. Adrienne felt drenched in the beauty of it all.

People milled about, dressed in their finest. The gentlemen wore tuxedos, their long coattails hitting their calves. They tipped their hats to everyone they met, their hands elegant in white gloves. The women sparkled like jewels, long white opera gloves visible beneath their cloaks. They swept through the grand doors in groups of three and four.

Lucie took Adrienne's arm as they moved toward the entrance. The entire family looked so dapper and refined tonight. Antoine stood straight and tall, enormously proud of himself in front of his father. Emelie's eyes were huge, sparkling sapphires; she moved as if she were in a dream. Genevieve leaned into Pierre's arm, flashing a brilliant smile that none of them had ever observed at home. Overnight, she had become young and beautiful again, all her worries swept away.

Pierre was not the father he normally was, either. His occasional visits to the castle had not prepared any of the family for this. At home, he was often preoccupied, busy with work that he brought with him. But for just these few hours, he brought together his friends and acquaintances in Paris with the family from the country estate.

Adrienne floated into the foyer of the grand opera house. A staircase stretched before them, a palace of gold marble, gold railings, gold statuary. Deep scarlet curtains framed each box of seats. Her eyes traveled to the balconies, the elaborate carvings, and the crystal chandeliers. The opera house glowed, gaslights spilling gold curtains of light on every surface. The shiny floors reflected it back again, light bouncing up onto their skirts.

Adrienne could feel that glow. It warmed her cheeks, her neck, the deep plunging V of her gown. She let it radiate through her being, felt as if she were glowing like one of the gas lamps. Luminous.

She clung to Lucie's arm. Her feet glided over each step on the staircase, as if she were some winged creature and not a human girl who had to climb the steps. The lights caught the coppery shimmer that wove through the teal threads of her gown—perfect reflections of her copper hair and water-colored eyes.

Pierre stopped to talk often. He knew many people in Paris society, and glowed as he introduced them to his wife and children. He put his hand on Antoine's shoulder many times on their way to the box, obviously proud of the young man. Marie hung at the edge of every introduction, still severe in black, but a lustrous black silk that was more appropriate to the situation than her normal attire.

Lucie leaned in close to Adrienne. "See that gentleman, in the balcony to our right?"

Adrienne let her eyes move up. A young man beamed at her, took his hat from his head, and bowed. Adrienne dropped her eyes back to the staircase they were climbing.

"He's been staring at you. Ever since we started up the stairs. His eyes were so intense, I had to look up," Lucie whispered.

The family trailed Pierre and Genevieve to the box reserved for embassy personnel and slipped into the lush velvet seats. The orchestra tuned their instruments in the pit below them, and Adrienne slid forward in her seat to watch. Pierre stood at the railing of the box, Antoine beside him, and pointed out various architectural details to his son. Antoine's hair was heavily greased; for once, it did not flop in his face. He looked surprisingly like his father.

"Isn't this incredible, Marie?" Genevieve leaned to her sister as they sat down together in the first row of the box. She could not contain her happiness; it flowed from her being, even to the point of including Marie.

Marie sighed. "I suppose. If one isn't used to this sort of thing, it could be overwhelming, I imagine. When Jacques was alive, we went to the opera quite often, and in some of the grandest opera houses in Europe."

Genevieve bit her lip and turned away.

Two gentlemen entered the box, and Pierre turned to greet them. He shook hands with both and then turned to present them to his family. "Monsieur Armand Devereux," Pierre began, holding out his gloved hand. "My wife, Genevieve. My daughters, Emelie and Adrienne." Pierre waved his hand in the direction of each girl. He turned behind him, to the railing where Antoine still stood, and directed the young man forward. "And this is my son, Antoine."

The gentleman kissed Genevieve's gloved hand, bowed to the girls, shook Antoine's hand. Adrienne stared. He had white hair, blue eyes, a thin white mustache. He was tall, slender, and stately, very well mannered. She couldn't help but think of Grand-père as she watched him bow to Marie and kiss her gloved hand.

"And this is Monsieur Devereux's grandson, Gerard."

Adrienne's eyes met those of the young man before her. He offered only the slightest of smiles as she met his gaze. It was the same man who had been staring at her as she climbed the steps. She swallowed.

"Gerard works with me at the embassy," Pierre continued as Gerard, in his turn, kissed Genevieve's and Marie's hands.

He reached for Adrienne's gloved hand, and pressed it to his lips. *"Enchanté, mademoiselle."* She blushed. For a moment, she forgot how to breathe. He dropped her hand and stepped back next to his grandfather.

The two men stood by the railing and chatted with Pierre. When Gerard laughed at something Pierre said, he threw his head back. The laugh came from somewhere deep inside him. Adrienne had never heard anyone laugh like that. The sound was rich and full. Real. It made her feel good to hear it, to see it. A smile played at the corners of her mouth.

Lucie touched Adrienne's arm, caught her gaze. Her eyebrows arched. She smiled. Adrienne ducked her head and pulled her lower lip between her teeth. She felt too warm, suddenly, and color rose in her cheeks and neck.

The lights in the opera house dimmed, and everyone took their seats. Gerard and his grandfather stayed in the embassy box. They sat next to Pierre, the adults filling the front row. Adrienne, Lucie, Emelie, and Antoine sat in the row behind them.

The music of the orchestra swept up through the room; the notes of Verdi's *La Traviata* danced and skipped over the balconies and balustrades. Adrienne leaned forward in her seat, transported, completely lost in the singing, and the costumes, and the music. She forgot where she was, forgot who she was. She forgot Marie, forgot Gerard with his auburn mustache, sitting a few seats away. She forgot that back home in Beaulieu, there were those who called her crazy. She forgot that her life had been filled with loneliness. She forgot everything. She felt as if she were sailing around the room, floating on the notes of the aria.

The second act began, and Adrienne continued to lean slightly forward. As she watched the stage below her, it turned dark, melted into one dark color, until everything disappeared. The music faded, replaced by the roar of waves, the crash of water hitting the side of a ship. She looked out at a wide expanse of sea, nothing but black as far as the eye could see. It was night, the sky a slightly paler shade of gray than the water below. She felt the swaying, rocking motion of the boat. Her own body swayed slightly with the movement. She stood at the railing. Moonlight lit a path of water that spread out before her, shimmering silver in the night.

Adrienne could feel the moisture in the air; she could smell the salt of the sea. She turned slowly, her eyes drawn to movement on deck in front of her. A woman, small in stature with a head of dark curls, was walking away. She wore a severe black dress, and moved quickly along the deck and into the hallway leading to the cabins of the ship. Adrienne followed, slowly becoming aware that the woman before her was Marie.

Adrienne continued to trail Marie, but now they were no longer on board ship. They were in the halls of a huge house, the corridor and rooms unrecognizable in Adrienne's vision. She watched as Marie stopped at one door, glancing to the right and the left, and unlocked it. She slipped inside, and Adrienne followed her. Marie turned, as if she knew someone was behind her, but Adrienne sensed that she herself could not be seen.

Marie turned her back, pulled out a small tapestry valise, and Adrienne watched as she placed a stack of papers inside. She locked the valise, and replaced it beneath the bed. Marie turned then, facing the invisible Adrienne in the vision. In slow, dreamlike motion, Adrienne's eyes wandered from Marie's face down the front of her gown. There were dark spots on Marie's dress, as if she had been splattered with ocean water. In the surreal quality of a dream, Adrienne focused intently on those dark splatters. The smell was overpowering, and the knowledge hit her like a wave. That was not seawater on Marie's gown. It was blood.

Adrienne gasped, and raised her hand to cover her mouth. For a moment, she lost her balance, swaying in her chair.

Lucie turned to look at her.

Emelie, on the other side of Adrienne, turned her head and looked at her sister. Adrienne could feel sweat break out on her upper lip, and she snapped her fan open and began to fan her face vigorously.

Lucie touched Adrienne's arm. She leaned forward and whispered, "Adrienne?"

Marie turned her head and looked over her shoulder. She took in Adrienne's glazed eyes, the sweat on her lip. Marie's lips went thin and firm, and she turned back to the opera stage.

Adrienne leaned back in her seat. She swallowed, turned her eyes toward Lucie. She was back in the opera house now, the music of the third act swelling around her. She could hear the soft movements of people breathing and shifting in their seats. She turned and met Lucie's dark eyes, wide with questions and concern.

Adrienne closed her fan and took a deep breath. Her heart continued to race.

She glanced to the left, to the row of seats in front of her. Gerard Devereux was sitting at an angle in his seat, and his eyes met hers. They stared at one another for a moment, and then he turned away. He was no longer smiling.

# CHAPTER NINETEEN

Adrienne left the cemetery on the hill and clicked the gate closed. She pulled her cloak around her, wrapped her hands in her muff. The wind was up. It brushed her cheeks with color. Her boots crunched on the icy pellets of snow, and she moved quickly toward the castle. December had come, with a vengeance.

Since the night at the opera house, since her vision of Marie, splattered with blood, Adrienne had spent many hours here. Despite the approaching winter, she came to the cemetery almost every day, sitting near the headstones of her grand-père and her grand-mère. She had begun to speak, silently, in her own mind, to the grandmother she had never known—the grandmother who also had visions. She knew nothing, really, and a dreamy, surreal vision did not seem like enough to make her break her promise of silence to her grand-père. But she desperately wanted one of them to guide her, to tell her how to handle these ominous feelings that were creeping into every corner of her mind.

Adrienne walked briskly on her return to the château. She stepped into the hall, pulled the string of her cloak, and let it drop from her shoulders. Emelie came skipping out of the parlor and danced in circles around the tiled floor of the hall. "He's coming!" she sang. "He's coming!" She grinned at Adrienne.

"Who's coming?"

Emelie stopped dancing. She sucked in her lower lip and let her eyes roll back in her head, as if she couldn't believe that Adrienne could be so dense. Then she beamed at her sister; her eyes danced. She stared at Adrienne, twisted back and forth. "He's coming! He's coming!"

Adrienne rolled her own eyes and walked into the parlor. She moved directly to the fireplace, held her reddened, brittle hands toward the warmth.

"Oh, Adrienne. I'm glad you're back." Genevieve sailed into the room, a letter in her hand. She stopped a few feet away. "We've had a letter from your father." Her face held the same impish grin that Emelie's did, as if they'd both swallowed tincture of mischief.

Adrienne said nothing.

"He's coming home this weekend." Genevieve's smile grew wider. "And he's bringing guests." She waited, as if she expected Adrienne to jump with excitement, to guess at who might be coming.

Adrienne stood perfectly still. A tingling sensation started crawling up her spine.

"The Devereuxs will be with him. They haven't seen this part of the country, and are anxious to get away from the city for a while." She smiled at her oldest daughter. "I find it difficult to believe that could be the only reason for their visit." There was a look in Genevieve's eyes that was new to Adrienne, as if this possible interest in her daughter took her back to her own days of courting.

Adrienne turned back to face the fire. She held her hands to the heat, but pulled them to her sides when she saw how much they trembled. She felt a blush flaming in her face, like a sleeping ember that blazes to life from a sudden gust of wind. Her heart raced. She did not want her mother or her sister to see the color, to notice her sudden nerves.

Genevieve sat down in the wing chair and looked through the letter once more. "Your father says they are a fine old family. Gerard has worked at the embassy for five years now. Your father says he is very capable, very intelligent."

Antoine ran into the room, Emelie close behind him. He stopped behind Adrienne on the rug and poked at her hair. "Adrienne has a beau-eau. Adrienne has a beau-eau." His voice had a singsong quality to it. His eyes twinkled with mischief.

Adrienne turned from the fire and reached for his collar. He sidestepped, and skipped around the room, grinning. "I wonder how many babies they'll have?"

"Antoine, young gentlemen do not behave like that," Marie's voice snapped from the table by the window. The drapes were pulled. Adrienne had not seen her sitting there. Four pairs of eyes shot over to the darkened area.

Antoine stopped skipping. He stood behind the divan. He grinned at Adrienne, raised his eyebrows.

Lucie met Adrienne's eyes. Adrienne tried to read Lucie's look, across the room, but the governess was mostly in shadow, and she could not.

Adrienne turned back to the fire, gazing into the flames as if they held the key to the future.

❦

Genevieve had rearranged the place cards on the dining room table several times now. She couldn't decide whether to put Adrienne and Gerard across from one another or next to one another. She finally settled on next to one another, with Pierre at one end of the table and Marie at the other. Genevieve would sit across from Adrienne, ready to help out if Adrienne should falter. And she would put Gerard's father, Armand, next to Marie. She thought he might be able to keep Marie occupied.

She had cut tuberoses from the greenhouse, and sent Antoine out for pine boughs. She hummed as she made three small arrangements for the table, another for the parlor after dinner.

The younger children, for the first time, were not allowed at the dinner table. They would eat upstairs, in their rooms, Lucie supervising to make sure that Antoine didn't sneak down the stairs and put pinecones on chairs or whistle inappropriately.

Candlelight danced on the walls, on the china and crystal, on the faces of the six people around the table.

Adrienne kept her eyes on her plate. Years of isolation, of learning to stay quiet, had made her completely uncomfortable around strangers. She had no idea what to say, or where to look. Every bite she took, every swallow, seemed vastly loud to her own ears. She stole glances at her mother, sitting directly across from her, and could tell that Genevieve was enjoying this immensely. Genevieve smiled often; her eyes danced. She met Adrienne's eyes and tipped her head toward Gerard, as if she could will the girl to speak, to be comfortable in this new situation.

Marie, at the other end of the table, looked regal and at ease. She spoke easily to both Armand and Gerard, who sat on each side of her. "When were you in the embassy, monsieur?" she asked Armand.

"From 1838 to 1872," he replied. "An exciting time, as you well know."

"Perhaps you remember my late husband, Jacques Morier?"

Armand studied the air in front of him for a minute, his white eyebrows knit together. "The ambassador to Russia, at one time, I believe?"

Marie nodded, obviously pleased.

"Yes, yes. I remember him. He had a gift, that young man. The gift of holding his tongue. I think some of the younger men do not understand how valuable that can be." He smiled at Marie, sipped his wine. "They haven't grown up around so many fine examples of men and women who lost their heads for speaking their minds."

"Indeed," Marie replied. "Diplomacy has much more to do with restraint, I think, than with speaking."

Gerard cast a sideways glance at Adrienne. "Did you enjoy the opera?" He kept his voice low, allowing Marie and Armand to continue their conversation.

Adrienne did not look up. "Very much," she murmured.

"Such a beautiful opera house. The sound carries very well, I think. Have you been often?"

Adrienne shook her head. "No. No, unfortunately, we don't often get to Paris."

Gerard turned slightly and looked at her directly. "That's a shame. I had hoped to see more of you there. You looked as if you were completely lost in the music a few weeks ago. As if you were absorbed in the story."

Adrienne flushed. Was that what he was thinking, when he turned to look at her that evening? She raised her eyes and met his own. They were brown and kind. She stared at him for a moment and dropped her eyes back to her meal. She stole a glance at her mother, across from her. Genevieve was radiant. She sipped her wine and smiled at her daughter and the handsome young man beside her.

⁓

After dinner, the group moved to the parlor. A fire blazed in the fireplace, and Lucie had brought Antoine and Emelie down to join the others. Stefan poured brandies and coffees for the men. The perfume of the tuberoses and pine boughs on the table competed with the men's cigars, the aromas twisting together.

"You must hear my daughter play," Pierre said. "She has a very light touch on the pianoforte. Lovely, actually."

Adrienne looked up from the divan, a cup of coffee balanced on her knee. "Oh, Papa, I . . ." Her hands had been trembling all evening. She knew there was no way she could play with anything resembling her usual acumen.

Lucie noticed her look of panic and stood. She held out her hand. "Come, Adrienne. Let's do one of the new duets from *Hänsel and Gretel.*"

Adrienne put her coffee on the table and took Lucie's hand.

Armand caught her gaze, his blue eyes twinkling. "Oh, that would be lovely. My wife used to play, may she rest in peace. I have so missed music in the house—the sound of a woman's voice."

Adrienne smiled at him and curtsied. He reminded her so much of her grand-père, she felt she would do almost anything for the man. She and Lucie sat down on the bench, and Adrienne stared at the keys for a moment. They moved into the prayer, from act 2, their two voices soaring into the height of the parlor ceiling.

Gerard stood back by the window. The curtains were pulled and his face obscured in the dim light. Armand moved to the side of the pianoforte, smiling wistfully, his eyes focused on some long-ago memory. Pierre stood slightly behind him, brandy snifter in his hand; the tip of his cigar glowed red.

Marie sat in the wing chair next to the fire. Adrienne could see her, behind and to the left of Armand. For one brief second, a single picture flickered in Adrienne's mind, a picture straight out of her vision at the opera house a few weeks before: Marie, turning slowly, her dark dress splattered in blood.

Adrienne's fingers faltered on the keys. The image disappeared as quickly as it had come, and she dropped her eyes to the keyboard, forcing herself to focus on the notes of the piece. She felt as if everyone were staring at her: Marie, in her chair by the fire; Armand, standing next to the pianoforte; her father, standing close beside him. Adrienne's fingers stumbled once again; her voice wavered. She forced herself to keep going.

When they finished, she looked up, horrified by both her vision and her errors. Armand stood, clapping enthusiastically. "Brava! Brava!" Adrienne sighed heavily, relief flooding through her that the song was over and that Armand could be so kind. She couldn't help but smile at him. She found herself falling slightly in love with him, with his enthusiasm and appreciation, with his eyes that were so like Grand-père's. For a moment, she felt safe and protected, as she had when Grand-père was alive. For a moment, she forgot about Marie.

She did not turn to look at her father for several heartbeats. When she did, her smile dropped. Her father was staring in her direction, but it was not Adrienne who had captured his attention. His eyes were glued to Lucie. Even as he sipped his brandy, and complimented the fine performance, he looked at no one but the governess.

"That was lovely," Gerard said, stepping out from the corner. His voice was very soft.

Adrienne turned to look at him. She met his eyes, as she had a few times at dinner, and in the warmth of his gaze, she forgot everything. She forgot her vision of Marie; she forgot the strange look in her father's eyes; and for a moment, at least, she forgot how badly she had hammered the song. She forgot the tension, the fear, the intense sensitivity that she felt in every nuance, every glance, when Marie was present. There was nothing at this moment but that glow in Gerard's eyes, the way his voice wrapped around his words. For several seconds, Adrienne let herself fall into that embrace.

"Yes, quite so." Armand placed his brandy snifter on the table. "But it's getting rather late. I hope this hasn't been an imposition."

Adrienne looked again at the older gentleman and felt all the gratitude she used to feel when Grand-père moved to rescue her from some uncomfortable situation. "Thank you, sir," she said, rising from the bench. "It was no imposition at all. I'm afraid I must be more tired than I thought—I seemed to have misplaced a few notes." She curtsied toward Monsieur Devereux. "Please forgive me."

Armand waved his hand. "On the contrary, young lady. It was absolutely beautiful."

"It is late," Marie observed, standing. "Perhaps we ladies should retire, and leave you gentlemen to your brandies."

Lucie and the children made their bows. Adrienne curtsied to Armand, turned slightly, and dipped her head toward Gerard. He bowed. *"Bonne nuit, messieurs."* She turned toward her father. *"Bonne nuit,* Papa." He bent and kissed her cheek.

# CHAPTER TWENTY

January arrived, colder and wetter than anything Adrienne could remember. She was oblivious, though, to the cold, the wind, the snow. Gerard and his grandfather were here for their third visit. Though she was still quiet, it was getting easier to talk to him. She found herself thinking about him far too often. There was something about him, something in his eyes, in the gentle way he spoke to her, that made her feel as if she already *knew* him, had known him forever. She had a hard time concentrating on her studies. All her concerns about Marie had vanished, dissolved by the warmth of Gerard's attention.

The two young people had pulled on hats and cloaks, gloves and mufflers. Adrienne rested her hands in her fox muff. She and Gerard strolled the grounds of the château, oblivious to the bite of the wind. This was their first time alone, though they were not, strictly speaking, alone. Lucie and Emelie trailed the two young people, a suitable distance behind: far enough that they couldn't hear what was said, close enough that the couple would still be considered adequately chaperoned.

They walked with no obvious destination in mind, and Adrienne looked up in surprise when they found themselves at the gate to the little cemetery. Gerard stopped walking, let his eyes drift over the stones, all of them brushed with windblown drifts of snow. The oak tree stood sentinel, its arms bare, reaching toward the gray skies.

"My grand-père is here," Adrienne said.

Gerard glanced at her face. "I wish I could have known him," he answered. "He is still highly regarded at the embassy . . . even after all this time."

Gerard wrestled with the gate, difficult to open in the icy drifts. They wandered through the stones. Gerard noted the comtesse, the tiny child-sized grave beside her. They stopped in front of the largest stone, dark gray granite carved with roses. Shadows stretched in front of the stone.

Adrienne stared into the distance. "He was my favorite person in the world," she whispered. "Strong, intelligent, kind. He had blue eyes." She smiled at his stone. Dead leaves skittered across the icy ground. She raised her eyes to Gerard. "Your grand-père reminds me of him."

"You were very young when he died?"

Adrienne nodded. "Seven. I still miss him." A gust of wind lifted the edge of her cloak.

Gerard stared at the stone. "I never really knew my parents. They died when I was very young. But I miss them, just the same."

Adrienne looked at his jawline, his eyes still glued to the comte's stone. His cheek was red. "How did they die?"

Gerard dropped his eyes to the ground in front of him. "My father was killed in the Franco-Prussian War. He was with Mac-Mahon. I was only a few months old."

There was a long silence, broken only by the moan of the wind. "And your mother?"

"She died when I was a year old. Fever, they said. My grand-père says she died of a broken heart. That after my father died, she lost the will to keep going."

The icy air crawled under their coats and hats, and both young people shivered. "It seems I've been alone most of my life," Gerard continued. "I have Grand-père, of course. Thank God. I don't know what I'd do without him."

They both looked into the distance. The turrets of the château reached into the gray skies. "I've never been very good at making friends. And I don't have any family, other than Grand-père . . . not like you."

Adrienne sighed. Her breath formed a white puff in the air. "Having family does not ensure that one won't be lonely." Her words were so soft; they were almost lost in the wind. She stared at the château grounds surrounding them. She wanted so much to tell him, to unburden herself and tell him the truth about her life. She had thought about it, over and over in the last few weeks. Telling him about her visions; telling him about the way she had been ostracized, the way the visions had marked her as different, defective. She wanted to tell him what it felt like to be left out, not quite accepted by anyone around her. She wanted to tell him that she was just as isolated, in this huge château and all this family, as if she'd been completely alone. That maybe, in some ways, it was worse than being alone. She had been judged and found defective for almost as long as she could remember, and it hammered at her relentlessly.

She looked at him again, his eyes still locked on the gravestones before him. Would he understand? Or would he, like so many others, judge her and push her away? She wished she had a vision that could tell her *that*. She wished that for just once in her life, the visions would come and tell her something that was actually useful. She waited, watching him, until he turned and looked at her. The moment passed. Adrienne swallowed; the words retreated to that deep space in her heart that held all of her secrets.

The wind gusted, lifting Adrienne's cloak, and she trembled with the cold.

"Come," Gerard said, taking her elbow. "We'd better be getting back."

She met his eyes, warm and kind and attentive. Someday, she thought. Someday she would tell him. Someday, maybe, she would be able to share all her secrets, all the things she held inside. But not yet. Not now.

They walked in silence, down the hill, past the lake, frozen now—a milky gray glass, flashing in the sun. Pine trees outlined the opposite shore. Occasionally, they heard Emelie laughing as she walked along behind them.

"This place is beautiful," Gerard murmured. He stopped walking. His body stood close to hers. She could feel his warmth. He put his hand at the small of her back, and she felt the slightest pressure against her cloak. "I have always been drawn to the quiet places." He turned and looked at her, raising his eyebrows. "Someday, perhaps. When I no longer work at the embassy."

They stood for a few moments, staring at the scene. A shared understanding of loneliness wrapped them, and Adrienne felt connected to Gerard in a way she had never felt before. His hand was still resting gently on her back, and she allowed herself to lean into him, his strength, his concern. For the first time since she was very little, she felt protected. Cared for. She wanted the moment to last forever.

Gerard turned to look at her, and he took her gloved hands in his own. "Adrienne, every time I visit, it is harder for me to leave. I think about you constantly." He looked away for a moment. "It feels as if . . . as if we understand each other. As if we are connected in some way that I do not really understand. It has reached the point where I cannot imagine life without you." He kissed first one hand, and then the other. His eyes locked on hers. "Would you do me the honor of becoming my wife?"

The gentlemen left at noon, and Adrienne spent the afternoon walking on air. They had agreed not to speak of their plans until Gerard had a chance to talk to her father. Pierre was in England, and was not expected back for a few weeks, but Gerard would speak with him as soon as Pierre returned to Paris.

For now, at least, Adrienne had to hold her happiness in check. She wandered from room to room, lost in a fog of dreaming. She pulled a book off the shelf in the library and opened it as if studiously interested, but if anyone had asked, she would not have been able to even produce the title. The afternoon was endless; dinner was a long ordeal in which she could not remember what they were served or whether or not she had eaten any of it.

They sat in the parlor after dinner, Genevieve and Marie, Lucie and the children. Genevieve's knitting needles clicked. The pendulum on the clock ticked. The fire crackled. Emelie sighed heavily every time she hit her finger with her embroidery needle, which was often. Antoine sat across from Lucie, playing chess. Occasionally, he would move a piece and beam his pride into Lucie's eyes. "Your turn," he announced, as if he knew that he had just performed so brilliantly that it made no difference what she did in response. Adrienne sat in the corner, a book in front of her, unable to focus on the words. She reread the same page, over and over again. Her mind kept slipping into the future, into her life with Gerard. Several times, she caught herself smiling, and had to force her face into a more composed expression.

Marie stitched. She had not said much at dinner. After the last several days with the gentlemen present, dinner had seemed abnormally quiet and subdued. Once or twice during the evening, Adrienne felt as if Marie were staring at her, but she would look up to find Marie engrossed in her stitching.

When the clock struck eight, they all knelt for prayers. Each of them counted off the decades, murmuring the words that had filled every evening of their lives. Antoine dropped his hands to scratch his leg, and Lucie put her hand over his, quietly forcing him to be still. Adrienne closed her eyes for a moment, the beads ticking through her fingers, the words so automatic that they no longer had meaning.

It hit her with a jolt—the same vision she had had at the opera house, the same vision that had struck her the night of Gerard's first visit: Marie turning, slowly, blood splattered on her dress and her hands.

This time, though, the vision hit her hard. Adrienne crumpled onto the floor, the wind leaving her as if she had been kicked. Everyone stopped praying to look at her, sitting in a pile on the rug, her beads dropped to the carpet and sweat breaking out on her face.

"Adrienne? Is something wrong?" It was Genevieve who spoke.

Adrienne raised a hand to her chest, forced herself to steady her breath. "I . . . I'm not feeling well, all of a sudden." She did not allow herself to look in Marie's direction, but she could feel the woman's eyes on her. She barely registered the stares of her mother and the two children.

Lucie stood and moved to Adrienne's side, bending low so that she could wrap her arms around the girl. "Come. I'll help you upstairs."

◠◡

It wasn't until after Lucie had tucked the younger children into their beds that she returned to Adrienne's room. The two women sat in the window seat, illuminated by the light of a crescent moon in the eastern sky and the candle on Adrienne's bedstand behind them.

"You've had another vision, haven't you?" Lucie whispered.

Adrienne nodded. She poured it all out, the relief so overwhelming it brought tears to her eyes. She described seeing Marie, surrounded by the dark water of the ocean. She described following her down a corridor, knowing that Marie had something she was hiding in that valise, watching her turn and seeing the blood on her dress, her hands.

Lucie sat quietly, taking it all in.

"The worst part . . . the part I can't stop thinking about . . . is that every time I've had this vision, three times now, it seems like Gerard has somehow been involved. That first night I met him at the opera, the first night they came to visit, when we played and sang. And now this, tonight, right after he left. It's been weeks since the last time. Why now, just when—" Adrienne caught herself and looked up into Lucie's dark eyes.

"Lucie, do you think it has something to do with him? Do you think that Marie might try to . . ." Adrienne found that she could not give voice to the thought. She did not want to speak the words, to put them out there in the air. She felt tears racing down her cheeks; she shook her head from side to side.

"Do you think that Marie might try to hurt him?"

∾

Lucie straightened her back and stretched her arms over her head. She had been at her desk, hunched over her journal, for the past hour. It was late: one in the morning, and she was exhausted. She put her plume back in its stand, blew on the ink of the page she had just finished.

It had been a while since she had written in the journal. For so long, there had been nothing to record. But she'd started writing again a few weeks ago. She had not told Adrienne, but Lucie had known, since the night at the opera, that Adrienne's visions were back. She had known the girl almost her entire life; she recognized the signs. She had not asked Adrienne about it. After the death of Madeline in childbirth, there was some part of Lucie that didn't want to know what Adrienne saw.

Lucie had watched as Gerard Devereux moved into their lives. She observed the way he looked at Adrienne, the way his eyes followed her around the room. She had seen Adrienne brighten; she had noticed the lilt in her step, the smiles that sometimes crept into her face when she thought no one was watching. Lucie wanted desperately to believe that Gerard was the answer, the handsome prince who would rescue Adrienne from her loneliness and isolation. The handsome prince who would rescue the maid from the evil witch.

She would never tell Adrienne this, but she had scratched it onto the pages of her journal, shivering with fear as she did. When Adrienne had described her vision—Marie on the dark ocean, Marie covered in blood—Lucie's whole body had frozen in apprehension. But it wasn't Gerard she feared for. Gerard was off in Paris; he was safe from Marie's clutches.

Adrienne was not. Lucie shivered again, looking at the words she had written on the page. Despite her own lack of clairvoyance, despite her inability to see or know the future, Lucie was certain about one thing. The blood on Marie's dress was not Gerard's.

She had to do something to protect Adrienne. She had to do something to get the girl out of here, away from Marie.

*I would never let Adrienne know this, and I hope she is distracted enough by her current circumstances that she does not notice, but I plan to watch Marie as I never have before. That woman is hiding something, I feel certain of it. And I intend to find out what it is.*

Lucie laid her pen on the desk and blew on the ink. She closed the journal and went to her closet, where she tucked it away in her tapestry valise.

# CHAPTER TWENTY-ONE

Adrienne let the book drop to her lap. She pulled her knees up inside her heavy wool dress, wrapped her arms around them, and leaned her cheek to rest on one knee. She stared out the window. It was so difficult to focus on a book these days. She would find herself at the bottom of the page with absolutely no idea of what she had just read.

The morning room was glazed in sunlight, still too winter-weak to provide much warmth. A fire crackled in the fireplace. Genevieve and Marie sat at their desks, attending to correspondence.

Adrienne stared out at the early March weather. The winds had been fierce the past few days, but there was movement in the air, a rustling and stirring. Like a whisper, it held the promise of spring. Adrienne could see the leaves of the crocus, poking through the soil in the garden, surrounded by the icy white of last evening's snow. The trees were thickening, like a woman in the early stages of pregnancy. Everything seemed ripe with the coming warmth and light and color.

Adrienne had been watching the plants, the trees, the garden, for as long as she could remember. But never, in all this time, had she allowed the promise of spring to seep into her bloodstream, to affect her heart or make her mind race. Since Grand-père's death, she had felt frozen inside, as if her heart and mind and emotions were locked in eternal winter. There was no reason to hope, no reason to look forward to anything. Every day was like the one before. Her life, until recently, had been just as solitary, just as barren and hard and cold, as the winter landscape.

Gerard Devereux had changed all that. He gave her a reason to believe, a reason to imagine a life different from the one she had always known. She found herself waking up with a smile on her face. She could see them, living together in an apartment in Paris. She couldn't help but smile when she imagined holding his child, their child, in her arms. She reached into the pocket of her dress, slipped a sideways glance at Marie, and pulled out his latest letter.

*Dearest,*
*I can hardly wait for your father's return from the north. It seems as if he is taking forever on this trip. I wish I had been able to speak with him right away, after leaving, but I suppose I shall have to be patient.*

*I told Grand-père, after we left you, that you had consented to marry me. I can't tell you how pleased he was. He likes you a great deal, Adrienne. That tells me that I have made a good choice, that he, too, can see our compatibility, our connection.*

*As soon as your father returns, I will speak with him. In the meantime, I remain,*

*Yours forever,*
*Gerard*

Adrienne brushed her fingers over the thick paper, folded it tenderly, and tucked it back into the pocket of her dress. She sighed, and laid her cheek against her knee again. She smiled at her reflection in the window glass. It was just like a fairy tale—the tall, handsome prince, the rescue from the wicked witch who sat at her desk in the corner. She took her hand from the letter in her pocket and made the sign of the cross once again, as she had every time she had thought of the vision of Marie. She'd been praying every morning, every night, trying to create a web of protection around Gerard.

Stefan entered the room with the morning's mail on a silver tray. Adrienne looked up, her eyes glued on his every move. He stopped first at Genevieve, with a nod of his head. "Madame." He turned and walked toward Marie, his heels clicking on the marble floor. "Madame." He bowed lower for Marie. Adrienne watched as he turned the tray on its side, tucked it under his arm. His eyes sought Adrienne's, briefly, as if he knew she expected mail. His eyes seemed to speak the words that he would not dare to say aloud: "I'm sorry, mademoiselle. Nothing today." He dipped his head toward her and left the room.

Adrienne sighed and turned back to the window. She stared at the snow on the ground, at the wind blowing in the treetops. She watched as the world outside her window faded and disappeared, and she was drawn into a scene half a world away.

It was night. A half moon hung in the sky, hazy with cloud cover. Her gaze dropped from the brilliance of the moon to a cobblestone street, curving up a hill. An enormous stone castle dominated the bend of the street. Four stories high, wood and granite and glass, and every window blazed with light. Carriages crowded the pavement; horses clip-clopped on the stones. She could hear the horses whinny and snort. She could hear laughter, voices rising and falling in the excitement of the evening.

One by one, the carriages stopped at the front door. Ladies and gentlemen spilled out, dressed in the costumes of a century before—the time of the American Revolution. The women wore wide skirts, the same skirts seen in the time of Louis XVI in France.

Their hair was powdered and poofed and pompadoured. The men wore powdered wigs and ruffled shirts, short white pants tucked into tight leggings, just below their knees. Ruffles cascaded over their hands as they reached to help the women down from the carriages. Music spilled from the doorways and windows and flowed down the street.

Around the castle, out of the way of the rich carriages and their ostentatious contents, sat the plain wagons and buggies of the townspeople. They had each paid a small fee to sit on the street, in the cold, and observe the participants in this costume ball in honor of George Washington's birthday. Everyone had heard about the huge castle, built by the French priest, completed just a few weeks before. And they had all ventured out, on this cold February evening, blankets wrapped around them, trying to catch a glimpse of the splendor inside, of the opulence and wealth of elite society in Manitou Springs, Colorado Springs, and Denver.

Unlike the frigid observers, Adrienne's vision took her through the doors of the castle, into the low-ceilinged entry, and up the steps. The parlor was to the left. People crowded the rooms, talking and laughing, sipping champagne. Against one wall stood a huge stone fireplace, the fire blazing high, light shimmering on the jeweled silks of the women's skirts. Beyond the parlor were glass doors, luxuriant green plants filling the conservatory behind. Julien stood at the top of the steps, greeting his guests.

"I understand you designed this yourself." A young woman smiled.

"Yes. Yes, I did. All my life, I've wanted to build a home like this, something like what I grew up with. I wanted to combine the styles and features that I've seen in all my travels. My father was a diplomat; we lived in some of the most beautiful places in Europe when I was young. I wanted to take the best of Europe, and still somehow manage to find something suitable for the mountains of

Colorado." He beamed with pride. "And I was afraid, mixing so many different architectural styles, that it would only confuse an architect. It just seemed easier to handle the design myself."

Adrienne's vision led her out of the parlor, up another staircase, to the picture gallery, a long, narrow room brimming with costumed ball-goers. Members of the orchestra filled the far end of the room; the discordant sounds of tuning up filled the air. They lifted their instruments, and at a nod from the conductor, broke into "Hail, Columbia!"

The ball-goers marched through the hall, down the stairs to the parlor below. Adrienne heard the voice of a costumed servant introducing "General and Mrs. Washington," "Mr. and Mrs. John Quincy Adams" as couples entered the parlor. Costumes of the American Revolution filled every available space.

Adrienne let her eyes sweep over the decorations. Potted plants and hothouse flowers bloomed in every corner; plants twisted through the railings. She stared at the two huge flags, draped over a balcony railing: one French, one American.

Adrienne watched as the guests sipped from crystal punch cups, nibbled on tiny sandwiches and cakes. She could hear the voices, the snippets of conversation. "It was so generous of the father to volunteer his castle for the ball. So glamorous. Such a perfect setting."

"Yes, I agree. And to think—every penny he raises tonight will go toward the new library."

"We are so fortunate to have the father here. And I understand that Manitou has been much better for his health than that . . . Santa . . . oh . . . Santa something-or-other. Another one of those dreary little mud towns in New Mexico Territory."

"Thick with Indians, is what I heard. Thank goodness he was transferred. I can't imagine someone like the father trapped in a place like that."

Adrienne drifted away from Manitou Springs and found herself once again sitting in the window seat in Beaulieu, staring at her own reflection in the glass.

Marie's voice filled the room, reading the letter from Julien, describing the George Washington ball that he had recently hosted at the castle. He had written about it all, just as Adrienne had seen it in her mind a few moments before. Adrienne turned and watched her aunt finish the letter. She watched as Marie folded it, tucked it back in the envelope, and placed it in a drawer of her desk.

Adrienne turned and stared out at the day. This was the first vision she had had for several weeks now. The castle was finished; Julien was living there; Marie would be joining him before too much longer. Marie had begun to have furnishings packed for shipping to the New World.

Adrienne let her hand drop to the letter in her pocket. She was tired of visions. Tired of trying to figure out what they meant. She was perfectly willing to let Marie go live in Manitou. She could take half of the château with her, for all that Adrienne cared. Before long, she would be married, living in Paris. Before long, she would have Gerard and his grandfather as her companions, and she could let all these vague, uneasy feelings go, nothing but dust in the wind.

# CHAPTER TWENTY-TWO

Adrienne sat in the window seat in the morning room. As she had so many times these past few months, she let the book drop to her lap. She stared out into the bright sunshine. The snow was gone. The buds on the maple trees were full and red, ripe with new leaves. She glanced at the tulips by the edge of the terrace. Not a cloud marred the blue sky.

Stefan entered the room, his silver letter tray before him. He bowed to Genevieve. "Madame." She took the letters he offered. Adrienne kept her gaze on the flowers outside. She dared not get her hopes up. It had been three weeks since she had last heard from Gerard. She had begun to think he had changed his mind. Perhaps he didn't love her after all.

Stefan bowed close to her, and she jumped. His eyes met hers with a twinkle. "Mademoiselle." She looked at him, at the gray hair, the gray eyebrows, and the absolutely emotionless expression on his face. Only his eyes showed the pleasure he felt in offering her this letter. She took it, her hands shaking.

He turned and left the room. Adrienne held the letter against her breast for a moment. She glanced at Genevieve, at Marie. They appeared to be absorbed in their own correspondence.

Adrienne slit the seal, pulled out the thick paper.

*Dearest,*

*I am sorry to have kept you waiting so long. My heart is so heavy, I could barely put pen to paper. I have been trans-ferred—to Brazil. I thought I was being groomed to work here, in Europe. I do not understand the sudden change of circum-stances. I leave tomorrow.*

*I have tried, repeatedly, to speak with your father. He returned ten days ago from his trip, but he has not allowed me an audience. I am baffled by his behavior. I caught him in the hallway this afternoon, told him I must speak with him. He smiled, and took my arm, and told me not to worry, that whatever it was, it could wait until I return from South America. I should have pressed him, perhaps, but I was afraid that it would only make my situation worse.*

*I have no idea how long I will be gone. I am stunned by all that has happened these past few days. And I do not think I can bear it, being so far from you. Will you wait for me? Is it too much to ask?*

*Yours forever,*
*Gerard*

Adrienne stared at the words on the paper. She read them again. Her mind refused to absorb them; her breath froze in her chest. She lowered the note to her lap, looked out the window at the sky. She picked up the note, read it again.

Adrienne turned her face back to the window and stared out at the scene that had, just a few moments ago, seemed so beautiful. Her eyes glazed; she could no longer see the daffodils, their yellow faces turned toward the sun. She could not see the blossoms on the chestnut tree, or the crystalline blue of the sky.

The clock ticked. Marie's pen scratched against the paper.

Adrienne turned slowly, and stared at the dark curls of her aunt's head. Hatred filled every pore of her being. Marie had made her life miserable, for as long as she could remember. With a venom that came from all the buried emotion of seventeen years, Adrienne sprang to her feet, her arms stiff at her side. "You did this, didn't you?" Her voice cut through the air like a knife. She faced Marie, her jaw clenched.

Marie raised her head slowly, removed her spectacles from her face. She let her eyes travel over Adrienne. She looked at the note in the girl's hand. "What are you talking about?"

"I'm sure you know very well what I'm talking about. He's been transferred to Brazil." Adrienne's hands shook, but she did not allow tears to come. She stood, her body a blade of steel in the cool morning. A hush fell over the room. She raised her eyes to Marie. Her voice was barely a whisper. "And you are behind it, aren't you?"

Every person in the room felt the change in barometric pressure. Genevieve's mouth hung open in a soft, round O. Emilie looked as if her own heart had been broken.

Marie sighed as if bored by Adrienne's hysterics. She sat, calm and cool, seemingly untouched by the heavy change in the room. She laid her pen on her desk and raised her eyes to her niece. "Has your mind come completely unhinged?"

Adrienne stopped. She blinked. Her eyes stung. She had no vision, no private information, to hurl at her aunt. She didn't actually *know* anything. But her fury, her pain, her years of suffering, all rose to the surface, and she could no more stop the words flying from her mouth than she could stop her heart from breaking.

"I have no power in the French embassy. Did it ever occur to you, Adrienne, that Gerard might not want to marry a woman with your . . . shall we say . . . encumbrances? Perhaps he heard about your vivid imagination. Perhaps *he* requested the transfer."

The words were delivered quietly, evenly, but Adrienne felt as if she had been kicked. Did someone tell him about her visions? Did someone tell him that she was defective? The silence in the room was overpowering. All eyes focused on Marie; everyone in the room held their breath.

Adrienne stared at Marie, heat smoldering in her cheeks at the suggestion. No, it had not occurred to her that Gerard himself might have requested the transfer. She ran her fingers over the letter she held in her pocket. Was it possible? Would he have done that to her? Would he have said the things he had in this letter, asking her to wait? Her entire life, she had felt different, unworthy, flawed in some irredeemable way, and this possibility just flamed the fires of her own self-doubt.

She turned and fled from the room, across the terrace and into the woods. Her stride was long; her arms swung, desperate to escape the tidal wave of thoughts and feelings and fears and questions that were slamming into her consciousness.

❦

Daylight faded from the sky. Dusk settled on the countryside. The keening of the wind seeped through the edges of the windows; branches bent and swayed, scratching at the sides of the château. Adrienne had been gone for hours. She had left without a sweater, without a cloak, without any kind of protection from the cold. Genevieve paced by the window. She stopped, looked out, bit her nail.

Marie sat, even now, at her desk. As if her work were too important to leave, under any circumstance. "Quit pacing, Genevieve," she ordered. "It won't help."

Lucie stood at the other window, staring into the woods where Adrienne had fled. She turned suddenly, and moved toward the hallway. "I'm going to go look for her," she announced, heedless of either of the women. She strode from the room, her fury clicking through her heels and onto the floor. She grabbed her own cloak and Adrienne's from the front hall.

Lucie flew down the path toward the lake, anger and worry boiling inside her, making her walk harder and faster than she ever had. She found Adrienne at the cemetery. The girl was crumpled in front of the comte's headstone, her face streaked with dirt and tears. Adrienne shivered, her teeth rattling. Lucie stooped and wrapped the cloak around her. She leaned close to Adrienne, pulled the girl into her arms.

"I've tried so hard. All these years, I've tried so hard to do the right thing. To be quiet. To hold my tongue. I did what Grand-père asked. I kept quiet." She looked up at Lucie, her eyes filled with fear. Adrienne wiped her hand under her nose. "I tried so hard."

She stopped for a moment, raised her tear-stained face to Lucie. "He's already gone. That letter was dated over a week ago." Adrienne stared at her grand-père's stone. "I hate her. I wish she was dead."

"How do you know? How do you know it was Marie? Could it have been a normal transfer?" Lucie did not speak the thought that Marie had planted in both of their minds, that Gerard himself might have requested the transfer.

Adrienne turned away. The wind gusted, whistling through the stones, singing with the spirits. It lifted Adrienne's skirt, set it back down. "I don't know. I didn't see anything, if that's what you mean. I don't know anything, except that she hates me and always has."

Lucie squeezed the girl's shoulders. "Did he say he was breaking the engagement?"

Adrienne wiped tears away, and shook her head. "No, nothing like that. Nothing about not wanting to marry me. Only that he had been transferred and had not been able to speak to my father."

"There, you see? Marie was just being mean. This will all work out—it just may take longer than we thought it would."

Both women watched as the last rays of sunlight turned the gravestones pink. Lucie said a silent prayer, asking the comte to help this girl, to protect her.

"Maybe. Maybe." She turned to her governess, her eyes filled to overflowing. "But that's not the way it feels."

Lucie put her hand on Adrienne's arm. "Would it help if I write to your father?"

Adrienne turned and looked at Lucie. "Write to my father? But why would *you* write to him?"

Lucie felt the girl's scrutiny, and she reddened. She could see Adrienne's thoughts lining up; she watched as Adrienne began to connect the pieces of the puzzle. She felt, once again, the heat of Pierre's gaze on the night that Gerard and his grandfather had first come to visit, the night she and Adrienne had performed the duet. She remembered the way she had blushed, remembered turning to see Adrienne looking first at her father and then at Lucie.

Adrienne leaned backward in the grass. She stared at Lucie. "Lucie? Has something happened? Between you and my father?"

Lucie met Adrienne's gaze. She swallowed. She wanted to protest, to ask Adrienne how she could think that, but when her eyes met those of the young girl, the words stuck in her throat. Adrienne would know. She would know the truth, no matter how Lucie tried to explain.

Lucie swallowed again, trying to force the truth back down, hidden, where it had stayed for so long. She drew a deep breath. She reached a hand to Adrienne, but the girl jumped up, refusing to be touched. She stared, her eyes wide with horror.

"I was seventeen when my father died. Alone. Penniless. I had nowhere to go." For years, Lucie had kept it all inside, shrinking away from the thought of what had happened. For years, she had cringed at the idea of what might become of her if the truth were known.

"After he died, I went to the embassy . . . to see if they might have some work for me. My father had known so many people there. Twenty years of his life, he worked there. He helped deliver the city during the siege of Paris. I thought there might be someone there who would be willing to help me."

Adrienne began shaking her head.

"Your father . . ." Lucie's cheeks flushed pink, like the sky in the dying sunlight. She drew in a breath. "Your father said he could find me a position as a governess. I was well educated. He knew I was proficient in music and painting and languages.

"I was so grateful to him. I had been so afraid. I . . ." Lucie glanced at Adrienne and let her eyes drop to the ground again. "I was afraid I would be forced . . . Sometimes there aren't a lot of choices for women. It often comes down to the convent or—" She stopped. Her eyes were brimming with moisture. She met Adrienne's gaze, wondering if the girl knew enough of the world to understand the implications.

Adrienne sank to her knees.

"When he told me that he knew of a family—a wealthy family—that needed a governess, I was so relieved." Lucie bit her lower lip. "The price . . . the price for being placed in such a good position . . . was only one night. Just one night." Lucie's words blew away from her, the sound fading in the dusk.

The branches on the tree swayed and creaked above their heads.

"I didn't know until I arrived here that he was sending me to be the governess to his own daughter. That I would be living with his own wife." Lucie stared into the sky, now almost completely drained of color. She shrugged. "I thought the worst was over. I needed the position."

Adrienne swiped her hand at her own tears. Lucie did the same.

"It was so hard. At first, I couldn't look Genevieve in the eye. I had these spells where I would feel like I was going to faint. I'd get light-headed . . . hot. But then, after a time . . . it got a little easier. Genevieve didn't know."

Lucie stole a sidelong glance at Adrienne. "You were so little. Just a baby, really. I fell in love with you, right off. I wanted you to be my daughter. And your grand-père. He reminded me of my own father. I felt so at home with him, and with you." She took a deep, quivering breath. "After a while, I was able to forget, to pretend it never happened." She looked at Adrienne's face again, barely visible in the dusk. "I had lost everything. Everything. I needed this position . . . I needed you. Oh, Adrienne! I never deliberately lied to you."

Lucie blinked, and stared off into the distance. All those years of fear, of dreading anyone ever knowing the truth, evaporated in an instant. It was over. The truth was out. She was swamped with relief, and with a horrible, aching guilt. As much as she wanted to tell Adrienne everything, she could not share the fact that it had happened again, on Pierre's most recent visit.

They sat in silence. Lucie did not move to comfort the girl, knowing that she would need time to absorb all the revelations of the past few hours.

Suddenly, Adrienne sat up straight and turned to Lucie, her eyes wide. "Do you think Marie knows?"

# CHAPTER TWENTY-THREE

Genevieve continued to stand by the window long after Lucie had disappeared down the path. She crossed her arms over her chest. She chewed her thumbnail. The clouds in the west were growing thicker, darker, like her thoughts. She had pinned all her own hopes on Adrienne and Gerard, on Adrienne's marriage, on a move to Paris. She had wanted it, she had dreamt of it, perhaps even more than her daughter.

Marie moved to the window and stood beside her sister, both of them staring at the approaching storm. "I really don't know how you've managed, all these years," Marie sighed.

A branch scraped against the window outside. "What do you mean?"

Marie snorted, a sound that clearly judged Genevieve's naïveté. "Someone as lovely as Lucie, right here in the same house."

Genevieve stood completely still, her breath arrested. She did not look at Marie, but she could see her reflection, dim and gray, in the window.

"Of course, your husband is not home that often. Perhaps it isn't anything to be concerned with." Marie shrugged, turned, and started back to her desk.

Genevieve stared outside. She remembered that evening, just a few months ago, when Lucie and Adrienne had played for the Devereuxs. She remembered that look in Pierre's eye, how his gaze had followed Lucie around the room.

"If it were me, though . . . I don't know that I would have been able to tolerate such a beautiful governess in such close proximity to my husband." Marie smiled above her papers. "But then, you are far more beautiful than I ever was."

Marie bent her head to her accounts.

Genevieve said nothing. She continued to stare out the window, watching as the sunset flamed and faded. She twisted her thumbs, chewed her nail. She remembered when Lucie had arrived at the castle, a letter from Pierre in her handbag. She'd been so young, her skin as fresh as the first snow of winter.

Genevieve paced the floor in front of the window. She tore at her thumbnail with her teeth. She went back, in her mind, to every time she could remember Pierre coming home. She tried to recall his facial expressions, his exact words. She searched her mind for images of the governess. She tried to remember if Pierre had gone for long walks, disappeared from her presence for a time. Had he actually stayed in the bed beside her all night, or had he slipped away, left her sleeping while he cheated on her under her own roof?

She remembered every time he laughed at something Lucie said; she recalled every song that Lucie and the girls had played and sung together. She remembered every compliment Pierre had paid Lucie, every time he had praised her work. Genevieve bit her thumbnail. It bled. She paced, her heels clicking on the floor. The clock ticked. The wind gusted against the windowpanes. They rattled in response.

What had she missed? There had to be some reason Marie mentioned it, and Genevieve was determined to find it. She stopped suddenly, her brow tense. That time he had brought Gerard and his grandfather out here, to Beaulieu. She had awakened halfway through the night, when Pierre crawled back into the bed. At the time, she had thought nothing of it. She was so enraptured by all the excitement of Adrienne's beau, of having visitors to the château, and Pierre home again. But now that moment came back, with all its burning questions. How long had he been gone? And where had he been?

Her shoulders deflated with the sudden sense of knowing. It was true, what everyone had been saying. And he had done it right under her nose. She stared out the window, suddenly furious. With Pierre, with the governess, with all the people who spread the gossip.

But more than anyone else, she was furious with herself. How could she have been such a fool?

∾

Each of the three women was trapped, locked in the solitude of their own violent emotions. Adrienne was buried in her grief. For most of her life, she had never dared to hope, never dared to dream. She had adjusted, accepted her loneliness. She had learned to tune out the whispers of the villagers. She had learned to live with the quiet, the isolation.

But Gerard had changed all that. She had looked into his eyes, and dared to dream. Dared to hope. Dared to believe that her life could be different. She had broken free, sailed into the air, escaped from the dreariness, only to be dashed back to earth, smashed on the rocks. She felt as if she had been shattered into a million pieces, that there was no way she could ever be pieced back together again.

She could not sleep. She could not eat. Lifting her head from the pillows in the morning took all the strength and concentration she could muster. She had to force herself to breathe.

Sometimes the pain would wash over her, through her, pulling her down to a depth of despair that threatened to swallow her, like some dark ogre in a fairy tale. When that happened, she grabbed her cloak and rushed out the door. She walked as hard and as fast as she could. She wanted to pound the pain through the soles of her feet, force it from her body. She wanted to walk so hard that her body rebelled and collapsed. Until she fell, exhausted, and all feeling ceased.

Genevieve stayed in her own room, down the hall. She paced. She chewed her nails until they were ragged and bloody. She was gripped by suspicion, suspicions that grew larger and more dreadful with each passing day.

She stood before her dressing table, bent forward, and ran her fingers over the fine lines at the corners of her eyes. Her skin was not as supple as it used to be, not as moist and dewy as Lucie's. She ran her fingers through her hair, thinner now, strands of gray laced through the gold.

She hadn't slept since that night, just a few days ago, when Lucie had run after Adrienne, the night that Marie had first mentioned the governess and her beauty. She would drift off, only to bolt awake, her heart hammering, her throat constricted. She remembered the way Pierre's eyes had followed Lucie, the way he twirled the ends of his mustache. She remembered the fire in his eyes. How long? How long had it been going on?

Genevieve looked in her mirror again. Her eyes were deep black cauldrons of worry. The lack of sleep, lack of food, had only added to her disheveled appearance. Her hair looked like rags. She thought of the witches in the fairy tales whom she now resembled. She chafed at the thought of how she now looked, and of the unspoiled youth of the governess in her room down the hall.

Genevieve paced to the window. She watched as Adrienne disappeared into the woods, her brown cloak sailing out behind her. She knew the girl would be gone for hours. Genevieve grabbed the shawl at the end of the bed and swung it around her shoulders. She moved into the hall, her heart pounding, the veins in her neck pulsing.

She stopped at the door to Lucie's room. She'd never done anything like this before. It was not in her nature to confront anyone. For a moment, she hesitated. Then she saw, once again, the look in Pierre's eyes, the way his gaze traveled over Lucie's figure. He was her husband. She had a right to protect her marriage, to protect what was hers.

The door stood open a few inches. Lucie stood at the window. Her hair was loose: thick, coffee-colored curls cascaded down her back like a deep, dark waterfall.

Genevieve pushed the door open. Lucie turned to face her. The look in the younger woman's face was so composed and quiet, almost serene, as if she had been expecting this confrontation for years.

Genevieve cleared her throat. "Lucie . . ."

Lucie watched her.

"Lucie, I've . . . made a decision. The children are older now. Adrienne is grown." Genevieve's eyes jumped to the bed, the fireplace, the dresser. She could not look at the woman standing before her, her eyes soft and bright.

Lucie exhaled, and in that soft breath, Genevieve heard all the accusations that Lucie would never dare to say aloud: accusations about her mothering, her inability to defend her own daughter, her weakness in front of Marie, her pathetic attempts to believe in her own marriage. Lucie said nothing. But her eyes were silent pools of truth, the deep brown of the earth after a rain. There was a strength, a confidence, that Genevieve, despite all her wealth and upbringing, had never possessed. Genevieve could understand why Pierre would find the young woman so attractive, and the thought made her hurry through the lines she had rehearsed in her own mind.

Genevieve swallowed. "I don't believe we will be needing your services any longer."

The words hung in the air, heavy and dense, like morning fog.

Genevieve took a deep breath. "I have prepared a letter of recommendation for you. My cousin, in Bordeaux, is looking for a governess." She stepped forward, laid the envelope on the bed cover. Her hands trembled.

"Renault will take you to the station. The train leaves at three. You will need to pack quickly to make it in time." Genevieve's hands shook; her throat burned as if she had swallowed acid. She stole one quick glance at the governess, and then turned and left, her heels clicking down the long hallway.

❧

Adrienne had just reached the cemetery, had only just opened the gate and gone inside, when the vision hit her. She grabbed at the wrought-iron posts to keep from falling. She was following Marie down that same long, dark hallway. She followed her into a room. She watched as Marie pulled a valise from under her bed. This time, in this vision, Adrienne moved closer to her aunt, standing just behind her. She looked over Marie's shoulder. She could see the valise, see the papers that Marie clutched in her hand. But in this vision, Marie wasn't putting papers *into* the valise; she was taking them out. And something about those papers was familiar. They weren't loose, but were part of a notebook, one Adrienne had seen before.

Adrienne's mind flashed to a scene when she was very young, before Grand-père had died. She had been standing in the doorway to Lucie's room, awakened by a nightmare and wanting to find her governess. Lucie was bent over her desk, her long brown braid hanging over one shoulder of her nightgown. On the corner of the desk, a candle flickered, the light dancing on Lucie's face. Adrienne could hear the scratch of her pen; she watched as Lucie looked up from her journal and laid her pen down. Her *journal*. The same journal where Lucie had recorded every vision, every dream, every suspicion that she and Adrienne had ever discussed.

Adrienne turned and ran from the cemetery, not bothering to take the time to lock the gate. Her feet pounded out the tempo of her thoughts. It wasn't Gerard who was in danger; it was Lucie. Adrienne ran, her boots painful on her feet as she tried to cover the distance quickly. She dropped her cloak on the floor of the great hall, raced up the stairs and down the long hall. Every step felt just as it had in her vision, following Marie. She was out of breath from her run, and choking on her own fear and dread.

The door to Lucie's room was open slightly, and Adrienne stopped, her heart pounding. She forced herself to breathe. Silently, with two fingers, she pushed the door open. Lucie stood with her back to Adrienne. On her bed lay dresses and gloves and handkerchiefs. Lucie was sniffling quietly, tears flowing down her cheeks. She turned and looked at Adrienne, her face contorted with pain and guilt. "Oh, Adrienne! I was so afraid I wouldn't get to see you. That I wouldn't get to say good-bye," she whispered.

Adrienne ran into her arms, and they held each other, crying. Adrienne was so relieved that Lucie wasn't dead that it took her a moment to soak in everything around her. "Say good-bye? What are you talking about?" She looked over Lucie's shoulder at the few items of clothing that Lucie owned lying across the bed.

"Your mother . . ." Lucie stopped and corrected herself. "They're sending me away."

"No. No." Adrienne shook her head, unable to absorb the idea.

She looked back at the bed. There, in one corner, lay a tapestry valise. The material was thick, gold and cream and burgundy. Adrienne blinked.

In slow motion, Adrienne pulled away from the arms of her governess. She moved to the side of the bed and stared at the valise. "Where did you get that?" She whispered. "Where did you find that?"

Lucie swallowed. "It's mine. I brought it with me when I came here. Why? What's wrong?"

Adrienne raised her hand, her finger pointing at the bag. "I've seen it before. In my visions. It's the same one Marie had in her hand. The one where she was getting all those papers."

The two women looked at each other.

Lucie's eyes grew wide. Her hand flew to her mouth. "My journal," she whispered. She reached for the bag, tore at the false bottom. She turned the bag upside down, inside out. She shook it, her movements growing more frantic with each second. The journal was gone.

Adrienne's heart hammered, remembering the vision, the valise. *The papers.* Those were the papers that had caused Marie to do something horrid, something that had splattered her with blood.

"Oh my God, Adrienne. I wrote down everything. *Everything.*" Their eyes locked on one another, trying to absorb the full extent of the information that had disappeared.

# CHAPTER TWENTY-FOUR

Marie's trunks lined the great hall. Servants bustled about, preparing bags and boxes and trunks for the trip to the train station. Julien's castle in Manitou Springs was completed. Marie had stripped the walls of the château, packing family heirlooms, paintings, a tapestry from Queen Isabella of Spain that had been in the family for generations. She had already shipped the four-poster bed that had once belonged to the empress Josephine.

Marie and Genevieve sat at the breakfast table. The children were already outside, paints and easels before them. Genevieve watched them as she sipped her coffee. It was difficult to contain the relief she felt. Marie would leave in a few hours. And maybe, with her departure, Genevieve could get past the nagging guilt, the shame, the feeling of inferiority that dogged her every time Marie turned to her with one of her stony looks.

Guilt sat on Genevieve's shoulders, lodged in her eyes, pulled at the corners of her mouth, ever since Lucie's departure. It snapped at her from every nook and cranny, like a snake. Adrienne's eyes were venomous. Emelie and Antoine were stunned when she announced that Lucie had taken another position. She shrugged it away, told herself time and again that they were only children, that they couldn't understand. She had done the right thing. She had done what was best for all of them. She had done what she had to do. But no matter how many times she repeated those phrases in her own mind, she couldn't shake the guilt she felt when she looked at any of the children.

Genevieve sipped from her coffee cup. She consoled herself with the idea that the first thing she'd do, after Marie had gone, would be to take the children and go to Paris. Perhaps she and the girls could go shopping. New dresses would cheer Adrienne, she felt certain. They could visit Pierre. Maybe see another opera. She had heard that *La Bohème,* the new one by Puccini, was quite good. Antoine could spend some time at the embassy with his father. She had had far too few occasions to indulge herself or the children.

She stared into the sunlight on the terrace, watched as Antoine threatened his sister with his paintbrush.

Marie cleared her throat. She held a cup of coffee in both hands, her elbows resting on the table. "Genevieve, I've been thinking." Marie raised her eyebrows. "Preparing for this trip has been quite tiring. I'm getting older. I'm not as energetic as I once was. You cannot imagine how difficult it is, a voyage of this magnitude, by oneself."

Genevieve turned to look at her sister. She felt the bitter pinch of her own limited existence. She had never sailed on an ocean liner; all her travels were limited to a few trips to Paris.

"Now that Julien has finished the castle, there will be a lot more work than there was in New Mexico. More entertaining involved." Marie put her cup into its saucer. Her eyes followed it.

Genevieve stared at her. Though Marie's hair was turning gray, she seemed just as formidable as she always had. Genevieve could not imagine Marie unable to manage any household, no matter how large. "You would like one of the maids? Henriette, perhaps?"

Marie lifted her cup again and sipped, her eyes examining Genevieve over the top. "No. No, not a maid. I was thinking that perhaps I would take Adrienne."

The words hung in the air, as heavy and dense as sleet, the atmosphere suddenly freezing.

Genevieve swallowed. She stared at her sister. "Adrienne? Why in the world would you want . . ."

Genevieve's body flushed with heat, as if she had developed a sudden fever. She knew immediately why Marie would want to take Adrienne. Keeping the girl quiet had been one of Marie's greatest missions. Genevieve felt it, knew it in her heart. She stared at her sister, and Marie stared back. And just as she had done her entire life, Genevieve was the first to look away, the first to give up. She pushed her forebodings aside, just as she had done countless other times, in countless other situations.

Marie continued talking, studiously oblivious to the rush of color and the sheen of sweat on Genevieve's face. "It might be good for her. She'll get to ride a train, see the ocean. An ocean voyage can be quite exciting. It might be just the tonic she needs to . . . to forget . . . to get past her heartbreak." Marie let her eyes flick to those of her sister.

Genevieve's skin prickled. Her stomach flipped. She blinked and looked outside. Her mind raced. A hundred thoughts crowded in and vied for her attention.

Adrienne had never been an easy child. The villagers had never forgotten the wild stories she had told as a child. Genevieve felt their staring eyes, the whispering gossip, every time she accompanied her daughter to church, every time she went to the village for buttons or cloth. She, like Adrienne, had become more reclusive in the years since Adrienne had first begun to tell stories.

She had never found a way to reconcile her feelings about her oldest daughter. There was so much about Adrienne that was disturbing, so much that had weighed on Genevieve. She hated the way the villagers whispered. She hated the way they looked in Genevieve's eyes, then away, quickly, as if they felt sorry for her. She hated the way Adrienne would sometimes tilt her head, the glazed look that would lock her eyes. When it happened, everyone in the family held their breath, waiting to see if she would speak, and what she would say. She hated the way she could never meet Adrienne's gaze, the way she never felt comfortable in the same room with her own daughter. And since Lucie's departure, Adrienne's looks had been hot with accusation, steaming with reproach.

Genevieve sighed. Her eyes flitted from the tablecloth, to the vase of lilacs in the center of the table, to the top of Marie's head, to a still-life painting on the opposite wall: an apple, a creamy white pitcher, three yellow daisies. It was one of Adrienne's paintings, and was really quite good. Genevieve moved her eyes away quickly.

"She can help me run the castle. Help me with my toilette— do my hair. That sort of thing. She does quite a wonderful job with Emelie's hair." Marie sipped again.

"It will do her good, Genevieve—a change of scenery. After all that's happened it is just what the girl needs. She could see America. We'd be taking a train across the country. Really, it might be just the thing. Get her out, let her see a little of the world."

Genevieve said nothing. She knew that those words were empty shells, designed to pull her attention away from the truth. She did not for one moment believe that Marie had Adrienne's welfare at heart. But somehow Marie's motivations were the least of her concerns. Relief had begun to seep into Genevieve's consciousness even before Marie had finished speaking. For the first time in years, she would be free of the burden of her strange daughter and her humiliating stories. Genevieve's mind raced with the possibilities. They could go to Paris. They might live with Pierre, unencumbered by the need to keep Adrienne out of sight.

Her racing thoughts hit an abrupt stop. Pierre. How would she ever explain this to Pierre? Genevieve focused on the children outside. Her stomach jolted and jumped; her heart skipped. She opened her mouth, tried to speak. And then she closed it again. Her brows pulled together. But she couldn't force the words to her throat. "Marie . . . I . . ."

"Most young girls Adrienne's age would jump at the chance to go abroad. Just a tour of the States, that's all. A few months in a completely different environment. It's exactly what she needs, after her disappointment." Marie's lips pursed.

"I took the liberty of writing to her father. I suggested that perhaps it would help Adrienne . . . a voyage. A diversion. Pierre agrees." Marie put her cup down again, and let her eyes drop to the tablecloth.

Genevieve stared at Marie. A lifetime of dealing with her older sister, of the countless ways in which she had witnessed Marie's manipulation and control, had not prepared her for what she felt at those words. Marie had certainly planned this well. Genevieve burned at the idea that Pierre had given his consent and never even approached his own wife about the situation.

"So, it's all settled, then. I've asked Henriette to help her pack. Really, dear"—Marie put her hand on top of Genevieve's limp white fingers—"this is for the best. Believe me. It will be good for everyone. We'll be back next spring."

Genevieve looked at her sister. Her eyes stung. A fever of guilt and shame and anger rose in her cheeks, stinging her throat. She couldn't swallow. "Marie . . ."

Marie had risen from her chair. She pushed it in, and the legs scraped on the marble floor. Her black crepe rustled. "Yes?"

Genevieve bit her lip. She locked her eyes on her own coffee cup. Her fists clenched and unclenched in her lap; her jaw tightened. But the words were caught, somewhere deep in her throat. They couldn't break through.

Marie watched Genevieve for a moment longer. Then she turned. Her heels click-click-clicked across the floor.

Genevieve put her elbows on the table, her forehead in her hands, her thoughts making her sick. What kind of a mother was she? She bent her head and bit her bottom lip.

Tears dropped on the white tablecloth; the dampness spread in splotchy pools. She whisked the tears from her cheeks and consoled herself with Marie's words. It was only a diversion, a trip abroad. Adrienne would be back next spring. The tour would be good for her.

# CHAPTER TWENTY-FIVE

Adrienne pressed her forehead to the glass window of the train. It was icy cold, like the blood in her veins. She stared vacantly at the French countryside passing by outside. The rich emerald greens of summer filed past the window. She watched the vineyards, green vines spotted with blue fruit. Her eyes registered small stone farmhouses, pastures, and cows, the occasional church on the hillside. But she felt nothing. She was interested in none of it.

She was dazed, numbed by all the events of the past few days. It had happened so fast, like a whirlwind sweeping into her life and taking everything with it. In less than two weeks, she had lost everything. Gerard and that blossoming of hope, pulled away from her, like a magician doing the tablecloth trick. Lucie, more like a mother than her own mother, the only friend and confidante she had ever known, banished. The knowledge, heavy as stone, that Marie had Lucie's journal and knew every vision that Adrienne had ever had. And now this—this sudden wrenching from her home and her family. It was too much, too sudden. Adrienne would doze off, and awaken with a start, wondering where she was. Like a person who has been pummeled, kicked, and beaten senseless, her mind and body were dazed, shocked, completely insensitive to everything and everyone around her. She didn't cry. She didn't speak. She didn't see the beauty that passed outside the window.

Adrienne never had the chance to speak to Emelie or Antoine. They had not been told. Adrienne watched, from the window of the buggy, as Emelie came running down the front steps of the castle, her eyes large, her mouth open. She saw the small oval of Adrienne's face in the window of the buggy, and lifted her hand.

Adrienne replayed the scene in her mind. Her eyes burned, stung by the memories. She felt it in her blood—Marie had orchestrated this whole fiasco. From Gerard's transfer to Lucie's sudden departure, to the way she herself had been whisked away, without a chance to see her father or her brother and sister. But no matter how Marie may have schemed, the worst pain was knowing that her mother had allowed this to happen. She had given up her daughter without protest. Adrienne's mind flared with the anger and shame of betrayal. She felt as if her insides had been wrenched out, robbed of everyone she had ever cared about. She heard the clicking of the train on the tracks, felt the rocking motion of the car, and the overwhelming need to escape the pain pulled at her, dragged her down into sleep.

And there she was again, this time in her dreams. She followed Marie down a long hallway, watched as her aunt stuffed papers, *Lucie's journal*, into her own valise. She watched, her subconscious bracing her for what she knew was coming. Marie turned, a glazed look in her eyes. Adrienne's gaze traveled the length of Marie's gown, took in the splatters of blood on the hem and skirt. Only this time, Adrienne could see Marie's hand, also covered in blood. She watched in horror as a knife slipped from Marie's grasp and clattered on the floor.

Adrienne lurched in her seat. Her eyes flew open. The train was slowing; she could see the bustle of the station ahead. She shook her head, trying to erase the eerie feeling of the dream. She was sick of it all: sick of visions that she didn't understand until it was too late, sick of dreams that never seemed to make sense.

Adrienne looked at the people waiting outside the station. Their faces, pale and gray in the dim light, looked just as tired, just as forlorn, as she felt herself. As if the whole world had been washed in sadness.

She looked at the sea, beating against the docks just a short distance away, a deep gray-blue in the light of evening. She heard the whistle of the train; she could see the lights of fishing boats on the water.

Fog rolled in, thick and dark, moving quickly, filling the streets of the little seaport village. She lost sight of the sea, the lights, everything that was not inside the train car. She looked at her aunt, standing and reaching for her traveling bag.

Darkness dropped around them as the train pulled into the station. The inside of the train glowed with amber light. Passengers stood and stretched, reached for their bags. A hum of anticipation filled the car. Adrienne stood, pulled her traveling bag from the seat, and walked slowly forward. Marie led the way, her gray hair bobbing. Adrienne followed, like a sleepwalker, into the fog.

# CHAPTER TWENTY-SIX

Adrienne stood at the railing of the ship, her eyes locked on the horizon, her arms wrapped across her chest. For the past three days, since they had boarded the ship, she had stood in this spot, transfixed. A swirl of green and blue and gray and black mixed together before her: a mesmerizing brew of sky and water. Adrienne spoke to no one. She ate nothing. She noticed none of the passengers or ship's mates as they moved around her.

She stared at the churning water. How easy it would be, to climb over the side of the railing, balance on the edge of the ship, raise her eyes, and step off. Just one step, one long drop along the side of the ship, and all this pain would be over with. No more of the ache that tore at her sides, no more of the anger that burned her eyes and stomach, no more of the hatred toward the woman who sat behind her, pretending to read a book as she kept careful watch over her niece.

One step, one slow plunge, almost like flying, would take her into the water. She could picture her hair, long strands streaming out around her like seaweed. She could see the light of the sun, filtering through the first few feet of ocean, turning it a glassy green.

She could feel her skirts, billowing up around her. Adrienne closed her eyes, felt the slow, dreamlike descent into darkness.

"Beautiful, isn't it?"

The voice beside her pulled her back onto the deck of the ship, out of the trance of water and darkness. Adrienne opened her eyes and turned toward the sound. A young man, a ship's mate, was winding a rope around two hooks just a few feet away from her. She looked at him. Brown eyes, brown hair, ruddy cheeks. He smiled.

"No matter how many times I've made the crossing, I never quite get used to it," he continued. His eyes sought the horizon, blue sky riding on gray-blue water.

He spoke French. Adrienne followed his gaze and stared out to sea. For the first time since boarding the ship, she felt awake. She could hear the slap of the water against the ship, feel the salt spray that tingled her skin. She could smell the ocean breeze. As if his words had pulled her back from the precipice.

The young man turned toward her again and smiled. "Good day, mademoiselle."

Adrienne met his eyes. She nodded. He walked farther, winding up a hose that had been used to wash down the deck.

Adrienne turned her gaze back to the sea. How long had they been on board? She could not remember when she first walked into their room, or how often she had lain on her own narrow bed in their cabin. She'd been lost in a fog of sadness and grief, unable to remember much of anything about the trip that took her away from her home.

The wind picked up and Adrienne pulled her cloak tight under her chin. She watched as the sun sank from the sky and perched on the edge of the horizon. The ship chased after it. Color spread over the water, like jewels of gold and copper, riches spilling out in all directions.

Adrienne stared at the water, at the feast of color before her. She straightened, her eyes locked on the golden sea. This was not the first time she had seen the ocean. The memory was vague, the edges tattered and frayed, but she closed her eyes and let her body soften into the smell, the sound, the feel of the sea.

She remembered walking on a beach at sunset, golden light spilling across the water and onto the sand. She could hear the cries of the seagulls. The waves lapped around her bare feet, and she laughed. Her grandfather held her hand, laughing with her. Adrienne smiled, filled with the warmth and the calm of that long-ago moment, filled with the overwhelming sense of protection she felt in her grandfather's presence. She couldn't have been more than four or five years old.

The memory faded. She opened her eyes and stared. The sky had turned to velvet. The water was black glass.

Grand-père. The thought of him brought comfort, like a warm woolen shawl around her shoulders. He had been gone for ten years now, but the memory of him filled her as if it had been only yesterday. Her grand-père. She smiled into the dark.

Never before had she thought of who he was, as a man. To her younger self, the only thing that mattered were his twinkling blue eyes, the way he winked at her when they shared a secret, the way he rushed to protect her from Marie's wrath. But as she stood in the dark, listening to the water, it occurred to her that he was much more than that, much more than her grand-père. He was a husband, a father, a comte. He had suffered his own heartaches: the loss of his son, less than a year old. The loss of his wife a few years later. He had raised his daughters without the benefit of a mother's love. He had spent the greatest part of his life without the woman he loved.

She began to try to fill in the details of his life, apart from the man she had known when she was small. She knew, from her studies with Lucie, of all the turbulence in French history during the comte's lifetime. He had survived the Napoleonic Wars, negotiated the turnings and intrigues of political upheaval. He had seen friends stripped of their possessions, banished from the country. He had seen others murdered, destroyed by the upheaval around them.

He knew what it was to be brokenhearted. He knew what it felt like to be betrayed. He knew what it meant to have to survive by one's wits. And Adrienne knew, too, that if he were here now, if he had suffered the same injustices that she had these past few months, he would not be standing here, at the railing of the ship, thinking of stepping over the edge.

She remembered the way he held his shoulders, straight and square and proud. She remembered the way the villagers were quick to greet him, the way the older ladies smiled and fluttered when he arrived at church. She remembered the way his jaw went firm and hard, the way his eyes turned to flint, when Marie was on the attack.

He had survived eighty-seven years of French politics, nine decades of ever-changing allegiances. Victor Hugo had been banished from the country for speaking his mind, but somehow, the Comte de Challembelles had managed to hold on to his lands, his title, his standing. He knew when to speak and when to stay silent. He knew when to be strong and when to ride the current.

Adrienne's thoughts drifted to the day the comte died. She remembered the smell of his room, metallic and sour. She remembered how frail and colorless he had looked, lying against the pillows. She felt the gentle squeeze of his fingers on her hand. She heard his words, "Be careful what you say, Adrienne."

When she heard those words at the age of seven, she thought that he meant she should stop speaking, should stay completely silent. But was that really what he intended?

Adrienne's thoughts churned, like the foam on the water. Perhaps he had never meant for her to withdraw from everything and everyone. Perhaps he had never meant to silence her completely. Perhaps he had only tried to tell her to be careful, to be discerning about what she said—to think about whom she could trust, and when it was safe to speak. Be careful. Not "be silent."

If he were here, now, what would he do? What would he say? How would he deal with Marie and all her schemes?

Adrienne paced the deck. She barely noticed the other passengers, dressed and heading to dinner. She watched as the stars decorated the sky. She noticed the glitter of light on the water, a scattering of tiny crystals. She felt the vastness of the ocean, the infinity of black space around her.

She chewed on every memory of him, every moment they had spent together, everything she had ever heard anyone say about him. If he were here, if this had happened to him, he would find a way to deal with it. He would not give up. He would not let Marie destroy him.

There had to be a way, somehow, to pick up the pieces, to find an answer. Adrienne stood straighter. She filled her lungs with the sea air. She squared her shoulders.

Grand-père would never let anything break him. And neither would she.

# AMERICA

# CHAPTER TWENTY-SEVEN

Adrienne woke early. The porthole in their cabin was a misty gray, but it was not the light that had pulled her from sleep. A vibration, a hum of energy, poured through the ship, buzzing through the wood, stirring in the blood of the passengers.

Adrienne dressed quickly and left Marie, still sleeping. She hurried to the railing, her eyes scanning the early-morning mist. She could feel it, even through the blanket of gray—the promise of the New World.

Passengers began to move and shift. Marie joined Adrienne at the railing, both women gazing into the fog. And then the sun broke through, the mist evaporated. New York Harbor loomed on the horizon. The Statue of Liberty rose out of the water, her torch held high, her face ripe with promise. Hope. Opportunity. The chance for a new life. The passengers crowded the railings, their eyes locked on the sight. Excitement surged through the ship, like the pounding of a big drum, pulling them all forward.

Smaller tugs crowded the water, whistles shouting into the morning. It seemed to take forever for the ship to dock, for the gangplank to be lowered, for the slow process of unloading the ship.

The docks were bustling with people and horses and buggies. Adrienne stood on solid ground for the first time in weeks, trying to adjust her body to the lack of movement beneath her. She scanned the skyline. Buildings stretched into the clear blue sky, taller than anything she had ever seen.

Marie had one of the dockworkers hail a hansom cab, and Adrienne followed. The energy of the city was infectious. Everywhere she looked, there were people, horses, buildings, a whirlwind of activity. She turned her head, her eyes glued to a sleek black motorcar, propelled forward as if by magic. The horses' hooves were loud on the pavement. She heard the crack of a whip, the curses of the drivers as they negotiated the swirling mass of humanity. Their own cab stopped often to let others go by. The streets were thick with milk carts, and vegetable stands, and dozens of carriages. And people. Clusters of people, everywhere Adrienne looked.

The cab rocked down Fifth Avenue, and Adrienne drank in the sight of the storefronts. They were filled with hats, bolts of satiny fabrics, sewing forms draped in the latest fashions. There were cigar stands and carts selling peanuts. Four boys in short pants and brown hats chased each other down the street, dodging people and vendors, laughing and shouting to one another.

The hansom cab swayed to a stop in front of the Waldorf Hotel, one of the few hotels that would allow a woman to stay without an escort. Marie had stopped here often on her voyages back and forth. A porter hurried to help the ladies down. He whistled at a bellboy to bring their bags. The boy, young and ruddy cheeked, stared at Adrienne for a moment. She barely noticed him. She stood on the sidewalk, staring up at the height of the hotel.

*"Merci."* Marie paid the cabdriver and tipped the porter. Adrienne turned just as the coin passed from Marie's black-gloved hand into the porter's white one. The coin glittered. Adrienne exhaled slowly. Money. She would need money. Her thoughts

whirled as she trailed Marie through the ladies' entrance. And that would mean learning about American money. She began to make a mental list of all the things she would need to learn in this new land.

Adrienne's gaze rose, taking in the height of the entryway, the heavy, glittering chandeliers, the marble tile on the floor, the rich burgundy velvet that covered the furnishings in the lobby. She was struck suddenly by the thrill of anticipation she had felt just a few months ago, on entering the Paris opera house. The memory pinched, mixed with the bitter losses of all that had happened since then. But the feeling, the excitement and activity, brought back the thrill of meeting Gerard.

Marie negotiated the process of checking in, made easier by the fact that the clerk spoke French. The bellboy took their bags upstairs, and Marie led Adrienne through the lobby to the Palm Room, the hotel restaurant that had attracted quite a following among European travelers to the city.

The hour was late for lunch, and the room was largely empty of people. Adrienne took in the circular space, lined with palm trees. It was light and airy, the ceiling high and rounded. The tables were draped in the finest white damask. A rose-patterned carpet stretched out before them. Marie sat down and spread her napkin on her lap.

Adrienne sat down across from her. She could not remember ever having eaten in a restaurant before. Unlike the ship, where all the first-class passengers had filled the dining hall with their conversation, this room was quiet. The late-afternoon sunlight filtered through the upper windows and turned the room into a tapestry of soft ambers.

A waiter appeared, a white towel folded over one arm, and filled their water glasses. He handed menus to Marie and Adrienne. He opened his mouth and words poured out. Adrienne stared at him, aware for the first time that she was in a *foreign* country. Aware that she could not speak or understand the language.

*"Je ne parle pas anglais."* Marie's clipped words cut him short. From the look on her face, it was quite clear that no one of good breeding could be expected to know anything other than French.

Adrienne stared at her aunt. She wondered how anyone could have traveled to America so often, lived here for years, and managed to remain ignorant of even the smallest smattering of English. Adrienne looked at the waiter and felt a wave of pity for the man. She watched his Adam's apple move as he swallowed.

A few tables away, a newspaper rattled and revealed a handsome, middle-aged man sitting behind it. He was smoking a cigar and had a glass of sherry on the table in front of him. He folded the paper and rose, stopping in front of Marie. "Might I be of assistance, madame?" he asked, in perfect French. "Francois Vionnet, at your service." He bowed to the two women. "He"—Monsieur Vionnet tipped his head toward the waiter—"was recommending the house specialty. They call it a Waldorf salad. Apples, celery, walnuts. Quite delicious, I can assure you."

Marie smiled, and nodded at him. "Thank you, monsieur. How very kind of you."

Adrienne watched as Monsieur Vionnet translated for the waiter and placed their orders. She looked away. She realized that if she were ever going to escape, if she had any hope of returning to France, then she would have to learn to speak English.

❦

Marie stopped at the front desk, at a box for outgoing mail, and Adrienne turned to look out the window. She watched the buggies and coaches and cabs on the street outside, heard the noises of the horses, the cracks of whips. She saw a young couple walking past, noticed the man's reddish mustache, his top hat. She watched the woman's skirt sway as they hurried forward. She watched the man's hand, pressing gently against her back. She inhaled, stung by the memory of Gerard's hand on her own back. She turned back toward the desk, and Marie.

Marie pulled a letter from her handbag, thick white paper adorned with the Morier crest. She dropped it in the box for outgoing mail. Adrienne watched as the envelope disappeared into the slot of the mailbox.

They started up the staircase to their rooms. Adrienne followed Marie, but the world around her changed. Time and movement slowed to a crawl; her heart pounded so loudly that she was certain everyone must be able to hear it. The staircase turned and Adrienne looked back down at the mailbox. Despite the fact that she could not see the letter inside the box, Adrienne could picture the envelope. It glowed, an eerie pale blue color that completely arrested her attention.

Adrienne followed Marie's black skirts up the stairs, turned and followed her down the hall, dark with deep coral walls and carpet, lined with dark wood doors to the rooms.

A scene flashed into her mind, and she nearly stumbled. Everyone stood at the family graveyard in France. She could see Emelie, her face red and wet; Antoine, back straight, his young face fighting away the tears. Genevieve stood in black dress, black veil, black gloves. Genevieve hated black, always said it made her look older, but there she was, swathed from head to toe. Adrienne's gaze turned slightly to the left, and there was her father, tall and handsome, his face like stone.

The family stood around a grave, not far from Grand-père's. Servants from the château surrounded them, standing a few steps behind. Adrienne could hear Père Henri's voice as he read from the Bible. In the vision, she was just behind her mother, and Adrienne moved slightly, so that she could see over her mother's shoulder. There was no casket at the grave in front of them. Only a granite headstone marked this as a grave, devoid of an actual body to bury. Adrienne's eyes locked on that stone.

ADRIENNE BEAUVIER
BELOVED DAUGHTER AND SISTER
1880–1897

Marie put the key in the lock and opened the door to their suite. Adrienne moved in behind her, still heavy with the images of her own funeral ticking through her mind. She knew it, then, with a certainty she had never experienced before.

Marie turned and looked at Adrienne, standing in the middle of the room, and their eyes met. Adrienne knew now why that letter had demanded her attention. She knew why she could see the images of her own funeral, without a body to bury. That letter, written in Marie's cramped hand and now on its way to her family in France, announced Adrienne's death at sea. She stared at Marie, marveling, once again, at the extent of the woman's scheming.

Marie had no intention of taking Adrienne back to France. Her family would not be waiting for her. No one would ever bother to come and look for her. Marie was hiding something, a secret so great that she had gone to unbelievable lengths to keep Adrienne from ever discovering the truth and speaking. And with the mailing of that letter, Adrienne was now totally and completely in Marie's grasp.

❧

It was two in the morning. Adrienne stood by the big window, looking out on the mostly darkened streets of New York. A few street-lights still glowed, globes of amber in the gray night. She heard one late buggy, the horses' hooves clip-clopping on the street below. She could smell the smoky remains of the fire in their parlor, a faint tinge of salt from the sea.

Adrienne turned and walked to the desk. She pulled out the chair, careful not to scrape the legs or make any sound, and sat down. She reached for Waldorf Hotel stationery and dipped the quill in the ink. She had to let someone know the truth.

She pulled a sheet of paper toward her and held the quill in her hand. Who would she write to? Not her mother. Her mother would never help her. She had done nothing, all these years, to help her. She had done nothing to protect her daughter, to stand up for her, to stop Marie from taking her away. Genevieve was powerless to help herself, much less her daughter.

She thought of Lucie, her best friend in the world. But she had no idea where Lucie now lived. She had been banished from the château just a few days before Adrienne herself was. Adrienne sighed. Even if she knew how to find Lucie, how to get a letter to her, Lucie did not have the resources or the power to help.

Adrienne held the quill in her hand. She thought of writing to her father, telling him of Marie's lies and schemes. But ever since the day of Lucie's departure, ever since the discovery that Lucie's journal was missing, Adrienne had not been able to shake the idea that the journal held evidence that Marie was using against him. She had no idea if Lucie had written about her relationship with Pierre, but there was always the chance that she had. Maybe it was her father who had sent Gerard to Brazil. Maybe he, too, was forced to acquiesce to Marie's demands.

Her mind kept coming back to the same idea. Her only hope was Gerard. So many times she had wanted to tell him the secret of her clairvoyance. So many times she had thought of telling him about her abilities, about the way her aunt was determined to keep Adrienne silent. How she wished now that she had been brave enough to do that.

She stopped and looked up at the dying fire across the room. A few red embers remained, glowing like the eyes of some wild creature from the ash. She could hear Marie, her breathing raspy as she slept in the adjoining room.

She laid the quill on the paper. Adrienne had lived a lifetime of isolation and loneliness, a lifetime of feeling different, inadequate, flawed. All those feelings came flooding back now, threatening to sweep her away. Perhaps Marie had spoken the truth that day in the morning room, when Adrienne had received word of his transfer. Perhaps he had already heard the rumors about his fiancée. Perhaps he had stopped for a pastry, and Madame LaMott had been quick to let him know all the talk about Adrienne Beauvier de Beaulieu, the granddaughter of the comte, the pretty girl who was quite mad. Perhaps Marie herself had found a way to inform him of Adrienne's failings.

Maybe he had asked to be transferred to Brazil. Perhaps he had chosen the easy way out—to take the assignment in Brazil and pretend that he was going against his own wishes.

Adrienne stared at the paper. Her thoughts swooped and swirled in the darkness, vampires that drank away every hope, every sweet memory of him. She hated herself in that moment. Hated what she was, hated what she could sometimes see. And now, when she needed a vision to guide her, to give her some spark of hope, to show her a way out, there was nothing. When she most needed guidance, her gift refused to cooperate.

Adrienne could count on one hand the people who cared about her, or had cared about her. Her sister, Emelie, only twelve, and just as helpless as Adrienne herself. Lucie, a servant, removed from the château in Beaulieu to God knew where. Her grand-père, dead for over ten years now. And Gerard. At least for a short time, it had really felt as if he cared. No matter how her doubts nagged at her, he was her only chance.

She picked up the quill and began to scribble the words.

*Dearest Gerard,*
*I have reason to believe that my aunt Marie is trying to stop us*
*from being together. She has taken me from my home, and we*
*are now in America, in New York. I believe she has sent word*
*to my family that I died at sea, but it is not true.*
*    Tomorrow we board a train heading west, to a place called*
*Manitou Springs, Colorado, and the home of my cousin, Julien*
*Morier. I cannot begin to fathom her motives for these actions,*
*but I beg you, if you get this letter, to please come for me.*

Adrienne laid the quill on the desk, rubbed her hands against
the sides of her face, searching for the words she needed. She had
always been so careful in her previous letters to Gerard to try to
strike just the right tone: intimate, but not too intimate. Her eyes
focused on the candle flame for a moment. She shook her head.
Tone was not important here. She was desperate.

She heard Marie in the next room, the rustle of covers, the
squeak of bedsprings. Adrienne didn't breathe for a moment. She
sat silently, completely still, waiting until she was certain that Marie
was asleep. Then she picked up the quill and bent over her paper.

*You are my only hope. Please come for me.*

*Yours faithfully,*
*Adrienne*

She folded the letter and slipped it into an envelope with the
hotel crest in the corner. She did not know the address, and so wrote
only his name, in care of the French embassy, Rio de Janeiro, Brazil.
She hated not having more information but consoled herself with

the thought that there could be only one French embassy in Rio de Janeiro. She ran her finger along the length of the stationery, wondering if Gerard would ever run his hand over the same thick paper. She put all her hope, all her love, in that touch, wanting desperately to convey all that she could not say.

She knew that Marie was watching her every move in the daylight hours, and of course she didn't dare leave the hotel room at this hour. Adrienne folded the letter and slid it into her wrist purse, a small black bag knitted in silk. Somewhere along the way, she would find an excuse to slip off to the restroom, and drop the letter into a mailbox.

So much depended on that one brief letter—so much that was completely out of her control. It could take months to reach him, if it did at all. It could take several more months for Gerard to travel to America and try to find her. And of course there was the chance that he would not choose to come at all.

Adrienne sighed and turned toward the window. The gray of the coming daylight was just beginning to stain the night sky. All her doubts and fears and insecurities vied for attention.

Adrienne pushed those thoughts away. None of that mattered now. He was her only hope.

# CHAPTER TWENTY-EIGHT

The train was hot and dusty, and Adrienne leaned her head against the window. She had watched the horizon for hours now, watched as the mountains grew from specks of blue to towering peaks as they drew nearer. The swaying of the train, the rhythmic clicking of the wheels pulled her, dragged her down into sleep.

She felt closed in, cramped, almost claustrophobic in the small space of her dream. The space was dark, gray, and unfocused, like walking in the fog, too confined. Like a prison. In the dream, Adrienne stood, looking out a small window. She was high up: the street below her looked small and far away. There were bars on the window. She knew, without turning to look, that she was locked in. From somewhere behind her, she heard a baby cry. Its wails pierced the walls of the room.

Adrienne's eyes shot open. A woman sat on the train seat to the left, holding her baby as it screeched, its face turning bright red with the effort. Adrienne swallowed and tipped her head to look out the window. The train was slowing. She could see the reddish stone of the station just ahead.

The train pulled into Colorado Springs, and Adrienne stood. Her legs and back felt numb, held too long in one position, and she was glad to move. She tried to get her bearings out the windows of the train, but they pulled inside the station and were swallowed by the darkness of the building. She could see very little.

Marie wove down the aisle in front of Adrienne, her body swaying from side to side, the feather of her hat bobbing and pointing, careening like a drunken bird. They stepped from the car and were immediately met by a muggy blast of station air.

Julien hurried over. Except for the collar that marked his ecclesiastical calling, he looked like many of the men in the station. His black beard was well trimmed, and he held his bowler in his hands as he moved toward them.

"Maman," he said, kissing his mother on her wrinkled, powdery white cheek. "I trust you had a good trip?"

"Adequate, I suppose," Marie replied. "Each time I make the journey, it seems longer and farther than the time before. But perhaps it is just my age."

Julien turned and took Adrienne's hand. "Adrienne! How good it is to see you! *Comment allez-vous?*" His eyes sparkled, and he raised her gloved hand to his lips. "You've grown into a lovely young woman, Adrienne. How long it has been since I saw you last. You were only a child, and now look at you." He held both her hands and raised her arms.

Adrienne smiled, gave the smallest of curtsies, and dropped her eyes to the ground. She had only vague memories of this cousin: his illness when she was very young, a visit he made to France when she was nine or ten. Like so many of the memories from her childhood, they were hazy and indistinct. She remembered nothing about him, nothing about his personality. Her stomach began to churn. She could not allow herself to think about what kind of life awaited her here.

Julien went off to make arrangements for their bags and then led the ladies to the waiting buggy, sitting in the red dust of Bijou Street, in front of the depot.

"I borrowed this buggy from the Gillis brothers," Julien explained as he climbed up and took the reins. "Mine isn't large enough to hold all of us. I suppose I will need to see about buying something larger. I didn't know you were coming, Adrienne"—he turned and looked over his shoulder at her—"until a few days ago when I got Maman's letter. I am so thrilled that you decided to come." He clucked to the horses, and they lurched forward. Adrienne made note of the fact that Julien had not been in on this scheme to bring her here; it was all Marie's doing.

"The Gillises are my neighbors on Ruxton Avenue. The same ones who built the castle. Remember, Mother? I think I wrote to you about them."

Marie nodded.

"They've got quite a reputation around here. Built the El Paso County Courthouse, the parish in Manitou, numerous other buildings." He waved his hand as he spoke. "And of course, I wanted the best when I started the castle. It pays to hire the best, don't you agree, Maman?"

Julien sat in the front seat of the carriage, Marie beside him. Adrienne sat in the seat behind. She could not remember ever having heard Julien talk so much at one time. He was animated about the castle, by the thought of showing it off to both of them.

"There were times when I thought we would never get it done," Julien continued. "I mean—so many architectural styles combined in one building. And it's built right into the hillside. That was a piece of work, too, I should tell you. There were old mining shafts in there that had to be covered up. Quite a structural challenge." Adrienne stared at the back of his head. His words sparked a vague memory. Was it a dream? A vision? Something about the castle, nestled against the hillside. But she could not remember.

"But, oh, Maman! Wait 'til you see it. I know it will remind you of France."

They turned right onto Colorado Avenue, and Adrienne gasped at the beauty spread before her. Mountains rose in front of them, purple against the blue sky, breathtaking in their size and proximity. She had read of the Rocky Mountains; she had watched from the train windows as they chugged across the prairie and the mountains drew nearer. But now, sitting right at their base in the open air, she was overwhelmed. She could see the thick green pines, red rock formations jutting through the trees, reaching into the sky.

"That mountain is Pikes Peak," Julien continued. "Discovered almost a century ago. Stunning, isn't it? Over fourteen thousand feet tall. And the castle is right at the base of it."

Adrienne could understand why Julien had wanted to build here. The mountains and pine trees and rock outcroppings were so much like the area around Beaulieu. It was beautiful. Her heart hammered; she fought the storm of pain that threatened to overtake her at the thought of home.

They drove through Colorado City, a few miles from the train station. "This area is a little rough," Julien said. "Lots of saloons, and miners, and . . . Well, not exactly the same caliber as Colorado Springs, I can tell you. General Palmer has been very careful to keep the Springs genteel, refined. He works hard to keep the rabble outside. Do you remember him, Maman? You met him when we were working on bringing the railroad into Santa Cruz."

Adrienne watched as the doors to a saloon flew open and a man came sailing out into the street. He sprawled in the mud facedown. She turned her head to watch as he dragged himself up. She could hear music spilling out of the dance hall after him. The buggy moved through the hubbub of Colorado City, and the road curved. A vista of red rocks towered in the near distance—every shade of scarlet and rose and apricot and sienna. Ponderosa pines stretched their feathery limbs around the rocks, and scrub oak covered the areas with any soil. The scene looked like a tapestry, like the finest work of a Persian master weaver.

Julien stopped the buggy, obviously pleased by Adrienne's appreciation. "Quite a sight, isn't it? The Indians consider it sacred ground. A while back a German man who lived here started calling it the Garden of the Gods. The name has stuck. Fitting, don't you think?"

"It's beautiful," Adrienne murmured. "I can see why you wanted to build here." The air was clear and crisp. The smell of pine trees was thick. The scenery lifted her spirits. She heard the call of a red-tailed hawk, and she shaded her eyes with a gloved hand, watching it glide through the sky.

Julien clucked to the horses, and they hurried forward, anxious and quick now that they were getting close to home. As they moved into the hills, the glimpse of Pikes Peak was lost, obscured by the hills and canyons of Manitou. Gray clouds piled up behind the mountains and spilled down into the town. The wind kicked up. Adrienne shivered.

They traveled the last half mile of Manitou Avenue at a trot, trying to beat the rain. The buildings, the red brick of the Presbyterian church, the town clock, the library, all blurred together in a jumble of stone and slanting rain. Adrienne hunched in her seat, her eyes blinking against the spattering of raindrops that hit her face. Julien turned left, up Ruxton Avenue. The street rose sharply and the horses slowed.

They turned right. The horses clipped over the bridge on Ruxton Creek, and despite all Julien's talk, she was still awed by the immensity of Miramont. The castle rose before them, four stories of wood and stone. The hill climbed sharply behind it, as if the castle had been carved from the mountain itself. Adrienne looked at the key-shaped windows on the third floor, at the glass conservatory below them, filled with greenery. She had seen it in visions, but in person, the building had a commanding presence.

Wind gusted. Lightning flashed in the dark skies overhead. Thunder bellowed. Rain beat the pavement in plate-sized splatters. An icy finger of wind raced across her shoulders and down her arms, and Adrienne shuddered. Julien pulled the carriage beneath the portico and jumped down, quick to help the women out of the rain. There were no servants to greet them.

Julien turned the key and pushed open the wooden door. The women stepped inside, shaking off the moisture from their skirts and shawls. Marie removed her hat, and drops splashed on the floor, the formerly proud plume now looking like a shipwrecked sailor. A wooden staircase rose to their right, and Julien led them up.

"I ordered the wallpaper from Paris," he said. "I wanted to bring France here—to make this place feel more like home."

Adrienne trailed behind Julien and Marie. She took in the pale blue, sage, and cream of the wallpaper. Her hands trailed over the honey-gold wood railing on the stairs. At the top of the staircase, to the left, was the parlor. The walls were deep sienna, almost the color of the red rocks and soil they had just passed through. Thick carpets and mahogany furnishings filled the room. Julien bent down and struck a match to the wood and kindling already set in the fireplace, a huge stone affair that covered one entire wall.

"You may recognize the secretary, Maman. From the Orleans family. The crystal is from that set that we had in Beaulieu . . . remember the one from Queen Isabella?"

Marie nodded and smiled her approval. "Julien, this is wonderful! The design is so original." She turned slowly, her eyes taking in every corner, every detail of the molding and pressed ceiling.

He led them down the hall to the right, past the dining room and kitchen. "The kitchen is unnecessary, really." Julien swept his hand up, indicating the dark wood cabinets. "We don't have any servants here, for doing our own cooking. But I put in a kitchen anyway. And I've made arrangements with the Sisters of Mercy to provide our meals." He beamed at his mother.

"I gave them that property on the hill, just above the castle. They're going to use it for a sanitarium. Word is out, it seems. Every tuberculosis patient in the world is coming to Colorado Springs and Manitou. Something about the dry mountain air has been very effective for many patients."

Julien moved around the room, his hand brushing over the countertops. "The only thing I asked in return for the property is that they provide us with our meals. Ingenious, don't you think? They'll be cooking for all the sisters and their patients, so it really won't take much extra to bring the three of us some of that food." He opened a cupboard, showing them the dishes and crystal that filled them. "But just in case we want to have someone in for tea, I went ahead and stocked the kitchen."

He opened a small door at the back of the kitchen. Marie and then Adrienne poked their heads into the small, narrow space. A staircase rose sharply along the back wall of the castle. Adrienne touched the stones lining the outside wall. They were cold, slightly damp. The air was close. She shivered, trying to shake the dark foreboding that inched its way along her back and neck.

"They can use this staircase. It connects to a tunnel that goes into the mountain and up into Montcalme. See, Maman." Julien smiled, obviously proud of his own foresight and planning. "They don't even have to go out in the weather to bring us our meals."

Marie smiled and laid her hand on Julien's forearm. "Wonderful, Julien. This is very well thought out."

They followed Julien to the third floor. The staircase opened onto a long, narrow room. The ceiling was made of pressed gold panels; the wallpaper was flecked with gold. The key-shaped windows they had observed from the street lined one wall of the room.

Julien had already hung the tapestry from Queen Isabella, the paintings that Marie had shipped. Adrienne turned slowly on the wooden floor. The room was exactly as she had seen it in her vision a few months before. She heard, once again, the orchestra at one end, watched as the costumed ball-goers danced.

Julien led them to a large bedchamber and balcony. The four-poster bed of the empress Josephine towered in one corner. Julien turned to his mother, his teeth gleaming from the center of his dark beard. "It arrived last week, Maman. I had some men from town put it together for you. It took eight men to get that bed upstairs."

He moved quickly to a little bathroom, next to Marie's dressing room. He sat on the edge of the tub and turned on the faucet. Water poured into the heavy bathtub. "And I put in all the latest amenities. Running water. Electricity. Radiators for heat. You'll see such a difference when winter gets here." Julien's voice was rapturous, as if he himself had invented steam heat.

The tour continued, Julien stopping and pointing and talking. His face glowed; his eyes sparkled. Adrienne did not remember this Julien, excited and talkative and proud. She remembered his pale coloring, his wracking cough, when he had come to France, ill from the poisoning. She had never seen him this animated.

They stopped in front of a small room, corners and nooks making it very different from the others. There was a small fireplace, surrounded with tile.

"The guest bedchamber," Julien explained.

"It's charming," Adrienne murmured, speaking for the first time since entering the castle. She turned a slow-motion circle in the center of the room. The twists and turns and corners gave the room sixteen sides. The fireplace, the dresser, reminded her in some small way of her own room in Beaulieu. A little like home. She sighed and followed Julien and Marie as the tour continued.

They turned, and Julien opened another door at the back of another hallway. Adrienne poked her head into another set of those dark, narrow stairs that laced the back of the castle, like a spider's web in their intricacy—the servants' stairs, despite the fact that there were no servants. Adrienne had never paid attention to the servants' stairs back home in Beaulieu. She only knew that except for a few high-placed servants, she rarely saw their comings and goings.

The group wandered back toward the long hall, filled with artwork. Adrienne's eyes traveled over the paintings and tapestries, so many of which she recognized from home. And there, at the end of the long, narrow room, was one more staircase, leading upward.

"Well. You ladies make yourselves at home. I'm going to see to the horses and buggy before they decide to go home on their own." Julien bowed, sweeping his arm out wide. Adrienne listened to his footsteps as he made his way back downstairs.

Adrienne turned and started back down the hall, back to the little bedchamber that felt so much like home. She had seen Marie's room, and Julien's. But he had made no mention of where she was to sleep. Perhaps . . . perhaps she would be allowed to have this little room, with its odd corners and marble fireplace. She stopped at the door and leaned against the doorjamb. She waited for some other bit of information, some other fragment of a vision.

Marie had followed her down the hall, and now stood just behind Adrienne's shoulder. Thunder roared, and Adrienne heard raindrops smashing against the roof and walls and windows.

"This room is for company, Adrienne. Julien often has church officials, visiting priests, sometimes even a bishop, as his guests." Marie's words were quiet. Adrienne shivered. There was a note in Marie's voice, slightly ominous, like the notes of a minor chord. "And we must have something nice for them. I'm sure you understand that."

Adrienne turned toward her aunt. "Where am I to sleep?"

Marie's gaze bore into Adrienne. Her eyes glimmered with some secret satisfaction. "Come. I'll show you."

Marie turned and led the way back through the long hall. She started up the steps—the ones leading to the fourth floor—as if she had already been here. As if she knew exactly where she was going.

Adrienne picked up her skirts and started up the steps behind Marie. She watched a flash of lightning electrify the walls; she heard the roar of thunder, close and loud as they reached the top of the stairs. Adrienne began to shake, her hands trembling, her stomach leaping. This place felt familiar, as if she had already spent countless hours here.

Marie led the way down a narrow hallway on the fourth floor and stopped in front of a small door. Adrienne moved to it. The room was narrow, cramped, and tiny. There was one small window, one narrow bed against the wall, barely enough space for her to walk next to the bed. Adrienne turned to Marie, her eyes wide, disbelief flaming like blue fire. This was a servant's bedroom.

She shook her head. Just as she had in her dreams, she wanted to scream, to shout, but there was nothing inside her to make the noise. Adrienne thought of the letter she had watched Marie mail. She remembered the vision of her "funeral" back home in France. She looked down at her black skirt and lifted it in her hand. She fingered the material, black and plain, like servants wore. Moments from the trip began to rise up and haunt her. Marie had not introduced her, anywhere. Not on board ship, not in the dining room, not at any of their stops along the way. She remembered the waiter at the Waldorf Hotel. He had never even looked at her. He assumed she was a servant. She was dressed like a servant. She was silent, like a servant.

She raised her eyes to Marie's. She shook her head. "You cannot do this," she whispered. "You cannot mean . . ."

Marie stood in the doorway, watching Adrienne turn slowly toward her.

Adrienne continued to shake her head. "How could you . . ." She searched for words, searched for some way to give voice to this latest form of her aunt's torture.

"You are really quite a clever girl. But you are no match for me. I may not have your *gift*, shall we say? But I have survived far more difficult circumstances than a niece who believes she is clairvoyant, and her governess, who faithfully records it all. Never think that you can outwit me." Marie fell silent for a moment, looking into Adrienne's eyes. "I survived all the political upheaval in France through my own wits. I can certainly manage a storyteller like you.

"My niece, Adrienne, died at sea of some mysterious fever. Her family has been notified, and quite likely, by this late date, have already conducted a funeral. I imagine she was honored in the family cemetery, despite not having an actual body to bury." Marie's lips met in a thin, determined line. "*You* are Henriette, my maid. Brought from France to help with my personal needs."

Adrienne stared. Despite all her experience with Marie's scheming, despite her own clairvoyance, she had not seen this coming. She had expected danger. She had wondered if Marie would try to kill her. But this? Life as a servant? In all her fears and visions, this had never occurred to her.

"Oh, and Henriette?" Marie stood by the door, looking back at Adrienne. "There is no one who will listen to any story you attempt to tell. I informed the Reverend Mother at Montcalme that I was bringing my maid, who is excellent except for her tendency to invent very colorful stories. All the sisters have been warned. They will pay no attention to anything you tell them."

Adrienne continued to shake her head. "But . . ." She could find no words. Marie stepped backward, pulling the door closed as she did so. She turned the key in the lock.

Adrienne heard the click as the bolt slid into place. She heard Marie's footsteps as she walked down the hall, the sound growing fainter as she descended the steps.

Adrienne slid to the floor, her bones turned to water. She collapsed, numb with fatigue and disbelief at this latest injustice, piled on top of all the others. She stared into the gray gloom of the small room. Her mind flooded with memories. Holding Grand-père's hand, walking to the village. The way the men tipped their hats, the way the women curtsied when they saw the comte. "*Bonjour*, Comte." She remembered the servants at home, Renault reaching to help her down from the carriage, Henriette serving every course, at every meal, in stoic silence. She remembered the night of the opera, all the eyes that had followed Pierre Beauvier and his wife, daughter of the Comte de Challembelles, and their three beautiful children. She remembered Armand Devereux, bending low to her; Gerard, his mustache twitching, as he kissed her gloved hand.

Adrienne turned her head, numb with disbelief, to stare at the locked door.

# CHAPTER TWENTY-NINE

Adrienne heard the key turn in the lock; she heard the bolt slide back and the door creak open. It was morning. The small window over the bed leaked a colorless gray light into the room.

Still completely clothed, Adrienne lay on top of the thin mattress, on her side. She stared vacantly at the wall across from her and did not look up at the sound of the key. She did not move. She did not even blink when the door swung open.

She felt weight at the foot of the bed. Julien sat down, let out a long whoosh of air. "I'm so sorry about all this, Adrienne." He looked around the room, waved his hand. Adrienne continued to stare at the wall.

"I tried to talk to her . . . to convince her that we could handle this some other way. But you know my mother. Once she makes up her mind, well . . ." Julien shrugged. "She can be tenacious." He glanced at the girl.

"I tried, when I was younger, to fight her. Just like you have. After a while, I realized that it isn't worth it—it didn't get me anywhere. The more I fought, the fiercer she became. She is a warrior, Adrienne. Tougher than anyone I've ever known. She never backs down. Never." Julien's voice betrayed no emotion. "You can never succeed by fighting her."

Adrienne did not move. Even her eyes stayed motionless.

"She's had to be tough. It was the only way to survive, what with everything that has happened in France in her lifetime." Julien looked down at his hands. "She's developed a keen sense of what needs to be done, of what to say, what to do . . . to protect herself. To protect me. To protect her family." He put his long, slender fingers together, tip to tip. "You know, we both know . . ." Julien sighed. His smile slipped away, and he turned to look at Adrienne. "We all know how dangerous it can be to be different. To have people start talking." His words hung between them.

Adrienne swallowed. "You think I'm dangerous?"

Julien exhaled a sharp huff. "No, that's not what I think. It's not you, Adrienne. It's the way you can . . . see things. Know things. It scares people. And when people are scared, when they don't understand, they talk. That's what is dangerous, Adrienne. Gossip. One can never tell where it might lead." Julien waited, as if expecting Adrienne to respond. She did not.

"And Maman has believed for a long time that your mother is ill-equipped to deal with the situation. So she took matters into her own hands."

Adrienne felt one tear filling her eye. She did not want to sniffle, did not want to dab her eye. She did not want Julien to see the tear hit the blanket beneath her. She swallowed.

"Adrienne, perhaps you should . . . play along." He looked down at his hands again, tapped the ends of his fingers together. "Let her think that she's in charge. Let her think . . . let her think what she wants to think. Let her think that she won, that you are willing to do what she says. If she sees that you aren't fighting her anymore, things will be much easier for you, believe me."

Julien stared at the wall across from the bed. "I fought her, too, when I was your age. I hated the way she always had to have the last word—always had to control everything." He let out a slow stream of air. "But I finally got smart. I let her think she's right. I nod my head; I go along. Just let her think you agree. You can think whatever you want, on the inside. Just don't say it. That's the trick."

He stood. His boots clicked on the floor as he walked to the door. He stopped, turned back, his voice soft. "I'll leave the door unlocked. Come down when you're ready. The sisters have been here. Your breakfast tray is in the kitchen."

❧

Adrienne opened the door and stuck her head out. To the left was the hallway that led to the main set of stairs, the ones she and Marie had climbed the day before. Those stairs, she knew, led down to the third floor, close to Marie's bedchamber. She could not, at this moment, stomach the thought of seeing Marie. To her right, another set of steep steps descended to the castle below: the servants' steps. They were sandwiched between the castle proper and the hillside it was built against. The outer wall was stone. She could feel the chill of the mountain seeping through the stones, the frigid air of that unlit, narrow space. She moved into the shadows, her hand trailing along the cold stones, her feet searching tentatively for each step. She waited for her eyes to adjust to the gloom.

At the bottom of the first staircase, a wooden door stood partially opened. Adrienne pushed it with one finger. The door creaked, and swung back slowly. Adrienne squinted and raised a hand to shade her eyes. The light of the morning was bright and harsh after the murky depths of the staircase.

She stepped into a large hallway and craned her neck, trying to get her bearings. Marie's suite of rooms was off to the right. Adrienne turned to the left. She opened the door to the little guest room that she had admired the day before.

She inched forward into the room and moved to the bed, twice as large as the one upstairs. She ran her fingers over the embroidered white linen, the silk quilt. She turned and ran her fingers along the edge of the dresser. A crystal vase, its arms overflowing with bachelor's buttons and pink roses, sat in the center, its bright beauty doubled by the mirror behind it. A picture of the morning room in Beaulieu flashed into her mind. She saw that same vase, sitting on the table behind the settee. A wisp of a smile brushed her face, the memory a flutter like a butterfly's wings.

Adrienne turned, ran her hand along the mantel of the fireplace. Silver candlesticks held long tapers of cream-colored wax. She turned again. On the wall, in one corner, was a painting. Adrienne moved toward it, her head tipped to one side as she took it all in. It was the Madonna, but not like any she'd ever seen before. This woman was surrounded by rays of light. There were roses streaming out around her, a snake under her feet. Her skin was a deep bronze.

"Lovely, isn't she?"

Adrienne jumped. Julien was standing just behind her shoulder. She had not heard him come into the room.

"That's the Indian version of the Madonna—the North American version. She's called Our Lady of Guadalupe."

"Her skin is so brown," Adrienne whispered, her eyes locked on the ebony eyes of the woman in the painting.

"Yes. Similar to the Black Madonna, in that respect. It is said that Our Lady appeared in Mexico. The roses—the ones all around her—were her way of proving to the bishop that it was really she."

They both stood quietly, observing the work. Adrienne stepped closer, looked in the dark eyes and dark skin of the Virgin Mother. She could see flakes of paint peeling away, revealing the smooth wood beneath. It drew her, pulled her closer. She could smell it, a type of cedar. With that one whiff of wood, she was suddenly standing in the church in Santa Cruz. The painting had hung at the front of the church, a poor adobe building with dirt floors. The walls were mud.

The furnishings were crude. Adrienne recognized the surroundings. It was the same church where Julien had been poisoned—the same church she had seen in her vision so many years before. He had been standing in front of this painting when it happened.

"My parishioners gave it to me, when I left Santa Cruz," Julien said. "I didn't want to take it—it was really the only fine piece of artwork that they had." He turned and caught Adrienne's eye. "But they insisted. I'd been there almost twelve years. I started the school. I taught many of their children personally. I guess they wanted to show their appreciation."

Adrienne turned to look at him. A shard of sunlight, bounced and reflected from the mirror across the room, shot into her eye as she turned. She blinked.

"*Bonjour*, Henriette."

Both Adrienne and Julien jumped at the sound of Marie's voice. She stood in the doorway and ran her eyes up and down Adrienne's wrinkled dress. "I'm glad to see you are up. Perhaps, if you are not otherwise engaged, you could help me with my toilette." Marie's eyes were stones.

Adrienne glanced at Julien. He looked at her, his eyes pushing her, encouraging her. He raised his hand and his fingers grazed her elbow.

She swallowed. She looked at Marie, who had already turned and started down the hall, as if there were no doubt that Adrienne would do as she was told. Adrienne turned her eyes to Julien. Silently, she pleaded with him, begged him for help. Anything but this. Anything but this stripping of her identity, this sudden plunge into servitude, this horrible sinking that left her without any semblance of her former self.

Julien met her gaze. "Pretend," he whispered. "Just pretend. Like an actress in a play." He nodded his head.

Adrienne turned slowly and started down the hall. Each step echoed on the wood floor, pounded in her mind. A maid. A maid.

How was this possible? Her mind wheeled and spun, crashing through every possible escape she could imagine. She wanted to run, wanted to scream. She pictured turning, running down the stairs and out the front door. But then what? Then where would she go?

Perhaps Julien was right. Every time she had fought her aunt, every time she had spoken up, Marie had only increased the pressure, as if gripping the girl in a vise, tightening the screws. Adrienne could think of nothing she could say, nothing she could do at this moment that would make things any better. Her steps carried her forward, down the hall, as if her feet knew what needed to be done, even if Adrienne herself did not.

She followed Marie into her dressing room and stood behind her as Marie sat down at her dressing table. Their eyes met in the mirror. There was hatred on both sides, and neither woman looked away. Marie reached for a comb, raised it up, holding it for Adrienne to take. Adrienne felt the fire in Marie's glare, bouncing back at her from the mirror in front of them. She took the comb, dropped her eyes, and began to arrange the gray curls.

Her jaw clenched. She wanted to yank Marie's hair, wanted to pull her head back and snap it. She imagined Marie's voice, crying out in pain; she imagined the look of surprise and horror in her eyes.

Adrienne combed. With every pull through the gray curls, she stood a little taller, a little straighter. Why should she do what she was told? Why should she give up, play along, lose herself in this woman's power? Perhaps there was another way.

Anger churned inside her, made her yank harder than she intended. She thought of ways to hurt Marie, to make her feel the pain that Adrienne had endured. She pictured holding a pillow over the woman's face, smothering her. She pictured Marie's body going limp and lifeless from the lack of air. The thought brought the tiniest sliver of a smile to her eyes. Marie caught her gaze in the mirror. Her eyes were small and hard, tiny black beads of hatred.

Adrienne looked back down at the curls, careful not to let a smile lift the corners of her mouth. A pillow. That would close those beady little eyes, silence that annoying whine in Marie's voice. She pictured it, standing over Marie's bed, her body silent and still, the dark of night pressed around both of them.

Adrienne moved slightly and caught the sight of the thick cord on the drapes behind her, flashing in the mirror. It was a deep blue, solid and sturdy. She pictured wrapping it around Marie's neck, pulling and twisting it, as tight as she could get it. She pictured Marie's eyes growing large and desperate. She saw the frantic movement of Marie's hands trying to tear the cord away. She pictured Marie's face blooming with color, like an exotic flower: red, then purple, and finally the quiet blue of death. She breathed slowly, enjoying this unexpected feeling of elation, the sense of power that filled her.

Adrienne combed. She felt Marie's glare, and looked up. Marie held pins in her hand. Adrienne laid the comb on the table, took the pins, fixed the gray curls in place. The scent of lavender wafted up from Marie's gown, and Adrienne swallowed. Lavender had always been the scent associated with Marie, the aroma of control. It was the one flower that Adrienne did not like, the one that made her want to retch.

"You may hang my nightclothes in the wardrobe," Marie ordered, never turning from her spot.

Adrienne moved slowly. She was suddenly completely calm, completely detached from this new role of ladies' maid. She picked up the heavy flannel gown, the wool dressing robe, and moved to the wardrobe. She could see Marie, still sitting at the dresser, her eyes locked on Adrienne's every movement in the glass before her. Adrienne turned her back and hung up the clothes. She pushed the wardrobe door shut. Their eyes met once again, Adrienne's reflection in the wardrobe mirror meeting Marie's reflection in the dressing mirror.

Marie turned around and faced her. "Your breakfast tray is in the kitchen. When you finish eating, you can start with the dusting." She stood and left the room, the scent of lavender lingering like a ghost.

Adrienne watched her walk away. She smiled. She felt better than she had in weeks. The thought of Marie, dead and quiet, unable to exert her iron will, brought with it a feeling of peace, a feeling as if all the clouds had lifted.

Maybe Julien was right. Perhaps if she pretended to go along, if she kept her face unreadable and her voice quiet, things would improve. She had to wait, had to bide her time. She had to give her letter the time it needed to reach Brazil. She had to give Gerard the time he needed to make arrangements, to make the trip, to find her here in Colorado. How long would it take? How long would she have to wait? How long would she have to do as Julien suggested, and *pretend*?

Adrienne moved to the window and looked out at the street below. She raised her hand to the drapes and let her fingers slide over the long silky cord. The traces of a smile moved the corners of her mouth. Yes, she would wait. And if, during this time of waiting, she sometimes imagined the ways in which Marie might die, what harm could there be in that? If it made Adrienne feel better, if it gave her the strength to keep going? Images of murder seemed an innocent consolation for all that she suffered at the hands of that woman.

# CHAPTER THIRTY

Adrienne followed Marie up the steps, just as she had the evening before. Her legs ached. She struggled to make the climb.

Marie stood in the doorway, key in hand. Her eyes followed Adrienne as she stepped into the room, into the small prison that was hers. Marie pulled the door closed. The key turned in the lock.

Adrienne collapsed on the narrow cot and stared at the ceiling. She did not light a candle. Complete darkness was a better fit for her thoughts. She was exhausted. "Acting," as Julien had called it, was draining. Every muscle in her body, every fiber of her being, felt strained and taut.

For years, she had spent most of her time alone, or with Lucie. Sometimes she painted, or played the piano with Emelie. The most stressful hours of her life had come on Sunday, when the family went to church and Adrienne was forced to endure the stares of the villagers.

Marie's visits to Beaulieu were distressing—she had to be constantly on her guard—but they never lasted more than a few months. Even when Marie was home in France, Adrienne had her own room with her own things, waiting for her at the end of the day. She had been allowed to wander the grounds, to paint, to read. And there had been long periods, sometimes a year or more, when Marie did not come home to France at all. Never, in all that time, had Adrienne faced the unrelenting prospect of day after day, hour after hour, in Marie's presence. Never, in all that time, had she faced the sheer stress of the past fifteen hours. Never before had she been faced with the incessant repetition of the same set of duties. Marie's eyes focused on every one of her movements, every one of her expressions.

Adrienne turned on her side and let out a sigh. Such effort, to hide her emotions, to swallow the burning anger that rose from her stomach. Several times, she had to remind herself to look away, to drop her gaze, when Marie would look up and see Adrienne staring. The humiliation, the degradation, of wielding a feather duster, of being consigned to take orders, only caused her hatred to burn more brightly, like blowing on the red coals of a dying fire. She was certain that her anger flared in her cheeks, caused her eyes to glint like steel.

She would not give in. She would not allow Marie to strip her of her birthright. There had to be *something* she could do, some way to extricate herself from this mess. As she had so many times in the past days, Adrienne allowed herself to imagine Marie gone, dead, erased from being. It was like tonic water, like a cool breeze. She closed her eyes and smiled. Marie—dead and gone. Out of her life. What a relief it would be! Such freedom. Adrienne could pick up the pieces. She could find Gerard. They could begin again. She might have a chance at an actual life.

She did not imagine how this might be accomplished; she only allowed herself to feel the sweet release of never having to deal with the woman again. Never having to face those eyes of flint, focused on Adrienne as if they could burn holes in the girl. Never having to face the incredible ways in which Marie had conspired to keep Adrienne under control.

It had started as a game, really, just a way to find consolation. It gave her a sense of power, picturing the ways in which Marie might die. Suffocation. Strangulation. An accidental fall down the stairs.

Adrienne had begun to pay particular attention to the inventory of pillows in the parlor. She had allowed herself to look at every curtain cord, in every room she entered.

She gauged the steepness and curve of each set of steps, took note of the steps that Marie used most often. She could picture it: Marie slipping at the top of the stairs, tumbling all the way to the bottom. Marie standing on the balcony outside her third-floor dressing rooms. She could see her, tumbling over the side of the railing. She could hear the thump of her body as it hit the street below, her arms and legs splayed out like those of a rag doll.

Adrienne held her hands out in front of her and examined them carefully: the long, slender fingers, the palms uncalloused, and until recently, completely free from work. Could she do it? Could she, Adrienne Beauvier de Beaulieu, commit murder? Could she silence forever that hateful poison that seeped from her own aunt, her own flesh and blood? She could imagine Marie gone, could imagine her dead and silent. But somehow, she could not actually see herself being the instrument that caused that fall, that caused her aunt's death.

Adrienne stood and walked to the small window. Her thoughts swooped around her, relentless birds of torture. Murder. She shook her head at the word. What horrible twists of fate had put her in a position where she could actually contemplate *murder*?

She shook her head, turned away from the window, and began to unbutton her plain black dress. The dress felt stiff with dirt. She had not changed in days, she realized. Not since their stay at the Waldorf Hotel in New York had she bothered to change into a nightgown. Adrienne slipped her arms from the dress and let it drop to the floor. She moved to her tapestry bag, the one small bag that Marie had allowed her to bring when they left France. She reached in and pulled out another plain black dress. She threw it across the end of the bed. Underneath it was her nightgown, a white flannel with tiny blue roses on the bodice. Adrienne pulled it out of the bag and dropped it over her head. She moved wearily toward the bed.

She stopped and turned, reached for the traveling bag. She sat down on the bed and pulled the bag to her lap. She searched desperately until her hand wrapped around the soft watery caress of velvet and silk. Smiling, Adrienne pulled the dress from the bag. She had forgotten all about it. Marie had insisted, in that final, frantic hour before their departure, that Adrienne needed nothing but plain black dresses for the trip. "Traveling is a dusty, dirty business," she explained.

She had insisted that once they reached America, she would take Adrienne shopping in New York and buy her a few new frocks. "The fashions are quite different in America, you'll see," she insisted. "They aren't nearly as sophisticated as Paris, but then, you want to fit in, don't you?"

Adrienne shook her head, remembering her own naïveté at Marie's explanations. But as soon as Marie had left the room, she had reached for one gown, her favorite dress. It was blue, the deep blue of dusk. Tiny rows of ruffles lined the bodice, fitted with pintucks and lace. The skirt was the same deep blue. Twin rows of velvet ruffles decorated the hem. Adrienne pulled it from the bag and held it to her chest. She buried her nose in the fabric, searching for the smell of France, a whiff of home. She held the fabric against her cheek, lost in the soft caress of her dream.

She pictured escaping, leaving the castle in her blue dress. She pictured Gerard at her side. She pictured them making their way back to France—riding the train across the country, staying in New York. She could see herself standing next to him on board ship, her gloved hand locked in his. She pictured a home in Paris, her sister coming to visit. For a few moments, all her pain and fatigue vanished. She was lost in the dream of living a normal, happy life, a dream she had begun to imagine the first time Gerard had come to Beaulieu.

"I will wait," she whispered to the dark. "I will pretend, just as Julien suggested. I will keep my head down and learn everything I can. I will give Gerard time to find me." She stared at the dark mound of material in her hand.

Adrienne stood, held the dress to her chest, and paced up and down the narrow room. And when he did find her, she would be ready. She would learn all she could about the castle, about the secret staircases and the doors and balconies. She would try to learn a few words of English. She would watch the sisters at Montcalme, on the hill just above them, and try to learn their habits. She would study Julien and Marie, observing the patterns in their days.

Adrienne hid the dress in the bottom of the bag. She lay down on the bed and pulled up the thin, scratchy gray blanket. She exhaled her fatigue into the dark air. Julien was right. Acting, that was the way to go. She would pretend to acquiesce. In the meantime, she would learn all she could about her surroundings. She would be ready when Gerard appeared. She would prepare for their escape.

Adrienne held her hands up in front of her again. For now, she would put away the thought of murder. For now, she would not worry about whether or not she was strong enough to silence Marie. For now, she would focus on some other way to escape from the clutches of her aunt's web.

# CHAPTER THIRTY-ONE

She did everything Marie asked of her, and she did it without uttering a word. She combed Marie's hair every morning, met those dark eyes in the mirror. But her heart was veiled. She did not allow a flicker of emotion to cross her face. She hung Marie's clothes, straightened the dressing room, her face a perfect blank. When Marie called, asked her to make tea or hang clothing, Adrienne complied. She did not speak. She curtsied, a mere wisp of a curtsy, a parody of a curtsy, dropped her eyes for a moment, and then looked Marie full in the eye once more.

And she used every opportunity, moving around that castle, feather duster in hand, to look for solutions. She used that feather duster as her excuse to examine every room in the building. She took note of every window, every door. She walked past the balcony doors on the third floor, stared at the wrought-iron railing that surrounded the small space. She calculated the chances of being able to climb over the railing, slide down the roof of the portico, and make it to the ground without injury.

She walked the back staircases, learned where each one ended, which door led to which room. She watched the clock, timing the appearance of the sisters with their meal trays. She watched Julien, trying to discern a pattern to when he left the castle and when he returned. He took the dogs for a walk every afternoon, close to four. Marie usually lay down for a nap while he was gone. She watched the windows, trying to see which direction he took when he left.

The afternoon sunlight slanted across the floor of the parlor. Marie sat by the fireplace, stitching. Adrienne stood by the bookcase, a cloth in her hand. She took down each book, wiped the spine and the tops of the pages where the dust gathered. She looked at each title. Her hand reached for the next volume, red with gold lettering. It was a dictionary, a French-English dictionary. Adrienne stole a glance in Marie's direction. The book was too large, too heavy, to slip into her skirt. Adrienne wiped the book slowly, thoroughly, trying to determine a way to sneak the book upstairs, to her prison in the attic.

She put it back on the shelf, reached for the next volume, a slim little work in black cloth. This was also a French-English dictionary, of the type that a person would use when traveling. Adrienne glanced up at Marie. She turned her body between the shelf and Marie, pulled another volume off the shelf, and held it up to dust it. She slipped the smaller dictionary into the pocket of her dress and prayed that it would not bulge and give her away.

The loud clopping of horses' hooves on the paving stones below caused both women to look up at the same time. Pounding fists thudded on the front door below them. No one had visited since Adrienne and Marie had first arrived. Adrienne wasn't sure what to do. She looked at Marie.

Marie held her stitching, arrested in midair. She met Adrienne's gaze. "Henriette, answer the door."

Adrienne put her dust rag on the table and hurried down the stairs. She pulled the heavy door inward. A man with a mustache stood on the step. He twisted his hat in his hands.

Adrienne curtsied.

"Hello. I mean . . . *bonjour*. Is the father at home?" he asked her.

Adrienne stood, looking into the man's eyes. *"Je ne comprends pas,"* she murmured.

"The priest?" The man looked troubled. He twisted his hat again. "Père Julien?"

Adrienne nodded. "Ahh . . . *Oui, monsieur.*"

She led the man up the stairs, through the parlor, and into the conservatory, where Julien was repotting a palm. Adrienne stopped at the glass doors and told Julien, in French, that a gentleman was here to see him.

Julien brushed the dirt from his hands. "Angus, how good to see you!" Julien held out his hand, and Angus Gillis stepped forward and took it. Adrienne curtsied and moved back into the parlor, pulling the double glass doors to the conservatory closed behind her. She moved back to the bookcase and took up her dust rag again.

She stood, working on books, not far from the two men in the next room, and strained her ears toward the sounds of the conversation. She almost smiled, thinking of the servants at home. The family had often forgotten they were in the room, and Adrienne realized now how perfectly suited servitude was to the game of spying. The voices of the two men drifted through the glass. She desperately wanted to be able to speak, to understand, English. Her fingers brushed the dictionary on the shelf.

Adrienne moved her body slightly, trying to watch the two men from under her lashes. Marie kept her head down on her stitching, but her body, too, was tense and taut, obviously strained toward any word she might understand. Adrienne shot a quick glance at Marie. The woman must certainly understand a lot more English than she let on. She had traveled back and forth so often over the years.

It was obvious that this was not a social call, despite the fact that Julien and Angus had been friends for some time. Adrienne could feel it in the air, even through her inability to understand the words that were spoken. The tension between the two men was palpable. Mr. Gillis reached inside his suit pocket and brought out a document, folded carefully. He held it out to Julien.

Julien's eyes narrowed; he waited several tense seconds before he reached for the document in Angus's outstretched hand. Their voices dropped, and Julien sank into a chair and unfolded the document, his face torqued with anger and with something that looked a lot like fear.

Adrienne almost forgot to use her duster, she was so intent on the energy of the exchange between Julien and this man who had built the castle. Angus muttered something and turned to leave, charging through the glass doors and coming straight at her. Adrienne looked up and saw his face, clouded with emotion. He held his hand up to her, a clear signal that he didn't need her to show him out, muttered something in English, and charged past her and down the steps. She heard the door close after him, the sound of the horses and buggy as they clip-clopped down the hill.

Marie put her stitching on the chair and moved quickly into the room that Angus Gillis had just vacated. She closed the doors behind her, but Adrienne could hear them, and this time she understood clearly what was being said. Marie asked him what was going on, what were those papers from Mr. Gillis. Why hadn't he stayed for tea?

Julien slouched in his chair; he did not look up at his mother. "A lawsuit. He's filed a lawsuit."

"A lawsuit? For what reason?" Marie's voice was overloud, and Adrienne stepped back slightly, hoping they would forget she was just outside the door.

"He says I haven't made a payment for over a year," Julien continued. "He went into a whole tirade about how he and his brother advanced the money for all of this." Julien waved his arm to indicate the castle. He shook his head, as if impatient and bored with the whole subject.

"But Julien, I sent you the money for the last payment over a year ago. What happened to those funds?" Marie's eyes were narrow and piercing.

"And I gave them some," Julien responded. He turned his eyes away from his mother. "But I used some of the money for a few other debts. A priest doesn't make a great deal of money, Maman."

The shouting continued, and Adrienne moved away from the conservatory. She had never heard the two of them argue, but this was obviously a topic that had come up more than once.

The glass doors opened, and Marie left the room, color glowing in her cheeks. She cast one stinging look at Adrienne and stormed through the parlor and up the stairs.

A crash erupted from the conservatory. Adrienne turned and saw that Julien had kicked over a huge potted palm. Dirt spilled across the floor; the palm splayed outward like the fingers of a hand. Julien kicked the half-empty pot again, and it skidded across the conservatory and crashed into the brick wall, pieces shattering across the floor.

Adrienne tensed. Her eyes took in the violence and anger smeared across the floor. She had never seen Julien like this. He'd always stayed calm, controlled, his voice always perfectly modulated. She stared at the broken pot and twisted palm, her stomach jumping. Her eyes rose and met his. His eyes were on fire, his jaw hard and set.

"What are you staring at?" Julien hissed at her. He strode from the room, the papers rolled tightly in his hand.

Adrienne watched him go. She took it all in—Marie's angry words, the raised voices, the broken pot. She turned back to the mess of dirt and plant all over the floor in the conservatory. She had never stopped to consider it before, but now she had to wonder where Julien had come up with the money to build this place. This castle, with its forty-six rooms and fancy wallpaper and pressed ceiling, had to have cost a fortune.

Was that the secret that Marie did not want known? Was this the information that she had schemed and lied and manipulated to protect? Was that the reason why she had brought Adrienne here? So that no one would learn of his financial mismanagement?

Adrienne turned slightly, and from the corner of her eye, she could see Marie, standing at the window on the landing of the staircase, staring out into the streets where her son had disappeared.

Adrienne could see how brittle and old Marie was becoming. She seemed smaller, somehow. For one brief moment, Adrienne almost felt sorry for her. Then Marie turned, and their eyes met. There was nothing fragile in Marie's look.

# CHAPTER THIRTY-TWO

Unlike the castle in France, Miramont Castle was often surrounded by activity. The sanitarium on the hill behind them bustled with goings-on. Nuns scurried back and forth between the tents spilling down the hill and the wooden structure of Montcalme, just above. They looked like blackbirds in their long habits, like blackbirds stooping to pick at seeds as they bent over their patients.

To the south of the castle, directly out the front windows, lay Ruxton Avenue. Every afternoon, a steady parade of tourists and townspeople walked by, some climbing the hill, others in their buggies, the horses clip-clopping on the steep, curvy road to Pikes Peak. Not far up Ruxton Avenue was the Iron Springs, one of the many natural springs for which Manitou had become famous. It was covered with a portico, surrounded by benches.

Adrienne stood at the window on the landing of the staircase, the lace curtain pushed to one side. She watched the steady stream of people, laughing and talking as they climbed the hill to the springs. The ladies looked like dolls, dressed in every stitch of finery they could manage. Adrienne looked at the wide hats, the ruffled parasols, the puff sleeves and slim-waisted dresses that seemed to be all the rage. She strained to see the lace and ribbons, the bodices thick with pintucks, the tiny buttons climbing to milky throats. Their skirts fluttered in the breeze, like the wings of butterflies, delicate, gossamer shimmers of material.

Adrienne stood on tiptoe, strained to catch every glimpse of beautiful clothing. She lowered her heels and fingered the heavy black crepe of her servant's dress. It crossed her mind that she was almost as bad as her mother, more concerned about the latest fashions than with what was happening in her life.

She sighed and let the lace curtain fall back into place. That wasn't entirely true. She was doing everything she could. In her rounds of dusting, she had the opportunity to find Julien's bowl of change that he kept in his room. Once a week, not enough to attract attention, she snuck a coin into her pocket, hiding it in her valise upstairs. She was practicing a few phrases in English every evening, locked in her room, quietly trying to whisper the pronunciation of the words. Preparing for the day that Gerard would arrive. "My name is Adrienne. I am from France. This is my husband, Gerard Devereux." She allowed herself to picture the two of them, walking up the street in Manitou, visiting the Iron Springs, talking to the other couples as they sat under the portico. An ordinary couple. An ordinary day.

She glanced down and saw Julien standing on the corner of the street just below the castle. He was speaking to a group of women, his two big dogs straining against their leashes, anxious to be home. Julien tipped his hat to them, fought the pull of the dogs as they moved up the hill toward the castle. She could see his teeth, a wide smile gleaming from his dark beard.

The door closed with a heavy thud, and Julien's voice rang out. "Maman? Henriette?"

Adrienne moved to the top of the steps and looked down at his dark head. Julien looked up at her. "We're having guests." He let the dogs loose and hung up the leads at the bottom of the steps. The dogs trotted off to their water dish, in a downstairs room. "I just ran into Dr. Creighton's wife and daughters. I've invited them to tea. They were headed to the Iron Springs but said they would stop on the way back."

Adrienne continued to stare at him. Julien met her gaze.

"We'll need tea. And cake, if there is any. And maybe a bottle of that ginger champagne as well."

Marie appeared on the landing opposite.

Adrienne turned and headed toward the kitchen. Guests. They were having guests. The novelty of it made her step lighter. She boiled water, cut slices of cake and fanned them out on a plate. She polished the silver teapot, the creamer and sugar bowl. She reached for the champagne glasses, arranged them, upside down, on a linen napkin on another tray.

Julien waltzed in, excitement coloring his eyes and the way he held his shoulders. He went through the pantry, searching for a bottle of ginger champagne. "Have you seen this before, Adrienne?" he asked, showing her the bottle. "Manitou Bottling Works" was printed on the label.

Adrienne shook her head.

"It's not really champagne. This company took some of the mineral water—there is a spring down the hill just by their shop— and came up with a secret recipe. Ginger and mineral water and . . . I don't know what else. But it's bubbly like champagne, without the alcohol, and completely delicious." He smiled at Adrienne, took the bottle, and headed to the parlor, where the guests had gathered.

Adrienne kept her eyes low, her face tranquil and composed as she moved around the room with the tea tray. She made a second round, passing out the empty champagne glasses, and Julien followed close behind her, proudly pouring ginger champagne.

Mrs. Creighton smiled at Julien as he filled her glass. "Eliza is quite fond of this." She nodded toward her youngest daughter. "Her favorite, in fact."

He poured a glass for the oldest daughter, a dark-haired, dark-eyed girl close to Adrienne's own age. The girl did not seem interested in anyone around her. She did not look at her mother, or Marie, or Julien. She seemed not to notice Adrienne as she served. Her eyes traveled to the pianoforte in the corner. She sipped her champagne absently.

Adrienne moved, head lowered, to the youngest daughter. Her hair hung in blond curls, just to her shoulder. Her eyes were blue. She looked like a china doll in her ruffles, clearly only nine or ten years old. She took an empty glass from the tray, accepted the piece of cake on delicate china that Adrienne held out to her.

*"Merci beaucoup."* She looked directly in Adrienne's eyes when she said it.

Adrienne smiled, dipped a slight curtsy. *"Je vous en prie."*

Julien followed behind her, pouring champagne. *"Parlez-vous français?"* He smiled at Eliza. She blushed and lowered her head.

Marie watched the girl intently.

"Only a little, I'm afraid," Mrs. Creighton answered for her. "We took a trip to the continent, just last summer. The girls and I, that is. Dr. Creighton is much too busy to get away."

"Yes, I see him on the hill with the patients, at all hours of the day and night. It must be difficult, to have him away so much."

"He does work long hours. But . . . we are glad he is able to help so many."

Eliza held her champagne glass up to Julien. Julien wrapped his hand around hers, held the glass, and poured. When he stopped pouring, his fingers slid slowly away from the child's. She dropped her eyes to the floor.

Adrienne looked at Julien. She could see the sparkle in his eyes, a gleam that was almost feverish. The look made her flinch. It held a light that was much too sharp, too bright. Adrienne had the fleeting thought that perhaps his stomach troubles were back; perhaps he was about to be bedridden again.

He moved to a seat not far away from the youngest child. His voice, though she could not understand what he said, held a note she had not heard before. Ingratiating. False. He put it on like perfume, as if he carried a bottle of disingenuousness in his pocket. "Aren't the roses just glorious this year?" He smiled at Mrs. Creighton. "Have you seen the churchyard?"

Mrs. Creighton nodded.

"I am fortunate to have so many of my young parishioners to help me with the gardens." Julien turned his smile toward Eliza.

Adrienne felt Marie's gaze burning into her and realized she'd been staring. She dropped her eyes. She turned the tray on its side under her arm, curtsied, and left. Several feet down the hallway, she stopped and turned, straining her neck to get another glimpse of Julien, smiling and chattering. Of the little girl, her head down, her glass held demurely in her lap. The little girl who spoke French.

# CHAPTER THIRTY-THREE

Uhhh," Adrienne gasped. Her eyes shot open; her body jerked. She let out a long stream of air. Her heart pounded. Only a dream. It was only a dream. She stared at the moonlight that spilled through the small window, painting the wall and floor in a blue glow. Only a dream, she told herself again. She was in her room, high up on the fourth floor of Miramont Castle. In America. In Manitou Springs. Only a dream.

Adrienne rolled onto her back. She stared at the ceiling, waiting for the thudding and lurching of her heart to slow. She sighed again and closed her eyes.

In the dream, she'd been sleeping, lying on her side. She was in her own bed at the château in France, a young girl of only nine or ten. She woke suddenly, her eyes flying open and her leg jerking. Moonlight flooded through the big picture window and onto the floor and the bed. But in the dream, she woke knowing that she was not alone. Someone was in the room with her.

She lay very still, trying to sense whom it was, to sense the quiet movements. She could feel the warmth of the body, feel hot puffs of air on her neck. Julien crawled into the bed and lay down behind her, his body curled around hers. His hand ran up and down her arm, down the side of her hip and thigh.

Adrienne rolled onto her back. "What are you doing?"

Julien brought his hand up quickly, pressing his fingers flat against her lips. "Shhh," he whispered.

She stared at him in the dark. His face was a pale oval in the moonlight. His mouth disappeared in the darkness of his mustache and beard. He removed the pressed fingers from her lips, slowly, cautiously, as if not sure she could be trusted to stay quiet.

"What . . ." she whispered.

His eyes held a sparkle, a feverish gleam. His eyelids drooped, a heavy-lidded look that made her squirm. She realized that he had his other hand on his own body, massaging himself slowly. He continued to rub himself with one hand, and with the other he trailed his fingers down her lips and her neck, through the dip of her collarbone, across her flat, little-girl chest, and slowly down her leg.

"Ahhh, Adrienne," he breathed. "Don't you ever get lonely?"

Adrienne blinked, tears stinging her eyes at the mention of the word. Yes. Yes. She was very lonely. She lay very still. She couldn't breathe, the word stabbing her chest like a knife. Lonely. Unbearably lonely. She had to have been nine or ten; her grand-père had been dead for over two years.

He moved his hand; she felt his body press closer to hers. "It's so difficult, isn't it? To be alone so much?"

Adrienne felt a tear filling her eye. She raised one hand, swiped at it angrily.

"I really don't believe that God wants us to be alone like that, to be so lonely," Julien whispered. He was moving against her now, pressing himself against her side, his hand trailing to the bone between her legs. She tried to shift away. His hand was insistent, firm, and she cried out.

"It's all right, Adrienne. I won't hurt you. God wants us to be touched. He wants us to feel good." Julien's breath came in ragged gasps next to her ear. Her hair felt hot and sticky where it caught his panting.

He made a groaning sound. His body shifted, almost covering her with its weight. He buried his face in the pillow. His hand stopped moving, his body stopped pressing. He lay there for a moment, utterly still.

His touch had felt dirty. She squirmed with shame, not understanding his movements or his breathing or anything about what was going on. She was afraid of him, in some way she had never known before. This was not normal.

"This is our secret, Adrienne. I'll help you . . . with your loneliness. I know how good it feels to be touched. To be held." He caressed the sides of her face, his fingers light and slow. "But we mustn't tell anyone. Only those who are truly lonely can understand." He held his fingers to his lips, as if shushing her. He rose from the bed, shifted the fabric of his pajamas, and moved to her bedroom door, his feet totally quiet on the floor. He turned back and looked at her, his eyes dark jewels in the night. "You understand, don't you?" He looked at her again, his eyes hard, almost threatening. "This is our secret." He snickered. "You don't want people to think that you're making up stories again, now do you?"

He closed the door with a gentle click.

෴

Adrienne's heart thudded; she stared into the dark of the room in Miramont, trying to force her mind to stop racing. *It is only a dream,* she told herself, over and over. Only a dream. But it didn't feel like a dream. It felt like a memory.

Her mind went back to the day before, the day that the Creightons had dropped in for tea. She saw, once more, the way Julien's tapered fingers had lingered over the hand of the little girl, Eliza. Adrienne raised her own hand from the covers and held it in front of her face. Had he touched her, that same way? She could *almost* see Julien's fingers, lingering over her own small hand. She could *almost* feel the brush of his fingers against hers, when he asked for her to pass the salt at the table, or when he handed her a book. She stared at her own hand in the semi-dark, felt the pitch and roll of her stomach at the thought.

Those years after Grand-père had passed were lost in a haze. She had tried so hard to keep her voice quiet, to keep her visions in check. She had blotted out huge pieces of her childhood. Now, at this distance, she tried to figure out if this were only a dream, or if it had really happened. The only thing she knew for certain was that it all made her feel sick, shame and revulsion mixing in a stomach-churning brew.

# CHAPTER THIRTY-FOUR

All thought of escape evaporated, like rain puddles in a harsh, hot sun. She could think of nothing but this cousin, this man she barely knew, this priest with his long, slender fingers and delicate constitution.

Who was he? What had he done? How much was he capable of? And what had he done to her? The questions flew up at her from the pages of the novel that she held open in front of her. She could not read. She tried to concentrate on a sentence and found her mind playing with some tidbit of memory, some long-forgotten knowledge.

The memories came back in wisps, like the scent of smoke left in a room after the smoker has gone. She remembered, in pieces, her vision at the church when she was very little. She remembered that younger version of Julien, standing in front of his congregation in Santa Cruz, raising the cup of wine to the heavens. She remembered the clattering sound as it fell to the floor, remembered the foam coming from his mouth.

At that young age, she never stopped to think about what the vision could possibly mean. To her young mind, it was just an interesting story. She would never have asked why—why anyone would hate their priest so much that they would want him dead. All the questions she had never asked at the time came tumbling back now, piling up in a jumbled mess that she felt compelled to try to sort through.

Slowly, bit by bit, she began to connect the dots—the pieces of information that she knew. If her memories of what Julien had done to her were truly *memories*, if her suspicions about why Julien was poisoned were correct, it might explain why Marie had gone to such lengths to get Adrienne away from France. It would explain Marie's overwhelming need to keep Adrienne silenced. Did Marie know about Julien? Or worse than actual knowledge, did she *suspect* that her son was abusing little girls? Is that why she had done all this?

Adrienne took up the feather duster and moved, absentmindedly, about the castle. She positioned herself at windows, looking out at the street below them or at the nuns on the hillside above. She moved through each room, hoping to catch a glimpse of him, trying to see where he went when he left the castle.

She wandered into his bedchamber, at the southwest corner of the castle. She moved around the room, her duster swishing back and forth, her eyes trailing over the objects on his dresser. There was nothing there to suggest something was amiss, only a hairbrush, a bottle of cologne, a folded handkerchief, the bowl of change that she had been slowly stealing.

She moved to the window. This room, Julien's room, was the only room in the castle that afforded a clear view of the church, a block up the hill. She held the curtains in one hand and stared at the church building, wishing she could use her vision to see inside, to see what he was up to.

Julien stepped out the side door of the church and locked the door behind him. Adrienne stepped back quickly and let the curtain drop. She watched him through the gauzy fabric as he looked around, up at the castle, and then moved up the hill, around the corner, and out of sight.

Adrienne exhaled slowly. She needed to be alone. She wanted a vision, craved a vision. For the first time that she could ever remember, she wanted to use her second sight, to know what was going on in this house. She wanted to know just what Julien was doing, and how much Marie knew.

After all those years of unwanted images, of knowledge she did not want or wish to have, now she needed it. And she had no idea how to make it work, how to trigger the mechanism that allowed her to see and hear and know. Nothing came to her. No words, no images, no sudden feeling of certainty. Nothing. All she had was this knot in the pit of her stomach, this vague *feeling* that something was dreadfully wrong.

How do you ever know the truth about another person? Without the knowledge that comes through clairvoyance, how could a person ever know when someone spoke the truth? How could you ever know with any certainty what happens behind closed doors?

Adrienne thought of her mother, of the feelings of doubt that had surrounded her like a fog. For years, she had carried an uneasy sense about her husband that she could never prove, never really know. Is this what it felt like? To suspect, to imagine, but to have nothing concrete to allow the relief of certainty?

Adrienne found herself staring at Marie much more often these days. Did she know some dreadful truth about her son? Was that why she had moved heaven and hell to keep Adrienne silent? Or was she, like Adrienne, left with just this vague foreboding, a sinister apprehension that amounted to nothing but shadows in the dark?

Adrienne sighed and turned her head toward the window. His loose change sparkled in the morning light, and she quickly slipped three coins into the pocket of her dress.

They knelt in the parlor—Julien, Marie, and Adrienne—heads bent, beads clicking, rosaries moving between their fingers. A fire blazed. Sparks popped and cracked.

Julien's eyes were closed; his voice rang in the room, leading them through the prayers. "I believe in God, the Father Almighty."

Adrienne whispered the words. "I believe in the Holy Spirit, the holy Catholic Church, the communion of saints . . ." Her mind popped and cracked like the sparks from the fire. She peeked at Julien, kneeling to her left.

Her mind raced to the vision of Julien, standing at the front of the church in Santa Cruz, drinking from the chalice. She saw, once more, the way his eyes bulged, the way he fell to the floor, his lips turning blue from the poison. She heard, once again, the crash of the potted palm after he had kicked it, just a few weeks ago, the way the pot hit the wall and shattered. She could hear one large piece that hadn't broken rolling back and forth on the floor.

Adrienne snuck another glance at him. His voice led the prayers, like a song. "Hail Mary, full of grace. The Lord is with thee. Blessed art thou amongst women, and blessed is the fruit of thy womb, Jesus."

Someone in that congregation had tried to poison their priest. Adrienne was convinced that no one would try to murder their priest unless he had done something truly awful. Had he stolen from them? Lied to them? Had he let his temper fly and actually hurt someone?

Her breath came faster; her heart pounded. She glanced at Julien again. She thought of the way his fingers had slid, slowly, over the fingers of that little girl, Eliza Creighton. Suddenly she knew, knew with certainty just what he had done.

He had touched one of the children in Santa Cruz, maybe even more than one. Maybe he had done more than just touch.

Her knowledge of the act was vague. But it would certainly explain attempted murder. That would certainly explain poison at the chalice.

Through the whirling of her thoughts, Adrienne could feel it, boring into her skull, drilling into the top of her head. She looked up through her lashes. Marie was directly across from her. Adrienne wondered if her thoughts had moved across her own face. Had she left her mouth open? Had she knit her brow? Had she stared too long at Julien?

Adrienne closed her eyes, tried to make her face calm and her heart slow. "Holy Mary, Mother of God, pray for us sinners . . ."

The prayers went on forever.

# CHAPTER THIRTY-FIVE

Marie and Adrienne placed their feet carefully as they walked down the stone street. It was cold, winter's chill making them hurry as fast as they could on the icy pavement. They turned at Ruxton Creek, walked up the path to the Chapel of Our Lady of Perpetual Help. Normally, Adrienne loved Sunday morning mass, if only for the opportunity it provided to leave the castle, to smell the pine trees, hear the birds, and look at the sky. She missed her long walks on the grounds of the castle in France, missed watching the trees and shrubs and grasses color and fade into their winter attire.

This morning, she watched her feet. She did not look around at the mountains, took no notice of the families walking to church or pulling up in their buggies. She didn't tip her head back, scanning the sky for hawks. She didn't stop to watch the water in the creek or the lacy patterns of ice; she didn't stop to listen to the sound of the water muffled beneath. Her mind was too full, too troubled, to enjoy the beauty of the winter morning.

She and Marie entered the small wooden building, made the sign of the cross, and moved to the pew at the left front. Adrienne stared at the floor. Her mind would not be still. She kept imagining Julien's eyes, that feverish sparkle, the lids heavy. She scanned the room, looking for children, for young girls Eliza's age, the age she herself had been in that horrible memory. She had to tell someone, didn't she? Had to do something to stop him. Or should she forget it all, concentrate on her own escape?

For days now, she had been making the arguments in her head. Even if she could speak the language, even if she could find the right person to speak to, what would she tell them? What did she have, really, as evidence? A disturbing dream. A long-ago vision of Julien being poisoned—a vision that Marie had covered with the story of working for the government in South America. Uneasy feelings and dreams were not enough to convict a man. She felt protective of every child that walked into the church, but she had no idea what she should do.

The bells chimed, and people stamped their feet at the door, walked the short aisle, and sat down, a heavy rustling of coats and scarves trailing from every pew. An older woman sat at the church organ. Her gray hat was huge, a cluster of bright-red cherries bobbed at its crown. She leaned far back in her seat as she played, her fingers insistent, her bosom heaving, the notes of Mozart filling the small space of the church.

Everyone rose. Adrienne kept her eyes on the floor. She didn't want to look at Julien, and she tried hard not to. She could feel him, though, as he swayed from side to side, walking slowly down the aisle. He swung the censer back and forth, and wisps of incense curled in the air. He walked to the front of the church, his stomach out, his shoulders back, almost swaggering in his chasuble.

In church, Julien was quite different from the Julien at home. Every movement ended with a flourish. Every sentence was strung out slightly longer than it needed to be. He seemed to love the power, the way every man and woman and child in the room hung on his every movement, every word. He stood now, at the front of the church, and closed his eyes. He held them closed, said not a word, for what seemed far too long. A man at the back of the church coughed.

Julien opened his eyes, gave a dramatic sigh, and started his homily, in English. She'd been practicing, trying to learn the words in the little dictionary upstairs. This morning she stared straight ahead. She did not want to know what he was saying. The tone of his voice was enough. She cringed at the way it rang out, stopped suddenly, and dropped to a lower register. Like an actor, she thought with a faint smile. Or a baritone at the opera. All melodrama and tragedy.

A weak, watery sunlight flooded through the eastern windows and caught the gold candlesticks on the altar. Adrienne stared, glad to have something to focus on other than Julien and his false speech and his slender hands waving dramatically.

A much younger Julien appeared before her, shining in the reflected light. He looked almost like a teenager, his skin smooth, his beard gone, and only thin wisps of hair sprouting on his upper lip. He and three other young men were walking down the street, laughing and joking.

"So, Julien, think your university education can help you with this?" One of his companions smiled broadly at Julien, and stopped. He stood outside the door to a bordello in Paris. Men came and went, laughing, smoking cigars. They could hear raucous laughter, the sound of a piano, and the laughter of women punctuating the deeper roars of the men.

Julien looked at the door and tried to see through the glass. His smile dropped from his face.

"How about it, fellows?" The first man raised his eyebrows and smiled suggestively. "A little drink, perhaps? Maybe a little . . ." He tipped his head toward the interior, smiled again, and opened the door.

The inside of the establishment was dark. Smoke filled the space. Along one wall was a huge bar, a mirror stretched behind it. Adrienne heard the sound of the bottles, tinkling and chiming as the bartender poured drinks. Laughter filled the air like smoke.

At the opposite end of the room, a woman stood on a small stage, singing a song that made Adrienne blush. The singer was very scantily dressed. She wore a tight corset, deep-blue velvet with tiny rows of black lace and black buttons up the center. Her breasts were barely contained; they threatened to spill with every shake of her shoulders. Her legs were long and thin, covered in black fishnet stockings. She wore tall black heels, in which she moved easily around the stage as she danced and sang. A man in white sleeves and a bowler hat, a cigar chomped between his teeth, played the piano.

She shimmied up to a table full of men, just to the right of the stage. She leaned down, putting her delicate hands on the face of one gentleman, turning his smile up to her as she sang. Then she pushed his head to her breasts. He shook his head back and forth between the two globes, and raised it, laughing, a deep red rising up his cheeks.

The woman shot up again, strutting around the room, shaking her derriere. She kicked one leg high in the air, swung it over another man's head. It came down neatly on the other side. Men sitting close by clapped and whistled.

The song ended, and she curtsied, just as if she were a fine lady. She bounced up, smiling. Some of the men stood, clapping, their cigars planted firmly between their teeth. Adrienne could see several other women at various locations around the room. All were clad like the singer, in garments that barely covered them, as if they had not bothered to dress completely. Some were sitting on the laps of men; others sat on chairs, leaning close to their companions, pushing their breasts against the men's arms.

The woman who had just finished singing sauntered over to the table where Julien sat with his companions. "Evening, boys." She smiled.

Julien blushed. She sat down next to him. "Could I have a cigarette?" she asked him. He pulled one from a silver case in his pocket, held a match to it. His hands shook. She smiled and blew smoke in his face. The corners of her mouth turned up, as if she enjoyed young men like Julien, obviously unschooled in the art of seduction. She talked to the young men for a few moments, laughing, blowing smoke at their jokes. Julien said very little.

She leaned forward and crushed her cigarette in a crystal ashtray. In one fluid movement, she rose, swung one leg up and over Julien, and ended in his lap, facing him with a bright smile. He almost jumped in surprise. She leaned close to him, rubbed her breasts against his jacket. She put one long-fingered hand at the back of his neck, caressed his hair, twisting it in small curls. Then she leaned toward him and whispered in his ear. Her left hand rested on his chest, and her slender fingers snaked between the buttons on his shirt.

She rose suddenly, grabbing his hand and pulling him up. One of his friends whistled. "About time, I'd say. This has been too long coming, if you ask me."

Julien glanced at his friend with a scowl. He turned and followed the young woman up a flight of stairs. She sashayed up, careful to keep her derriere in front of his face as she led him up the stairs. His face burned scarlet in the dim, smoky light.

They walked down a long hallway. Julien heard grunts, moans, giggles, coming from behind the closed doors they passed. The woman pushed open a door to the left, and they stepped inside. The room was tiny, barely able to contain a brass bed and oak washstand. Red satin spilled over the mattress; an oil lamp cast a soft golden glow on the walls and ceiling.

Julien stopped in the center of the room. He swallowed. The woman closed the door, turned to look at him, and in one polished movement, she ripped the hooks at the top of her corset. Her breasts spilled out. The nipples were dark and huge in the dim light.

Julien gasped, his breath arrested. She finished the ripping motion, and her corset dropped to the floor. Her black fishnet stockings were held up by garters, wrapped high on her slender thighs. Her waist was lean. He let his eyes drop to the reddish brown hair below her belly.

She smiled and moved toward Julien, her hand moving smoothly to his chest. She pulled his shirt up; her fingers worked the buttons of his trousers. She leaned into his neck, her tongue flicking back and forth over the sparse stubble. His trousers dropped to the floor. His penis stood straight and hard, brushed against her belly as she continued to kiss him.

She moved to the bed, smiling, her hand guiding him to her. She lay back, spread her legs, and guided his hand to the warmth between them. Julien lay awkwardly beside her. He panted, his eyes closed. She moved one hand to hold his penis; with the other she tried to guide him inside her. Julien's body stiffened. He moaned, and collapsed at her side. He had not lasted long enough to get inside her. He lay now, next to her on the bed, gasping.

She dropped her hands from his body and rolled her eyes at the ceiling. She reached over him to the bedside table and lit a cigarette. Julien rolled onto his back.

"Well, that didn't last long, did it?" Her words were sharp. "What's the matter, little boy? Having trouble keeping a stiffie?" She moved her hand from side to side. She blew smoke in the air, snorted.

"I love the young ones," she whispered, running her fingers over the hair on his chest. "Sometimes they can go on and on forever. So young. So eager. So energetic." She looked down at Julien, shriveled and soft. "Well, don't worry about it. When you're older, when you have a little more experience, you'll be able to hold on longer." She smiled and pushed herself up from the bed.

She stood on the rug, tugging her corset back up over her hips. She fingered the hooks, reached the top, adjusted her breasts. She turned toward Julien and leaned down close to him, her breath puffing into his face. "Thanks, honey. It was two seconds of absolute bliss." She stood up straight, winked at him, and flounced out of the room.

⁓

Adrienne's breath caught. She stared up at Julien, stately and dignified in his white robes, his gold collar marking him as someone special, someone different. Someone who held ultimate authority, someone who could not be questioned. Someone that no one would dare to tease or make fun of. She stared, watching his every move.

She knew now, without any doubt, why he had gone into the church. Not one week after his humiliation in the Paris brothel, he had withdrawn from university, moved away from his companions of that wretched evening. He had insisted that God called him. That God needed him. He had not mentioned to anyone that it was he who needed the church—needed the protection, the authority, the standing offered in the robes of Christ. He needed the perfect excuse to never marry. He needed to make certain he would never face humiliation and shame in front of an adult woman, ever again.

And with that vision, Adrienne understood why he was drawn to the children. They wouldn't laugh at him. They wouldn't make fun of him. They were completely in his power. The weak, the helpless, the quiet.

Adrienne swallowed. She shifted in her seat, glanced at Marie, to her right. She sucked in her lip and sighed. At last, a vision. The corners of her mouth rose slightly. They weren't gone; she wasn't broken. And with that vision, one that made her blush thinking of it, she understood her cousin. She understood why he craved power and prestige, why he needed to build a forty-six-room castle for just him and his mother. And more disturbing than all that, she understood why he might turn to children when he needed human touch.

# CHAPTER THIRTY-SIX

Julien and Marie sat in the parlor. It was midmorning, but November's chill had permeated every inch of the castle, and a fire blazed in the fireplace. Marie stitched. Julien sat on the divan, his feet up under a blanket. He held a book in front of him. He coughed and the sound crackled in the air and made Adrienne's throat hurt when she heard it. Marie glanced up at him.

"Would you like more tea, Julien?"

He continued to cough, held his hand up in a gesture of denial, and shook his head. The coughing stopped, and he lay back against the cushions, exhausted.

Adrienne dusted by the bookcase. She ran her feather duster over the volumes, over the edge of shelf that protruded from the spines of the books. She tipped her head to the side, her eyes caught on the French-English dictionary. She remembered the dictionary upstairs and mentally started practicing the words she'd been teaching herself. *I need help. I need help.*

Her head jolted up at the sound of pounding on the front door. Marie looked up at her. Adrienne put her duster down and hurried down the stairs.

A young man stood outside, his cheeks flushed red from the cold. He wore the collar of a priest, a black overcoat to protect against the cold. He held his hat in his hands. "Is the father at home?" he asked, looking past Adrienne's shoulder. "Monsieur Morier?"

*"Oui, monsieur,"* she answered, standing to the side while he entered.

She led him up the steps to the parlor. Julien hurried to lower his feet to the floor, to toss aside the blanket he'd been wrapped in. He slipped his feet into his slippers and stood, holding his hand out. "Father Michael. This is a surprise. Come in, please." The young priest stepped into the room. "This is my mother, Madame Morier," Julien said, his hand sweeping to indicate Marie in the wing chair.

"Nice to meet you, madame." Father Michael bowed and held Marie's hand for a moment.

*"Enchanté,"* Marie replied.

"Uh . . . Father Morier." The young man seemed to stumble on his own words. He twisted his hat in his hand. "Might I have a word with you?" He glanced at Marie. "Privately?"

Julien raised his eyebrows. "Certainly. *Pardonnez-moi*, Maman." He bowed to his mother and started down the hall, to an office at the other end of the castle.

Adrienne curtsied as the men walked past her, and said to Julien in French, "Shall I bring tea?"

"Yes, please, Henriette. We'll be in my office."

She walked to the kitchen, just behind Julien's office, and began preparing a tray. She could hear their voices, rising and falling.

"I'm sorry you've not been well," Father Michael began, as soon as he and Julien were seated in the office.

"This cough seems to haunt me, I'm afraid," Julien replied. "Ever since that trip to South America, so many years ago. I haven't been the same since." As if to emphasize his point, he began to cough. It took him a few minutes to recover. "And these cold temperatures only make it worse."

The younger man nodded. "Unfortunate. I understand you were in the service of your country when this started."

"Quite so," Julien said, putting his hands together, fingertip to fingertip. "But . . . I could hardly refuse the French government, now could I?"

"I suppose not," Father Michael replied.

Adrienne entered with the tray. She placed it on the desk, poured tea into the cups. She turned to face the young priest. *"Crème? Sucre?"* she asked.

"Sugar, please," he replied.

She fixed his cup, handed it to him. She poured Julien's and placed it on the desk beside him. She walked to the door, curtsied, and went back to the kitchen.

Julien watched her leave. He waited a moment before turning back to the young priest before him.

The younger man's eyes darted nervously. "Father, I . . . I have received a letter from the archbishop. He's very concerned about your health. He worries that . . ." The young priest was breathless, almost panting. "He worries that . . . Well, that this may be too much for you—the rigors of maintaining a parish."

"Nonsense." Julien waved his hand. As if to contradict him, his cough began again.

Father Michael waited patiently for the cough to stop, his face full of emotion. He placed his teacup on the desk, reached into the pocket of his coat, and pulled out an envelope, the crest of the archbishop glowing in the corner. "He's asked me to bring you this." Father Michael laid the envelope on the desk between them. His hands trembled.

Julien stared at it. He put the tips of his fingers together again, steepled, and leaned back in his chair.

The younger priest swallowed. "He . . . the archbishop . . . does not want to see your health get any worse." Father Michael swallowed again. His leg shook, almost rattling as it vibrated, as he sat stiff and straight in his chair. "He thinks it might be better if . . . well . . . if you . . . if you were relieved of your parish duties." The young man's eyes jumped.

Julien took a deep breath. He eyed the young priest, held his fingers pressed together, just under his chin. "I see." He turned his gaze to the window on his left and summoned every ounce of calm he could find. He searched for the right way to respond. After a moment, he sighed heavily. "Well, he may be right. It has been rather difficult, these past few months." Julien glanced at the face of the younger priest. "I certainly haven't had the energy that I would like."

Father Michael nodded, his face flooded with relief.

Julien coughed again and reached for his handkerchief. As if substituting for words, the cough went on and on.

Father Michael sat on the edge of his chair, waiting for a moment of respite. He twisted his hat again. The cough subsided, and Julien leaned back in his chair with his handkerchief pressed to his lips. The younger man stood. "Well, I guess I'd better be going." He extended his hand.

Julien looked at it, and turned away, his gaze seeking the window.

Father Michael brushed his hand, damp with sweat, against his pant leg. "I'll see myself out," he finished. He strode to the door, and stopped, his hand on the door handle. "Good luck to you, Father." He walked away, his footsteps clicking down the hall, down the steps. The front door opened and closed.

Julien waited another heartbeat. Then he swept his arm against the tea tray, anger giving him strength that he didn't normally possess. Cups and sugar and cream smashed against the wall in his office, china shattering in a million pieces across the floor.

# CHAPTER THIRTY-SEVEN

A drienne stood behind Marie at the dressing table. Marie's eyes were locked on her; they followed Adrienne's every move in the glass. Adrienne combed the gray curls, trying to look absorbed in her work, trying to avoid Marie's dark eyes in the mirror.

Adrienne's skin crawled, as if there were tiny spiders let loose on her back and shoulders and arms, creeping through her hair. Everything had changed in the few days since the visit of the younger priest. The air in the castle was different, brittle, as if all the secrets that each of them carried were shards of glass, suddenly spilled all over the floor. All three did their best to avoid stepping on anything that held the stab of truth. All three were doing their best to ignore the shattered remains of Julien's life.

Julien had told them that he had decided to give up the parish, that his health would not allow him to continue, and he had coughed almost incessantly ever since, as if the cough could convince them all that what he said was true. Adrienne knew differently. She may not have been able to understand the words of that conversation, but there was no question that throwing a tea tray at the wall did not reflect Julien's version of events. Adrienne did not know what Marie had heard, but she suspected that Marie, too, knew that Julien was lying.

Last night, Adrienne had bolted awake, early in the morning hours. She'd been dreaming again, a dream that she had not had since before she left France. It was so familiar, following Marie down the long, dark hallway. She watched as Marie stuffed a notebook full of papers into her valise. She watched, the dreamer already knowing what was coming, watching as Marie turned, her dress splattered with blood.

The dream shook her. For the first time in months, Adrienne thought more about her own situation than she did about what Julien was doing and what Marie knew. For the first time, she began to wonder how all of this would end. These were thoughts that she had not allowed herself before; she knew Marie wanted her quiet, wanted to keep her from spreading stories about Julien. But until now, her only thought of the future had been her rescue when Gerard showed up and took her away.

All her life, Marie had managed to stay one step ahead of her. She had come up with her plans and schemes before Adrienne had even had a chance to think about it. This time, Adrienne was determined to stay one step ahead of her aunt.

She thought of the times that she pictured Marie dead and gone. She thought of the times she had pictured holding a pillow over the woman's face, or wrapping the curtain cord around her neck. She thought of Marie slipping on the top step and tumbling to the bottom. She thought of her own horror at committing murder. And now she couldn't help but wonder if Marie was thinking the same kinds of things, if she had already concocted some way to rid herself of her niece once and for all. Which of them was strong enough, mentally and physically, to get rid of the other?

Marie held up the hairpins in her left hand. Her eyes continued to follow Adrienne in the mirror, searching the girl's face and eyes for evidence of what she knew.

Adrienne glanced at her aunt. The woman must have had suspicions about Julien. How could she not suspect that *something* was wrong? He had been poisoned at the chalice, after all, and it was only Marie's quick thinking that had saved his life.

Adrienne laid the comb on the dresser and reached for the pins. Her fingers fumbled and the hairpins dropped to the floor. *"Pardonnez-moi,"* she murmured, and stooped to retrieve them. She used that moment, kneeling on the floor, reaching for the pins, to calm her breathing, to arrange her face. How long had Marie suspected her son? Since the poisoning in Santa Cruz? Or even longer?

Adrienne's fear had grown sharper with each passing day. Danger crackled in the air, seeped from the walls. She could see it in the drawn face of her cousin; she smelled it in the brandy that was often on his breath. It jumped off of Marie's skin and hair and eyes, like sparks from the fire.

Marie was truly worried now. It was not the same as when Adrienne was younger and Marie was only interested in making sure that Adrienne's stories were not allowed to get out. This was different. She might not know exactly what her son had done, but she knew that something was dreadfully wrong, something much more substantial than a failure to pay his debts. The feeling made Marie even more determined, more formidable than Adrienne had ever before known. More dangerous.

Adrienne's eyes darted from the staring face in the mirror before her to the gray curls. Her hands shook as she pressed in the pins. She patted the curls in place.

Marie gazed at Adrienne's reflection in the mirror, and stood. She walked away from the dressing room, never turning to face the girl directly. The scent of lavender lingered, wafting toward Adrienne's nose, wrapping itself in the curtains.

Adrienne leaned against the wall after she had gone. Her breath escaped in a long, slow sigh. Her hands trembled. She held them to her chest, willed herself to breathe. Breathe. Slowly. Normally. She leaned her forehead against the glass of the window.

Where was Gerard? It had been over a year now since she dropped that letter in a mailbox when they had changed trains in St. Louis. That should have been plenty of time for the letter to reach him. It should have been plenty of time for him to come for her.

She turned and began to straighten the items on Marie's dressing table. The letter caught her eye, a beacon from her former life. The paper was thick and creamy, the gold crest of the Challembelles family across the top, tendrils of gold trailing down the sides of the page. How many times had she seen that stationery sitting on her mother's desk in Beaulieu? Adrienne almost couldn't breathe with the thought. A letter. A letter from home.

Her heart felt as if it might stop; her entire mind filled with longing, with memories of the château and the grounds and the lake. All the places she had walked, all the things and people she had lived with for most of her life, came swimming back, and she blinked rapidly to keep the tears at bay.

She let her fingers drop to the thick paper, and for a moment, she allowed herself to touch her former life. The letter was folded into thirds and had been tossed carelessly on top of the dressing table. Adrienne lifted it in her fingers, her hands shaking, her stomach tossing. Home. A letter from home. She opened it slowly, sinking to the low stool in front of the mirror. Her mother's handwriting, all its loops and flourishes, filled the page. Adrienne read slowly, drinking in every word.

*The children are doing well, although it is probably not appropriate to call them children any longer. Emelie has become quite a beautiful young woman. It seemed as if it happened overnight. She has finished her studies at the convent school. Antoine has grown taller, and his voice is beginning to find the lower registers. He takes after his father a great deal.*

Adrienne stared at the page, her eyes filling with images of her brother and sister. She swallowed, trying to keep from sobbing at the thought of them.

*We've had some very sad news. Do you remember Gerard Devereux, the young man who worked at the embassy with Pierre? He and his grandfather came here to visit a few times. It seems that he did not adjust well after his transfer to Brazil. He requested leave from the embassy, quite suddenly it seems, and took passage on a freighting vessel, bound for New York. Whatever it was that upset him so, he could not wait for the next passenger ship, and left with a small freighter and crew, apparently determined to get to America. The ship went down, somewhere off the coast of Florida. All aboard were lost. Pierre is quite worried for Gerard's grandfather. He had a hard time adjusting to Gerard's transfer, and Pierre fears that this news will be the death of him.*

Adrienne read the words again, as if they had been written in a language she did not understand. She dropped the letter on the dressing table; her hand covered her mouth. She couldn't breathe; her vision clouded as if she were going to faint. No, it couldn't be true. No. Her mind screamed, unable to accept this. Gerard, dead. Gerard, lost somewhere in the dark depths of the ocean. He *had* received her letter. He *had* tried to come for her. Her mind raced, careening from one ugly thought to another. Gerard. No. No. It could not be. Dead, because of her.

Adrienne slipped into the chair in front of the dressing table. She read the letter again and raised her eyes to the mirror. Not half an hour before, Marie had sat at this very table, looking into this very mirror, watching Adrienne's every move.

She was stunned, shocked to her core, her mind refusing the information in front of her. Marie knew. Marie knew that Gerard had been on his way to America. She must know that Adrienne had tried to contact him. Had she left this letter here, on purpose, for Adrienne to find? Marie had a desk, in her bedroom, where she managed most of her correspondence.

Adrienne looked at her reflection in the mirror, the face looking back at her a montage of shock and fear and the slow dawning of understanding. Marie knew. Adrienne swallowed. Time was up. She had to get out of here, and quickly.

∽

Adrienne's thoughts found focus. She stopped waiting, knowing that Gerard would not be coming for her. She stopped concentrating on Julien, on what he had done to her and what he might now be doing to other little girls. She stopped wondering what Marie knew about all of it. If she allowed it, the overwhelming pain of Gerard's death would surge up at her, threatening to pull her under its dark depths. She pushed it away. Later, she would let herself grieve. Right now, she had to focus; she had to gather all her resources to get out of there.

She moved around the castle, dust rag in hand, and found a plan clicking into place. In her mind, she practiced the phrases from the little English dictionary. *My name is Adrienne Beauvier. I need your help.* She conjured her escape, imagined every phase of the plan. She had rehearsed it a thousand times. Tonight, when they locked her in her room, she would pack her tapestry bag. Her one good dress, her one nightgown, the cloak from France that she wore when they went to church. She would find some opportunity, during her daily rounds of dusting tomorrow, to move that bag into the dark, damp staircase that laced the back of the castle, the servants' stairs. She had the dictionary packed inside, along with the coins she had managed to steal from Julien's dresser over the past months.

She sat in the kitchen, her plate of scrambled eggs in front of her. On the counter nearby was the tray that the nuns brought down, without fail, three times a day. Adrienne had seen the nun who delivered their meals. Her name was Hortense and she was very young, probably close to Adrienne's own age. If Adrienne or Marie were in the room when she came down, she always smiled and whispered "Good morning." Adrienne had never once been alone with her. Marie always hovered near the kitchen when it was time for the trays to arrive.

Adrienne stared at that tray. She turned and looked at the door in the kitchen, the one leading to the servants' stairs that laced the back of the castle. She remembered Julien telling them how one particular staircase entered a tunnel, an old mine shaft, that went up to Montcalme, to the sanitarium on the hill. Tomorrow, she would take that tapestry bag, sneak through that door and into the tunnel. She would need a candle for that time in the tunnel, and she had already planned to take the one that was in her bedroom on the fourth floor. She could picture walking into the kitchen at Montcalme. She could picture the surprise on the faces of the nuns when she walked through.

Adrienne stood and took her dishes to the sink. She began to wash, as she did every morning, her own plates and those of Marie and Julien. She dried them, stacked them neatly in the cupboard. Plates and cups and silverware stayed here in the kitchen, along with the things needed to make tea or coffee. The nuns brought only covered serving dishes, filled with food. Adrienne looked again at that tray. The nuns must have several. They carried one down, heaped with food, and another back up, piled high with the serving dishes from the meal before.

Adrienne dried her hands, hung the dish towel over the edge of the sink, and smoothed the front of her skirt. She leaned to one side, searching for signs of Marie in the adjoining dining room. Marie had finished her coffee and left the dishes at her place at the table. Sunlight flooded the table and chairs and the heavy wool rug beneath them. The table cast a glare into Adrienne's eyes.

Adrienne moved quietly to the door of the back staircase. She pulled it open, softly, just a few inches, and peeked inside. She knew there was more than one staircase; they went to every floor of the castle. She had no idea which one might lead to the tunnel, but it had to be somewhere off of the staircase that led here, into the kitchen.

"You can attend to my cup and saucer, since you have finished everything else." Marie stood in the doorway to the kitchen.

Adrienne jumped, and turned to her aunt. "Of course," she muttered.

"And I believe my bedroom needs dusting," Marie continued. Her eyes were locked on her niece.

"As you wish." Adrienne let her eyes drop to the floor between them, not trusting her face or her eyes. She felt certain that they would betray her if she looked directly at Marie.

All day, she watched. She watched the clock, waiting to see when Marie would go for her nap. Marie was very structured in her day and had become even more so as Julien's life fell apart in front of her. At three, Marie stood and placed her stitching on the chair behind her. "I'm going to lie down for a bit," she murmured.

Adrienne nodded, without looking up, trying to keep her eyes focused on her own stitching, trying to keep her face calm and serene. She heard Marie's shoes as they clicked up the stairs and across the floor overhead. Adrienne continued to stitch. She stabbed herself with the needle and drew her finger away to suck on the blood.

The door to Julien's study opened, and she heard him call the dogs. They whined; they pranced around the hall, anxious to go out. She heard Julien walking down the stairs, heard the crashing and bumping and boisterousness of the dogs, heard the click of the front door and the sudden quiet after the dogs went out. It was three thirty. Julien was usually gone for thirty or forty minutes.

Adrienne heard the ticking of the clock. If she was careful, if she timed it exactly right, she would have about half an hour between the time Julien left and Marie woke up from her nap. She prayed that it would be enough time to grab her bag, find the door to the tunnel, escape to the nuns, and somehow convince them to protect her should Julien appear at Montcalme looking for her.

One more day. Twenty-four more hours. Adrienne forced herself to breathe. She forced herself to keep stitching. Just one more day.

# CHAPTER THIRTY-EIGHT

They sat in the parlor. Night had folded around the castle. The fire burned; red-orange reflections danced on the wood floor. Julien sat at the pianoforte. He took a deep breath, started the melancholy air of Schubert's *Winterreise*. The notes rose in the air, sorrow moving across the room, pressing on Adrienne's shoulders.

She was jittery with anxiety, her plans knocking around in her head, almost making her feel dizzy. She swallowed, and the workings of her own throat seemed impossibly loud in the quiet night. She knew she would have to find something to keep her occupied this evening: something to keep her eyes down, away from Marie's gaze. She was certain her face would give her away if she didn't. Adrienne stood and moved to the bookshelves across the room. She ran her fingers along the top edges of the bindings, pretending to scan titles when in truth she wasn't quite sure what was on the shelf before her.

Adrienne reached for a book, *Les Misérables,* and moved back to her seat by the fire, carefully avoiding looking directly at Marie. She opened the book, forced her eyes to find the words. Marie moved to the sofa and held a glass of wine in front of Adrienne, the merlot like a liquid garnet in the crystal.

Adrienne reached for the glass and held it with one hand, trying to pretend absorption in her book. Marie moved across the room, placed a glass of wine on the pianoforte. Julien did not look at her. His eyes were closed; his shoulders swayed with the anguish of the piece he played.

Marie sat down in the wing chair, her black skirts swishing as she moved.

Adrienne did not look in her direction. She did not trust her eyes, did not trust her face. She willed herself to stay completely calm, tried to make her features look blank and peaceful and lost in the novel before her. For the third time, her eyes traveled over the opening sentence: "An hour before sunset, on the evening of a day in the beginning of October, 1815, a man traveling afoot entered the little town of D—"

Julien finished the piece he was playing. He raised his hand and shuffled through the sheet music lying on top of the pianoforte. Adrienne could see his long fingers; she almost retched with the thought of those fingers brushing over the hands of the little girls. Brushing over her own hands all those years ago.

She shook her head and tried again to concentrate on the words of the book in front of her. The amber light of the fire glowed on everything: on one side of Marie's face, on the polished wood of the floor. Marie looked up from her stitching. Her eyes caught Adrienne's. She lifted her wineglass and sipped, her eyes never leaving the face of her niece.

Adrienne dropped her eyes back to the book. She raised her eyes and her glass of wine at the same time. She took a long, slow sip. She glanced at Julien, who had stopped playing, his hands arrested over the keys, as if he had lost his train of thought. Adrienne was acutely aware of every sound, every sensation in the room. The clock ticked. The fire crackled and popped. She could hear the thread as it pulled through the fabric of Marie's stitching.

She turned her gaze back to the page. She took another sip of her wine, starting to feel slightly sick. Her pulse raced; her face grew warm. She felt dizzy, as if the entire world had started to spin.

"Drink, Adrienne. It is getting late." Adrienne raised her eyes to the face of her aunt. Marie's eyes gleamed in the firelight, a glint of triumph in their dark depths, a hint of a smile brushing the corners of her mouth.

Adrienne raised the glass to her lips and drained it. Slow liquid warmth flowed down her throat and into her chest.

Adrienne. Marie had called her Adrienne. Adrienne lowered the glass, stared at the fire. She couldn't remember the last time Marie had called her Adrienne. For a moment, she felt as if she were at the back of some long tunnel, sound coming to her from far away, muffled and indistinct. Marie and Julien and the fire in the grate seemed a tremendous distance away.

Julien raised his head, took his own glass of wine. She watched his Adam's apple move as he swallowed. She could hear it, a swallow that seemed inordinately loud and far too slow. This was not normal. She could almost hear the workings of his throat, could hear the swishing of the wine as it made its way down his esophagus. Nothing that she looked at or heard was normal.

Adrienne rubbed her hand against her forehead. The beginnings of a headache pinched at her temples and between her eyes. The corners of the room began to move forward and back, as if she were in the throes of fever.

The word slammed into her consciousness with the sudden bang of a drum. *Poison.* She shuddered, swallowed, sat up straighter. Her breath caught. Poison. Adrienne lowered the glass to her lap, trained her eyes on the flames of the fire. She cast a sidelong glance at Marie, her own eyes held low, trying to see Marie through her lashes.

Marie sat in the wing chair. She was stitching again, her needle poking through the fabric, her arm extending as she pulled the thread. Every now and then she stopped, raised her own glass of wine, and sipped. She appeared to be absorbed in what she was doing.

Adrienne moved her glass in a slow circle, staring at the few drops of crimson liquid that still lay in the bottom. She wrapped both hands around it. Wasn't it normally Julien who poured the wine? Adrienne tried to pull back the memories of every other night in the parlor. One evening floated into the next, a relentless repetition. They were all alike. Marie stitched. Julien played. Adrienne read. They drank a glass of wine. They knelt on the carpet, prayed the Rosary. Marie followed her up the stairs and locked the door behind her. But she could swear that it was Julien who usually poured the wine.

She raised her eyes to Marie, who continued to stitch. She felt light-headed, queasy, as if she had already drunk far too much of whatever potion Marie had concocted. Her head pounded. She was lost in a fog, her body sitting in the parlor, her mind fuzzy. She could not begin to sift through the thoughts that pounded in her brain, the foreboding that crept up her arms and raised the hair on the back of her neck.

"I'm . . . I'm not feeling very well this evening," Adrienne murmured. She leaned forward, and with a shaky hand, placed her wineglass on the low table before her. "I don't think I can manage . . ." She swallowed hard and looked up at Marie again. "I feel as if I might be sick." As if to corroborate her words, sweat broke out on her forehead and upper lip. Her face went completely pale.

"Hmmm," Marie murmured, eyeing her own wine. Her eyes flicked up to Adrienne. "You cannot manage prayers this evening?"

Adrienne felt herself flush with color. A rush of heat spread up her spine and into her face. Sweat pooled on her lip. "No, I . . . I think I had better lie down," she whispered. She rose, swaying slightly on her feet.

*"Bonne nuit."* Adrienne bent her head slightly to Marie. She turned and ducked her head toward Julien. He didn't look in her direction.

# CHAPTER THIRTY-NINE

Adrienne lay on the narrow bed upstairs, turning first to face the wall next to the bed, and then back again, facing the wall just a few feet away. She couldn't stop the fluttering in her stomach. Her mind raced. Too many thoughts fought for her attention, and she could not concentrate on any of them, her mind swimming with murky, surrealistic images.

Adrienne turned on her side again. Her mind was playing tricks on her. She was dizzy and dazed and could not focus. The walls of her narrow room pushed in on her, as if she were caught in a vise. It reminded her of the time when she was six years old and had the chicken pox. Her fever had gone dangerously high. She remembered the way the room receded and then grew large again, making her dizzy. Just how much poison had she ingested? She wished she knew more about it, knew of some way to counteract the effects of whatever this drug was.

Adrienne turned over again, her eyes searching the darkness of the room. The sounds of life below her had stopped. The castle was quiet. The grandfather clock in the ballroom below her pounded out twelve strokes. They reverberated through the floor. Tomorrow. She was leaving tomorrow. She chanted it in her head like a mantra, like a prayer. Tomorrow. She was leaving tomorrow. If she didn't die tonight from the poison, if her body could fight off the effects for just a few more hours, she would be gone.

She rolled onto her back and lay staring at the ceiling. She let out one long breath, trying to quiet her racing mind and queasy stomach. Mice ran along the rafters in the roof above her. She could hear them scratching and chewing somewhere over her head. She watched as the ceiling started playing tricks on her. One corner of the room stretched away from her, as if the room had grown to ten times its normal size. Her breath caught; her stomach clenched with the flutterings of panic. She kept her eyes on the corner of the ceiling, cringed as it began to grow larger and larger, before moving back toward her as if the room were shrinking.

The sound slipped under the door and into her consciousness, as imperceptible as a feather falling. Something, someone, was outside her room, moving quietly in the dark. She strained her ears, wondering if her mind had failed her completely. Was the poison making her imagine things? She wondered if she could trust any of her own perceptions right now. But no, there was the sound again, closer. She heard footsteps, soft and deliberate, on the back stairs. The sound was on the servants' stairs: the ones only Adrienne and the nuns from Montcalme ever used. She stared into the dark, waiting. Her body focused and tensed toward the sound. Listening.

The footsteps reached the fourth floor, moved tentatively down the hallway toward Adrienne's door. Adrienne scanned the dark. Marie. Come to find out if the poison had worked or if she would have to use more. Or would she try something more serious? Had she, like Adrienne, been dreaming of ways to commit murder? Ways to rid herself of her troublesome niece?

She heard the door to the room push inward, just a breath of sound as it moved against the floor. Adrienne closed her eyes and pretended to sleep.

The footsteps moved forward, slow, conscious, steps that skimmed carefully in the dark, barely brushing across the floor. Adrienne felt a pressure on the mattress next to her, felt the warmth of another person sitting next to her on the bed. She heard breathing. She forced herself to breathe, forced the slow, unhurried breaths of a sleeper. She felt her eyelids flutter, willed them to stay still.

Someone slipped off the mattress to the floor and knelt beside the bed. Cold fingers reached under the covers and brushed against her arm. Adrienne pictured the syringe, could almost feel the sting of the needle in her vein, poison pushing into her bloodstream, rushing its way toward her heart.

The hand moved away from her arm. Long, slender fingers lingered on her breasts, moving slowly toward her belly, and between her legs.

Adrienne's eyes shot open; she jerked. She tried to sit up.

"Adrienne," Julien whispered. "You're awake."

She gasped. He moved up from the floor and perched on the side of the bed, his hip next to hers. His hand pressed against her shoulder, pushing her back against the mattress.

"I saw you," he murmured into the dark. "Tonight. Watching me. Staring at me." The lids of his eyes drooped, heavy and curved. His breath smelled of wine, and beneath that, brandy. "I've seen you watching me, for a while now. You watch me from the windows." His eyes held that feverish gleam that she had seen before—that same feverish gleam she had noticed when Eliza Creighton had come to visit. "The windows in my room." He smiled, his breath a puff of amusement. "I know exactly what you're doing. I know exactly what you want."

He shoved her shoulder down and leaned toward her face. His breath was sour. Adrienne started to squirm, tried to tear away from the force that bore down on her. He brought his other hand up and clamped it over her mouth. His eyes glowed, fire sparkling in their dark depths. She fought as hard as she could, terrified that he was there to kill her, to silence her forever.

With one hand, he continued to hold Adrienne's mouth shut, his arm stretching across her body with a strength that seemed far beyond his size, his infirmity. He pushed her into the thin, hard mattress. Adrienne squirmed harder. She raised her back, trying to force him up. She kicked against the mattress, the covers flying up.

Julien brought his right hand back and slapped her, hard, on the side of the head. "Hold still," he hissed. Adrienne stopped moving. Her head throbbed with pain; for a moment, her vision blurred.

He fumbled with his pajama bottoms with one hand, the other still clamped on Adrienne's mouth. He pulled the covers back, yanked her gown up, and pushed himself on top of her. She writhed and fought, but he held her tightly and fought harder, forcing her legs apart with his knee. When he thrust himself inside, she gasped. Her back arched. The pain shot up through her spine, straight to her eyes. They smarted and stung.

"Ah!" she gasped, her mouth growing hot and wet inside his palm. She tried to fight him with her free arm, and he drove into her harder. Her blood pulsed, her pelvis throbbed with a red-hot light, like holding a hand over the flame. She felt as if she might faint.

He gasped, moved again, his breath coming out in ragged, sour puffs right over her face. His eyes were closed; he drove into her again and again and again with an angry force.

Tears escaped, running down the sides of her face and onto the pillow. She wanted to cry, wanted to scream, but his hand held her tight, squeezed against her lips, forced her head against the pillow. His elbow trapped her hair. Every time he moved, it pulled against her scalp. She stopped moving, stopped trying to fight. Every motion sent her reeling, a throbbing, aching, burning pressure against her limbs, her back, her pelvis.

Julien moaned, fell on her, his body knocking the wind out of her. He lay there, his body heavy against her. He panted. Adrienne felt tears running from her eyes, pooling in her hair.

He took his hand away from her mouth and rolled off of her. He smiled, his teeth bright in the dim light. He stood, straightened his nightclothes, and looked down. She stared at him through her tears, this man who could be so brutal. Her thighs burned. Her insides screamed with a white-hot pain. She felt wet, sticky, and dirty, like during her monthly.

"I've been watching you, Adrienne. Watching you, watching me. Keeping an eye on me. You can hardly keep your hands off of me, can you?" He humphed into the air. "I knew it. I knew you wanted it. That glow . . . that stare . . ." He turned and ran his hand over her breast. He smiled again, into the dark. "Anytime, my dear. Anytime at all." He turned and moved softly to the door.

"Don't worry," he whispered, his hands on the door. "I won't tell my mother what a little whore you are."

She heard him turn the key in the lock.

# CHAPTER FORTY

Morning light seeped through the window and spread through the room, but Adrienne was only dimly aware of it. Marie unlocked the door and pushed it open. Adrienne lay on her side on the bed, curled into a ball. She did not turn to look at her aunt; she did not acknowledge the woman's presence.

"Are you ill?" Marie asked.

Adrienne did not respond.

Marie took another step into the room. "Adrienne? Are you ill?" she asked again.

Adrienne said nothing. She did not shift on the bed.

Marie took another slow step forward. Adrienne heard her swallow, heard her turn and leave the room. The door closed with a soft click.

Adrienne curled tighter, put her hands between her knees. Pain gripped her, flashes of red light behind her eyelids. Her jaw hurt where he had pinched it; her neck and shoulders ached from the pressure of his arms on her. The lower part of her body burned. She knew there was blood trickling between her legs, drying on the sheets, but she did not want to move, did not want to look at the evidence of what had happened.

Worse, though, than the physical pain was the swirl of emotions in her mind. She had been living in a dream world, waiting for rescue, waiting for escape. She had managed, somehow, to banish all the loss, all the pain, that she had sustained in the last few years. Like dolls on a shelf, she had neatly put away the thoughts of Lucie, Gerard, Emelie, and Antoine, her home in Beaulieu, her former life. She had foolishly believed that some day, she would see them all again. Now the wreckage of her life came crashing down on her, crushing her lungs, stealing her breath. Tears trickled from the corners of her eyes. Her losses were enormous. And now this final act of robbery.

Adrienne knew little about the act of love. Certainly she knew none of the details. But when Gerard had touched the small of her back as they walked on the castle grounds, when she felt his eyes on her as she moved about the drawing room, she had imagined. She had imagined kissing him, holding him, spending every night in his arms.

Adrienne cringed and drew her body closer, tighter, as if she could curl into a ball that no horror could ever penetrate. It was not supposed to be like this. It was not supposed to have happened like this. Again, yet again, the things that were most precious to her had been stolen, ripped away, like spring blossoms in a terrifying wind.

She had no one to turn to, no shoulder to cry on. Loneliness had followed her since she was little, always at her side. Now it took on a force like a hurricane, a wide swath of destruction left in its wake. It was too much. Grand-père—gone. Lucie—gone. Her family—gone. Gerard—gone. Marie, filling her glass with some slow-acting poison. And now this.

Adrienne turned onto her back and stared up at the ceiling. All thought of escape had fled. She no longer cared if she lived or died. If it were true that Gerard was dead, then there was no reason to go on. And if it were not true, if he were still alive, still somewhere waiting for her, she knew she could never go to him. Not like this. Not damaged and soiled and shamed as she was.

Adrienne raised her hand to her mouth and bit her finger. Tears rolled down her cheeks. No. No. She could never tell anyone about this. She could not go to the sisters on the hill. Shame washed through her, and her hands trembled at the thought of the way they would look at her. Questioning the truth of what she said. Judging her. Condemning her. Just like the villagers in Beaulieu had done when she was a child. No matter what awful things Julien might have done, Adrienne knew that it was she who would bear the heavy burden of shame.

She had not asked for it, not for this; he was wrong about that. But she had been watching him, for some time now. There had been moments in the evenings, before prayers, when she had caught herself staring at him. Trying to see inside his soul, trying to figure out who he really was and what he might be up to.

She turned on her side again and stifled a small sob. She knew far more about him than she wanted to. She wished, now that it was too late, that she had never started spying on him, had never attempted to learn the truth.

Hatred surged up from the core of her being. "I want him dead," she whispered to her quiet room. She wanted both of them dead. She wanted him to twist and writhe in pain, to burn with shame and humiliation. She wanted them to suffer, both of them, for what they had done to her.

But more than anything else, she just wanted to be left alone.

# CHAPTER FORTY-ONE

Nothing changed. Everything changed.

The sun still came up every morning. Marie still climbed the stairs and unlocked the door to Adrienne's attic room. Adrienne still got dressed, still took the back stairs, the servants' stairs, down to the kitchen. She took the cover off her breakfast tray, stared at the food the nuns had brought. She went through all the same motions, just like she'd been doing for months.

But everything inside her was dead. She had no appetite. She poked at the food, pushed it around the plate. She no longer did anything to help Marie. She did not do her hair; she did not pick up her clothing. She no longer dusted. She did not pretend to be the maid, Henriette. And miraculously, Marie did not ask her to.

There was nothing to fuel her any longer. She had no desire to stand at the front windows and stare at the ladies walking by in their fine dresses. She had no interest in where Julien went, or what he did. She didn't care if Marie lived or died, spoke or stayed silent. She did not read. She did not stand at the window, drinking in the sight of the mountains. She did not watch for the birds to return. She did nothing. She sat in a chair, staring, seeing nothing. Feeling nothing.

Her life was a blank slate, a pale, wasted gray. She felt no anger, no revulsion, no hatred, no shame, because she felt nothing. She knew that if, for one moment, she allowed one sliver of emotion to slip through, it would destroy her, like a wooden stake through the heart of a vampire.

She sat, mostly in her own room at the top of the stairs. It was the one place that neither Julien nor Marie would frequent. She stared. She held her hands in her lap, still and quiet.

And when evening came, and she was expected in the parlor, she found a seat in the corner. She was careful not to look anywhere near Julien's direction. When he touched his fingers to the pianoforte, when the notes sailed up into the room, she heard only a distant sound, like a long-forgotten memory.

Marie poured wine, every evening. Three glasses. She always took Adrienne's glass to her first. Adrienne wrapped her hands around it, stared into the rich liquid garnet, raised the glass to her lips, and drained it. She could almost feel the look of satisfaction on Marie's face. She knew the vial of poison was in the pocket of Marie's skirt. Sometimes she stared, as if she could see the bottle through the fabric. She only hoped it was strong enough: strong enough to erase everything, strong enough to get the job done, and soon.

This night was just like every other. They sat, bathed in the red glow of firelight. Marie made a feeble attempt at stitching, her eyes traveling back and forth between the linen in her lap and Adrienne's face, hard and indifferent, her eyes locked on the fire. Julien played.

Marie stood, laid her stitching on her chair, and walked to the bar in the corner. Her heels clicked on the floor. The clock ticked; the pendulum squeaked. The chime rang the time: eight thirty. Marie poured the wine.

She moved to Adrienne, held the glass out. Adrienne let her eyes brush over Marie's face. She took the glass in her hand and held it in her lap. Marie carried another glass to Julien. He stopped playing and took the glass. He, too, seemed distracted, his attention lost in some other time, some other place.

Marie took her own wine, lifted her stitching, and sat down in the wing chair.

Adrienne held her glass up toward the light of the fire. She watched the way the golds and oranges of the flames flickered behind the crystal. "Wouldn't arsenic be quicker?" Her words cut like ice in the quiet room.

Julien looked at her, then at Marie.

"What are you talking about?" Marie glared. One tiny flicker of fear moved over her face.

"Laudanum is fine, I guess," Adrienne continued, still staring into the wineglass she held to the light. She lowered the glass, met Marie's eyes. "It's just so damn slow." Adrienne had never before used a curse word, and she found it gave her a feeling of power.

Marie swallowed. She glowered at Adrienne.

Julien looked from one to the other. "Maman, what is she talking about?"

Marie did not look at him. Her eyes were locked on her niece.

"What are you saying?" He turned to Adrienne, his face still filled with shock.

Adrienne smiled. Here was a power she never knew she had: the power to use her words, whether true or not, to cause trouble. She was frightening to them because it was just possible that she knew the truth about them both. And the truth carried far more force than she had ever believed. The truth could destroy them both. Adrienne stared at her aunt.

"I know you are poisoning my wine, Marie. I've known for quite some time." Adrienne rotated the glass in front of her, allowing the flames of the fire to shoot through the crystal. "I just wish you would use something stronger. Something quicker. Arsenic, maybe. Or strychnine. Isn't that what you used with Julien's father?

Strychnine?" Adrienne lowered her glass and let her eyes rest on Marie's face.

From the corner of her eye, she watched as Julien's eyes grew wide. She watched him turn to his mother, anguish written in every centimeter of his features.

"Let me think . . . he was what . . . thirty-seven when he died? Is that right?" Adrienne stared. The sense of power she felt, the look of horror on Julien's face, the look of hatred and loathing on Marie's, was much more gratifying than she could have imagined. "Awfully young, at any rate."

"How dare you?" Marie rose from her seat and stood in the middle of the room, her arms clenched and tight by her sides.

"I always wondered how you knew so much about poison— and antidotes—when Julien was poisoned. You must have made a study of them? Is that required training in French diplomacy?"

Julien rose from the pianoforte. He moved slowly to the middle of the room, looking from one face to the other. Adrienne slouched in her chair, her wineglass held in one hand. She didn't bother to look at either one of them, only stared at the flames before her, half a smile playing on her lips. There was none of the fear, none of the panic that would have filled her face and posture just a few weeks ago.

Adrienne raised her wineglass to her lips, and drained it. She stood, put the wineglass on the table. *"Bonne nuit."* She dipped in a small curtsy, dropped her eyes, just as a proper servant would.

She turned and left the room, but she felt herself grow taller, her steps sure and confident as she climbed the stairs to her room. She smiled in the dark. Why had she never thought of this before? She had had no vision, possessed no knowledge that Marie had poisoned her own husband. But it didn't matter. They didn't know that. Adrienne sucked her bottom lip between her teeth, fighting a smile. The satisfaction was enormous.

# CHAPTER FORTY-TWO

Like the deep waters of the ocean, currents of electricity flowed through the castle. Each of the two older people took pains to avoid getting caught in them. Julien and Marie no longer took meals together in the dining room. When their trays arrived, carried through the servants' stairway by one of the nuns, Julien would take his to his office. Marie took hers to the dining room. They were careful to avoid going into the kitchen at the same time. Neither one of them ate much.

Adrienne was no longer asked to perform any of the duties of a maid. Julien and Marie seemed to forget that she existed at all. Marie did not come up the stairs in the evening; she no longer locked Adrienne in her attic room. They did not gather in the parlor. Julien did not play the piano. Marie did not stitch. No one drank wine. No one said prayers together.

Julien spent his time sitting at the desk in his office, his fingers pressed together at the tips, going back over his childhood. He wondered what secrets Marie had hidden from him, wondered what atrocities the woman was actually capable of. Anyone who could manage the torture she had inflicted on Adrienne could be capable of a great deal. And perhaps that explained why she had taken such pains to keep Adrienne isolated, unable to spread stories to the family or servants.

Marie spent her time wondering what Julien had done, wondering what Adrienne knew. There were whole days that she stayed in bed, coughing, too tired to get up.

For Adrienne, the whole world had turned gray, had lost every small stroke of color. For the first time since arriving at the castle, no one watched her; no one locked her up at night. She could have wandered the rooms. She could have stepped outside and inhaled the cold, crisp air of winter. She could have walked away. But she did none of those things. She went down to the kitchen each morning, drank the tea left by the nuns, knowing that Marie had begun to put the laudanum there, since the family no longer drank wine in the parlor at night.

She was dreaming of Gerard. It had happened several times now, always the same dream. She was on a ship, in the middle of the ocean. Night had turned everything to gray and black. Pale moonlight washed the water, making it a slightly lighter gray than the sky above it. She stood at the railing, felt the salt breeze on her face and her hair. She closed her eyes. It was a feeling she had not had before, a feeling of freedom. In the dream, she smiled, just slightly, and tipped her head to the side.

And there he was, coming up out of the water, as if he had been somewhere in its depths. He appeared magically on the horizon, moving toward the ship. Walking on water. Like the sea and sky around her, he was gray. Shades of gray, his face paler than the rest of him. He smiled when he saw her. She smiled back.

And then she woke. The first time the dream had come to her, she cried when she realized where she was—that she was still in her dim attic room. But lately, she woke with a smile on her face. She could feel him, close to her. Feel him, as if he were just outside the door and would be here any moment. As if he were, indeed, coming to rescue her.

Adrienne sat in the kitchen. Morning light, the weak, watered-down sunlight of winter, streamed across the floor. She lifted the cover from her breakfast tray and stared at the eggs on the plate. Her head hurt. She was tired. The eggs stared up at her, greasy orbs that made her retch. She dropped the cover on the table and rushed to the sink, trying not to be sick on the floor.

The clatter of the dishes brought Julien to the door of the room. He looked at the spattered eggs on the table and turned to hear Adrienne retching in the sink. "Adrienne?"

She leaned over the sink, spitting. She was clammy with sweat, so nauseated she could barely stand. She turned on the cold water, rinsed the sink, and cupped water to her face. She cupped another handful, carried it around to the back of her neck. It dripped onto her dress, wet the curls that had escaped from the knot of hair at her neck.

She turned. Julien stood in the doorway. She felt her legs grow weak and she swayed, slowly, like a dancer. Then she dropped to the floor.

Julien gasped, horror filling his bloodstream. "Adrienne?" He moved to her crumpled form, patted her face. "Adrienne?"

Marie appeared in the kitchen door. "What's wrong?"

Julien turned to look at her. "You've given her too much," he spat.

Marie glared back at him. "I didn't do this," she hissed.

Julien shot her a piercing stare. He turned back to Adrienne. Her eyes were rolled back; her breathing was shallow; her face and hands were a pale yellow color. "I'll lay her in the chapel. Bring some tea."

Despite Adrienne's slender frame, he struggled with her weight. His chest heaved, and he coughed as he carried her across the hall and into the small room that he sometimes used for prayer. He laid her on a narrow couch, straightened her limbs and her head.

Marie came behind him. She had poured a cup of tea from the teapot Adrienne had left on the table. Julien looked at the cup and then raised his eyes to his mother. "Is this clean? No poison?"

Marie glowered at him. "Only tea."

Julien held Adrienne's head, and Marie attempted to pour liquid into her mouth. Adrienne sputtered. Tea poured from the sides of her mouth, darkening the collar of her dress and the silk upholstery of the couch. Julien laid her head back again. She did not open her eyes.

He stood. He knew now that he could not just stand by and watch the girl die. "I'll go find Doctor Creighton." He turned and faced his mother. "Don't touch her."

"Julien, I—"

"I said don't touch her." He watched as his mother sank down onto a chair, her eyes glued to Adrienne's pale, limp form. He pushed past his mother. The front door slammed.

It was half an hour before the voices of Julien and Dr. Creighton carried in the cool air. Their boots thudded on the steps as they hurried up. Dr. Creighton moved into the room. He nodded to Marie and knelt beside the couch. He opened his bag, took out his stethoscope, held it to Adrienne's chest. He raised her eyelids, examined her eyes.

He turned back toward Julien and Marie. "Leave us," he ordered.

Marie stood and trailed Julien out of the room. Julien closed the door. Marie found a chair in the great hallway, ran her hand on the cushion, and sank into it, as if she could not see, as if she were blind and feeling her way into a chair. Julien did not look at her. He paced up and down the hall, his hands held behind his back.

Ages passed before the door opened, and Dr. Creighton stood, leaning against the doorframe. His stethoscope hung around his neck; his shirt collar was unbuttoned, his jacket off, his sleeves rolled to the elbows. Julien stopped pacing.

Dr. Creighton began unrolling his sleeves, fastening the cuffs. "Has she been eating?" he demanded. He looked from Julien to Marie, and back again.

"I . . . I don't really know," Julien answered. "We don't . . . She doesn't take her meals with us." He looked nervous. He turned to Marie, asked the question in French.

Marie shook her head, held her hands to the sides. "I do not know if she has been eating," she answered in French.

The doctor turned from Marie to Julien. Julien translated Marie's answer.

The doctor stared at Julien. "Well, she needs to. The girl is pregnant."

Julien's eyes grew wide. He swallowed. His eyes flickered back to his mother's face.

Marie looked at him, puzzled.

"Baby . . . *bébé*," Dr. Creighton said to her. He held his hands in front of his stomach, illustrating.

Marie's hand flew to her mouth. "No." She shook her head. "No. That's not possible . . . How could she possibly be . . ." She stopped, and her eyes found Julien's. He couldn't have. He couldn't have. Her eyes went back to Dr. Creighton, down to the floor, traveled to the partially opened door that hid Adrienne behind it. She looked back at Julien. The dart of his eyes, the twitch of his mouth, told her that it was, indeed, possible.

Dr. Creighton took the stethoscope from his neck and put it back in his bag. He raised his eyes to Julien. "She needs rest. She needs to eat. Make sure it happens. I'll be back to check her in a day or two." His jaw clenched. Dr. Creighton grabbed his bag and strode down the stairs, anger pounding through his heels, bouncing and echoing on the walls.

# CHAPTER FORTY-THREE

Adrienne turned on her side on the narrow couch. Tears slid slowly from the edges of her eyes and dropped onto the satin fabric. She stared at the bay window across the room. Beveled glass caught the sunlight, bent it, spread geometric shapes around the walls and ceiling and floor. How could she not have known? If her powers to see, to hear, were truly so great, how could she not have known that she carried a child—his child—inside her?

She felt dirty. Shamed to the very core of her being. She blushed, even now, at the look she had seen in the doctor's eyes. She heard his broken attempts to tell her, to explain what was wrong. She heard him, standing in the hall, breaking the news to Julien and Marie.

She saw her grand-père's face, and bit her lip, burying her head in the couch cushion. She could not look him in the eye, not even in her imagination, with this new development. She pictured Gerard—saw his eyes, dark and gentle, as the two of them had stood at Grand-père's grave in the blustery winds of winter twilight. She shook her head, trying to blot out the image. What would Gerard think of her now? What would anyone think?

Marie pushed the door open and carried a tray into the room. She laid it on the floor, pulled a small table next to the couch. Its legs scraped against the wood. She bent, picked up the tray, and placed it on the table. She looked at Adrienne. Adrienne did not meet her eyes; she did not speak. Marie stood for another moment, her skirts still moving slightly. She turned and left the room.

Adrienne glanced at the tray: teapot, cup and saucer, sugar and creamer, a delicate silver spoon. There was a plate with two slices of buttered toast. Adrienne looked away. She would never feed this . . . this . . . Her breath caught, hung in her throat. This baby. This child of a nightmare. She would never eat again.

She lay on her side, staring out the windows. She watched as the light changed, slowly, from the bright glare of morning to a softer, clouded gold of afternoon. When the color had started to fade, when the room had dimmed, the door opened.

Marie looked at the tray beside Adrienne, untouched. The cold toast was shriveled and hard. Marie picked it up and carried it out of the room. Several minutes later, she came back, another tray in hand.

Adrienne almost smiled into the cushion: Marie, waiting on her. Marie, carrying a tray, just like a servant. Marie, forced to be the one to care for Adrienne. Julien could not, would not. And Marie was unwilling to take the chance and ask the nuns on the hill for help. There was always the chance that they might talk about Julien, that the sisters might spread word of Adrienne's "illness."

Marie slid the tray onto the table. She turned toward Adrienne. She picked up the cup, poured the tea out in a slender, steaming stream. She dropped in a lump of sugar, poured the cream. The spoon clinked against the sides of the cup.

Marie held the cup in front of Adrienne's unfocused eyes. "Drink your tea, Adrienne," she whispered. "It will make you feel better."

Adrienne's eyes shot up to her aunt's face, dim and smoky in the waning light. She'd heard that tone before . . . Where was it? It seemed many lifetimes ago. "Drink your tea, Adrienne. Drink your tea, Adrienne." The words echoed in Adrienne's head. "Drink your wine, Adrienne."

Adrienne looked up at Marie, who stood holding the teacup in her hand. Adrienne looked at it, at the thin, almost translucent china of the cup. She pushed herself to a sitting position, took the cup and saucer in hands that shook. The cup rattled and sloshed. Adrienne brought it down to her lap, raised the cup in her right hand, and sipped.

Marie breathed a long, slow sigh.

Adrienne looked up at her. She sipped again. She stared at Marie, as she slowly drank every drop. She held the cup and saucer out to Marie. *"Merci,"* she whispered. She only thought the rest: there was no need to say the words out loud. "Thank you. Thank you for the poison. Thank you for helping me get this over with. I certainly hope you've been able to find something stronger than laudanum." They knew, they both knew, all the ways that Marie had been wrong. Adrienne lay back down on the couch, on her side. She pulled her legs up, curled into herself, like a baby.

Marie took the tray and pulled the door closed when she left.

Baby. Baby. The word bounced around the room. It screamed inside her head. Baby. Julien's baby.

Adrienne sat up, threw off the blanket. She paced to the window, pulled back the lace curtain, stared into the blue dark of twilight. She laid her head against the cold glass. Tears made silent trails down her face, glistening in the pale light of the moon. The decision came quickly. After all this time, after all this loss, her determination was rigid and unyielding. She had tolerated far too much suffering.

She turned, walked across the room, turned the handle, and softly pulled the door open. She leaned forward into the hallway, looking, listening. The castle was dark. Everything was quiet. She heard no noise in the parlor, could see no glow from the fire, or the lamps. She moved across the hall, into the kitchen. She opened the drawer with the knives, the same knives she had used to cut the cake for the Creighton family not so long ago. She reached in, picked up a long, slender handle, the blade curving slightly at the end. She looked at it, ran her finger over the tip of the blade.

She laid the knife against her skirt and moved quietly back across the hall. She closed the door of the chapel behind her, the click just a soft note in the quiet room. She sat down on the couch and held the knife in front of her. She ran her fingers over it, again and again, stroking the silver blade.

Adrienne looked up. She looked into the dark eyes of Archbishop Lamy, a portrait Julien had purchased when he left New Mexico. Her eyes rose to the rosary draped on the wall next to it. They flicked to the statue of Jesus hanging on the cross. It clung to a narrow strip of wall between the windows. His shoulders were slumped, his forehead dripping blood from his crown of thorns. His eyes, like hers, were unfocused, unseeing, as he waited for the agony to be over.

She stared at him. Waiting for the agony to be over. That was a feeling that she knew far too well. Here she was, not twenty years old, and her life had been one agony after another. She could not remember anything else; all that had been good in her life was lost, ripped away. All she felt at this moment was a horrible, swirling soup of shame, fear, revulsion, anger. But the worst of all was the hopelessness. She no longer expected God to help her. She no longer believed that *anyone* could help her.

Adrienne's eyes dropped to the knife. She pictured Marie sitting at the dressing table in her room. She pictured standing behind her at the dressing table, the knife held hidden in the folds of her skirt. She pictured grabbing Marie by the hair, yanking her head backward. She pictured drawing the blade across that neck, blood shooting onto the mirror, and the floor, and all over her hands.

In her mind, she walked, in a trance, down the hall to Julien's bedroom. She pictured sneaking up on him, the way he had snuck up on her. She pictured standing next to his bed, watching as he became aware of her—watching as he woke from sleep to find her standing over him, holding the knife in both hands. She pictured raising her arms above her head and driving that blade as hard as she could into his chest. She could see the fountain of blood; she could see his eyes fill with shock and horror as life escaped his body.

Adrienne ran her finger along the blade. She looked at the way the silver caught the moonlight, sending slender streams of pale white light flashing around the room. She turned the knife slowly and then laid it against her wrist, testing the weight of it, the feel of it in her hand. She watched her vein pulse from the pressure. She looked up again, at Jesus. At the savior. She thought of all the teachings of the church, all the words of Père Henri as he cautioned a much younger Adrienne about the "wages of sin."

She would go to hell. She knew that. For what she'd just thought—for what she was about to do. Hellfire. Eternal damnation. But could hell be any worse than this? Hell was living in this prison, tortured by two people she hated, pregnant with the child of a man she abhorred.

Her eyes dropped to her wrist, pale and creamy in the moonlight. She turned the blade on its edge. She drew a deep breath, pulled the blade across her wrist, as deep as she could make it cut. The pain caused her eyes to water. Blood oozed, and then began to pour. Her hand grew wet and sticky. Blood ran down her arm, onto her skirt. She dropped the knife. It bounced on the floor.

She sat, staring into the moonlight coming through the windows, waiting for her life to leak away. Her eyes grew heavy. An exhaustion heavier than anything she had ever known pulled at her, dragging her down into its murky depths. She lay down on her side, her bloody arm between her body and the couch, but held out, like a stiff branch. Blood poured onto the floor, a slender river cascading from her arm. She closed her eyes. Sighed. A smile turned up the corners of her mouth. It was almost over. The fear, the pain, the shame. Almost over. Relief. At long last . . . relief.

# CHAPTER FORTY-FOUR

Marie opened the door to the chapel the next morning, tray in hand. For a moment, her mind could not register the sight before her. She dropped the tray; it clattered on the floor. China shattered, tea poured along the floorboards. Marie's hands rose to her mouth. The smell was sickening, metallic and rusty. She moved forward slowly, her skirts dragging through the blood. She reached for the knife that had fallen to the floor and held it, blood marking her hands.

She bent over, blood rushing to her head, forcing her to reach for a wall and slide her body slowly to the floor. The smell, the blood, was overpowering. She held her hand over her mouth and nose, tried to fight back the bile that threatened to erupt from her throat.

Julien appeared behind her, drawn by the crash. "Oh my God!"

He rushed past Marie, knelt on the floor next to Adrienne, his pants growing damp from the pool of thickening blood. He held his hand to her neck and reached for a pulse. Marie knew there was no need. Her body was cold and rigid.

He knelt next to her, his hand resting on her shoulder. Her eyes were closed. She looked almost peaceful. As if she'd gone to sleep.

Marie sat slumped against the wall, staring at the pool of blood. The knife dropped from her now-bloody hand and clattered on the floor.

The seconds ticked by, both of them utterly quiet.

For a moment, Marie was paralyzed with memory, no longer sitting in a room in Manitou Springs, but back again at Beaulieu. She was thirteen years old. She could hear the baby, Genevieve, wailing and crying. She moved toward the door of her mother's bedroom, an overwhelming dread filling her being. She heard the creak of the bedroom door as it swung open. Baby Genevieve lay in her bassinet, her screams punctuating the stillness in the room. The smell was the same; the pool of blood was the same. She moved closer to the body of her mother, lying on the bed. Her arm lay close by her side; blood had pooled under the wrist and leaked onto the bedding, onto Marguerite's nightgown. It pooled on the floor. Marie moved closer, her head shaking back and forth. Her foot hit against something. She bent down and picked up the knife that Marguerite had used to take her own life.

Marie could not scream. It caught in her throat and stayed there, frozen into stillness, as the baby's nurse rushed in behind her, her own screams loud and almost ludicrous in their ferocity. Marie had held the knife close against her own skirt, unwilling to let the nurse see it. Her father charged in a moment later, banishing the nurse from the room and quickly taking charge.

She remembered the months, the years, of walking into a room and seeing the dark eyes of the servants on her, their voices suddenly hushed. She remembered the stares of the people in the village. Her father had done his best to change the story, to make it sound as if Marguerite had died from complications of childbirth. He made a very large contribution to the church. Marguerite was buried in the family cemetery, with a full Christian burial. But the gossip never really died, and neither had the shame and humiliation and anger.

Marie had spent her whole life trying to make sure that no one would ever gossip about them again. She had spent her whole life trying to protect herself, and those she loved, from any further pain and disgrace. She had spent her whole life, and especially these past few years of controlling Adrienne, trying to avoid the pain and fear of that awful moment.

"We should . . . we need . . ." Marie began. She fought nausea, pulled a handkerchief from her pocket, and held it to her mouth and nose. She pushed herself up to her feet. "We . . . we have to get her out of here. The sisters will be coming with our trays . . . We cannot let anyone see this."

Julien nodded at her words. He could not meet her eyes, and she stared at the back of his head. How could he have done this? Here she was, nearing the end of her life, and worried, once again, that word of a suicide would travel through town. Worried that Dr. Creighton might reveal the reason that the young girl had taken her own life. All the nightmares that she had spent a lifetime trying to avoid were back again, slamming against her. And *he* was the cause. The son for whom she would do anything. The son she had bent heaven and earth to protect. Marie thought quickly, as she always had. It was February; the ground outside was frozen. Trying to dispose of the body outside was out of the question. Besides, what if someone, what if one of the nuns, should see him? She looked around the room, let her mind travel through the castle. Where could they put her? She thought of staircases, closets, the coal room in the basement. She thought of the many fireplaces. None of those would work. The smell would permeate the building. When the sisters came down from Montcalme with their trays of food, they would notice it immediately.

Julien stood, walked to the other side of the couch, out of the pool of blood, and knelt, sliding his arms under Adrienne's legs and shoulders. Heaving from the weight, he stood on shaky legs and turned toward the door. Adrienne's head tipped back; her hair fell in a sheet of reddish gold.

"I'll bury her," he whispered. "In my private chapel, at the other end of the parlor. There's a tunnel, an old mining tunnel, behind the north wall. We found it during construction. I think I can get her in there."

Marie nodded.

Julien shifted the weight in his arms. Adrienne's arm fell to the side. He maneuvered her through the door. "Could you . . ."

Marie stared at the puddles of blood on the floor. She held the handkerchief to her mouth. "I'll clean up," she whispered.

༄

Julien turned and walked down the hallway, to the other end of the castle. He laid Adrienne on the floor, next to the chapel door, while he fumbled with his keys. This was his personal chapel. He never allowed anyone in here. He found the key, jammed it into the lock. The door swung open.

He bent, and picked up the body once again. He panted, as if her slender weight had turned to lead with the alchemy of death. He carried her to the other end of the room. The room was stone on all four sides. Only one window shone in the space. It was small, high up on the wall. He laid her, again, on the floor.

He moved back to the door, went through to the parlor, and looked for some tool to work with. He returned with the letter opener, removed his jacket, and closed the door to the chapel behind him. He began to chip at the mortar between the stones, the stones that lined the back wall of the room, next to the mountainside.

It took several hours. The light in the window had paled to gray when he had finally removed enough of the stones to fit himself through. He wiped the dust from his hands, lit a candle, and stepped into the dark, damp space. He shivered. The belly of the mountain swallowed him in its eerie silence.

Julien went back, slipped his hands under Adrienne's arms, and pulled, sliding her, one tug at a time, into the tunnel. He crouched, pulled her several feet into the tunnel, and laid her body on the cold, damp earth. He arranged her limbs, which had grown stiff in the hours of digging. He thought of getting a blanket, her cloak, something to wrap her in, but it was more trouble than he could manage. He wanted nothing more than to get this over with, to get out of this dark space, away from the eerie feeling of death. He wanted to pretend it had never happened. He wanted to erase the words of the doctor; he wanted to eradicate the look on his mother's face.

He knelt, shivering, tired in every limb, every muscle. It crossed his mind, briefly, that he should pray—that he should whisper a "Hail Mary" or an "Our Father." He shivered again and started to cough.

He knelt and made the sign of the cross on her forehead. But the words caught, stuck in his craw. He could not speak. He could not pray. He looked at her body, at the wisp of a frame that held a baby. Not his baby, he insisted to the dark. With a girl like Adrienne, how could you ever be sure? She had been trouble from the moment she was born. There was no telling what other secrets she held.

He turned and hurried away from her, rushed to evade his own guilt. Inside the little chapel, he knelt and began to put the stones back in place. He felt exhausted, unable to continue. The only light in the room was the flicker of the candle, the window having gone dark and black while he was inside the tunnel. He sat back on his heels, staring into the dark crevice.

The thought of going to bed, upstairs, just above this room, sent a shiver down his spine. He could not leave the space open, her body stiff and cold, uncovered. No matter how tired he felt, he knew he had to continue, to get those stones back into place.

He could mortar them later. But tonight, he had to close that dark opening, shut off that ghastly sight. Erase her from memory. Block her in, as if she had never existed.

He worked into the early-morning hours. When he had finished, he moved to the door of the little chapel, shut it hard, and locked it behind him. He could barely hold his head up, barely move his feet through the parlor.

He stopped, staring down the hall toward the other chapel, the one by the kitchen. He moved slowly, holding his candle before him. The door swung backward slowly when he pushed it, a soft swoosh against the floor.

The room was clean. The broken dishes were gone, the spilled tea wiped from the walls. The knife no longer lay on the wooden planks. There was no sign of blood on the floor. The couch looked pale silver in the night. He could feel the dampness where Marie had cleaned it. But he could see no sign of blood.

He turned and dragged himself to bed.

# CHAPTER FORTY-FIVE

Julien was slow in getting up the next morning. He turned in his bed, looked out the window at the mountains. Storm clouds billowed behind the peaks, spilled over into the canyons. The first fat flakes of snow swirled in the air. He stood and dressed. He did not kneel to the statue of the Virgin in his room. He did not pray.

The morning was half gone when he left his own room and walked into the grand ballroom. His mother sat in the corner, dressed in black, a hat and veil on her head. Her hands were tiny and lost in black gloves. She held her handbag in her lap.

"I'm going back to France," she said, not looking at him but addressing her words to the tapestry hanging on the wall in front of her. It was the tapestry the family had had for generations, the one from Queen Isabella of Spain.

Julien dropped his eyes to the floor, swallowed hard, and sighed. "When?"

She turned her eyes to his. "Now. Today."

Julien pursed his lips. Her announcement brought nothing except a profound feeling of relief. He sighed. "As you wish."

"You can take me to the train station." She had turned her eyes away again. It was not a question.

❧

Julien sat in the parlor, slumped in the wing chair, his feet propped on the table in front of him. He held a brandy snifter in his hand, twirled it in his fingers. The only light in the room came from the fire. Amber spirits danced on the floor.

He sighed, a long, slow breath, heavy with fatigue. Marie had taken only one trunk. She had left most of her belongings; all of the treasures that had been in the family for years were still here, just as she had left them.

He had helped her board the train and find a compartment. He held her elbow and helped her into her seat. She leaned back against the cushion, stared out the window into the dark of the station. She did not turn to him. She did not look at him. She did not say good-bye.

Julien took a slow sip of the brandy and leaned back into the chair. The warmth of the liquid burned its way down his throat, through his chest, into his belly. He closed his eyes. He was exhausted—physically, emotionally, mentally. He felt adrift in a dark sea, untethered from the one woman who had always been there, always a hindrance to his desires and yet always able to help when he needed it.

The sound, when it finally penetrated his awareness, was soft, barely discernable. The flames of the fire crackled. But underneath that sound, wrapped around it, coming through it, he heard the sound of a door, pushing, slowly, along the floor.

Julien opened his eyes. He looked through the glass doors of the conservatory, opening into the parlor. Blue moonlight filled the space beyond, plants reaching up to touch the frosty light. He leaned forward, and stared into the icy blue darkness. The creaking sound of a wooden door reached his ears. He listened, his body strained for every sound, every breath of movement.

It grew quiet once again. He leaned forward for what seemed like ages, but could hear nothing else. At last, he shook his head, sighed, and leaned back in the chair. He took another drink of the brandy, closed his eyes.

Again, that soft sound: a heavy door, tight in its frame, pushing slowly against the floor. Julien's eyes shot open. He stood and walked to the door of the conservatory. He moved into the blue glow of the moonlight in the glass-enclosed room and turned, slowly, trying to find the sound.

He stopped, and gasped. His mouth fell open. The door to his private chapel—that heavy wooden door that he had so carefully locked last night—stood open. He felt a rush of cold air on his right side. He forced himself to move, one slow, deliberate step at a time, toward the opened door. He cocked his head, trying to see into the darkened room of the private chapel. He held his breath, every fiber of his being tense with listening. Behind him, the doors of the conservatory slammed shut, the glass rattling in the doorframes.

# CHAPTER FORTY-SIX

Julien sat at his desk. His beard was unkempt; his eyes looked like those of a wild animal. His hair stood in spikes on his head, uncombed. He brushed his hand through it and rested his head in his hands.

In the weeks since his mother had left, he had barely slept. Every time he lay down, he pictured Adrienne's body, lifeless and bloody, as he carried her to his private chapel and buried her in the tunnel. And every time he did manage to drift off for a few moments, his mind fought its way back to consciousness, listening as the music carried toward his room. The first time it happened, he got out of bed, walked down the hall, his ear cocked toward the sound. Someone was playing the piano in the great hall. Notes of the night serenade drifted into the room, like a dream. He would walk to the edge of the hall, keeping his feet hushed. But no matter how quiet he was, the minute he stood there, his hand on the switch for the light, the music suddenly stopped. He turned, more and more often, to the bottle of brandy he kept by his bed.

The pounding on the front door made him jump. Julien shot up, walked to the window, and pulled the curtain aside, trying to see to the street below. The angle of the roof was wrong; he could see nothing but the top of the portico. The banging on the door sounded again.

Julien ran his hands through his hair, swallowed. He took a deep breath. He straightened his clothes. He noticed how disheveled, how wrinkled and dirty he looked. He stopped, thought about not answering the door.

The pounding sounded again, more insistent. "Father?" a woman's voice called.

Julien swallowed again. He clenched his jaw and went downstairs, pulled the door open. Mother Mary Meyers, the superior for the Sisters of Mercy at the sanitarium, stood on the stoop, the skirts of her white habit billowing out around her.

"Good morning," she barked. Her eyes were hard and cold, and she took in his unkempt appearance. "Might I have a word with you?" She stepped through the door without waiting for his reply.

Julien ground his teeth. "I'm rather busy this morning, Mother."

"Yes. Well." She ran her eyes over his beard, over the hair on his head standing up in tufts. She could probably smell the alcohol on his breath. "This won't take long."

Julien turned to walk up the stairs and waved his hand for her to follow.

He led her to the parlor. She moved in, her stride swift and strong.

"Please have a seat," he snapped, annoyed with the interruption. He was too exhausted to deal with her today and wished only to get this encounter over with as quickly as possible.

"No," she bellowed. "As I said, this won't take long." She watched him as he walked to the edge of the room and dropped into a wing chair.

She straightened her back, held her hands folded in front of her, rough and red against her white habit. "I'll be frank, Father," she stated.

Julien moved his eyes to the window across the room.

"There have been reports . . ." She stopped. Her hands fidgeted. "I have received reports that . . . There are allegations . . ."

Julien moved his eyes to her face. "What allegations?" He glared at her.

"Allegations that . . . that you have been touching the children."

Julien's jaw clamped shut, his face flushed with anger. His eyes burned into her. "Is that so?"

She did not wither at his look. "Yes, Father. Several of the sisters have come to me. It seems that some of the children have told them . . ." She took another breath, threw her shoulders back. "The children are telling some very alarming stories."

"And you believe them?" Julien ground his teeth. His fists clenched and unclenched at his sides. "Children are well known for making up stories."

"I didn't . . . not at first. But I have spoken to some of the children myself. Their stories are . . ." She raised her eyebrows. "Convincing. Far too detailed to be childish imagination. I felt I must confront the situation."

Julien rose from his chair. They stood facing each other, locked in a battle of wills.

"Have you been touching . . ." she began.

Julien slammed his hand on the table. A paperweight jumped and wobbled. "Don't you dare speak to me like that!" His words were clipped and slow, low and heavy, like thunder. He slammed his hand down again.

Mother Meyers jumped at the sound, but she did not drop her eyes.

"I won't have it! Do you hear?" He started to move around the table, staring at the woman before him, wanting to put his hands around her neck. "You will not come into my home and speak to me like this!"

303

"I didn't believe it," she said quietly. "Not at first. Even as I walked over here today, I didn't quite believe it."

Julien's jaw was hard. Color flamed in his neck.

"Now . . ." She tipped her head, just slightly. "Seems like a rather strong reaction, from a man who has done nothing."

Julien took another step toward her, his arms taut, like violin strings pulled too tight, ready to snap.

He stopped, two feet from her face, and stared at her. "You'll be dead within a year," he hissed.

"Are you threatening me?" She pulled her shoulders up and stared right back at him.

His breathing was ragged. The sour smell of brandy filled the air.

She met his gaze. Then she turned sharply on her heel. Her shoes snapped and clicked across the floor and down the steps.

Julien heard the door slam. He paced to the window, pulled the curtain aside, watched as she strode away, her white habit sailing out behind her. He stood watching, long after she had disappeared.

He turned and went to the bar, poured another brandy, despite the early-morning hour. He returned to the window, sipping, and stared out at the street. His mind reeled with her accusations. Who spoke? Which children? Who dared to tell such stories? He wanted to march into town, grab children by their collars, shout into their small, frightened faces. "Was it you? Or you?" He imagined their fright, tears popping into their eyes.

Anger pounded in his face, in his ears, in his neck. He was furious. He paced back and forth in the parlor. And then he heard it, once again: the swish of wood, the door brushing along the floor. He turned slowly. Sunlight washed across the conservatory. Potted palms lifted their arms to the light. The door to his chapel moved slowly, as if some invisible force was pushing it open.

# CHAPTER FORTY-SEVEN

D r. Creighton finished measuring the elixir. He tightened the lid, put a label on the small bottle, and walked back to the counter at the front of the drugstore. For a few hours every afternoon, while he wasn't busy with patients at the sanitarium, he dispensed remedies from this tiny shop on Manitou Avenue.

Fred Parker stood by the front window, staring into the street. Red mud filled the street in heavy clumps and mounds, churned up by the many horses and carriages. He turned, and Dr. Creighton noticed the dark circles under his eyes, the twitch at the corners of his mouth. His eyes jumped uneasily around the room.

"Fred? Are you all right?" Dr. Creighton took the gold coin that Fred held out to him, payment for the elixir. "You seem a little jumpy." Dr. Creighton stopped. He'd never seen Fred act like this before. He looked guilty, like he'd just robbed a bank.

Fred glanced back at the street. He turned back toward the doctor, leaned slightly to look behind the doc into the shelves at the back. He leaned one hand on the counter, his eyes coming up to Dr. Creighton. "Couple of us boys is getting together this evenin'." He smiled, a slick, oily smile. He glanced behind the doctor again, turned his body to look at the door. "Gonna clean up the neighborhood a little."

"What do you mean?"

Fred stroked his mustache. "You know that priest? Father Morier?" Fred drew the syllables out in a false attempt at the proper French pronunciation.

Dr. Creighton nodded.

Fred looked behind the doctor again, searching the shadows for spies. "Rotten bastard! Word is he's been touching the kids. Little kids. Same age as my Sallie." Fred shook his head. "Goddamned rotten bastard!"

Dr. Creighton let out a slow leak of air. "Fred, are you . . . are you certain? This is a very serious accusation. Are you absolutely sure?" Dr. Creighton remembered the French maid that he had been called to look in on a few weeks ago. She was young, but certainly not a child. He'd gone back to check on her a few days later, and Julien had informed him that the maid and his mother had gone back to France. Probably best, given her condition, the doctor had thought at the time.

Fred leaned forward again. "You know that little Tyler girl? Ain't but seven year old? Her mama said she cried and carried on like she'd been kilt! And once she told her mama, then the lid came off." Fred puffed. "Then other kids started talking. Makes me sick, that piece of French scum."

"Fred, even if this is true . . . shouldn't you let the law handle it? He's a priest. He deserves the chance to defend himself." Dr. Creighton fought the anger, the nausea that rushed over him. He thought of his own little girl. She was nine.

"The law?" Fred exploded. "Let the law handle it? And drag those kids through the courts? A trial? Let everyone in town see who they are? Make 'em get up in front of people, and have to tell their story? Are you crazy?"

Dr. Creighton swallowed.

"Seems to me them kids been through enough. Rotten god-damned son of a bitch."

Fred stopped, turned slowly toward the doctor. "You ain't . . . you ain't a friend a his, is ya?"

Dr. Creighton pulled his shoulders up. "What are you saying, Fred Parker?"

They met each other's eyes.

They stared at each other for several moments. Dr. Creighton lowered his gaze to the countertop. He quieted his breath. He looked back at Fred. "I just think maybe you ought to let the law handle it."

Fred spat in the direction of the spittoon in the corner. "Well . . . I guess I ain't asked what you thought." He turned and left, letting the door slam behind him. The bell on the handle jangled.

◦⌒⊙

Basil Creighton stood still, staring out at Manitou Avenue. Pockets of snow lay heaped at the sides of the street, only churned into mud where the horses had done their work. Basil stared at the mud. He never had liked the father. He'd always found him arrogant, a little too full of his own importance. And that thing with the maid—that had made him want to choke the priest.

He gulped. His Adam's apple strained against his shirt collar. The last thing in the world he wanted to do was to help that sorry excuse for a man and even sorrier excuse for a priest—a man of God. But it didn't matter what the man had done; he still had the right to a trial. He still had the right to face his accusers, to have his day in court.

Basil moved to the front door, pulled his key out of his pocket, and locked the bolt. He turned the sign in the window to "Closed."

He stared out into the street. It was growing quiet; only a few people stirred in the late winter afternoon.

He turned and hurried out the back of the shop. He carried his bag, pulled the collar of his coat up against the chill of the wind blowing off the mountain. He hurried up the steep grade of Ruxton Avenue.

Light shone from inside the houses. They looked warm and safe, protected from the weather, safe from harm. Basil looked around, wondering how many of these homes were actually secure. If this horrible rumor was true, how many homes had been violated? How many children had that man touched? His stomach churned. He thought about going home, abandoning this fool's errand and walking the block and a half to his own wife and children, probably this moment sitting down to dinner.

But the thought of sitting in his own home, warm in front of the fire, his daughters relaxed and comfortable in the room around him, while somewhere in the streets, the priest was being beaten to death, or shot, or maybe hung . . . Basil rushed past the turnoff to his own home and continued up the hill on Ruxton Avenue.

He stopped at number sixteen, climbed the steps to the porch, and banged on the front door. It was the dinner hour, but it couldn't be helped. There was no time to waste.

Angus Gillis answered the door, a white napkin stuck in his shirt collar. Angus reached for it and pulled it away. "Basil! Good to see you. Come in, come in." Basil stepped inside, shook the thick hand that Angus offered. "Have you eaten?"

Basil looked up at Angus Gillis, glad he'd chosen to come here. The builder was as open and honest and straightforward as any man in this town. Basil admired his clear thinking, his even temper, the way he had handled the situation with the priest over his unpaid debts on the castle. Somehow, even through all that, Angus had managed to stay friends with Morier.

Basil glanced toward the dining room, where Mrs. Gillis and their daughter, Lenore, sat waiting. He turned and looked Angus in the eye. "Thanks for offering, Angus, but I'm short on time. Can we speak privately?"

Angus nodded, and leaned into the dining room to address his wife and daughter. "You two go ahead. I'll finish a little later." He led Basil into the parlor and closed the sliding pocket door behind him. A few minutes later, the door rolled open and both men moved swiftly. Angus reached for his coat and hat from the hat tree in the hallway. Mrs. Gillis stood, staring at her husband.

Angus paused for a moment at the door to the dining room. He looked at his wife and dropped his voice. "There's a lynch mob, going after Father Morier."

Her hand rose to her throat, a napkin clutched tightly in her fist. "Be careful, Mr. Gillis," she whispered. "He is not worth your life."

He nodded to her and clamped his hat on his head. The two men left, the door shutting with a sharp thud behind them.

"You go down to the town clock," Angus murmured. "See if you can find out where they are. Slow them down, if you can." Dr. Creighton nodded, and started down the hill he'd just come up.

Angus went behind his house and hitched the horses to his buggy. He threw a couple of wool blankets into the back, a buffalo robe on top. He climbed up in the seat and clucked to the horses. They turned to the right, up Ruxton Avenue, toward the castle.

❦

Julien heard the pounding on the door, but he was slow in responding, as if waking from a dream. His shirt was untucked, wrinkled, and messy. He noticed the bottle of brandy in his hand and moved to put it on the table. He raised a hand to his face. His beard had grown shaggy and unkempt. His eyes stung; he could smell the odor on his clothes and body and breath. He waited, but the pounding on the front door was loud and insistent, and he forced himself down the stairs.

"Why, Angus. What a pleasant surprise," Julien began, his words slurred and sloppy.

Angus stepped abruptly through the door and closed it behind them. Julien stepped back in surprise. "Get your coat, Father. There's no time to waste."

"What in the world? What are . . ." Julien shook his head, trying to clear it. "What are you talking about?"

"Father? Now. Get your coat. There's a lynch mob, down the hill. They want your hide, and they'll be here soon. You need to get out of here. There's no time to lose."

Julien's eyes darted from Angus's face to the floor to the stairs leading up to the parlor. His throat worked in a series of gulps. He stared at his home around him.

"Father? Get your coat."

Julien raised his eyes to Angus Gillis. He turned, let his eyes glide over the golden wood on the stairs, the wallpaper from Paris. He looked at the fire in the parlor, the huge wall of carefully cut stone surrounding it. Light danced on the ceiling and the molding, shipped from a cabinetmaker in New York, that surrounded the room. He moved slowly, as if it were too much to ask. Too much to be borne. How could he leave this castle? The one he had designed, the one Angus and his brother had built?

His hand moved to the side of his head. All that time, all those years, at the parish in New Mexico, waiting, hoping, for a chance to go somewhere where he would feel at home, where the people would appreciate him. Somewhere where his every move wasn't shadowed by the stares of the dark-eyed people who so obviously disliked him, somewhere where there were more Europeans, more of the wealthy, privileged set that he felt so at home with.

Julien let his eyes travel over every corner, every plant. He could see the painting his mother had shipped from Beaulieu, the still life that had hung at the castle in France since long before Julien was born.

Angus reached for his elbow, held it firmly in his large hand. "We have to go."

Julien nodded. He took his coat from the hook, pulled it over his arms and shoulders. He reached for his hat, clamped it on his head. He glanced up the stairs, one last time, and then let Angus guide him out the front door. Julien climbed into the back of the buggy and curled up on the floor. Angus covered him with blankets, the buffalo robe on top.

Julien felt the buggy dip as Angus climbed up on the seat. He heard the crack of the whip, the sharp clop-clop of the horses' hooves on the pavement. He felt the steep pitch of the hill as the buggy started down. Under the covers, in the dark, he followed every turn and twist of the road: left onto Ruxton Avenue, the curve of the street where Angus's own house stood, the right turn onto Manitou Avenue at the bottom of the hill.

He heard their voices, rising in volume as the buggy drew close to the group of men waiting by the town clock. The buggy stopped.

"Evenin', Angus." Julien recognized the timbre of the voice. He couldn't remember where he'd heard it before, what face it might belong to.

"Evenin', boys." Angus's voice was friendly and even, completely calm. "Having a party?"

Stanley Reed laughed. "Guess you could say that, huh, boys?" Julien could hear the laughter of several men.

Reed turned back toward Angus. "More like housecleaning, actually."

"That so?" Julien was impressed by how normal Angus made his voice sound.

"Certain French priest has made a little mess around here," Reed continued. "Want to join us?"

"I would. I would, indeed. No room for that kind of thing around here."

Julien's heart pounded. The sound was deafening, like the ocean in a storm. He wondered how the men outside the buggy could keep from hearing it. For a moment, Julien wondered if Angus was going to turn him over to the men.

"But I'm afraid I can't—not this evening anyway," Angus said. "Got an appointment in Colorado Springs. We're looking at house plans. But I wish you boys success. Any man that would do something like . . . like what I've heard. Well, he doesn't deserve to live, far as I'm concerned. A man of the cloth, at that!" Julien held his breath. The tension was strong enough to sober him completely. He could feel the quiet in the men outside the wagon; he could feel the way Angus held his breath, as if uncertain whether they would let him go. Julien heard the rattle of a harness, heard Angus cluck to the horses, and they lurched forward. The wheels on the buggy creaked and moaned.

The voices grew quieter as the buggy moved away from them. Julien let out a long sigh.

Angus didn't say another word the rest of the drive. The buggy pitched and rocked and swayed with the dips in the road, the turns they made. The five miles lengthened, and to Julien, crouched in the back, it felt like fifty. Despite the pile of blankets, he found his body shaking, whether from fear or cold, he could not tell. He didn't feel safe, had no idea where Angus might be taking him. Maybe Angus was driving him into the mountains, in the darkness, ready to dispatch the priest by himself. Maybe that group of men had already gone to the castle, already thrown open the door, searched the premises. Perhaps, at this very moment, they were racing after the buggy.

The buggy stopped moving. Angus stayed still on his seat. "You can get up now, Father," he whispered.

Julien pushed the heavy robes aside and sat up. He was cramped and stiff. The cold had seeped in under the blankets and locked in his joints. He looked at the tall, dark brick building beside them. They were at St. Mary's Church, on Bijou Street in Colorado Springs.

Angus climbed down from his seat. He sighed, stretched his back and shoulders. He did not look at Julien. He moved to the door of the rectory and pounded.

They waited several moments. Angus pounded again. The housekeeper for Father Byrne pulled the door open and stared into the dark. It was long past time for visitors, and she was in her housecoat and slippers. Her hair hung in a long gray braid down the side of her neck. She looked at Father Morier, dusty and wrinkled, brushing at his clothes, and she stepped aside to let the two men pass.

Father Byrne appeared at the top of the stairs, also in housecoat and slippers. He had obviously been sleeping. His face was creased from the pillowcase. His silky white hair, thin and sparse, stood at odd angles. He put his glasses on his nose, peered down the stairs at the two men below. "Why, Father Morier! Mr. Gillis! This is unexpected!"

He started down the stairs. "Come in, come in." He waved his hand, indicated the parlor to their left. The fire from earlier in the evening glowed with red coals.

Angus twisted his hat in his hands. "I'm afraid I've brought you nothing but trouble," he began, his eyes flicking over to Morier beside him.

"Oh?" Father Byrne's eyes were large and gray, almost pop-eyed behind his glasses.

"I've brought Morier to you for hiding. There's a lynch mob after him. We barely made it out of Manitou." Angus's voice was gruff and deep.

313

Father Byrne examined the two men. Julien kept his eyes pinned on the rug beneath them, leaves of ivy trailing and twisting on the deep-green background.

"And just why would they want to lynch the good father?"

Julien shrugged but did not meet the eyes of the older priest. "I have no idea," he began. His eyes skipped and flittered from the floor to the chairs to the window.

Angus interrupted. "They say he's molesting kids."

Father Byrne stared at Morier.

Angus turned to Julien, his eyes running up and down the small-statured man. "I don't know if it's true or not. But I heard some things myself, even before tonight." Angus pushed a heavy breath into the room. "I don't know if I done the right thing, really. Bringing him here. Maybe I should have just let them—"

He stopped, and Julien shuddered.

"But no matter what a man has done, I guess I never believed that turning him over to vigilantes is the right way to handle a problem." He looked off into the darkened corner of the room. "Myself . . . I'd like to see him go to trial. Face his accusers."

He looked back at Julien again. Julien could not meet his gaze.

Father Byrne clapped a hand on Angus's shoulder. "You've done the right thing, Mr. Gillis. We can't allow anyone to take the law into his own hands."

Angus nodded.

"I'll take care of things. I believe there is a train, for the east, first thing tomorrow morning. Perhaps Father Morier should be on it."

Angus caught Julien's eye.

Without a word, he turned and walked to the door, pulling it closed behind him.

# EPILOGUE

Over a hundred years have passed since Julien first built the castle, over a hundred years since Adrienne arrived from France in the guise of a servant. It's been over a hundred years since the night she picked up the knife and did what she felt she had to do. But the two who perpetrated the events, who instigated the torture, are no longer stuck. They are completely removed from the horror that took place inside these walls, completely oblivious to how their actions have continued to affect Adrienne, to hold her prisoner.

For over a hundred years, she has paced these halls, climbed these stairs, stared out these same windows. She watched as the world changed around her. She watched as the town of Manitou Springs grew, as houses crowded around the castle, as the very fabric of life has been rewoven by technology and industry. She watched while the Manitou Springs Historical Society took over the castle and worked to restore it to its original form. She watches the visitors come and go; sometimes she eavesdrops on their conversations, smiling at the all-too-frequent question "Is there a ghost in the castle?"

Yes, there is, and she's made her presence known in dozens of harmless ways. The preservation architect from Denver, who came down to begin the process of restoration, was convinced there was a ghost present. He spent hours in the castle, tearing at false walls and boarded-over fireplaces, trying to get down to what the castle had been like originally. He pored over plans, read everything he could find that had been written about the building when Julien was there.

Adrienne did what she could to get his attention. He'd unlock a door, gather up his papers, and before he could get inside, she would close and lock it again. Sometimes he would close a door, turn the key in the lock, and start toward his car. Adrienne would push it open and watch the expression on his face as he turned to see it swing inward. She moved his papers. He was so certain of a presence that he mentioned the "ghost" in his preservation report.

And she's made her presence known to the ladies who work there, with a variety of benign parlor tricks. She moved the crocheted antimacassars, right after the cleaning lady had finished placing them on the sofa. The woman turned her back for a moment, and suddenly they were on the chair. Adrienne sat in the rocking chair and rocked, making the chair creak and moan, watching as the woman's face filled with fright. She moved dolls and dishes in the gift shop, sometimes to the opposite side of the room. She removed the coffee from the coffeemaker one morning when someone had started a pot for a meeting. The woman returned a few minutes later to find nothing but pale gray water coming out of the spout. Once, she even whispered "Happy birthday" to a woman working alone on the fourth floor. She loved to watch their reactions. She loved watching as they shook off their shivers.

But after one hundred years, none of that is even remotely satisfying. They might acknowledge the presence of a ghost. They have even named her Henrietta, a name that makes her shudder with its reminders of the life she led inside these walls. Once in a while a child, or some particularly sensitive person, walks through the door, sensing her presence. When that happens, Adrienne follows him or her from room to room, whispering to them, sometimes lightly touching a shoulder or a strand of hair. She loves it when someone can actually feel her presence—when someone almost stops and waits for her to say something.

It is not enough. It is not enough to spend eternity playing parlor tricks, all the while drowning in loneliness, just as she had in her physical life. Even after all this time has passed, she is still capsizing in the negative emotions that come charging up over her at the oddest times, like a storm at sea. She walks through the parlor, past the big fireplace, and stops suddenly, remembering those evenings by the fire, Marie pouring the wine and watching Adrienne's every move. She walks into the kitchen and is suddenly hit with the feeling of looking at the breakfast tray that the nuns sent down and feeling, once again, like she's going to retch. Some man with dark hair and a dark beard will visit the castle with his wife and family, and Adrienne finds herself gritting her teeth, the feeling of hatred so strong she's surprised that the living don't sense it. Once, she passed a woman on the stairs, a woman with graying curls and a grim expression, and for a moment Adrienne thought about shoving her, watching her tumble and roll down the staircase, as if she were the cause of Adrienne's distress. As if she were the one who had kept Adrienne a prisoner here, all these years after the real culprits had left.

That is one thing she has discovered in the past hundred years: the emotion, the energy of anger and revulsion and shame and horror has not gone away. Adrienne's actions on that long-ago evening allowed her to escape their physical presence, the physical torture that she endured at their hands. But the mental agony, the emotional suffering, has continued, as if it has an energy all its own, unrelated to whether or not there is a physical presence to claim it.

She stands at the window on the stairs, staring out at the night, as she has for hours now. There is a sliver of moon in the dark sky; Venus tags along like a puppy, twinkling with a joy promised to those who can get *out*, who can manage to leave it all behind. She knows now that it is not Julien or Marie who is keeping her a prisoner of this never-ending torment. There is no punishment that has been meted out by some great power, forcing her to stay locked inside these walls, reliving the same drama over and over again. The only thing keeping her here is *herself*, the energy of her own thoughts and emotions, her own inability to let go.

For years, she stood at this window and asked why. She wondered what she had done to deserve this treatment, what was wrong with her, what was it that had set off the whole chain of events. For a while, she believed that if she only understood why, then she would be able to escape.

She has quit asking why; she has quit seeking the answer. Even if she knew the answer, it would not free her from this prison. For years, she had believed that if they were caught, if they were punished for what they had done, that would be enough. That would make her feel better, would bring her a sense of justice and closure and allow her to let it all go.

She spent ages waiting for that to happen, for some Old Testament god to seek them out and make them pay. But that was long, long ago; too many years have passed for such a possibility. Julien and Marie are long dead; there will be no punishment; there will be no justice.

Adrienne swallowed. Below her, the blue house was dark. She could picture that little girl with the bike snug in her bed, completely unaware of the torture that went on in this castle all those years ago. Completely unaware of the steps Adrienne took to solve her problem. Completely unaware of all the awful events that took place behind these walls, just a few steps away.

Adrienne did not believe that she could ever *forgive* Julien and Marie for what they had done to her. She could never condone their actions, could never erase the pain they had caused. Forgiveness, the way she understood it, was not possible. But the way she had hung on, all these years, to her anger, to her need to blame them, her need for revenge, had not done anything to hurt Julien or Marie. It was *she* who continued to suffer, over a hundred years later. It was *she* who was still trapped here, still unable to find peace.

The thought occurred to her: *What if I just let go?* Not forgiveness, exactly, but just release. What if she unchained herself from all the pain, the anger, the shame, the sadness, all of it. Just put it down, like a heavy suitcase that she had been carting around for far too long. For the first time in over a century, Adrienne thought that perhaps she was ready, willing even, to detach. Forget about being able to forgive. Forget everything. Just let it go. For the first time, she *wanted* to let it go. She was willing to let it go.

She raised her hand to the lace curtain, her vision clear now as she studied the way the moonlight poured across the roof of the blue house. She watched the shadows of the trees spilling across the walls, watched as leaf shadows danced and flickered. Moonlight, pale and weak, came through the lace curtain in front of her, and her gaze was drawn to the soft shadows playing on her own hand. She watched, fascinated, as the shadows continued to sway and dance, only now on the curtain itself. She watched as her hand began to fade and disappear, like morning fog when the sun comes out.

# AFTERWORD

This story is a work of fiction but was inspired by the real people, and some of the real events, connected with Miramont Castle, in Manitou Springs, Colorado.

Sometime in the early months of 1900, Father Jean Baptiste Francolon and his mother, Marie Plagne Francolon, left Miramont Castle under mysterious circumstances, leaving behind furniture, works of art, and family heirlooms, including the four-poster bed that had belonged to the empress Josephine Bonaparte. They also left many unpaid debts. The Gillis brothers did file a lawsuit against Father Francolon for nonpayment on the castle; they contacted his bishop first, reticent to sue the man they had worked so closely with.

Marie Francolon died in France a few months later.

Jean Baptiste Francolon died in New York in 1922. He was never given another parish after being relieved of his duties in Manitou Springs.

Francolon was born in France in 1854, the grandson of the Comte de Challembelles. His father, who worked in the diplomatic corps of the French government, died when Jean was just thirteen years old. Francolon studied at the university in Paris and prepared to go into diplomacy as well.

Just before he was to finish, he showed a sudden change of heart and entered the theological seminary in Clermont, France. Archbishop Lamy had also attended the seminary at Clermont and returned often to recruit priests for his large diocese in the New Mexico Territory. Jean Baptiste Francolon was one of those recruits. He was ordained in Santa Fe, New Mexico, in 1878, and served as secretary and then chancellor to the archbishop. He was given his own parish in 1881, at Santa Cruz de la Cañada, twenty-five miles north of Santa Fe. The parish covered over seventy square miles and included three Indian pueblos.

The journals of Adolph Bandelier, a Swiss anthropologist who spent many years in the New Mexico Territory, record that Father Francolon was poisoned at the chalice in 1885. He never fully recovered his health. Francolon was transferred to Manitou Springs, Colorado, to the Chapel of Our Lady of Perpetual Help, in 1892.

Francolon never revealed to anyone in Manitou that he had been poisoned. The story he told was that he had been sent to South America on a secret mission for the French government in 1885–86 and it was there that his health was compromised.

The stories of the George Washington ball were well documented in Colorado newspapers of the time, and were well attended by the elite of Denver and Colorado Springs society.

Francolon was proud of having helped bring the Denver and Rio Grande Railroad into Española, New Mexico, close to his parish. A spur of the D&RG, called the Chili Line, did exist between Antonito, Colorado, and Española. Francolon also boasted of his friendship with General William Palmer, who was instrumental in the building of the Denver and Rio Grande. There is some question as to the business practices of the railroad company in dealing with the acquisition of lands for the railroad from native peoples.

Francolon donated his original residence on the hill behind the castle, a wooden structure called Montcalme, to the Sisters of

Mercy. They operated a sanitarium for tuberculosis patients in that structure. He also arranged with the sisters to have them provide meals for himself and his mother.

The Sisters of Mercy, in a history written by Kathleen O'Brien, RSM, entitled *Journeys: A Pre-Amalgamation History of the Sisters of Mercy, Omaha Province*, document the rumors of pedophilia about Francolon. The Sisters also share the story, through oral tradition, of Francolon having cursed the mother superior when she confronted him about the allegations of pedophilia. Whether he cursed her or not cannot be verified. On August 29, 1901, Mother Mary John Baptist Meyers was killed in a train accident as she traveled from Denver to Durango, slightly more than a year after the alleged curse.

The Sisters also share, in this same document, the story of Francolon's being whisked away to St. Mary's Church, under cover of darkness, with a vigilante committee on his heels.

Stories of the ghost were documented in the preservation report of the preservation consultant, Philip Lawrence Hannum, who helped restore the castle to its original form. Other members of the Manitou Historical Society, and some who have worked at the castle, have also reported mysterious occurrences, which they attribute to the ghost. They call her Henrietta.

The rest of the story is fiction.

# BIBLIOGRAPHY

Copp, Shirley. *Miramont Castle: A Brief History.* Manitou Springs, Colo: Manitou Springs Historical Society, 1985.

Hanks, Nancy, PhD. *Lamy's Legion: The Individual Histories of Secular Clergy Serving in the Archdiocese of Santa Fe from 1850 to 1912.* HRM Books, Santa Fe, c. 2000.

Hannum Preservation Report. Philip Lawrence Hannum.

Horgan, Paul. *Lamy of Santa Fe, a biography.* Farrar, Strauss & Giroux, New York, 1975.

Kessell, John L. *The Missions of New Mexico Since 1776.* Albuquerque: University of New Mexico Press, 1980.

Lange, Charles H. and Carroll L Riley, eds and anns. 1966. *The Southwestern Journals of Adolph F. Bandelier, 1880-1882.* Albuquerque: University of New Mexico Press.

Mensing, Marcia. *Miramont Castle: The First Hundred Years.* Manitou Springs Historical Society, Manitou Springs, Colorado, 1995.

O'Brien, Kathleen, R.S.M. *Journeys: A Pre-Amalgamation History of the Sisters of Mercy, Omaha Province.* Omaha, Nebraska.

Tenhaeff, W.H.C. *Telepathy and Clairvoyance.* Charles C. Thomas Publisher, Springfield, IL, 1972; translation of Dutch edition 1965 by W. de Haan, N.V. Zeist.

Salpointe, Rev. Jean-Baptiste. 1967. *Soldiers of the Cross: Notes on the Ecclesiastical History of New Mexico, Arizona and Colorado.* Albuquerque, Calvin Horn.

Sipe, A.W. Richard. *Sex, Priests, & Power: Anatomy of a Crisis,* Brunner Mazel Publishers, New York, 1995.

The Denver Republican, February 23, 1897.

# ACKNOWLEDGMENTS

Many people were helpful as I struggled to learn about the lives of those who were involved in the castle and to weave those facts into the narrative. I would like to thank Linda Pineda at Miramont Castle, Marcia Muensing, the staff of the Pioneer Museum in Colorado Springs, Melissa Salazar of the New Mexico State Archives, Sister Mary Lavey, and Maria Mondragon-Valdez. Several early readers of all or part of the manuscript were also very helpful, including Jodine Ryan, Alberta Bouyer, Jennie Shortridge, Barb Kolupke, and Misa Lobato. My agent, Alison Fargis, has been wonderful every step of the way, as well as my editors, Danielle Marshall and Charlotte Herscher. I am deeply appreciative.

# ABOUT THE AUTHOR

*Collin Brothers, 2014*

Elizabeth Hall is a writer, fiber artist, and teacher, transplanted to Washington after spending most of her life in Colorado. *Miramont's Ghost* is her first novel.